It's Washington, D.C.; it's the last night of the year, and people are dying . . .

At 9 am on New Year's Eve a man gets onto the packed escalator of a metro station and fires a silenced machine gun into the crowd. He escapes without being spotted in the confusion caused by the horror of this vicious attack, which leaves dozens of people killed and injured.

One hour later, a note is delivered to the mayor: twenty million dollars, or the writer will instruct the killer to strike again; at 4 pm, at 9 pm, at midnight . . . hundreds more will die.

The money has to be found, the ransom will have to be paid. But then a hit-and-run victim is identified as the mastermind behind the operation, and suddenly there's no way of stopping the psychotic gunman killing again, and again, and again . . .

The only thing the FBI have to go on is the note. Parker Kincaid, forensic document expert, and agent-in-charge, Margaret Lukas, could be the only people who can stop the killer.

Praise for Jeffery Deaver's bestselling thrillers:

The Bone Collector

'Those who were gripped by Deaver's last novel, *A Maiden's Grave*, will not be surprised at the double-take finalé, but I am willing to bet they still won't get it. Another genuinely compulsive chiller from the best psychological thriller writer around' Peter Millar, *The Times*

'Sophisticated chiller . . . compulsive reading' *Guardian*

A Maiden's Grave

'Not since *Children of a Lesser God* has there been such a moving and in this case unequivocally unpatronising depiction of the world of the Deaf, which they themselves spell with a capital D as a socio-political statement . . . But where this book really sings is in the psychology: Potter's self-conscious exploitation of his own emotional vulnerability to empathise with the hostage-taker. His skill is to descend with the potential killer to a mutual resignation, while avoiding the danger of empathy turning into sympathy. Deaver knits a seamless fabric of tightening tension right-up to an explosive double-whammy ending. *A Maiden's Grave* is a gripping sleight of hand and an explosive punctuation mark. It is Deaver's best book yet' *The Times*

'The shifts in the balance of power and testing of limits between predator and prey build crisis after crisis into this excellent siege thriller' *Daily Mail*

'A real chiller, seething with violence and heart-stopping suspense . . . Deaver skilfully builds the tension . . . to a climax, before adding a stunning twist to the story' *Sunday Telegraph*

The Devil's Teardrop

Jeffery Deaver

CORONET BOOKS

Hodder & Stoughton

First published in Great Britain in 1999
by Hodder and Stoughton
First published in paperback in 2000
by Hodder and Stoughton
A division of Hodder Headline

A Coronet Paperback

10 9 8 7 6 5 4 3 2 1

A CIP catalogue record for this title is available
from the British Library.

ISBN 0 340 71253 8

Typeset by Palimpsest Book Production Limited,
Polmont, Stirlingshire

Printed and bound in Great Britain by
Clays Ltd, St Ives plc

Hodder and Stoughton
A division of Hodder Headline
338 Euston Road
London NW1 3BH

With thanks to Madelyn

Acknowledgments

The author would like to thank Vernon Geberth, whose excellent book *Practical Homicide Investigation* is a milestone work in police procedure and has provided invaluable information in researching this and the author's other books. The puzzles described in this book are variations on several contained in *Perplexing Lateral Thinking Puzzles* by Paul Sloane and Des MacHale.

I

THE LAST DAY OF THE YEAR

A thorough analysis of an anonymous letter may greatly reduce the number of possible writers and may at once dismiss certain suspected writers. The use of a semicolon or the correct use of an apostrophe may eliminate a whole group of writers.

—Osborn and Osborn,
Questioned Document Problems

1

08.55

The Digger's in town.

The Digger looks like you, the Digger looks like me. He walks down the wintry streets the way anybody would, shoulders drawn together against the damp, December air.

He's not tall and not short, he's not heavy and not thin. His fingers in dark gloves might be pudgy but they might not. His feet seem large but maybe that's just the size of his shoes.

If you glanced at his eyes you wouldn't notice the shape or the color but only that they don't seem quite human, and if the Digger glanced at *you* while you were looking at him, his eyes might be the very last thing you ever saw.

He wears a long, black coat, or a dark blue one, and not a soul on the street notices him pass by though there are many witnesses here – the streets of Washington, D.C., are crowded because it's morning rush hour.

The Digger's in town and it's New Year's Eve.

Carrying a Fresh Fields shopping bag, the Digger dodges around couples and singles and families and keeps on walking. Ahead, he sees the Metro station. He was told to be there at exactly 9 A.M. and he will be. The Digger is never late.

The bag in his maybe-pudgy hand is heavy. It weighs eleven pounds, though by the time the Digger returns to his motel room it will weigh considerably less.

A man bumps into him and smiles and says, "Sorry," but the Digger doesn't glance at him. The Digger never looks at anybody and doesn't want anybody to look at him.

"Don't let anybody . . . ." *Click*. ". . . let anybody see your face. Look away. Remember?"

I remember.

Click.

Look at the lights, he thinks, look at the . . . *click* . . . at the New Year's Eve decorations. Fat babies in banners, Old Man Time.

Funny decorations. Funny lights. Funny how nice they are.

This is Dupont Circle, home of money, home of art, home of the young and the chic. The Digger knows this but he knows it only because the man who tells him things told him about Dupont Circle.

He arrives at the mouth of the subway tunnel. The morning is overcast and, being winter, there is a dimness over the city.

The Digger thinks of his wife on days like this. Pamela didn't like the dark and the cold so she . . . *click* . . . she . . . What did she do? That's right. She planted red flowers and yellow flowers.

He looks at the subway and he thinks of a picture

he saw once. He and Pamela were at a museum. They saw an old drawing on the wall.

And Pamela said, "Scary. Let's go."

It was a picture of the entrance to hell.

The Metro tunnel disappears sixty feet underground, passengers rising, passengers descending. It looks just like that drawing.

The entrance to hell.

Here are young women with hair cut short and briefcases. Here are young men with their sports bags and cell phones.

And here is the Digger with his shopping bag.

Maybe he's fat, maybe he's thin. Looking like you, looking like me. Nobody ever notices the Digger and that's one of the reasons he's so very good at what he does.

"You're the best," said the man who tells him things last year. You're the . . . *click, click* . . . the best.

At 8:59 the Digger walks to the top of the down escalator, which is filled with people disappearing into the pit.

He reaches into the bag and curls his finger around the comfy grip of the gun, which may be an Uzi or a Mac-10 or an Intertech but definitely weighs eleven pounds and is loaded with a hundred-round clip of .22 long-rifle bullets.

The Digger's hungry for soup but he ignores the sensation.

Because he's the . . . *click* . . . the best.

He looks toward but not at the crowd, waiting their turn to step onto the down escalator, which will take them to hell. He doesn't look at the couples or the men with telephones or women with hair from Supercuts, which is where Pamela went. He doesn't look at the families. He clutches the shopping bag to his chest, the way anybody would if it were full of holiday treats. One hand on the grip of whatever kind of gun it is, his other hand curled – outside the bag – around what somebody might think is a loaf of Fresh Fields bread that would go very nicely with soup but is in fact a heavy sound suppressor, packed with mineral cotton and rubber baffles.

His watch beeps.

Nine A.M.

He pulls the trigger.

There is a hissing sound as the stream of bullets begins working its way down the passengers on the escalator and they pitch forward under the fire. The *hush hush hush* of the gun is suddenly obscured by the screams.

"Oh God look out Jesus Jesus what's happening I'm hurt I'm falling." And things like that.

Hush hush hush.

And all the terrible clangs of the misses – the bullets striking the metal and the tile. That sound is very loud. The sounds of the hits are much softer.

Everyone looks around, not knowing what's going on.

The Digger looks around too. Everyone frowns. He frowns.

Nobody thinks that they are being shot. They believe that someone has fallen and started a chain reaction of people tumbling down the escalator. Clangs and snaps as phones and briefcases and sports bags fall from the hands of the victims.

The hundred rounds are gone in seconds.

No one notices the Digger as he looks around, like everyone else.

Frowning.

"Call an ambulance the police the police my God this girl needs help she needs help somebody he's dead oh Jesus my Lord her leg look at her leg my baby my baby . . ."

The Digger lowers the shopping bag, which has one small hole in the bottom where the bullets left. The bag holds all the hot, brass shells.

"Shut it off shut off the escalator oh Jesus look somebody stop it stop the escalator they're being crushed . . ."

Things like that.

The Digger looks. Because everybody's looking.

But it's hard to see into hell. Below is just a mass of bodies piling up, growing higher, writhing . . . Some are alive, some dead, some struggling to get out from underneath the crush that's piling up at the base of the escalator.

The Digger is easing backward into the crowd. And then he's gone.

He's very good at disappearing. "When you leave you should act like a chameleon," said the man who tells him things. "Do you know what that is?"

"A lizard."

"Right."

"That changes color. I saw it on TV."

The Digger is moving along the sidewalks, filled with people. Running this way and that way. Funny. Funny . . .

Nobody notices the Digger.

Who looks like you and looks like me and looks like

the woodwork. Whose face is white as a morning sky. Or dark as the entrance to hell.

As he walks – slowly, slowly – he thinks about his motel. Where he'll reload his gun and repack his silencer with bristly mineral cotton and sit in his comfy chair with a bottle of water and a bowl of soup beside him. He'll sit and relax until this afternoon and then – if the man who tells him things doesn't leave a message to tell him not to – he'll put on his long black or blue coat once more and go outside.

And do this all over again.

It's New Year's Eve. And the Digger's in town.

While ambulances were speeding to Dupont Circle and rescue workers were digging through the ghastly mine of bodies in the Metro station, Gilbert Havel walked toward City Hall, two miles away.

At the corner of Fourth and D, beside a sleeping maple tree, Havel paused and opened the envelope he carried and read the note one last time.

Mayor Kennedy—

> *The end is night. The Digger is loose and their is no way to stop him. He will kill again – at four, eight and Midnight if you don't pay.*
>
> *I am wanting $20 million dollars in cash, which you will put into a bag and leave it two miles south of Rt 66 on the West Side of the Beltway. In the middle of the Field. Pay to me the Money by 1200 hours. Only I am knowing how to stop The Digger. If you ▓▓▓ apprehend me, he will keep killing. If you kill me, he will keep killing.*

If you dont think I'm real, some of the Diggers bullets were painted black. Only I know that.

This was, Havel decided, about as perfect an idea as anybody could've come up with. Months of planning. Every possible response by the police and FBI anticipated. A chess game.

Buoyed by that thought, he replaced the note in the envelope, closed but didn't seal it and continued along the street. Havel walked in a stooped lope, eyes down, a pose meant to diminish his six-two height. It was hard for him, though; he preferred to walk tall and stare people down.

The security at City Hall, One Judiciary Square, was ridiculous. No one noticed as he walked past the entrance to the nondescript stone building and paused at a newspaper vending machine. He slipped the envelope under the stand and turned slowly, walking toward E Street.

Warm for New Year's Eve, Havel was thinking. The air smelled like fall – rotten leaves and humid wood smoke. The scent aroused a pang of undefined nostalgia for his childhood home. He stopped at a pay phone on the corner, dropped in some coins and dialed a number.

A voice answered, "City Hall. Security."

Havel held a tape recorder next to the phone and pressed PLAY. A computer-generated voice said, "Envelope in front of the building. Under the *Post* vending machine. Read it now. It's about the Metro killings." He hung up and crossed the street, dropping the tape recorder into a paper cup and throwing the cup into a wastebasket.

Havel stepped into a coffee shop and sat down in a window booth, where he had a good view of the vending machine and the side entrance to City Hall. He wanted to make sure the envelope was picked up – it was, before Havel even had his jacket off. He also wanted to see who'd be coming to advise the mayor. And whether reporters showed up.

The waitress stopped by his booth and he ordered coffee and, though it was still breakfast time, a steak sandwich, the most expensive thing on the menu. Why not? He was about to become a very wealthy man.

2

10.00

"**D**addy, tell me about the Boatman."

Parker Kincaid paused. He set down the cast-iron skillet he was washing.

He'd learned never to be alarmed by anything the children asked – well, never to *appear* alarmed – and he smiled down at the boy as he dried his hands with paper towels.

"The Boatman?" he asked his nine-year-old son. "You bet. What do you want to know?"

The kitchen of Parker's house in Fairfax, Virginia, was fragrant with the smells of a holiday meal in the works. Onion, sage, rosemary. The boy looked out the window. Said nothing.

"Go ahead," Parker encouraged. "Tell me."

Robby was blond and had his mother's blue eyes. He wore a purple Izod shirt and tan pants, cinched at the waist with a Ralph Lauren belt. His floppy cowlick leaned to the starboard this morning.

"I mean," the boy began, "I know he's dead and everything . . ."

"That's right," Parker said. He added nothing more. (*"Never tell the children more than they ask."* This was one of the rules from Parker Kincaid's *Handbook for the Single Parent* – a guide that existed solely in his mind yet one he referred to every day.)

"It's just that outside . . . sometimes it looks like him. I mean, I looked outside and it's like I could see him."

"What do we do when you feel like that?"

"I get my shield and my helmet," the boy recited, "and if it's dark I put the lights on."

Parker remained standing. Usually, when he had serious conversations with his children, he subscribed to the eye-level approach. But when the subject of the Boatman arose a therapist had recommended that Parker stand – to make the boy feel safe in the presence of a strong, protective adult. And there *was* something about Parker Kincaid that induced a sense of security. Just forty, he was tall – a little over six feet – and was nearly in as good shape now as he'd been in college. Thanks not to aerobics or health clubs but to his two children – and their soccer scrimmages, basketball, Frisbee tourneys and the family's regular Sunday morning runs (well, *Parker's* run – he usually brought up the rear behind their bicycles as they looped around a local park).

"Let's take a look. Okay? Where you think you saw him."

"Okay."

"You have your helmet and your shield?"

"Right here." The boy patted his head and then held up his left arm like a knight's.

"That's a good one. I've got mine too." Parker mimicked the boy's gestures.

They walked to the back door.

"See, those bushes," Robby said.

Parker looked out over his half acre in an old development twenty miles west of Washington, D.C. His property was mostly grass and flower beds. But at the back of the lot was a tangle of forsythia and kudzu and ivy he'd been meaning to cut back for a year. Sure enough, if you squinted, some of the vegetation *did* resemble a human form.

"That looks spooky," Parker conceded. "Sure does. But you know the Boatman was a long time ago." He wasn't going to minimize the boy's fear by pointing out that he'd been scared only by some scruffy bushes. But he wanted to give Robby a sense of distance from the incident.

"I know. But . . ."

"How long ago was it?"

"Four years," Robby answered.

"Isn't that a *long* time?"

"Pretty long, I guess."

"Show me." He stretched his arms out. "This long?"

"Maybe."

"I think it's longer." Parker stretched his arms out farther. "As long as that fish we caught at Braddock Lake?"

"That was *this* long," the boy said, starting to smile and holding his own arms out.

"Naw, it was *this* long." Parker gave an exaggerated frown.

"No, no, it was *this* long." The boy danced from one foot to the next, hands up high.

"It was longer!" Parker joked. "Longer."

Robby ran the length of the kitchen, lifting one arm. Then he ran back and lifted the other. "It was *this* long!"

"That's how long a shark is," Parker cried. "No, a whale, no, a giant squid. No, I know – a Tufted Mazurka!" A creature from *If I Ran the Zoo*. Robby and Stephie loved Dr. Seuss. Parker's nickname for the children was the "Whos" – after the creatures in *Horton Hears a Who*, which was their absolute favorite story of all time, beating even Pooh.

Parker and Robby played a game of indoor tag for a few minutes then he caught the boy in his arms for a brief tickle fest.

"Know what?" Parker asked, gasping.

"What?"

"How 'bout tomorrow we cut down all those bushes."

"Can *I* use the saw?" the boy asked quickly.

Oh, they're ready for any opportunity, he thought, laughing to himself. "We'll see," Parker said.

"All right!" Robby danced out of the kitchen, memories of the Boatman lost under euphoria at the promise of power tools. He ran upstairs and Parker heard some gentle bickering between brother and sister about which Nintendo game to play. Stephanie, it seemed, won and the infectious Mario Bros. theme wafted through the house.

Parker's eyes lingered on the brush in the backyard. The Boatman . . . He shook his head.

The doorbell rang. He glanced into the living room but the children hadn't heard it. He walked to the door and swung it open.

The attractive woman offered a broad smile. Her

earrings dangled below her sharp-edged hair, which was bleached blonder than usual by the sun (Robby's was her shade while Stephanie's was closer to Parker's brown). Her tan was scrupulous.

"Well, hello," Parker said tentatively.

He glanced past her and was relieved to see that the engine of the beige Cadillac parked in the driveway was still running. Richard was behind the wheel, reading the *Wall Street Journal*.

"Hi, Parker. We just got in to Dulles." She hugged him.

"You were . . . where were you?"

"St. Croix. It was wonderful. Oh, relax. God, your body language . . . I just stopped by a minute."

"You look good, Joan."

"I feel good. I feel really good. I can't tell whether you look good, Parker. You look pale."

"The kids're upstairs—" He turned to call them.

"No, that's all right," Joan started to say.

"Robby, Stephie! Your mommy's here."

Thuds on the stairs. The Whos turned the corner fast and ran up to Joan. She was smiling but Parker could see that she was miffed he'd called them.

"Mommy, you're all tan!" Stephie said, tossing her hair like a Spice Girl. Robby was a cherub; Stephanie had a long, serious face, which, Parker hoped, would start to look intimidatingly intellectual to boys by the time she turned twelve or thirteen.

"Where were you, Mommy?" Robby said, frowning.

"The Caribbean. Didn't Daddy tell you?" A glance at Parker. Yes, he'd told them. Joan didn't understand that what the children were upset about wasn't miscommunication about her destination but the fact she hadn't been in Virginia for Christmas.

"Did you have a nice holiday?" she asked.

"We got an air hockey and I beat Robby three games this morning."

"But I got the puck in four times in a row!" he said. "Did you bring us something?"

Joan looked in the direction of the car. "Of course I did. But, you know, I left them in the suitcase. I just stopped by for a minute now to say hi and to talk to your father. I'll bring your presents tomorrow when I come to visit."

Stephie said, "Oh, and I got a soccer ball and the new Mario Bros. and the whole set of Wallace & Gromit—"

Robby stepped on his sister's recitation. "And *I* got a Death Star and a Millennium Falcon. And tons of Micro Machines! And a Sammy Sosa bat. And we saw *The Nutcracker.*"

"Did you get my presents?" Joan asked.

"Uh-huh," Stephie said. "Thank you." The girl was impeccably polite but a Barbie doll in a pageant dress no longer held any interest for her. Eight-year-olds now were not the eight-year-olds of Joan's childhood.

"Daddy took back my shirt," Robby said, "and got one the right size."

"I told him to do that if it didn't fit," Joan said quickly. "I just wanted you to have *something.*"

"We didn't get to talk to you on Christmas," Stephie said.

"Oh," Joan replied to her daughter, "it was so hard to call from where we were staying. It was like *Gilligan's*

Island. The phones were never working." She tousled the boy's hair. "And after all you *weren't* home."

She was blaming them. Joan had never learned that nothing was ever the children's fault, not at this age. If you did something wrong it was *your* fault; if they did something wrong it was *still* your fault.

Oh, Joan . . . It was subtle lapses like this – the slight shifting of blame – that were as bad as slaps in the face. Still, he said nothing. (*"Never let the children see their parents argue."*)

Joan stood. "Richard and I have to go now. We have to pick up Elmo and Saint at the kennel. The poor puppies have been in cages all week."

Robby was animated once more. "We're having a party tonight and we're going to watch the fireworks on TV and play *Star Wars* Monopoly."

"Oh, that'll be fun," Joan said. "Richard and I are going to Kennedy Center. For an opera. You like the opera, don't you?"

Stephie gave one of the broad, cryptic shrugs she'd been using a lot lately in response to adults' questions.

"That's a play where people sing the story," Parker said to the children.

"Maybe Richard and I'll take you to the opera sometime. Would you like that?"

"I guess," Robby said. Which was as good a commitment as a nine-year-old would ever make to high culture.

"Wait," Stephie blurted. She turned and pounded up the stairs.

"Honey, I don't have much time. We—"

The girl returned a moment later with her new soccer outfit, handed it to her mother.

"My," said Joan, "that's pretty." Holding the clothes awkwardly, like a child who's caught a fish and isn't sure she wants it.

Parker Kincaid, thinking: First, the Boatman, now Joan . . . How the past was intruding today. Well, why not? After all, it was New Year's Eve.

A time to look back . . .

Joan was obviously relieved when the children ran back to Stephie's bedroom, buoyed by the promise of more presents. Then suddenly her smile was gone. Ironically, at this age – she was thirty-nine – she looked her best with a sullen expression on her face. She touched her front teeth with the tip of her finger to see if they were dotted with lipstick. A habit of hers he remembered from when they were married. "Parker, I didn't have to do this . . ." She was reaching into her Coach purse.

Hell, she got me a Christmas present. And I didn't get her one. He thought quickly: Did he have any extra gifts he'd bought but hadn't yet given away? Something he could—

But then saw her hand emerge from the purse with a wad of papers.

"I could've just let the process server take care of it on Monday."

Process server?

"But I wanted to talk to you before you went off half-cocked."

The top of the document read: "Motion to Modify Child Custody Order."

He felt the blow deep in his stomach.

Apparently, Joan and Richard *hadn't* come directly from the airport but had stopped at her lawyer's first.

"Joan," he said, despairing, "you're not . . ."

"I want them, Parker, and I'm going to get them. Let's not fight about it. We can work something out."

"No," he whispered. "No." He felt the strength leach from his body as the panic swept through him.

"Four days with you, Fridays and weekends with me. Depending on what Richard and I have planned – we've been doing a lot of traveling lately. Look, it'll give you more time to yourself. I'd think you'd look forward to—"

"Absolutely not."

"They're my children . . ." she began.

"Technically." Parker had had sole custody for four years.

"Parker," she said reasonably, "my life is stable. I'm doing fine. I'm working out again. I'm married."

To a civil servant in county government, who, according to the *Washington Post*, just missed getting indicted for accepting bribes last year. Richard was just a bug-picking bird on the rump of Inside-the-Beltway politics. He was also the man Joan'd been sleeping with for the last year of her marriage to Parker.

Concerned the children would hear, he whispered, "You've been a stranger to Robby and Stephie practically from the day they were born." He slapped the papers and rage took him completely. "Are you thinking about them at all? About what this'll do to them?"

"They need a mother."

No, Parker thought, *Joan* needs another collectible. Several years ago it had been horses. Then championship weimaraners. Then antiques. Houses in fancy neighborhoods too: She and Richard moved from

Oakton to Clifton to McLean to Alexandria. "Moving up in the world," she'd said, though Parker knew she'd simply grown tired of each previous house and neighborhood when she failed to make friends in the new locale. He thought of what uprooting the children that frequently would do to them.

"Why?" he asked.

"I want a family."

"Have children with Richard. You're young."

But she wouldn't want *that*, Parker knew. As much as she'd loved being pregnant – she was never more beautiful – she had fallen apart at the work involved with infants. You can hardly have children when, emotionally, you're one yourself.

"You're completely unfit," Parker said.

"My, you *have* learned how to take the gloves off, haven't you? Well, maybe I *was* unfit. But that's in the past."

No, that's in your nature.

"I'll fight it, Joan," he said matter-of-factly. "You know that."

She snapped, "I'll be by tomorrow at ten. And I'm bringing a social worker."

"What?" He was dumbfounded.

"Just to talk to the kids."

"Joan . . . On a *holiday?*" Parker couldn't imagine that a social worker would agree to this but then he realized that Richard must have pulled some strings.

"If you're as good a father as you think you are you won't have any trouble with them talking to her."

"*I* don't have any trouble. I'm thinking of them. Just wait until next week. How do you think they'll feel having some stranger cross-examining them on the holiday? It's ridiculous. They want to see *you*."

"Parker," she said, exasperated, "she's a professional. She's not going to cross-examine them. Look, I have to run. The kennel's closing soon because of the holiday. Those poor puppies . . . Oh, come on, Parker. It's not the end of the world."

But, yes, he thought, that's exactly what it is.

He began to slam the door but halfway through the gesture he stopped, knowing that the sound would upset the Whos.

He closed the door with a firm click. Turned the dead bolt, put the chain on, as if trying to lock this cyclone of bad news out. Folding the papers without looking at them, he walked into the den and stuffed them into the desk. He paced for a few minutes then climbed the stairs and stuck his head in Robby's room. The children were giggling and tossing Micro Machines at each other.

"No bombardiering on New Year's Eve," Parker said.

"So it's okay to bombardier tomorrow?" Robby asked.

"Very funny, young man."

"He started it!" Stephie sniped, then returned to her book. *Little House on the Prairie*.

"Who wants to help me in the study?" he called.

"I do," Robby cried.

Together, father and son disappeared down the stairs into his basement office. A few minutes later Parker heard the electronic music again as Stephie exchanged literature for computer science and sent intrepid Mario on his quest once more.

*   *   *

Mayor Gerald Kennedy – a Democrat, yes, but not *that* strain of Kennedys – looked at the piece of white paper on his desk.

> *Mayor Kennedy—*
> *The end is night. The Digger is loose and their is no way to stop him.*

Attached to the sheet was an FBI memo, which was headed, "Annexed document is a copy. METSHOOT case, 12/31."

METSHOOT, Kennedy thought. Metro shooting. The Bureau loved their labels, he recalled. Sitting hunched like a bear over the ornate desk in his Georgian office in the very un-Georgian Washington, D.C., City Hall, Kennedy read the note once more. Looked up at the two people seated across from him. A trim, attractive blond woman and a tall, lean gray-haired man. Balding Kennedy often thought of people in terms of their hair.

"You're sure he's the one behind the shooting?"

"What he said about the bullets," the woman said, "them being painted? That checked out. We're sure the note's from the perp."

Kennedy, a bulky man comfortable with his bulk, pushed the note around on his desk with his huge hands.

The door opened and a young black man in a double-breasted Italian suit and oval glasses walked inside. Kennedy gestured him to the desk.

"This is Wendell Jefferies," the mayor said. "My chief aide-de-camp."

The woman agent nodded. "Margaret Lukas."

The other agent gave what seemed to Kennedy to be a shrug. "Cage." They all shook hands.

"They're FBI," Kennedy added.

Jefferies's nod said, Obviously.

Kennedy pushed the copy of the note toward the aide.

Jefferies adjusted his designer glasses and looked at the note. "Shit. He's gonna do it again?"

"So it seems," the woman agent said.

Kennedy studied the agents. Cage was from Ninth Street – FBI headquarters – and Lukas was the acting special agent in charge of the Washington, D.C., field office. Her boss was out of town so she was the person running the Metro shooting case. Cage was older and seemed well connected in the Bureau; Lukas was younger and appeared more cynical and energetic. Jerry Kennedy had been mayor of the District of Columbia for three years now and he had kept the city afloat not on experience and connections but on cynicism and energy. He was glad Lukas was the one in charge.

"Prick can't even spell," Jefferies muttered, lowering his sleek face to read the note again. His eyes were terrible, a malady shared by his siblings. A good portion of the young man's salary went to his mother and her two other sons and two daughters in Southeast D.C. A good deed that Jefferies never mentioned – he kept it as quiet as the fact that his father had been killed on East Third Street while buying heroin.

For Kennedy, young Wendell Jefferies represented the best heart of the District of Columbia.

"Leads?" the aide asked.

Lukas said, "Nothing. We've got VICAP involved, District police, Behavioral down in Quantico, and Fairfax, Prince William and Montgomery County police. But we don't have anything solid."

"Jesus," Jefferies said, checking his watch.

Kennedy looked at the brass clock on his desk. It was just after 10 A.M.

"Twelve hundred hours . . . noon," he mused, wondering why the extortionist used twenty-four-hour European, or military, time. "We have two hours."

Jefferies said, "You'll have to make a statement, Jerry. Soon."

"I know." Kennedy stood.

Why did this have to happen now? Why here?

He glanced at Jefferies – the man was young but, Kennedy knew, had a promising political career ahead of him. He was savvy and very quick; Jefferies's handsome face twisted into a sour expression and Kennedy understood that he was thinking exactly the same thing that the mayor was: *Why now?*

Kennedy glanced at the memo about the special reviewing stand at the New Year's Eve fireworks tonight on the Mall. He and Claire, his wife, would be sitting with Representative Paul Lanier and the other key congressional zookeepers of the District.

Or they would have been if this hadn't happened.

Why now?

Why my city?

He asked them, "What're you doing to catch him?"

It was Lukas who answered and she answered immediately. "We're checking CIs – confidential informants – and Bureau handlers who've got any contact with domestic or foreign terrorist cells. So far, nothing.

And my assessment is this isn't a terrorist profile. It smells like a by-the-book profit crime. Then I've got agents comparing past extortion schemes to try to find a pattern. We're looking at any other threats the District or District employees have received in the past two years. No parallels so far."

"The mayor's gotten some threats, you know," Jefferies said. "About the Moss situation."

"What's that?" Cage asked.

Lukas answered, "The Board of Education whistle-blower. The guy I've been baby-sitting."

"Oh, him." Cage shrugged.

To Jefferies, Agent Lukas said, "I know about the threats. I've looked into them. But I don't think there's a connection. They were just your routine anonymous threats from pay phones. No money was involved and there were no other demands."

Your routine anonymous threats, Kennedy thought cynically.

Except that they don't sound so routine if your wife picks up the phone at 3:00 in the morning and hears, "Don't push the Moss investigation. Or you'll be as fucking dead as he's gonna be."

Lukas continued. "In terms of standard investigation I've got agents running license plates from every car parked around City Hall this morning. We're also running the tags from cars around Dupont Circle. We're checking out the drop area by the Beltway and all the hotels, apartments, trailers and houses around it."

"You don't sound optimistic," Kennedy grumbled.

"I'm *not* optimistic. There're no witnesses. No reliable ones anyway. A case like this, we need witnesses."

Kennedy examined the note once again. It seemed odd that a madman, a killer, should have such nice handwriting. To Lukas he said, "So. I guess the question is – should I pay?"

Now Lukas looked at Cage. He answered, "We feel that unless you pay the ransom or an informer comes forward with solid information about the Digger's whereabouts we won't be able to stop him by 4 P.M. We just don't have enough leads." She added, "I'm not recommending you pay. This's just our assessment of what'll happen if you don't."

"Twenty million," he mused.

Without a knock the office door opened and a tall man of about sixty, wearing a gray suit, stepped inside.

Oh, great, Kennedy thought. More cooks in the kitchen.

U.S. Representative Paul Lanier shook the mayor's hand and then introduced himself to the FBI agents. He ignored Wendell Jefferies.

"Paul," Kennedy told Lukas, "is head of the District Governance Committee."

Though the District of Columbia had some autonomy, Congress had recently taken over the power of the purse and doled out money to the city like a parent giving a reckless child an allowance. Especially since the recent Board of Education scandal Lanier had been to Kennedy what an auditor is to a set of accounting books.

Lanier missed the disparaging tone in Kennedy's voice – though Lukas seemed not to – and the congressman asked, "Can you give me a heads-up on the situation?"

Lukas ran through her assessment once more. Lanier remained standing, all three buttons of his Brooks Brothers suit snugly secured.

"Why here?" Lanier asked. "Why Washington?"

Kennedy laughed to himself. The prick's even stolen my rhetorical question.

Lukas answered, "We don't know."

Kennedy continued, "You really think he'd do it again?"

"Yes."

The congressman asked, "Jerry, you're not seriously thinking of paying."

"I'm considering all options."

Lanier was looking dubious. "Well, aren't you concerned with what it'll look like?"

"No, I don't care how it looks," Kennedy snapped.

But the congressman continued in his politician's perfect baritone. "It's going to send the wrong message. Kowtowing to terrorists."

Kennedy glanced at Lukas, who said, "It *is* something to think about. The floodgates theory. You give in to one extortionist there'll be others."

"But nobody knows about this, do they?" Kennedy nodded to the note.

"Sure, they do," Cage said. "And more'll know pretty soon. You can't keep something like this under wraps for long. Notes like this have wings. You bet they do."

"Wings," Kennedy repeated, disliking the expression and all the happier that Lukas was running the show. He asked her, "What can you do to find him if we *do* pay?"

Lukas again responded. "Our tech people'll rig the

drop bag – with a transmitter. Twenty million will weigh a couple hundred pounds," she explained. "It's not something you can just hide under the seat of a car. We'll try to track the perp to his hideout. If we're lucky, get both him and the shooter – this Digger."

"'Lucky,'" Kennedy said skeptically. She was a pretty woman, he thought, though the mayor – who'd been married to his wife for thirty-seven years and had never once considered cheating on her – knew that beauty is mostly expression of eye and mouth and posture, not God-given structure. And Margaret Lukas's face hadn't once softened since she'd walked into his office. No smile, no sympathy. Her voice was flinty now as she said, "We can't give you percentages."

"No. Of course you can't."

"Twenty million," mused Lanier, the controller of the purse strings.

Kennedy rose, pushed his chair back and stepped to a window. Looked out on the brown lawn and trees speckled with brown leaves. The winter in Northern Virginia had been eerily warm for the past several weeks. Tonight, the forecasters were predicting, would be the first big snow of the year but at the moment the air was warm and humid and the scent of decomposing vegetation wafted into the room. It was unsettling. Across the street was a park, in the middle of which was a big, dark, modern statue; it reminded Kennedy of a liver.

He glanced at Wendell Jefferies, who took the cue and joined him. The aide wore aftershave; he must have had twenty different scents. The mayor whispered, "So, Wendy, the pressure's on, huh?"

The aide, never known for his restraint, responded, "You got the ball, boss. Drop it and you and me both, we're gone. And more than that too."

And more than that too . . .

And Kennedy had thought things couldn't get any worse after the Board of Education scandal.

"And so far," Kennedy said, "no leads. Nothing."

So far twenty-three people dead.

So far all they knew was that this psychopath was going to try to kill more people at 4 o'clock and more after that and more after that.

Outside the window the eerily warm air stirred. Five lacy brown leaves twisted to the ground.

He turned back to his desk. Looked at the brass clock. The time was 10:25.

Lanier said, "I say we don't pay. I mean, it seems to me that when he finds out the FBI's involved he might just balk and head for the hills."

Agent Lukas offered, "Bet he had an idea the Bureau'd be involved before he started this."

Kennedy picked up on her sarcasm. Lanier, again, remained oblivious.

The congressman continued, speaking to her, "I didn't think you were in favor of paying."

"I'm not."

"But you also think he'll keep shooting if we don't pay."

"Yes," she answered.

"Well . . ." Lanier lifted his hands. "Isn't that inconsistent? You don't think we should pay . . . but he's going to keep killing."

"That's right."

"That doesn't give us much guidance."

Lukas said, "He's a man who's prepared to kill as many people as he needs to, just to make money. You can't negotiate with somebody like that."

"Will paying make your job harder?" Kennedy asked. "Harder to catch him?"

"No," she said. A moment later: "So," she asked, "are you going to pay or not?"

The desk lamp shone on the note. To Kennedy it seemed that the piece of paper glowed like white fire.

"No, we're not paying," Lanier said. "We're taking a hard line. We're standing tough on terrorism. We're—"

"I'm paying," said Kennedy.

"You sure?" Lukas asked him, not seeming to care one way or the other.

"I'm sure. Do your best to catch them. But the city's going to pay."

"Hold on," the congressman said, "not so fast."

"It's not fast at all," Kennedy snapped. "I've been considering it since I got this goddamn thing." He gestured at the fiery note.

"Jerry," Lanier began, laughing sourly, "you don't have the right to make that decision."

"Actually he does," said Wendell Jefferies, who could append the letters J.D. and LL.M. after his name.

"Congress has jurisdiction," Lanier said petulantly.

Cage said to Lanier, "No, it doesn't. It's exclusively the District's call. I asked the attorney general on my way over here."

"But we've got control of the money," Lanier snapped. "And I'm not going to authorize it."

Kennedy glanced at Wendy Jefferies, who thought

for a moment. "Twenty million? We can draw on our line of credit for discretionary spending." He laughed. "But it'll have to come out of the Board of Education reserve. They're the only account that's majorly liquid."

"That's the only place?"

"That's it. It's debt or nickels and dimes everywhere else."

Kennedy shook his head. How goddamn ironic — the money to save the city was available only because someone had cut corners and landed the administration in the middle of a huge scandal.

"Jerry, this is ridiculous," Lanier said. "Even if they get *these* men somebody else could try the same thing next month. Never deal with terrorists. That's the rule in Washington. Don't you read Department of State advisories?"

"No, I don't," Kennedy said. "Nobody sends 'em to me. Wendy, get started on that money. And Agent Lukas . . . go catch this son of a bitch."

The sandwich was okay.

Not great.

Gilbert Havel decided that after he got the money he was going to the Jockey Club and having a real steak. A filet mignon. And a bottle of champagne.

He finished his coffee and kept his eye on the entrance to City Hall.

The chief of police of the District had come and gone quickly. A dozen reporters and camera crews had been turned away from the front door, directed toward an entrance on the side of the building. They hadn't looked happy. Then a couple of what were clearly FBI agents had disappeared into City Hall some time ago, a man and a woman, and hadn't emerged. It was definitely a Bureau operation. Well, he'd known it would be.

So far no surprises.

Havel looked at his watch. Time to go to the safehouse, call the helicopter charterer. There was a lot to get ready for. The plans for picking up the $20 million were elaborate – and the plans for getting away afterward were even more so.

Havel paid his check – with old, crumpled singles – and pulled his coat and cap on again. He left the coffee shop, turned off the sidewalk and walked quickly through an alley, eyes down. The Judiciary Square Metro stop was right beneath City Hall but he knew it would be watched by police or agents so he headed for Pennsylvania Avenue, where he'd get a bus down to Southeast D.C.

White man in a black man's 'hood.

Life sure is funny sometimes.

Gilbert Havel emerged from the alley and turned onto a side street that would take him to Pennsylvania. The light changed to green. Havel stepped into the intersection. Suddenly, a flash of dark motion from his left. He turned his head. Thinking: Shit, he doesn't see me! He doesn't see me he doesn't—

"Hey!" Havel cried.

The driver of the large delivery truck had been looking at an invoice and had sped through the red light. He glanced up, horrified. With a huge squeal of brakes the truck slammed directly into Havel. The driver screaming, "Christ, no! Christ . . ."

The truck caught Havel between its front fender and

a parked car, crushing him. The driver leapt out and stared in shock. "You weren't looking! It wasn't my fault!" Then he looked around and saw that the light had been against him. "Oh, Jesus." He saw two people running toward him from the corner. He debated for a moment. But panic took over and he leapt into his truck. He gunned the engine and backed away then sped down the street, skidding around the corner.

The passersby, two men in their thirties, ran up to Havel. One bent down to check for a pulse. The other just stood over him, staring at the huge pool of blood.

"That truck," the standing one whispered, "he just took off! He just left!" Then he asked his friend, "Is he dead?"

"Oh, yeah," the other man said. "Oh, yeah, he's dead."

3

12.45

*W*here?
     Margaret Lukas lay on her lean belly on a rise overlooking the Beltway.

Traffic sped past, an endless stream.

She looked at her watch again. And thought: Where *are* you?

Her belly hurt, her back hurt, her elbows hurt.

There'd been no way to get a mobile command post near the ransom drop zone – even a disguised MCP – and not be seen by the extortionist if he was anywhere near. So here she was, in jeans, jacket and cap turned backward, like a sniper or gangsta, lying on the rock-hard ground. Where they'd been for an hour.

"Sounds like water," Cage said.

"What?"

"The traffic."

He lay on his belly too, next to her, their thighs nearly touching – the way lovers might lie on a beach watching the sunset. They studied the field a hundred yards away. They were overlooking the money drop near Gallows Road – yes, "Gallows," an irony so rich that not one of the agents had bothered to comment on it.

"You know how that happens?" Cage continued. "Something gets under your skin and you try not to think about it. But you can't help it. I mean, it sounds like water."

It didn't sound like water to Lukas. It sounded like cars and trucks.

Where was the unsub? There's 20 million bucks there for the taking and he's not taking it.

"Where the hell is he?" muttered another voice. It belonged to a somber man of about thirty, with a military hairstyle and bearing. Leonard Hardy was with the District of Columbia police and was part of the team because, even though the Bureau was handling the operation, it would look bad not to have a District cop on board. Lukas would normally have protested having non-Bureau personnel on her team but she knew Hardy casually from his assignments at the Bureau's field office near City Hall and didn't mind his presence – as long as he kept doing what he'd done so far: sitting quietly by himself and not bothering the grown-ups.

"Why's he late?" Hardy mused again, apparently not expecting an answer. His immaculate hands, with perfectly trimmed nails, continued to jot notes for his report to the District chief of police and the mayor.

"Anything?" She turned her head, calling in a whisper to Tobe Geller, a curly-haired young agent also decked out in jeans and one of the same navy-blue, reversible windbreakers that Lukas wore.

Geller, in his thirties too, had the intensely cheerful face of a boy who finds complete contentment in any product filled with microchips. He scanned one of three portable video monitors in front of him. Then he typed on a laptop computer and read the screen. "Zip," he responded. If there was any living thing larger than a raccoon for a hundred yards around the ransom bags Geller's surveillance equipment would detect it.

When the mayor had given the go-ahead to pay the extortion money, the cash had made a detour en route to the drop. Lukas and Geller had Kennedy's aide shepherd the money to an address on Ninth Street in the District – a small, unmarked garage that was up the street from FBI headquarters.

There, Geller had repacked the ransom into two huge Burgess Security Systems KL-19 knapsacks, the canvas of which looked like regular cloth but was in fact impregnated with strands of oxidized copper – a high-efficiency antenna. The transmitter circuitry was in the nylon handles, and batteries were mounted in the plastic buttons on the bottom. The bag transmitted a Global Positioning System beacon cleaner than CBS's main broadcast signal and couldn't be shielded except by several inches of metal.

Geller had also rewrapped forty bundles of hundred dollar bills with wrappers of his own design – there were ultrathin transmitting wafers laminated inside them. Even if the perp transferred the cash from the canvas bag or it was split among accomplices Geller could still track down the money – up to a range of sixty miles.

The bag had been placed in the field just where the note had instructed. All the agents had backed off. And the waiting began.

Lukas knew her basic criminal behavior. Extortionists and kidnappers often get cold feet just before a ransom pickup. But anyone willing to murder twenty-three people wasn't going to balk now. She couldn't understand why the perp hadn't even approached the drop.

She was sweating; the weather was oddly warm for the last day of the year and the air was sickly sweet. Like fall. Margaret Lukas hated autumn. She'd rather have been lying in the snow than waiting in this purgatory of a season.

"Where are you?" she muttered. "Where?" She rocked slightly, feeling the pain of pressure on her hipbones. She was muscular but thin, with very little padding to protect her from the ground. She compulsively scanned the field once more though Geller's complex sensors would have picked up the unsub long before her blue-gray eyes could spot him.

"Hmm." C. P. Ardell, a heavy-set agent Lukas worked with sometimes, squeezed his earphone and listened. Nodded his bald, pale head. He glanced at Lukas. "That was Charlie position. Nobody's gone off the road in the woods."

Lukas grunted. So maybe she was wrong. She'd thought the unsub would come at the money from the west – through a row of trees a half mile away from the expressway. She believed that he'd be driving a Hummer or a Range Rover. Would snag one of the bags – sacrificing the other for the sake of expediency – and disappear back into the woods.

"Bravo position?" she asked.

"I'll check," said C. P., who worked undercover a lot because of his unfortunate resemblance to a Manassas drug cooker or a Hell's Angel charter member. He seemed to be the most patient of all the agents on the stakeout; he hadn't moved his 250-pound frame an inch since they'd been here. He made the call to the southernmost surveillance post.

"Nothing. Kids on a four-wheeler is all. Nobody older than twelve."

"Our people didn't chase 'em away, did they?" Lukas asked. "The kids?"

"Nup."

"Good. Make sure they don't."

More time passed. Hardy jotted notes. Geller typed on his keyboard. Cage fidgeted and C. P. did not.

"Your wife mad?" Lukas asked Cage. "You working the holiday?"

Cage shrugged. It was his favorite gesture. He had a whole vocabulary of shrugs. Cage was a senior agent at FBI headquarters and though his assignments took him all over the country he was usually primary on cases involving the District; he and Lukas worked together often. Along with Lukas's boss too, the special agent in charge of the Washington D.C. field office. This week, though, SAC Ron Cohen happened to be in a Brazilian rainforest on his first vacation in six years and Lukas had stepped up to the case. Largely because of Cage's recommendation.

She felt bad for Cage and Geller and C. P., working a holiday. They had dates for tonight or wives. As for Len Hardy she was happy he was here; he had some pretty good reasons to keep himself busy on holidays and this was why she had welcomed him to the METSHOOT team.

Lukas herself had a comfortable home in Georgetown, a place filled with antique furniture, needlepoints and embroideries and quilts of her own design, an erratic wine collection, nearly five hundred books, more than a thousand CDs and her mixed-breed Labrador, Jean Luc. It was a very nice place to spend a holiday evening though in the three years she'd lived there Lukas had never once done so. Until her pager had signaled her ascencion to the METSHOOT command she had planned to spend the night baby-sitting that Board of Education whistle-blower, Gary Moss, the one who'd broken the school construction kickback scandal. Moss had worn a wire and had picked up all sorts of good incriminating conversations. But his cover had been blown and the other day his house had been firebombed, his daughters nearly killed. Moss had sent his family to stay with relatives in North Carolina and he was spending the weekend in federal protection. Lukas had been in charge of his protection as well as handling the investigation into the firebombing. But then the Digger arrived and Moss was, at the moment, nothing more than a bored tenant in the very expensive apartment complex referred to among law enforcers as "Ninth Street" – FBI headquarters.

She now scanned the field again. No sign of the extortionist.

"He might be staking *us* out," a tactical agent crouched behind a tree said. "You want a perimeter sweep?"

"No."

"It's standard procedure," he persisted. "We could use five, six handoff cars. He'd never spot us."

"Too risky," she said.

"Uhm, you sure?"

"I'm sure."

Abrupt responses like this had earned Lukas the reputation in the Bureau for being arrogant. But she believed that arrogance is not necessarily a bad thing. It instills confidence in those who work for you. It also gets you noticed by your bosses.

Her eyes flickered as a voice crackled in her earphone, speaking her name.

"Go ahead," she said into the stalk mike, recognizing the voice of the deputy director of the Bureau.

"We've got a problem," he said.

She hated dramatics. "What?" she asked, not caring a bit about the abrasion in her voice.

The dep director said, "There was a hit-and-run near City Hall a little while ago. White male. He was killed. No ID on him. Nothing at all, just an apartment key – no address – and some money. The cop who responded'd heard about the extortion thing and, since it was near City Hall, thought there might be a connection."

She understood immediately. "They compared prints?" she asked. "His and the ones on the extortion note?"

"That's right. The dead guy's the one who wrote the note, the shooter's partner."

Lukas remembered part of the note. It went something like:

If you kill me, he will keep killing.

Nothing can stop the Digger . . .

"You've got to find the shooter, Margaret," the

deputy director said. There was a pause as, apparently, he looked at his watch. "You've got to find him in three hours."

Is it real? Parker Kincaid wondered.

Bending over the rectangle of paper, peering through his heavy, ten-power hand glass. Joan had been gone for several hours but the effect of her visit – the dismay – still lingered, trying though he was to lose himself in his work.

The letter he examined – on yellowing paper – was encased in a thin, strong poly sleeve but when he eased it closer to him he did so very carefully. The way you'd touch a baby's red, fat face. He adjusted the light and swooped in on the loop of the lowercase letter *y*.

Is it real?

It *appeared* to be real. But in his profession Parker Kincaid never put great stock in appearances.

He wanted badly to touch the document, to feel the rag paper, made with so little acid that it could last as long as steel. He wanted to feel the faint ridge of the iron-gallide ink, which, to his sensitive fingers, would seem as raised as braille. But he didn't dare take the paper from the sleeve; even the slightest oil from his hands would start to erode the thin letter. Which would be a disaster since it was worth perhaps $50,000.

If it was real.

Upstairs, Stephie was navigating Mario through his surreal universe. Robby was at Parker's feet, accompanied by Han Solo and Chewbacca. The basement study was a cozy place, paneled in teak, carpeted in forest-green pile. On the walls were framed documents – the less valuable items in Parker's collection.

Letters from Woodrow Wilson, FDR, Bobby Kennedy, the Old West artist Charles Russell. Many others. On one wall was a rogues' gallery – forgeries Parker had come across in his work.

Parker's favorite wall, though, was the one opposite the stool he sat on. This wall contained his children's drawings and poems, going back over the past eight years. From scrawls and illegible block letters to samples of their cursive writing. He often paused in his work and looked at them. Doing so had given him the idea about writing a book on how handwriting mirrors children's development.

He now sat on the comfortable stool at an immaculate white examination table. The room was silent. Normally he'd have the radio on, listening to jazz or classical music. But there'd been a terrible shooting in the District and all the stations were having special reports on the slaughter. Parker didn't want Robby to hear the stories, especially after the boy's flashback to the Boatman.

He hunched over the letter, eagerly, the way a jeweler appraises a beautiful yellow stone, ready to declare it false if that's how he saw it but secretly hoping that it will turn out to be rare topaz.

"What's that?" Robby asked, standing and looking at the letter.

"It's what came in the truck yesterday," Parker said, squinting as he checked out an upper-case *K*, which can be written a number of different ways and therefore is very useful in handwriting analysis.

"Oh, the armored car. That was neat."

It *was* neat. But it didn't answer the boy's question. Parker continued, "You know Thomas Jefferson?"

"Third president. Oh, and he lived in Virginia. Like us."

"Good. This's a letter that somebody thinks he wrote. They want me to check it and make sure."

One of the more difficult conversations he'd had with Robby and Stephie was explaining what he did for a living. Not the technical part of being a questioned document examiner. But that people would forge letters and documents and try to claim they were real.

"What's it say?" the boy asked.

Parker didn't answer right away. Oh, answers were important to him. He was, after all, a puzzle master – his lifelong hobby was riddles and word games and brain-teasers. He believed in answers and he tried never to defer responding to his children's questions. When a mother or father said, "Later," it was usually for *their* convenience, hoping the child would forget the question. But the content of this letter made him hedge. After a moment he said, "It's a letter Jefferson wrote to his oldest daughter." This much was true. But Parker didn't go on and tell the boy that the subject of the letter was Mary – his second daughter – who had died of complications from childbirth, as had Jefferson's wife some years before. He read:

> *Back here in Washington I live under a sorrowful pall, haunted as I am by visions of Polly on horseback and running along the porch in good-natured defiance of my prescriptions to her to exercise more caution . . .*

Parker, certified document examiner, struggled to

ignore the sadness he felt reading those words. Concentrate, he told himself, though the terrible image of a father being deprived of one of his children kept intruding.

A sorrowful pall . . .

Concentrate.

He observed that the girl's nickname in the letter was what Jefferson would have used – born "Mary," the girl was called "Polly" by her family – and that the punctuation-sparse style was typically Jeffersonian. These attested to authenticity. So did some of the events that the letter referred to; they had in fact occurred in Jefferson's life and had done so around the time the letter had purportedly been written.

Yes, textually at least, the letter seemed real.

But that was only half the game. Document examiners are not only linguists and historians, they are scientists too. Parker still had to perform the physical examination of the letter.

As he was about to slip it under one of his Bausch & Lomb compound microscopes the doorbell rang again.

Oh, no . . . Parker closed his eyes. It was Joan. He knew it. She'd picked up her dogs and returned to complicate his life further. Maybe she had the social worker with her now. A surprise commando raid . . .

"I'll get it," Robby said.

"No," Parker said quickly. Too quickly. The boy was unnerved by his abrupt reaction.

Father smiled at son. "I'll go." And slid off the stool, climbed the stairs.

He was mad now. He was determined that the

Whos would have a fun New Year's Eve, despite their mother. He flung the door open.

Well . . .

"Hello, Parker."

It took him a second to remember the name of the tall gray-haired man. He hadn't seen the agent for years. Then he recalled. "Cage."

He didn't recognize the woman standing beside him.

4

"How you doin', Parker? Never expected to see me in a month of blue Mondays, did you? Wait, I'm mixing up my expressions. But you get the picture."

The agent had changed very little. A bit grayer. A little more gaunt. He seemed taller. Parker remembered that Cage was exactly fifteen years older than he. They shared June as a birth month. Gemini. Yin-yang.

From the corner of his eye Parker saw Robby appear in the hallway with his coconspirator, Stephie. Word of visitors spreads fast in a household of children. They edged closer to the door, gazing out at Cage and the woman.

Parker turned and bent down. "Don't you two have something to do up in your rooms? Something *very* important?"

"No," Stephie said.

"Uh-uh," Robby confirmed.

"Well, I think you do."

"What?"

"How many Legos are on the floor? How many Micro Machines?"

"A couple," Robby tried.

"A couple of *hundred?*"

"Well," the boy said, grinning.

"Upstairs now . . . Up, up, or the monster'll take you up there himself. Do you want the monster? *Do* you?"

"No!" Stephie shrieked.

"Go on," Parker said, laughing. "Let Daddy talk to his friend here."

As they started up the stairs Cage said, "Oh, not hardly a friend. Right, Parker?"

He didn't respond. He closed the door behind him and turned back, appraising the woman. She was in her thirties, with a narrow, smooth face. Pale, nothing like Joan's relentless tan. She wasn't looking at Parker but was watching Robby climb the stairs through the lace-curtained window beside the door. She then turned her attention to him and reached out a strong hand with long fingers. She shook his hand firmly. "I'm Margaret Lukas. ASAC at the Washington field office."

Parker recalled that within the Bureau assistant special agents in charge were referred to by the acronym, pronounced A-sack, while the heads of the offices were called S-A-C's. An aspect of his former life he hadn't thought about for years.

She continued, "Could we come inside for a minute?"

A parental warning alarm went off. He responded, "You mind if we stay out here? The children . . ."

Her eyes flickered and he wondered if she considered this a snub. But that was just too bad; the kids' exposure to the Bureau was limited to sneaking a look at Scully and Mulder on *The X-Files* when sleeping over at friends' houses. He planned on keeping it that way.

"Fine with us," Cage said for both of them. "Hey, last time I saw you . . . man, it was a while ago. We were at Jimmy's, you know, his thing on Ninth Street."

"That's right."

It was in fact the last time Parker Kincaid had been at the Bureau headquarters. Standing in the large courtyard surrounded by the somber stone building. A hot July day two years ago. He still got occasional e-mails about what a fine speech he'd delivered at the memorial service for Jim Huang, who was one of Parker's former assistants. He'd been gunned down on his first day as a field agent.

Parker remained silent.

Cage nodded after the kids. "They're growing."

"They do that," Parker answered. "What exactly is it, Cage?"

The agent gave a shrug toward Lukas.

"We need your help, Mr. Kincaid," she said quickly, before the stream of breath accompanying Parker's question evaporated.

Parker tilted his head.

"It's nice out here," Cage said, looking up. "Fresh air. Linda and I should move. Get some land. Maybe Loudon County. You watch the news, Parker?"

"I listen."

"Huh?"

"Radio. I don't watch TV."

"That's right. You never did." Cage said to Lukas, "'Wasteland,' he'd call TV. He read a lot. Words're Parker's domain. His bailiwick, whatever the hell a bailiwick is. You told me your daughter reads like crazy. She still do that?"

"The guy in the subway," Parker said. "That's what you're here about."

"METSHOOT," Lukas said. "That's what we've acronymed it. He killed twenty-three people. Wounded thirty-seven. Six children were badly injured. There was a—"

"What is it you want?" he interrupted, worried that his own children might hear this.

Lukas responded, "This's important. We need your help."

"What on earth could you possibly want from me? I'm retired."

Cage said, "Uh-huh. Sure. Retired."

Lukas frowned, looked from one to the other.

Was this rehearsed? A good cop/confused cop thing? It didn't seem to be. Still, another important rule in his invisible parental *Handbook* was: "*Get used to being double-teamed.*" He was on his guard now.

"You still do document examination. You're in the Yellow Pages. And you've got a web site. It's good. I like the blue wallpaper."

He said firmly, "I'm a *civilian* document examiner."

Lukas said, "Cage tells me you were head of the Document Division for six years. He says you're the best document examiner in the country."

What weary eyes she has, Parker thought. She's probably only thirty-six or thirty-seven. Great figure, trim, athletic, beautiful face. Yet what she's seen . . . Look at those eyes. Like blue-gray stones. Parker knew about eyes like that.

Daddy, tell me about the Boatman.

"I only do commercial work. You know, is this letter from JFK real or a forgery? I don't do any criminal forensics."

"He was also candidate for SAC Eastern District. Yeah, yeah, I'm not kidding." Cage said this as if he hadn't heard Parker. "Except he turned it down."

Lukas lifted her pale eyebrows.

"And that was years ago," Parker responded.

"Sure it was," Cage said. "But you're not rusty, are you, Parker."

"Cage, get to the point."

"I'm trying to wear you down," the graying agent said.

"Can't be done."

"Ah, I'm the miracle worker. Remember?" To Lukas he said, "See, Parker didn't just find forgeries; he used to track people down because of what they wrote, where they buy writing paper, pens, things like that. Best in the business."

"She already said you said that," Parker said acerbically.

"Déjà vu all over again," Cage said.

Parker was shivering – but not from the cold. From the trouble these two people represented. He thought of the Whos. He thought of their party tonight. Thought of his ex-wife. He opened his mouth to tell lanky Cage and deadeye Lukas to get the hell out of his life. But she was there first. Bluntly she said, "Just listen. The unsub—"

Parker remembered: unknown subject. An unidentified perp.

"—and his partner, the shooter, have this extortion scheme. The shooter lights up a crowd of people with an automatic weapon every four hours starting at four this afternoon unless the city pays. Mayor's willing to and we drop the money. But the unsub never shows up. Why? He's dead."

"You believe the luck?" Cage said. "On his way to collect twenty million and he gets nailed by a delivery truck."

Parker asked, "Why didn't the *shooter* pick up the money?"

"'Cause the shooter's only instructions're to kill," Lukas said. "He doesn't have anything to do with the money. Classic left-hand/right-hand setup." Lukas seemed surprised he hadn't figured it out. "The unsub turns the shooter loose with instructions to keep going if he doesn't get a call to stop. That way we'll hesitate to cap the perp in a tac operation. And if we collar the unsub he's got leverage to work out a plea bargain in exchange for stopping the shooter."

"So," Cage said. "We've gotta find him. The shooter."

The door behind him started to open.

Parker quickly said to Lukas, "Button your jacket."

"What?" she asked.

As Robby stepped outside Parker quickly reached forward and tugged her jacket closed, hiding the large pistol on her belt. She frowned at this but he whispered, "I don't want him to see your weapon."

He put his arm around his son's shoulders. "Hey, Who. How you doing?"

"Stephie hid the controller."

"I did not," she called. "Didn't, didn't!"

"I was winning and she hid it."

Parker said, frowning, "Wait, isn't it connected with a cord?"

"She unplugged it."

"Stephie-effie. Is that controller going to appear in five seconds? Four, three, two . . ."

"I found it!" she called.

"My turn!" Robby cried and charged up the stairs again.

Once more Parker noticed Lukas's eyes follow Robby as he climbed to the second floor.

"What's his name?" Lukas asked.

"Robby."

"But what did you call him?"

"Oh. 'Who.' It's my nickname for the kids."

"After Wahoo?" she asked. "Your alma mater's team?"

"No. It's from a Dr. Seuss book." Parker wondered how she knew he'd gone to the University of Virginia. "Look, Cage, I'm sorry. But I really can't help you."

"You understand the problem here, boy?" Cage continued. "The only link we've got – the *only* clue at all – is the extortion note."

"Run it by PERT."

The Bureau's Physical Evidence Response Team.

Lukas's thin lips grew slightly thinner. "If we have to we will. And we'll get a psycholinguistic from Quantico. And I'll have agents check out every god-damn paper and pen company in the country. But—"

"—that's what we're hopin' you'd take over on," Cage filled in. "You can look at it, you can tell us what's what. Stuff nobody else can. Maybe where he lived. Maybe where the shooter's going to hit next."

Parker asked, "What about Stan?"

Stanley Lewis was the current head of the Bureau's Document Division. Parker knew the man was good; he'd hired Lewis years ago as an examiner. He recalled that they'd spent an evening drinking beer and trying to outdo each other forging John Hancock's signature. Lewis had won.

"He's in Hawaii for the *Sanchez* trial. Even in a Tomcat we can't get him back here before the next deadline."

"It's at four," Lukas repeated.

"It won't be like last time, Parker," Cage said softly. "That'll never happen again."

Lukas's head swiveled between the two men once again. But Parker didn't explain what Cage had meant. He wasn't talking about the past; he'd had enough past for one day.

"I'm sorry. Any other time, maybe. But I can't now." He was imagining what would happen if Joan found out he was working on an active investigation.

"Shit, Parker, what do I have to do?"

"We have nothing," Lukas said angrily. "No leads. We have a few hours until this crazy shoots up another crowd of people. There were children shot down—"

Parker waved his hand abruptly to silence her. "I'll have to ask you to leave now. Good luck."

Cage shrugged, looked at Lukas. She handed Parker her card, with the gold-embossed seal of the Justice Department on it. Parker had once had cards just like these. The typeface was Cheltenham condensed. Nine-point.

"Cell phone's on the bottom . . . Look, if we have any questions, you at least mind if we call?"

Parker hesitated. "No, I don't."

"Thank you."

"Goodbye," Parker said, stepping back into the house.

The door closed. Robby stood on the stairs.

"Who were they, Daddy?"

He said, "That was a man I used to work with."

"Did she have a gun?" Robby asked. "That lady?"

"Did you *see* a gun?" Parker asked him.

"Yeah."

"Then I guess she had one."

"Did you work with her too?" the boy asked.

"No, just the man."

"Oh. She was pretty."

Parker started to say, For a lady cop. But he didn't.

•   •   •

Back here in Washington I live under a sorrowful pall, haunted as I am by visions of Polly on horseback . . .

•   •   •

Parker, back in his basement study, alone now, found himself thinking of the letter in front of him as Q1. FBI document lab procedures dictated that questioned documents were called Q's. Authentic documents and handwriting samples – also called "knowns" – were referred to as K's. It had been years since he'd thought of the suspect wills and contracts he analyzed as Q's. This intrusion of police mindset into his personal life was unsettling. Nearly as troubling as Joan's appearance.

Forget about Cage, forget about Lukas.

Concentrate . . .

Back to the letter, hand glass in front of his face.

He now noted that the author – whether it had been Jefferson or not – had used a steel pen; he could see the unique flow of ink into fibers torn by the nib. Many forgers believe that all old documents were written with feather quills and use those exclusively. But by 1800 steel pen points were very popular and Jefferson did most of his corresponding with them.

One more tic on the side of authenticity.

I think of your Mother too at this difficult time and though my dear I do not want to add to your burden I wonder if I might impose on you to find that portrait of Polly and your Mother together, do you recall it? The one Mr. Chabroux painted of them by the well? I meant to bring it with me that their faces might sustain me in my darker moments.

He forced himself not to think about the context of the letter and examined a line of ink where it crossed a fold in the paper. He observed there was no bleeding into the gully of the crease. Which meant the letter had been written before it was folded. He knew that Thomas Jefferson was fastidious about his writing habits and would never have written a letter on a piece of paper that had been previously folded. Score another point for the document . . .

Parker looked up, stretched. He reached forward and clicked on the radio. National Public Radio was broadcasting another story about the metro shootings.

"*. . . report that the death toll has risen to twenty-four. Five-year-old LaVelle Williams died of a gunshot wound. Her mother was wounded in the attack and is listed in critical—*"

He shut the radio off.

Looking at the letter, moving his hand glass over the document slowly. Swooping in on a lift – where the writer finishes a word and raises the pen off the surface of the paper. This lift was typical of the way Jefferson ended his strokes.

And the feathering of the ink in the paper?

How ink is absorbed can tell you many things about the type of materials used and when the document was made. Over the years ink is drawn more and more into the paper. The feathering here suggested it had been written long ago – easily two hundred years. But, as always, he took the information under advisement; there were ways to fake feathering.

He heard the thud of the children's feet on the stairs. They paused, then there were louder bangs as first one then the other jumped down the last three steps to the floor.

"Daddy, we're hungry," Robby called from the top of the basement stairs.

"I'll be right there."

"Can we have grilled cheese?"

"Please!" Stephie added.

Parker clicked out the brilliant, white examination light on his table. He replaced the letter in his vault. He stood for a moment in the dim study, lit only by a fake Tiffany lamp in the corner, beside the old couch.

> *I meant to bring it with me that their faces might sustain me in my darker moments.*

He climbed the stairs.

5

"The weapon," Margaret Lukas called abruptly. "I want the deets on the shooter's weapon."

"You want what?" Cage asked.

"Deets. De-tails." She was used to her regular staff, who knew her expressions. And idiosyncracies.

"Any minute now," C. P. Ardell called back. "That's what they're tellin' me."

They were in one of the windowless rooms in the Bureau's new Strategic Information and Operations Center on the fifth floor of headquarters on Ninth Street. The whole facility was nearly as big as a football field and had recently been expanded to let the agency handle as many as five major crises at once.

Cage walked past Lukas and as he did so he whispered, "You're doing fine."

Lukas didn't respond. She caught sight of her reflection in one of the five-by-fifteen-foot video screens on the wall, on which was displayed the extortion note. Thinking: Am I? Am I doing fine? She hoped so. Lord, how she hoped that. The legend that went around the Bureau was that every agent got one chance to strike gold in his or her career. One chance to get noticed, one chance to move up exponentially.

Well, this sure as hell was hers. An ASAC running a case like this. It never happened. Not in a . . . what had Cage said? Not in a month of blue Mondays.

Looking past her reflection at the note, which glowed white with spidery black letters on the huge screen. What am I not thinking of? Lukas wondered. In her mind she ran through what she *had* thought of. She'd sent the dead unsub's fingerprints to every major friction ridge database in the world. She had two dozen District cops trying to find the delivery truck that hit him on the chance the unsub uttered some dying words to the driver (and had had miracle-worker Cage secure an immunity-from-prosecution waiver on the hit-and-run charge to induce the driver to talk). She had two dozen agents tracking down wits. Hundreds of tag numbers were being checked out. Handlers were milking CIs all over the country. Phone records in and out of City Hall for the past two weeks were being checked. She was—

A call came in. Len Hardy started to pick up the phone but Cage got to it first. Hardy had shed the trench coat, revealing a white polyester shirt with thin brown stripes and razor-crease slacks and a brown tie. Despite lying in a Northern Virginia field for an hour his marine-officer hair was still perfectly in place and there was not a bit of dirt on him. He looked less like a detective than a clean-cut Jehovah's Witness about to offer you some brochures on salvation. Lukas, who wore a new Glock 10, thought the thin

Smith & Wesson .38 revolver on Hardy's hip was positively quaint.

"You doing okay, Detective?" Lukas asked him, seeing his disgruntled expression as Cage swept the phone out from under his nose.

"Right as rain," he muttered, not too sardonically.

She gave a faint laugh at the expression, which she knew was an indigenous Midwestern phrase. She asked if he was from there.

"I grew up outside Chicago. Downstate. Well, that's what they call it – even though my hometown was northwest of the city."

He sat down. Her smile faded. *Right as rain . . .*

Cage hung up. "Got your *deets*. That was Firearms. Gun was an Uzi. About a year old and there was a lot of barrel spread. That weapon's seen some serious action. Mineral cotton in the silencer. Hand packed, it looked like. Not commercial. The shooter knows what he's doing."

"Good!" Lukas said. She called to C. P. Ardell, across the room, "Have somebody check out Web sites that give instructions for homemade silencers and converting Uzis to full auto. I want e-mail addresses of recent hits."

"Do they have to give up that info?" C. P. asked.

"Not without a warrant. But make 'em think they do. Be *persuasive*."

The agent made a call and spoke for a few minutes. He reported, "Com-Tech is on it." The Bureau's crack computer and communications unit, headquartered in Maryland.

To Cage, Lukas said, "Hey, got an idea."

The agent lifted an eyebrow.

She continued. "What we can do is get that guy from Human Resources?"

"Who?" Cage asked.

Lukas continued. "That guy examines applicants' handwriting and writes up their personality."

"The District does that too," Len Hardy said. "It's supposed to weed out the wackos."

"Whatta you mean?" C. P. asked Lukas. "We already sent it to Quantico."

The big agent was referring to a copy of the note that had been sent to the Bureau's Behavioral section for psycholinguistic profiling. Tobe Geller sat at a computer terminal nearby, waiting for the results.

"No, no, that's to link him to similar MOs and profile his education and intelligence," Lukas said. "I'm talking about profiling his personality. Graphoanalysis."

"Don't bother," a voice from behind them said.

Lukas turned and saw a man in jeans and a leather bomber jacket. He walked into the lab. He wore a visitor's badge around his neck and was carrying a large attaché case. It took a moment to recognize him.

Cage began to speak but stopped himself. Maybe afraid that he'd scare him off.

"Artie let me up," Parker Kincaid said. The Bureau's employee entrance night guard. "He still remembers me. After all these years."

This was a very different image of Kincaid, Lukas thought. He'd seemed frumpy at his house. It hadn't helped that he'd been wearing some god-awful sweater and baggy slacks. The gray crew-neck sweater he wore now, over a black shirt, seemed much more *him*.

"Mr. Kincaid," Lukas said, nodding a greeting. "Don't bother with what?"

"Graphoanalysis. You can't analyze personality from handwriting."

She was put off by his peremptory tone. "I thought a lot of people do it."

"People read tarot cards too and talk to their dear departed. It's bogus."

"I've heard it can be helpful," she persisted.

"Waste of time," he said matter-of-factly. "We'll concentrate on other things."

"Well. All right," Lukas said and pledged that she'd try not to dislike him too much.

Cage said, "Hey, Parker, you know Tobe Geller? Doubling as our computer and communications man tonight. We tracked him down on his way to a ski trip in Vermont."

"It was New Hampshire," the trim agent corrected, offering Kincaid one of his ready grins. "For holiday pay I'll do anything. Even break a date. Hi, Parker. I heard about you."

They shook hands.

Cage nodded to another desk. "This's C. P. Ardell. He's from the District field office. Nobody knows what C. P. stands for but that's what he goes by. I don't think even he knows."

"Did a while ago," C. P. said laconically.

"And this is Len Hardy. He's our District P.D. liaison."

"Nice to meet you, sir," the detective said.

Kincaid shook his hand. "Don't really need the 'sir.'"

"Sure."

"You Forensic? Investigative?" Kincaid asked him. Hardy seemed embarrassed as he said, "Actually I'm

Research and Statistical. Everybody else was out in the field so I got elected to liaise."

"Where's the note?" he asked Lukas. "I mean, the original?"

"In Identification. I wanted to see if we could raise a few more prints."

Kincaid frowned but before he could say anything Lukas added, "I told them to use the laser only. No ninhydrin."

His eyebrows lifted. "Good . . . you've worked in forensics?"

She had a sense that, even though she was right about not using the chemical, he was challenging her. "I remember from the Academy," she told him coolly and picked up the phone.

"What's that?" Hardy asked. "Nin . . ."

As she punched in a number Lukas said, "Ninhydrin's what you usually use to image fingerprints on paper."

"But," Kincaid finished her thought, "it ruins indented writing. Never use it on suspect documents."

Lukas continued to make her phone call – to ID. The tech told her that there were no other prints on the document and that a runner would bring the note up to the Crisis Center stat. She relayed this to the team.

Kincaid nodded.

"Why'd you change your mind?" Cage asked him. "About coming here?"

He was silent for a moment. "You know those children you mentioned? The ones injured in the subway? One of them died."

With a solemnity that matched his, Lukas said, "LaVelle Williams. I heard."

He turned to Cage. "I'm here on one condition.

Nobody except the immediate task force knows I'm involved. If there's a leak and my name gets out, whatever stage the investigation's in, I walk. And I deny I even know you people."

Lukas said, "If that's what you want, Mr. Kincaid, but—"

"Parker."

Cage said, "You got it. Can we ask why?"

"My children."

"If you're worried about security we can have a car put on your house. As many agents as you—"

"I'm worried about my ex-wife."

Lukas gave him a quizzical glance.

Kincaid said, "I've had custody of my children since my wife and I got divorced four years ago. And one of the reasons that it's me who has custody is that I work at home and I don't do anything that'd endanger them or me. That's why I only do commercial document work. Now it looks like my wife's reopening the custody case. She can't find out about this."

"Not a single problem in the world, Parker," Cage reassured him. "You'll be somebody else. Who d'you want to be?"

"I don't care if you make me John Doe or Thomas Jefferson as long as I'm not me. Joan's coming by the house tomorrow morning at ten with some presents for the kids. If she finds out I went off on New Year's Eve to work on a case . . . it'll be bad."

"What'd you tell them?" Lukas asked.

"That a friend of mine was sick and I had to go visit him in the hospital." He pointed a finger at Cage's chest. "I hated lying to them. *Hated* it."

Recalling his beautiful boy, Lukas said, "We'll do our best."

"It's not a question of best," Kincaid said to her, easily holding her eye. Which is something very few men could do. "It's either keep me out of the picture or I'm gone."

"Then we'll do it," she said simply, looking around the room. C. P., Geller and Hardy all nodded.

"All right." Kincaid took his jacket off, pitched it onto a chair. "Now, what's the plan?"

Lukas ran through the status of the investigation. Kincaid nodded, not saying anything. She tried to read his face, see if he approved of what she was doing. Wondered if she cared whether he did or not. Then she said, "The mayor's going on the air soon to make a plea to the shooter. He's going to suggest that we'll pay the money to *him*. Not come right out and say it but hint at it. We're hoping he'll contact us. We've got the money downstairs in a couple of trace bags. We'll drop them wherever he wants."

Cage took over. "Then Tobe here'll track him back to his hidey-hole. Jerry Baker's tactical team's on call. We'll nail him when he gets back home. Or take him down on the road."

"How likely is it he'll go for the cash?"

"We don't know," Lukas said. "When you take a look at the note you'll see the unsub – the guy who got killed – was pretty slow. If his partner, this Digger, is just as dumb he might not go for it." She was thinking of the criminal psychology she'd learned at the Academy. Slower perps were far more suspicious than intelligent ones. They tended not to improvise even when circumstances changed. Lukas added, "Which means he might just keep on shooting the way he's been instructed to."

Cage added, "And we don't even know if the shooter'll hear Kennedy's broadcast. But we just don't have a single damn lead."

Lukas noticed Kincaid glance down at the Major Crimes Bulletin. It was about the firebombing of Gary Moss's house. Bulletins like these described the crime in detail and were used to brief subsequent officers on the specifics of a case. This one mentioned how Moss's two children had just escaped being burned to death.

Parker Kincaid stared at the bulletin for longer than he seemed to want to, apparently troubled by the stark report of the attempt to murder the family.

The two children of the Subject were able to effectuate an escape from the structure with only minor injuries.

Finally he pushed it away. Looked around the center, taking in the banks of phones, computers, desks. His eyes ended up on the video monitor displaying the extortion note.

"Can we set up the ready-room someplace else?"

"This is the Crisis Center," Lukas said, watching him scan the note. "What's wrong with here?"

"We're not using most of the space," Kincaid pointed out. "And hardly any of the equipment."

Lukas considered this. "Where did you have in mind?"

"Upstairs," he said absently, still staring at the glowing note. "Let's go upstairs."

Parker walked through the Sci-Crime document lab, looking over the array of equipment he knew so well.

Two Leitz binocular stereo microscopes with a

Volpi Intralux fiber optic light source, an old Foster + Freeman VSC4 video spectral comparator and the latest of their video spectral comparators – the VSC 2000, equipped with a Rofin PoliLight and running QDOS software through Windows NT. Also, sitting well-used in the corner were a Foster + Freeman ESDA – an electrostatic detection apparatus – and a thin-layer gas chromatograph for ink and trace analysis.

He noticed the glass windows the tourists paraded past every day, nine to four, as part of the FBI headquarters tour. The corridor was now dark and ominous.

Parker watched the other members of the team find seats at desks and lab tables. The room was cluttered, smelly and uncomfortable, the way real working laboratories were. But he preferred to be here – rather than in the glitzy Crisis Center – because he firmly believed in something he'd learned from his father, a historian who specialized in the Revolutionary War. "Always fight your battles on familiar ground," the professor had told his boy. He'd chosen not to give this answer to Lukas; another thing William Kincaid had told his son was "You don't have to share everything with your allies."

He glanced into Stan Lewis's office again. Saw the books that he himself had used when this had been his department: Harrison's *Suspect Documents*, Housely and Farmer's *An Introduction to Handwriting Identification*, and *Scientific Examination of Questioned Documents* by Hilton. And the Bible of the profession: *Questioned Documents* by Albert S. Osborn. He looked at the credenza behind the office chair and recognized the four bonsai trees he'd cultivated then left for Lewis.

"Where's the note?" he asked Cage impatiently.

"On its way. On its way."

Parker turned on several of the instruments. Some hummed, some clicked. And some were silent, their dim indicator lights glowing like cautious eyes.

Waiting, waiting . . .

And trying not to think about his talk with the children an hour before – when he'd told them that their holiday plans were changing.

Both of the Whos had been in Robby's room, the floor still awash with Legos and Micro Machines.

"Hey, Whos."

"I got to the third level," Stephie'd said, nodding at the Nintendo. "Then I got bomped."

Robby'd had a full-scale invasion of his bed underway – with helicopters and landing craft.

Parker had sat on the bed. "You know those people who were here before?"

"The pretty lady you kept looking at," his son had said coyly.

("They're sharper than you'll ever guess," reports the *Handbook.)*

"Well, they told me that a friend of mine is sick and I have to go visit him for a little while. Who do you want to baby-sit?"

In addition to the standard cast of high-school and college sitters, Parker had a number of friends in the neighborhood – parents he socialized with – who'd gladly take the children for the evening. There was also his friend Lynne, who lived in the District. She would have driven to Fairfax to help him out but he was sure she'd have a date tonight (it was impossible to imagine Lynne without a date on New Year's Eve) and their relationship was no longer at the level where he could ask for a sacrifice like that.

"You *have* to go?" Robby'd asked. "Tonight?"

When he was disappointed, the boy would become very still, his expression remaining unchanged. He never pouted, never grumbled – which Parker would have preferred. He just froze, as if sadness threatened to overwhelm him. As Robby had looked up at him, unmoving, holding a tiny toy helicopter, Parker'd felt his son's disappointment in his own heart.

Stephie was less emotional and wore those emotions less visibly; her only response had been to toss her hair from her face and give him a frown, asking, "Is he going to be all right? Your friend?"

"I'm sure he'll be okay. But it would be a good thing for me to see him. So – do you want me to call Jennifer? Or Mrs. Cavanaugh?"

"Mrs. Cavanaugh!" they'd said, almost in unison, Robby coming out of his dolor. Mrs. Cavanaugh, the neighborhood grandmother, baby-sat on Tuesdays – when Parker sat in on a local poker game.

Parker had stood up, surrounded by the sea of toys.

"But you'll be back before midnight," Robby'd asked, "won't you?"

(*"Never make promises if there's any chance you can't keep them."*)

"I'm going to try as hard as I can."

Parker had hugged both of the children and then walked to the door.

"Daddy?" Stephie had asked, pure innocence in her baggy black jeans and Hello Kitty T-shirt. "Would your friend like me to make him a get-well card?"

Parker had felt his betrayal as a physical blow. "That's okay, honey. I think he'd like it better if you just had fun tonight."

Now, intruding on these difficult thoughts, the door to the document lab swung open. A lean, handsome agent with swept-back blond hair walked into the room. "Jerry Baker," he announced, walking up to Parker. "You're Parker Kincaid."

They shook hands.

He looked across the lab. "Margaret," he called in greeting. Lukas nodded back.

"You're the tactical expert?" Parker asked him.

"Right."

Lukas said, "Jerry's got some S&S people lined up."

Search and Surveillance, Parker recalled.

"Some good shooters too," Baker said. "Just dying for a chance to light up this beast."

Parker sat down in the gray chair. He said to Lukas, "You've processed the unsub's body?"

"Yes," Lukas said.

"Do you have the inventory?"

"Not yet."

"No?" Parker was troubled. He had very definite ideas of running investigations and he could see Lukas would have definite ideas too. He wondered how much of a problem he'd have with her. Handle it delicately or not? Glancing at her tough face – pale as pale marble – Parker decided he had no time for niceties. In a case with so few leads they needed as many K's – known aspects of the unsub – as they could find. "We better get it," he said.

She responded coolly, "I've ordered it sent up here ASAP."

Parker would have sent somebody – Hardy maybe – to pick it up. But he decided not to fight this skirmish. He'd give it another few minutes. He looked at Baker. "How many good guys do we have?"

"Thirty-six of ours, four dozen District P.D."

Parker frowned. "We'll need more than that."

"That's a problem," Cage said. "Most actives are on alert because of the holiday. There're a couple hundred thousand people in town. And a lot of Treasury and Justice agents're on security detail, what with all the diplomatic and government parties."

Len Hardy muttered, "Too bad this happened tonight."

Parker gave a short laugh. "It wouldn't have happened at any other time."

The young detective gave him a quizzical look. "What do you mean?"

He was about to answer but Lukas said, "The unsub *picked* tonight because he knew we'd be short-handed."

"And because of the crowds in town," Parker added. "The shooter's got himself a fucking firing range. He . . ."

He paused, listening to himself. He didn't like what he heard. Living with the children, working largely alone, he'd softened since he'd left the Bureau; the rough edges were gone. He never swore and he tempered everything he said with the Whos in mind. Now he found himself back in his former life, his hard life. As a linguist, Parker knew that the first thing an outsider does to adapt to a new group is to talk their talk.

Parker opened his attaché case – a portable document examination kit. It was filled with the tools of his trade. Also, it seemed, a Darth Vader action figure. A present from Robby.

"'The Force be with you,'" Cage said. "Our mascot for the night. My grandkids love those movies."

Parker propped it up on the examination table. "Wish it were Obi Wan Kenobi."

"Who?" Lukas frowned, shook her head.

Hardy blurted out, "You don't *know*?" Then blushed when she glanced at him coldly.

Parker was surprised too. How could somebody not know about *Star Wars*?

"Just a character in a movie," C. P. Ardell told her.

Without a reaction she turned back to a memo she was reading.

Parker found his hand glass, which was wrapped in black velvet. It was a Leitz lens, twelve power, and was the essential tool of a document examiner. Joan had given it to him for their second anniversary.

Hardy noticed a book in Parker's attaché case. Parker saw the cop looking at it and handed it to him. *Mind Twisters Volume 5*. Hardy flipped through it then passed it to Lukas.

"Hobby," Parker explained, glancing at her eyes as she scanned the pages.

Cage said, "Oh, this man loved his puzzles. That was his nickname 'round here. The Puzzle Master."

"They're lateral thinking exercises," Parker said. He looked over Lukas's shoulder and read out loud, "'A man has three coins that total seventy-six cents. The coins were minted in the United States within the last twenty years, are in general circulation and one isn't a penny. What are the denominations of the coins?'"

"Wait, one of them *has* to be a penny," Cage said.

Hardy looked at the ceiling. Parker wondered if his mind was as orderly as his personal style. The cop reflected for a moment. "Are they commemorative coins?"

"No, remember – they're in circulation."

"Right," the detective said.

Lukas's eyes scanned the floor. Her mind seemed to be elsewhere. Parker couldn't tell what she was thinking.

Geller thought for a minute. "I'm not wasting my brain cells on that." He turned back to his computer.

"Give up?" Parker asked.

"What's the answer?" Cage asked.

"He has a fifty-cent piece, a quarter and a penny."

"Wait," Hardy protested, "you said he didn't have a penny."

"No, I didn't. I said *one* of the coins wasn't a penny. The half-dollar and the quarter aren't. But one of them is."

"That's cheating," Cage grumbled.

"It sounds so easy," Hardy said.

"Puzzles are always easy when you know the answer," Parker said. "Just like life, right?"

Lukas turned the page. She read, "'Three hawks have been killing a farmer's chickens. One day he sees all three sitting on the roof of his chicken coop. The farmer has just one bullet in his gun and the hawks are so far apart that he can only hit one. He aims at the hawk on the left and shoots and kills it. The bullet doesn't ricochet. How many hawks are left on the roof?'"

"It's too obvious," C. P. observed.

"Wait," Cage said, "maybe *that's* the trick. You think it should be complicated but the answer really *is* the obvious one. You shoot one and there're two left. End of puzzle."

"Is that your answer?" Parker asked.

Cage said uncertainly, "I'm not sure."

Lukas flipped to the back of the book.

"*That's* cheating," Parker said.

She kept flipping. Then frowned. "Where are the answers?"

"There aren't any."

She asked, "What kind of puzzle book is that?"

"An answer you don't get on your own isn't an answer." Parker glanced at his watch. Where the hell was the note?

Lukas turned back to the puzzle, studied it. Her face was pretty. Joan was drop-dead beautiful, with her serpentine cheekbones and ample hips and buoyant breasts. Margaret Lukas, wearing a tight-fitting black sweater, was smaller on top and trimmer. She had thin, muscular thighs, revealed by tight jeans. At her ankle he caught a glimpse of sheer white stockings – probably those knee-highs that Joan used to wear under her slacks.

She was pretty, Daddy.

For a lady cop . . .

A slim young man in a too-tight gray suit walked into the lab. One of the young clerks who worked in the Mail and Memo Distribution Department, Parker guessed.

"Agent Cage," he said.

"Timothy, what've you got for us?"

"I'm looking for Agent Jefferson."

Parker was saved from asking "*Who?*" by Cage. "Tom Jefferson?"

"Yessir."

He pointed to Parker. "This's him."

Parker hesitated for only a moment then took the envelope and signed for it, carefully writing "Th. Jefferson" the same way the statesman had done, though with a much more careless hand.

Timothy left and Parker cocked an eyebrow at Cage, who said, "You wanna be anonymous. Poof. You're anonymous."

"But how—"

"I'm the miracle worker. I keep telling you."

The Digger is standing in the shadows outside his motel $39.99 a day kitchenette and free cable we have vacancies.

This is a lousy part of town. Reminds the Digger of . . . *click* . . . where, where?

Boston, no, White Plains . . . *click* . . . which is near New . . . New York.

Click.

He's standing beside a smelly dumpster and watching the front door to his comfy room.

He's watching people coming and going, the way the man who tells him things told him to do. Watching his front door. Watching the room through the open curtain.

Come and go.

Cars speed by on the lousy street, people walk past on the lousy sidewalk. The Digger looks like them, the Digger looks like no one. Nobody sees the Digger.

"Excuse me," a voice says. "I'm hungry. I haven't eaten—"

The Digger turns. The man looks into the Digger's blank eyes and can't finish his sentence. The Digger shoots the man with two silenced bullets. He falls and the Digger hefts the body into the big blue dumpster, thinking the silencer needs repacking; it's not that . . . *click* . . . not that silent anymore.

But nobody's heard. Too much traffic.

He picks up the shell casings and puts them into his pocket.

The dumpster is a pretty blue.

The Digger likes colors. His wife grew red flowers and his wife grew yellow flowers. But no blue flowers, he believes.

Looking around. Nobody else is nearby.

"If somebody looks at your face, kill them," said the man who tells him things. "Nobody can see your face. Remember that."

"I'll remember that," the Digger answered.

He listens to the dumpster. Silence.

Funny how when you're . . . *click* . . . when you're dead you don't make any noise.

Funny . . .

He goes back to watching the door, watching the window, watching the people on the sidewalk.

He checks his watch. He's waited for fifteen minutes.

Now it's okay to go inside.

Have some soup, reload his gun, repack the silencer. Which he learned how to do on a pretty fall day last year – was it last year? They sat on logs and the man told him how to reload his gun and repack the silencer and all around them were pretty colored leaves. Then he would practice shooting, spinning around like a whirligig, spinning around with the Uzi, as leaves and branches fell. He remembers the smell of hot, dead leaves.

He liked the forest better than here.

Opening the door, walking inside.

He calls his voice mail and methodically punches in his code. One two two five. There are no messages from the man who tells him things. He thinks he's a little sad that he hasn't heard from the man. He hasn't heard a word since this morning. He *thinks* he's sad. But he isn't sure what sad is.

No messages, no messages.

Which means he should repack the silencer and reload his clips and get ready to go out again.

But first he'll have some soup and put on the TV.

Have some nice hot soup.

6

Mayor Kennedy—

The end is night. The Digger is loose and their is no way to stop him. He will kill again – at four, eight and Midnight if you don't pay.

I am wanting $20 million dollars in cash, which you will put into a bag and leave it two miles south of Rt 66 on the West Side of the Beltway. In the middle of the Field. Pay to me the Money by 1200 hours. Only I am knowing how to stop The Digger. If you ~~will~~ apprehend me, he will keep killing. If you kill me, he will keep killing.

If you don't think I'm real, some of the Diggers bullets were painted black. Only I know that.

Documents have personalities. The Jefferson letter sitting in Parker's vault at home – whether a forgery or not – was regal. Scripty, and rich as amber. But the extortion note sitting on the FBI examination table here in front of him was choppy and stark.

Still, Parker was examining it the way he approached any puzzle: with no assumptions, no preconceptions. When solving riddles the mind is like fast-drying plaster; first impressions last. He'd resist drawing any conclusions until he'd analyzed the note completely. Deferring judgment was one of the hardest parts of his job.

Three hawks are killing a farmer's chickens . . .

"The bullets at the Metro?" he called. "You found some painted?"

"Yup," Jerry Baker said. "A dozen or so. Black paint."

Parker nodded. "Did I hear you say you'd ordered a psycholinguistic?"

"We did." Geller nodded at his computer screen. "Still waiting for the results from Quantico."

Parker looked at the envelope that had contained the note. It had been placed in an acetate sleeve to which was attached a chain-of-custody card headed with the word METSHOOT. On the front of the envelope was written, in the same handwriting as the note: *To the Mayor – Life and Death.*

He donned rubber gloves – not worried about fingerprints but rather about contaminating any trace materials that might be found on the paper. He unwrapped his Leitz hand glass. It was six inches across, with a rosewood handle and a glistening steel ring around the perfect glass lens. Parker examined the glue flap on the envelope.

"What've we got, what've we got. Anything?" he muttered under his breath. He often talked to himself when he was analyzing documents. If the Whos were in his study while he was working they assumed his comments were directed at them and got a kick out being included in Daddy's job.

The faint ridges left by the glue application machine at the factory were untouched.

"No spit on the glue," he said, clicking his tongue angrily. DNA and serologic information can be lifted from saliva residue on envelope flaps. "He didn't seal it."

Lukas shook her head, as if Parker had missed something obvious. "But we don't need it, remember? We took blood from the corpse and ran it through the DNA database. Nothing."

"I figured you'd run the *unsub's* blood," Parker said evenly. "But I was hoping the Digger'd licked the envelope and we could run *his* spit through the computer."

After a moment she conceded, "Good point. I hadn't thought about that."

Not too full of herself to apologize, Parker noted. Even if she didn't seem to mean it. He pushed the envelope aside and looked at the note itself again. He asked, "And what exactly *is* this 'Digger' stuff?"

"Yeah," C. P. Ardell piped up. "We have a wacko here?"

Cage offered, "Another Son of Sam? That Leonard Bernstein guy?"

"David Berkowitz," Lukas corrected before she realized it was a joke. C. P. and Hardy laughed. You could never exactly tell when Cage was fooling with you, Parker recalled. The agent was often jokey when investigations were at their most grim. It was a type of invisible shield – like Robby's – to protect the man inside the agent. Parker wondered if Lukas had shields too. Maybe, like Parker himself, she sometimes wore her armor in full view, sometimes kept it hidden.

"Let's call Behavioral," Parker said, "and see if they have anything on the name Digger."

Lukas agreed and Cage made the phone call down to Quantico.

"Any description of the shooter?" Parker asked, looking over the note.

"Nope," Cage said. "It was spooky. Nobody saw a gun, saw muzzle flash, heard anything other than the slugs hitting the wall. Well, hitting the vics too."

Incredulous, Parker asked, "At rush hour? Nobody saw anything?"

"He was there and then he was gone," C.P said.

Hardy added, "Like a ghost." Parker glanced at the detective. He was clean-cut, trim, handsome. Wore a wedding ring. Had all the indicia of a contented life. But there seemed to be a melancholy about him. Parker recalled that when he was leaving the Bureau the exit counselor explained to him – unnecessarily – about the high incidence of depression among law enforcers.

Bending over the letter again, studying the cold paper and the black type. He read it several times.

The end is night . . .

Parker noted that there was no signature. Which might seem like a pointless observation, except that he'd assisted in several cases in which perps had actually signed ransom or robbery notes. One had been fake, intended to lead them off (though the scrawled signature provided handwriting samples that ultimately convicted the perp). In another case the kidnapper had actually signed his real name, perhaps jotted automatically in the confusion of the abduction.

The perp was arrested seventeen minutes after the victim's family received the ransom demand.

Parker moved the powerful examining light closer to the note. Bent over it. Heard a neckbone pop.

Talk to me, he silently urged the piece of paper. Tell me your secrets . . .

The farmer has just one bullet in his gun and the hawks are so far apart that he can only hit one . . .

He wondered if the unsub had tried to doctor his handwriting. Many criminals – say, kidnappers writing ransom notes – will try to disguise their writing to make comparisons more difficult. They'll use odd slants and formations of letters. But usually they can't do this smoothly; it's very difficult to suppress our natural hand and document examiners can usually detect "tremble" – a shakiness in the strokes – when someone's trying to disguise his writing. But there was no tremble here. This was the unsub's genuine writing.

Normally the next step in an anonymous writing case would be to compare the suspect document with knowns — compare Q's with K's — by sending agents to public records offices with a copy of the extortion note and have them plough through files to find a match. Unfortunately for the team on the METSHOOT case, most writing in public records are in uppercase block, or "manuscript", style ("Please Print," the directions always admonish) and the extortion note had been written in a form of cursive. Even a document examiner with Parker Kincaid's skill couldn't compare printing with cursive writing.

But there was one thing that might let them search public files. A person's handwriting includes both general and personal characteristics. General are the elements of penmanship that come from the method of handwriting learned in school. Years ago there were a number of different methods of teaching writing and they were very distinctive; a document examiner could narrow down a suspect's location to a region of the country. But those systems of writing – the flowery "Ladies Hand," for instance – are gone now and only a few methods of writing remain, notably the Zaner-Bloser System and the Palmer Method. But they're too general to identify the writer.

Personal characteristics, though, are different. These are those little pen strokes that are unique to us – curlicues, mixing printing and cursive writing, adding gratuitous strokes – like a small dash through the diagonal stroke in the letter *Z* or the numeral 7. It was a personal characteristic that first tipped examiners off that the Hitler diaries "discovered" a few years ago were in fact fake. Hitler signed his last name with a very distinctive uppercase *H* but he used it only in his signature, not when writing in general. The forger had used the ornate capital *H* throughout the diary, which Hitler would not have done.

Parker continued to scan the extortion note with his hand glass, looking to see if the unsub had had any distinctive personal characteristics in his handwriting.

Daddy, you're funny. You look like Sherlock Holmes . . .

Finally he noticed something.

The dot above the lowercase letter *i*.

Most dots above *i*'s and *j*'s are formed by either tapping the pen directly into the paper or, if someone is writing quickly, making a dash with a dot of ink to the left and a tail to the right.

But the METSHOOT unsub had made an unusual mark above the lowercase *i*'s – the tail of the dot went straight upward, so that it resembled a falling drop of water. Parker had seen a similar dot years before – in a series of threat letters sent to a woman by a stalker who eventually murdered her. The letters had been written in the killer's own blood. Parker had christened the unusual dot "the devil's teardrop" and included a description of it in one of his textbooks on forensic document examination.

"Got something here," he said.

"What?" Cage asked.

Parker explained about the dot and how he'd named it.

"Devil's teardrop?" Lukas asked. She didn't seem to like the name. He guessed she was more comfortable with science and hard data. He remembered that she'd had a similar reaction when Hardy had said that the Digger was like a ghost. She leaned forward. Her short blond hair fell forward and partially obscured her face. "Any connection with your perp?" she asked. "In that stalker case?"

"No, no," Parker said. "He was executed years ago. But this" – he nodded toward the sheet – "could be the key to finding out where our boy lived."

"How?" Jerry Baker asked.

"If we can narrow down the area to a county or – even better – a neighborhood then we'll search public records."

Hardy gave a short laugh. "You can actually find somebody that way?"

"Oh, you bet. You know Michele Sindona?"

C. P. shook his head.

Hardy asked, "Who?"

Lukas searched through her apparently vast mental file cabinet of criminal history and said, "He was the financier? The guy who handled the Vatican's money?"

"Right. He was arrested for bank fraud but he vanished just before trial. He showed up a few months later and claimed he was kidnapped – thrown in a car and taken someplace. But there were rumors he hadn't been kidnapped at all but'd flown to Italy, then returned to New York. I think it was an examiner in the Southern District got samples of Sindona's handwriting and found out he had this personal handwriting quirk – he made a dot inside the loop when he wrote the numeral nine. Agents went through thousands of customs declaration forms on flights from Italy to New York. They found a dot in the number nine in an address of a card filled in by a passenger who, it turned out, had used a fake name. They lifted one of Sindona's latents from it."

"Man," C. P. muttered, "collared because of a dot. A little thing like that."

"Oh," Parker said, "it's usually the little things that trip up the perps. Not always. But usually."

He placed the note under the scanner of the VSC. This device uses different light sources – from ultraviolet to infrared – to let examiners see through obliterations and to visualize erased letters. Parker was curious about the cross-out before the word "apprehend." He scanned the entire note and found no erasures other than under the obliteration. He then tested the envelope and noticed no erasures.

"What'd you find?"

"Tell you in a minute. Don't breathe down my neck, Cage."

"It's two-twenty," the agent reminded.

"I can tell time, thanks," Parker muttered. "My kids taught me."

He walked to the electrostatic detection apparatus. The ESDA is used to check documents for indented writing – words or markings pressed into the paper by someone writing on pages on top of the subject document. The ESDA was originally developed as a way to visualize fingerprints on documents. But the device turned out to be largely useless for that purpose because it also raised indented writing, which obscured any latent prints. In TV shows the detective rubs a pencil over the sheet to visualize the indented writing. In real life it would be malpractice for a document examiner to do this; it would probably destroy most indented writing. The ESDA machine, which works like a photocopier, reveals lettering that was written as many as ten sheets above the document being tested.

No one quite knows why the ESDA works so efficiently but no document examiner is without one. Once, after a wealthy banker died, Parker was hired to analyze a will that disinherited his children and left his entire estate to a young maid. Parker was very close to authenticating the document. The signatures looked perfect, the dates of the will and the codicils were logical. But his last test – the ESDA – revealed indented writing that said, "This one ought to fool the pricks." The maid confessed to hiring someone to forge the will.

Parker now ran the unsub's note through the machine. He lifted a plastic sheet off the top and examined it.

Nothing.

He tried the envelope. He lifted off the thin sheet and held it up to the light. He felt a bang in his gut when he saw the delicate gray lines of writing.

"Yes!" he said excitedly. "We've got something."

Lukas leaned forward and Parker smelled a faint floral scent. Perfume? No. He'd known her for only an hour but he'd decided that she was not the perfume sort. It was probably scented soap.

"We've got a couple of indentations," Parker said. "The unsub wrote something on a piece of paper that was on top of the envelope."

Parker held the electrostatic sheet in both hands and moved it around to make the writing more visible. "Okay, somebody write this down. First word. Lowercase *c-l-e*, then a space. Uppercase *M*, lowercase *e*. Nothing after that."

Cage wrote the letters on a yellow pad and looked at it. "What's it mean?" The agent gave a perplexed shrug.

C. P. tugged a pierced earlobe and said, "Don't have a clue."

Geller: "If it's not bits and bytes I'm helpless."

Lukas too shook her head.

But Parker took one look at the letters and knew immediately. He was surprised no one else could see it.

"It's the first crime scene."

"What do you mean?" Jerry Baker asked.

"Sure," Lukas said, "Dupont C-i-r-c-l-e, capital *M* – Metro."

"Of course," Hardy whispered.

Puzzles are always easy when you know the answer.

"The first site," Parker mused. "But there's something written below it. Can you see it? Can you read it?" He jockeyed the sheet again, holding it out to Lukas. "Jesus, it's hard to see."

She leaned forward and read, "Just three letters. That's all I can make out. Lowercase *t-e-l*."

"Anything else?" Hardy asked.

Parker squinted. "No, nothing."

"*T-e-l*," Lukas pondered.

"Telephone, telephone company, telecommunications?" Cage asked. "Television?"

C. P. offered, "Maybe he's going to hit one of the studios – during a broadcast."

"No, no," Parker said. "Look at the position of the letters in relation to the *c-l-e Me*. If he's writing in fairly consistent columns then the *t-e-l* comes at the end of the word." Then Parker caught on. He said, "It's a—"

Lukas blurted, "Hotel. The second target's a hotel."

"That's right."

"Or motel," Hardy suggested.

"No," Parker said. "I don't think so. He's going for crowds. Motels don't have big facilities. All the events tonight will be in hotel banquet rooms."

"And," Lukas added, "he's probably sticking to foot or public transportation. Motels're in outlying areas. Traffic's too bad tonight to rely on a car."

"Great," Cage said then pointed out, "but there must be two hundred hotels in town."

"How do we narrow it down?" Baker asked.

"I'd say go for the bigger hotels . . ." Parker nodded toward Lukas. "You're right – probably near public transportation and high population centers."

With a loud bang Baker dropped the Yellow Pages on the table. "D.C. only?" He flipped them open. C. P. Ardell walked over to the table and began looking over the tactical agent's shoulder.

Parker considered the question. "It's the District he's extorting, not Virginia or Maryland. I'd stick to D.C."

"Agreed," Lukas said. "Also we should eliminate any place with 'Hotel' first in the name, like 'Hotel New York.' Because of the placement of the letters on the envelope. And no 'Inns' or 'Lodges.'"

Cage and Hardy joined C. P. and Baker. They all bent over the phone book. They started circling possibilities, discussing whether this choice or that was logical.

After ten minutes they had a list of twenty-two hotels. Cage jotted them down in his own precise handwriting and handed the list to Jerry Baker.

Parker suggested, "Before you send anybody there, call and find out if any of the functions tonight are for diplomats or politicians. We can eliminate those."

"Why?" Baker asked.

Lukas responded, "Armed bodyguards, right?"

Parker nodded. "And Secret Service. The unsub would've avoided those."

"Right," Baker said and hurried out of the room, opening his cell phone.

But even eliminating those, how many locations would remain? Parker wondered.

A lot. Too many.

Too many possible solutions . . .

Three hawks have been killing a farmer's chickens . . .

7

02.45

M y fellow citizens . . .
They powdered his forehead, they stuck a plug in his ear, they turned on the blinding lights.

Through the glare, Mayor Jerry Kennedy could just make out a few faces in the blackness of the WPLT newsroom, located just off Dupont Circle.

There was his wife, Claire. There was his press secretary. There was Wendell Jefferies.

My fellow citizens, Kennedy rehearsed in his mind. *I want to reassure you that our city's police force and the FBI*, no, *the federal authorities are doing everything in their power to find the perpetrators*, no, *the persons responsible for this terrible shooting.*

One of the station's senior producers, a thin man with a trim, white beard, came up to him and said, "I'll give you a seven-second countdown. I'll go silent after four and use my fingers. At one, look into the camera. You've done this before."

"I've done this before."

The producer glanced down and saw no papers in front of Kennedy. "You have anything for the TelePrompTer?"

"It's in my head."

The producer gave a brief chuckle. "Nobody does that nowadays."

Kennedy grunted.

. . . responsible for this terrible crime. And to that person out there, I am asking you please, please . . . no, just one please *. . . I'm asking you please to reestablish contact so that we can continue our dialog. On this, the last day of a difficult year, let's put the violence behind us and work together so that there'll be no more deaths. Please contact me personally . . .* no *. . . Please call me personally or get a message to me . . .*

"Five minutes," the producer called.

Kennedy waved aside the makeup artist and motioned Jefferies over to him. "You heard anything from the FBI? *Anything?*"

"Nothing. Not a word."

Kennedy couldn't believe it. Hours into the operation, the new deadline approaching, his only contact with the feds had been a fast phone call from some District detective named Len Hardy, who was calling on behalf of that agent, Margaret Lukas, to ask Kennedy to make this appeal to the killer over the air. Lukas, Kennedy reflected angrily, hadn't even bothered to call him herself. Hardy, a District cop who sounded intimidated by the feds he was supposed to be liaising with, hadn't known any details of the investigation – or, more likely, didn't have permission to give out any. He'd tried to call Lukas but she'd been too busy to take his call. Cage too. The mayor had spoken briefly with the head of the District's police department but short of providing cops to work under FBI supervision the chief had had nothing to do with the case.

Kennedy was furious. "They don't take us seriously. Jesus. I want to do something. I mean, other than this." He waved his hand at the camera. "It's going to sound like I'm begging."

"It's a problem," Wendy Jefferies conceded. "I've called the press conference but half the stations and papers aren't sending anybody. They're camped out at Ninth Street, waiting for somebody at the Bureau to talk to them."

"It's like the city doesn't exist, it's like I'm sitting on my hands."

"That's sort of what it's looking like."

The producer started toward him but the mayor gave him a polite smile. "In a minute." The man veered back into the shadows.

"So?" Kennedy asked his aide. He'd seen a cagey look behind the young man's Armani glasses.

"Time to call in some markers," Jefferies whispered. "I can do it. Surgically. I know how to handle it."

"I don't—"

"I don't want to do it this way either," Jefferies said fiercely, never one to glove his advice to his boss, "but we don't have any choice. You heard the commentary on WTGN."

Of course he had. The station, popular with about a half-million listeners in the metro area, had just aired an editorial about how, during his campaign, Kennedy had pledged to take back the streets of Washington from criminals and yet had been more than willing to pay terrorists a multimillion-dollar ransom today. The commentator, a surly, old journalist, had gone on to cite Kennedy's other campaign promise of cleaning up corruption in the District while being completely oblivious to, and possibly even participating in, the Board of Education school construction scandal.

Jefferies repeated, "We really don't have any choice, Jerry."

The mayor pondered this for a minute. As usual, the aide was right. Kennedy had hired the man because, as a white mayor, he *needed* a senior black aide. He didn't apologize for such tactical hiring. But he'd been astonished that the young man possessed a political sense that transcended grassroots community relations.

His aide said, "This is the time for hardball, Jerry. There's too much at stake."

"Okay, do what you have to." He didn't bother to add, Be careful. He knew Jefferies would.

"Two minutes," came a voice from above.

Kennedy thought to the Digger: Where are you? Where? He looked up at a darkened camera and stared at it as if he could see through the lens and cables to some TV set out there – see through the screen to the Digger himself. He thought to the killer, *Who* are you? And why did you and your partner pick *my* city to visit like the angel of death?

. . . in the spirit of peace, on this last day of the year, contact me so that we might come to some understanding . . . Please . . .

Jefferies bent close to the mayor's ear. "Remember," he whispered, waving his hand around the TV studio, "if he's listening, the killer, this might be the end of it. Maybe he'll go for the money and they'll get him."

Before Kennedy could respond the voice from on high called out, "One minute."

The Digger's got a new shopping bag.

All glossy red and Christmasy, covered with pictures of puppies wearing ribbons 'round their necks. The Digger bought the bag at Hallmark. It's the sort of bag he might be proud of though he isn't sure what proud means. He hasn't been sure of a lot of things since the bullet careened through his skull burning away some of his spongy gray cells and leaving others.

Funny how that works. Funny how . . .

Funny . . .

The Digger's sitting in a comfy chair in his lousy motel, with a glass of water and the empty bowl of soup at his side.

He's watching TV.

Something is on the screen. It's a commercial. Like a commercial he remembers watching after the bullet tapped a hole above his eye and did a scorchy little dance in his crane crane cranium. (Somebody described the bullet that way. He doesn't remember who. Maybe his friend, the man who tells him things. Probably was.)

Something flickers on the TV screen. Brings back a funny memory, from a long time ago. He was watching a commercial – dogs eating dog food, puppies eating puppy food, like the puppies on the shopping bag. He was watching the commercial when the man who tells him things took the Digger's hand and they went for a long walk. He told him that when Ruth was alone . . .

"You know Ruth?"

"I, uhm, know Ruth."

When Ruth was alone the Digger should break a mirror and find a piece of glass and put the glass in her neck.

"You mean—" The Digger stopped talking.

"I mean you should break the mirror and find a long piece of glass and you should put the glass in Ruth's neck. What do I mean?"

"I should break the mirror and find a long piece of glass and I should put the glass in her neck."

Some things the Digger remembers as if God Himself had written them on his brain.

"Good," said the man.

"Good," repeated the Digger. And he did what he was told. Which made the man who tells him things happy. Whatever that is.

Now the Digger is sitting with the puppy bag on his lap in his room at the motor lodge, kitchenettes free cable reasonable rates. Looking at his bowl of soup. The bowl is empty so he must not be hungry. He thinks he's thirsty so he takes a drink of water.

Another program comes on the TV. He reads the words, mutters them out loud, "'Special Report.' Hmm. Hmmm. This is . . ."

Click. This is . . .

Click.

A WPLT Special Report.

This is important. I should listen.

A man the Digger recognizes comes on the air. He's seen pictures of this man. It's . . .

Washington D.C. Mayor Gerald D. Kennedy. That's what it says on the screen.

The mayor's talking and the Digger listens.

"My fellow citizens, good afternoon. As you all

know by now, a terrible crime was committed this morning in the Dupont Circle Metro station and a number of people tragically lost their lives. At this time the killer or killers are still at large. But I want to reassure you that our police force and the federal authorities are doing everything in their power to make sure there will be no recurrence of this incident.

"To the persons responsible for this carnage, I am asking you from my heart, please, please, contact me. We need to reestablish communication so that we can continue our dialog. On this, the last night of the year, let's put the violence behind us and work together so that there'll be no more deaths or injuries. We can—"

Boring . . .

The Digger shuts the TV off. He likes commercials for dog food with cute puppies much better. Car commercials too. *Ohhhhhh, everyday people* . . . The Digger calls his voice mail and punches in the code, one-two-two-five. The date of Christmas.

The woman, who doesn't sound like Pamela his wife but does sound like Ruth – before the glass went into her neck, of course – says that he has no new messages.

Which means it's time for him to do what the man who tells him things told him.

If you do what people tell you to do, that's a good thing. They'll like you. They'll stay with you forever.

They'll love you.

Whatever love is.

Merry Christmas, Pamela, I got this for you . . . And you got something for me! Oh my oh my . . . A present.

Click click.

What a pretty yellow flower in your hand, Pamela. Thank you for my coat. The Digger pulls this overcoat on now, maybe black, maybe blue. He loves his coat.

He carries his soup bowl into the kitchenette and puts it in the sink.

He wonders again why he hasn't heard from the man who tells him things. The man told him that he might not call but still the Digger feels a little ping in his mind and he's sorry he hasn't heard the man's voice. Am I sad? Hmmmm. Hmmmm.

He finds his leather gloves and they are very nice gloves, with ribs on the backs of the fingers. The smell makes him think of something in his past though he can't remember what. He wears latex gloves when he loads the bullets into the clips of his Uzi. But the rubber doesn't smell good. He wears his leather gloves when he opens doors and touches things that are near where he shoots the gun and watches people fall like leaves in a forest.

The Digger buttons his dark coat, maybe blue, maybe black.

He smells his gloves again.

Funny.

He puts the gun into the puppy bag and puts more bullets in the bag too.

Walking out the front door of his motel, the Digger closes the door after him. He locks it carefully, the way you're supposed to do. The Digger knows all about doing things you're supposed to do.

Put glass into a woman's neck, for instance. Buy your wife a present. Eat your soup. Find a bright new shiny shopping bag. One with puppies on it.

"Why puppies?" the Digger asked.
"Just because," said the man who tells him things.
Oh.
And that was the one he bought.

8

03.00

Parker Kincaid, sitting in the same gray swivel chair he himself had requisitioned from GSA many years ago, did a test that too few questioned document examiners performed.

He read the document.

And then he read it again. And a half dozen times more.

Parker put much faith in the content of the document itself to reveal things about the author. Once, he was asked to authenticate a letter supposedly sent by Abraham Lincoln to Jefferson Davis, in which Lincoln suggested that if the Confederacy surrendered he would agree to allow certain states to secede.

The shaken director of the American Association of Historians sent Parker the letter, which would have thrown U.S. history into turmoil. The scientists had already determined the paper had been manufactured in the 1860s and the ink used was iron gallide, contemporary to the era. The document showed time-appropriate absorption of the ink into the paper fibers and was written in what clearly seemed to be Lincoln's handwriting.

Yet Parker didn't even pull out his hand glass to check the starts and lifts of the penstrokes. He read it once and on his analysis report wrote, "This document is of dubious origin."

Which was the forensic document examiner's equivalent of a Bronx cheer.

The reason? The letter was signed "Abe Lincoln." The sixteenth president abhorred the name Abe and would never let it be used in reference to him, let alone would he sign an important document with the nickname. The forger was arrested, convicted and – as is often the case with the crime of forgery – sentenced to probation.

As he now read the extortion note yet again Parker took careful note of the unsub's syntax – the order of the sentences and sentence fragments – and his grammar, the general constructions he'd used in composition.

An image began to emerge of the soul of the man who'd written the note – the man lying cold and still six floors below them in the FBI morgue.

Tobe Geller called, "Here we go." He leaned forward. "It's the psycholinguistic profile from Quantico."

Parker gazed at the screen. He'd often used this type of computer analysis when he'd overseen the Document Division. The entire text of a threatening document – sentences, fragments, punctuation – is fed into a computer, which then analyzes the message and compares it with data in a huge "threat dictionary," which contains more than 250,000 words, and then a standard dictionary of millions of words. An expert, working with the computer, then compares the letter to others in the database and decides if they were written by the same person. Certain characteristics of the writer can also be determined this way.

Geller read, "'Psycholinguistic profile of unsub 12-31A (deceased), METSHOOT. Data suggest that above-referenced unknown subject was foreign-born and had been in this country for two to three years. He was poorly educated and probably spent no more than two years in what would correspond to an American high school. Probable IQ was 100, plus or minus 11 points. Threats contained in subject document do not match any known threats in current databases. However, the language is consistent with sincere threats made in both profit and terrorist crimes.'"

He printed out a copy and handed it to Parker.

"Foreign," Lukas said. "I knew it." She held up a crime scene photo of the unsub's body, taken at the scene where he'd been killed by the delivery truck. "Looks Middle European to me. Serb, Czech, Slovak."

"He called City Hall security," Len Hardy said. "Don't they tape incoming calls? We could see if he had an accent."

Parker said, "I'll bet he used a voice synthesizer, right?"

"That's right," Lukas confirmed. "It was just like the 'You've got mail' voice."

Geller said, "We should call IH."

The Bureau's International Homicide and Terrorism Division.

But Parker crumpled up the psycholinguistic profile sheet and tossed it into a wastebasket.

"What— ?" Lukas began.

From C. P. Ardell's fat throat came a sound that could only be called a guffaw.

Parker said, "The only thing they got right is that the threat is real. But we *know* that, don't we?"

Without looking up from the extortion note he said, "I'm not saying IH shouldn't be involved but I *can* say he wasn't foreign and he definitely was smart. I'd put his IQ at over one hundred sixty."

"Where do you get that?" Cage asked, waving at the note. "My grandkid writes better than that."

"I wish he had been stupid," Parker said. "It'd be a hell of a lot less scary." He tapped the picture of the unsub. "Sure, European *descent* but probably fourth generation. He was extremely smart, well educated, probably in a private school, and I think he spent a lot of time on a computer. His permanent address was someplace out of this area; he only rented here. Oh, and he was a classic sociopath."

Margaret Lukas's laugh was nearly a scoff. "Where do you get *that?*"

"It told me," Parker said simply. Tapping the note.

A forensic linguist, Parker had been analyzing documents without the benefit of psycholinguistic software for years – based on the phrases people chose and the sentences they constructed. Words alone can make all the difference in solving crimes. Some years ago Parker had testified at the trial of a young suspect arrested for murder. The suspect and his friend had been shoplifting beer in a convenience store when the clerk caught them and came at them with a baseball bat. The friend grabbed the bat and was threatening the clerk. The suspect – the boy on trial – had shouted, "Give it to him!" The friend had swung and killed the clerk.

The prosecutor claimed the sentence "Give it to him" meant "Hit him." The defense claimed the suspect had meant, "Give the bat back." Parker had testified that "Give it to him" had, at one point in the history of American slang, meant to do harm – to shoot, stab or hit. But that usage had fallen by the wayside – along with words like "swell" and "hip." Parker's opinion was that the suspect was telling his friend to return the bat. The jury had believed Parker's testimony and though the boy was convicted of robbery he escaped the murder charge.

"But that's how foreigners talk," Cage pointed out. "'I am knowing.' 'Pay to me.' Remember the Lindbergh kidnapping? From the Academy?"

All FBI trainees at Quantico had heard the story in their forensic lectures. Before Bruno Hauptmann was arrested and charged with the Lindbergh baby abduction, document examiners in the Bureau deduced from the expressions in the ransom notes that the person who'd written them was a German immigrant who'd been in the United States for probably two or three years – which described Hauptmann accurately. The analysis helped narrow the search for the kidnapper, who was convicted primarily on the basis of handwriting comparisons between a known of his writing and the ransom notes.

"Well, let's go through it," Parker said and put the note on an old-fashioned overhead projector.

"Don't you want to scan it and put it on the video screen?" Tobe Geller asked.

"No," Parker answered peremptorily, "I don't like digital. We need to be as close to the original as we can get." He looked up and gave a fast smile. "We need to be in bed with it."

The note flashed onto a large screen mounted on one wall of the lab. The ashen document seemed to stand in front of them like a suspect under interrogation. Parker walked up to it, gazed at the large letters in front of him.

Mayor Kennedy—

The end is night. The Digger is loose and their is no way to stop him. He will kill again – at four, eight and Midnight if you don't pay.

I am wanting $20 million dollars in cash, which you will put into a bag and leave it two miles south of Rt 66 on the West Side of the Beltway. In the middle of the Field. Pay to me the Money by 1200 hours. Only I am knowing how to stop The Digger. If you ~~usea~~ apprehend me, he will keep killing. If you kill me, he will keep killing.

If you don't think I'm real, some of the Diggers bullets were painted black. Only I know that.

As Parker spoke he pointed to parts of the note. "'I am knowing' and 'pay to me' *sound* foreign, sure. The form of the verb 'to be' combined with a present participle is typical in a Slavic or Germanic Indo-European-root language. German or Czech or Polish, say. But the use of the preposition 'to' with 'me' is not something you'd find in those languages. They'd say it the way we do. 'Pay me.' That construction is more common in an Asian language. I think he just threw in random foreign-sounding phrases. Trying to fool us into thinking he's foreign. To lead us off."

"I don't know," Cage began.

"No, no," Parker persisted. "Look at how he tried to do it. Those quote foreign expressions are close together – as if he'd gotten the fake clues out of the way then moved on. If a foreign language was really his first he'd be more consistent. Look at the last sentence of the letter. He falls back to a typical English construction: 'Only I know that.' Not 'Only *I am knowing* that.' By the way, that's also why I think he spent time on a computer. I'm on-line a lot, browsing through rare document dealers' Web sites and news groups. A lot of them are foreign but they write in English. You see bastardizations of English just like these all the time."

"I agree with that, about the computers," Lukas told Parker. "We don't know for sure but it's likely that he learned how to pack silencers and rig the Uzi for full auto on the web. That's how everybody learns things like that nowadays."

"But what about the twenty-four-hour clock?" Hardy asked. "He demanded the ransom by '1200 hours.' That's European."

"Another red herring. He doesn't refer to it that way earlier – when he writes about when the Digger's going to attack again. There, he says, 'Four, eight and Midnight.'"

"Well," C. P. said, "if he's not foreign he's *got* to be stupid. Look at all the mistakes." To Lukas he said, "Sounds just like those rednecks we took down in Manassas Park."

Parker responded, "All fake."

"But," Lukas protested, "the very first line: 'The end is night.' He means 'The end is *nigh*.' He—"

"Oh," Parker continued, "but that's not a mistake you'd logically make. People say, 'Once *and* a while,' even though the correct expression is 'Once *in* a while,' because there's a certain logic to using the conjunction '*and*' and not the preposition '*in*.' But 'The end is night' makes no sense, whatever his level of education."

"What about the misspellings?" Hardy asked. "And the capitalization and punctuation mistakes?" The detective's eyes were scanning the letter carefully.

Parker said, "Oh, there're plenty more mistakes than those." Look how he uses the dollar sign *and* the word 'dollars.' A redundancy. And when he's talking about the money he's got an improper object of the sentence." Parker touched a portion of the screen, moving his finger along the words:

> *I am wanting $20 million dollars in cash, which you will put into a bag and leave it two miles south of Rt 66 on the West Side of the Beltway.*

"See, he says, 'leave it,' but the object 'it' isn't necessary. Only that isn't the sort of mistake that makes sense – most grammatical errors are reflections of errors in speaking. And in everyday vernacular we just don't add unnecessary direct objects. If anything we're lazy – we tend to streamline our speech and leave *out* words.

"And the misspellings?" Parker continued. He paced slowly in front of the projected note and the letters moved across his face and shoulder like black insects. "Look at the sentence 'their is no way to stop him.' 'Their' is a homonym – words that are spelled differently but are pronounced the same. It should be t-h-e-r-e. But most people only make those mistakes when they write quickly – usually when they're on computer. Their mind sends them the spelling phonetically not visually. The second-highest incident of homonymic mistakes is by people typing on typewriters. But with handwriting they're rare.

"The capitalizations?" He glanced at Hardy. "You only find erroneous uppercasing when there's some logical basis for it – concepts like art or love or hate. Sometimes with occupations or job titles. No, he's just trying to make us *think* he's stupid. But he isn't."

"The note tells you that?" Lukas asked, staring as if she were seeing an extortion note entirely different from the one Parker was studying.

"You bet," the document examiner responded. He laughed. "His other mistake was *not* making some mistakes he should have. For instance, he uses a comma in adverbial clauses correctly. A clause beginning a sentence should end with a comma. The 'if' clause." He touched it on the wall screen.

If you kill me, he will keep killing.

"But with a clause at the *end* of the sentence you don't need one."

He will kill again – at four, 8 and Midnight if you don't pay.

"He also used a comma before 'which.'"

I am wanting $20 million dollars in cash, which you will put into a bag . . .

"That's a standard rule of grammar – a comma before the nonrestrictive 'which' and not before the restrictive 'that' – but generally only professional writers and people who've gone to good schools follow it anymore."

"There oughta be a comma before 'which'?" C. P. grumbled. "Who cares?"

Parker silently responded, *We* do. Because it's little things like this that lead us to the truth.

Hardy said, "It looks like he tried to spell 'apprehend' and couldn't get it right. What do you make of that?"

"Looks like it," Parker said. "But you know what's under the mark-out there? I scanned it with an infrared viewer."

"What?"

"Squiggles."

"Squiggles?" Lukas asked.

"A term of art," Parker said wryly. "He didn't write anything. He just wanted us to *think* he was having trouble spelling the word."

"But why'd he go to all this trouble to make us think he's stupid?" Hardy asked.

"To trick us into looking for either a stupid American or a slightly less stupid foreigner. It's another smokescreen." Parker added, "And to keep us underestimating him. Of *course* he's smart. Just look at the money drop."

"The drop?" Lukas asked.

C. P. asked, "You mean at Gallows Road? Why's that smart?"

"Well . . ." Parker glanced up, then from one to the other of the agents. "The helicopters."

"What helicopters?" Hardy asked.

Parker frowned. "Aren't you checking out helicopter charters?"

"No," Lukas said. "Why should we?"

Parker remembered a rule from his days working at the Bureau. Never assume a single thing. "The field where he wanted the money dropped was next to a hospital, right?"

Geller was nodding. "Fairfax Hospital."

"Shit," Lukas spat out. "It has a helipad."

"So?" Hardy asked.

Lukas shook her head, angry with herself. "The unsub picked the place so a surveillance team would get used to incoming choppers. He'd chartered one himself and was going to set down, pick up the money and take off again. Probably fly at treetop level to a getaway car."

"I never thought about that," Hardy said bitterly.

"None of us did," C. P. said.

Cage added, "I've got a buddy at the FAA. I'll have him check it out."

Parker glanced at the clock. "No response from Kennedy's news conference?"

Lukas made a call. She spoke to someone then hung up.

"Six calls. All cranks. None of them knew anything about the painted bullets so they were bogus. We've got their names and numbers. Nail 'em later for interference with law enforcement activity."

"You think the unsub wasn't from around here?" Hardy asked Parker.

"Right. If there was any chance he thought we could compare his handwriting with public records in the area he would've disguised his writing or used cutout letters. Which he didn't. So he's not from the District, Virginia or Maryland."

The door swung open. It was Timothy, the runner

who'd brought the note. "Agent Lukas? I've got the results from the coroner."

Parker thought, It's about time.

She took the report and as she read it. Cage asked, "Parker, you said he was a sociopath. How do you figure that?"

"Because," Parker said absently, his eyes on Lukas, "who'd do something like this *except* a sociopath?"

Lukas finished and handed it to Hardy. He asked, "You want me to read it?"

"Go ahead," she answered.

Parker noticed that the young man's sobriety lifted, maybe because he was, for a moment, part of the team.

The detective cleared his throat. "'White male approximately forty-five years old. Six foot two. One hundred eighty-seven pounds. No distinguishing. No jewelry except a Casio watch – with multiple alarms," Hardy looked up. "Get this. Set to go off at four, eight and midnight." Back to the report: "'Wearing unbranded blue jeans, well worn. Polyester windbreaker. J. C. Penney workshirt, also faded. Jockey underwear. Cotton socks, Wal-Mart running shoes. A hundred twelve dollars in cash, some change.'"

Parker stared at the letters on the screen in front of them as if the words Hardy was reading described not the unsub but the note itself.

"'Minor trace elements. Brick dust in hair, clay dust under nails. Stomach contents reveal coffee, milk, bread and beef – probably inexpensive grade of steak – consumed within the past eight hours.' That's it." Hardy read another METSHOOT memo, attached to the coroner's report. "No leads with the delivery truck – the one that hit him." Hardy glanced at Parker. "It's so frustrating – we've got the perp downstairs and he can't tell us a damn thing."

Parker glanced at another copy of the Major Crimes Bulletin, the one he'd seen earlier. About the firebombing of Gary Moss's house. The austere description of the near deaths of the man's daughters had shaken Parker badly. Seeing that bulletin he'd very nearly turned around and walked out of the lab.

Parker shut off the projector, put the note back on the examining table.

Cage looked at his watch. He pulled on his coat. "Well, we've got forty-five minutes. We better get going."

"What do you mean?" Lukas asked.

The senior agent handed her her windbreaker and Parker his leather jacket. He took it without thinking.

"Out there." He nodded toward the door. "To help Jerry Baker's team check out hotels."

Parker was shaking his head. "No. We have to keep going here." He looked at Hardy."You're right, Len. The unsub can't tell us anything. But the note still can. It can tell us a lot."

"They need everybody they can get," Cage persisted.

There was silence for a moment.

Parker stood with his head down, opposite Lukas, across the brightly lit examining table, the stark white extortion note between them. He looked up, said evenly, "I don't think we'll be able to find him in time. Not in forty-five minutes. I hate to say it but this is the best use of our resources – to stay here. Keep going with the note."

C. P. said, "You mean you're just going to write 'em off? The victims?"

He paused. Then said, "I guess that's what I mean. Yes."

Cage asked Lukas, "Whatta you think?"

She glanced at Parker. Their eyes met. She said to Cage, "I agree with Parker. We stay here. We keep going."

9

03.15

From the corner of her eyes Lukas saw Len Hardy, standing motionless. After a moment he smoothed his hair, picked up his coat and walked over to her.

Right as rain . . .

"Let *me* go at least," he said to her. "To help with the hotels."

She looked at his earnest young face. He kneaded his trench coat in his large right hand, the nails perfectly trimmed and scrubbed. He was a man, she assessed, who found comfort in details.

"I can't. I'm sorry."

"Agent Cage is right. They'll need everybody they can get."

Lukas glanced at Parker Kincaid but he was lost in the document once more, easing it carefully from its clear acetate shroud.

"Come on over here, Len," Lukas said, gesturing him into the corner of the document lab. Cage was the only one who noticed and he said nothing. In his long tenure at the Bureau the senior agent would have had plenty of talks with underlings and knew that the process was as delicate as interrogating suspects. More delicate – because these were people you had to live with day after day. And whom you might have to depend on to watch your back. Lukas was grateful Cage was giving her rein to handle Hardy the way she felt best.

"Talk to me," she said. "What's eating you?"

"I want to *do* something," the detective replied. "I know I'm second-string here. I'm from the District. I'm Research and Stats . . . But I want to help."

"You're only here as liaison. That's all you're authorized for. This is a federal operation. It's not task-forced."

He gave a sour laugh. "Liaison? I'm here as a *stenographer*. You and I both know that."

Of course she knew it. But that wouldn't have stopped Lukas from giving him a more active role if she thought he'd be valuable elsewhere. Lukas was not one who lived her life solely by regs and procedures and if Hardy had been the world's best sniper she'd kick him out the door and onto one of Jerry Baker's shooting teams in an instant, whatever the rules dictated. After a moment she said, "All right, answer me a question."

"Sure."

"Why are you here?" she asked.

"Why?" He frowned.

"You volunteered, didn't you?" Lukas asked.

"Yeah, I did."

"Because of your wife, right?"

"Emma?" He tried to look confounded but Lukas could see right through it. His eyes fell to the floor.

"I understand, Len. But do yourself a favor. Take your notes, kick around ideas with us and stay out of the line of fire. Then when this prick's tagged go on home."

"But it's . . . hard," he said, avoiding her eyes.

"Being home?"

He nodded.

"I know it is," Lukas answered sincerely.

He clung to the trenchcoat like a child's security blanket.

In fact if it had been anybody but Len Hardy who'd shown up as the District police liaison she would have kicked them right back to police headquarters. She had no patience with ass covering or interagency turf wars and no time to coddle employees of a corrupt, nearly bankrupt city. But she knew a secret of Hardy's life – that his wife was in a coma, the result of an accident when her Jeep Cherokee had skidded off the road in a rain storm near Middleburg, Virginia, and hit a tree.

Hardy had been to the District field office several times to compile statistical data on crime in the metro area and had gotten to know Betty, Lukas's assistant. She'd thought at first that the man was trying to pick up the attractive woman but had then overheard him talking emotionally about his wife and her injury.

He didn't have many friends, it seemed, just like Lukas herself. She'd gotten to know him slightly and had learned more about Emma. Several times they'd had coffee in the Policemen's Memorial Park, next to the field office. He'd opened up slightly but, also like Lukas, he kept his emotions tightly packed away.

Knowing his tragedy, knowing how hard it would be for him to sit home alone on a holiday, she had welcomed him onto the team and resolved to cut him some slack tonight. But Margaret Lukas would never jeopardize an operation for the emotional health of anyone.

Right as rain . . .

He now told her, "I can't sit still. I want a piece of this guy."

No, she thought. What he wants is a piece of God or Fate or whatever force of nature broke Emma Hardy's life, and her husband's, into a thousand pieces.

"Len, I can't have somebody in the field who's . . ." She looked for a benign word. "Distracted." "Reckless" would have been closer and "suicidal" was what she meant.

Hardy nodded. He was angry. His lip trembled. But he dropped his coat on a chair and returned to a desk.

Poor man, she thought. But seeing how his intelligence, his sense of propriety and perfection shone through his personal anguish, she knew he'd be all right. He'd survive this terrible time. Oh, he'd be changed, yes, but he'd be changed the way iron is changed into steel in a refinery's white-hot coals.

Changed . . .

The way Lukas herself had.

If you looked at Jacqueline Margaret Lukas's birth certificate, the document would reveal that she'd been born on the last day of November 1963. But in her heart she knew she was just over five years old, having been born the day she graduated from the FBI Academy.

She recalled a book she'd read a long time ago, a children's story. *The Wyckham Changeling.* The picture of a happy elf on the cover didn't hint at the eeriness of the story itself. The book was about an elf who'd sneak into homes in the middle of the night and switch babies – kidnap the human child and leave a changeling – an elfin baby in its place. The story was about two parents who discover that their daughter had been switched and go on a quest to find her.

Lukas remembered reading the book, curled up on a couch in her comfortable living room in Stafford, Virginia, near Quantico, postponing going to Safeway because of an unexpected blizzard. She'd been compelled to finish it – yes, the parents had found the girl and traded the elf baby back for her – but she had shivered at the unpleasant aftertaste of the book and had thrown it out.

She'd forgotten about the story until she'd graduated from the Academy and been assigned to the Washington field office. Then one morning, walking to work, her Colt Python snug on her hip, a case file under her arm, she realized: That's what *I* am – a changeling. Jackie Lukas had been a part-time librarian for the Bureau's Quantico research facility, an amateur clothing designer who could whip up outfits for her friends and their children over a weekend. She'd been a quilter, needlepointer, wine collector (and drinker too), a consistently top finisher in local five-K races. But that woman was long gone, replaced by Special Agent Margaret Lukas, a woman who excelled in criminalistics, investigative techniques, the properties of C4 and Semtex explosives, the care and handling of confidential informants.

"An FBI agent?" her perplexed father asked during

a visit to her parents' Pacific Heights townhouse in San Francisco. She'd gone home to break the news to them. "You're going to be an agent? Not like with a gun? You mean, you'll work at a desk or something."

"With a gun. But I'll bet they give me a desk too."

"I don't get it," the burly man, a retired loan officer for Bank of America, said. "You were such a good student."

She laughed at the apparent non sequitur though she knew exactly what her father meant. An honor student at both St. Thomas High in Russian Hill and Stanford. The lean girl, who accepted dates too rarely and raised her hand in class too often, was destined for high places in academia or on Wall Street. No, no, he didn't mind that Jackie was going to be toting guns and tackling killers; it was that she wouldn't be using her *mind*.

"But it's the FBI, Dad. They're the *thinking* cops."

"Yeah, I guess. But . . . is this what you want to do?"

No, it was what she *had* to do. There was a gulf of a difference between the two verbs, *wanted* and *had*. But she didn't know if he'd understand that. So she said a simple "Yes."

"Then that's good enough for me." Then he turned to his wife and said, "Our girl's got mettle. You know what mettle is? M-e-t-t-l-e."

"I know," Lukas's mother called from the kitchen, "I do crosswords, remember. But you'll be careful, Jackie? Promise me you'll be careful."

As if she were about to cross a busy street.

"I'll be careful, Mom."

"Good. I made coq au vin for dinner. You like that, right?"

And Jackie hugged her mother and her father and two days later flew back to Washington D.C. to change into Margaret.

After graduating she was assigned to the field office. She got to know the District, got to work with Cage, who was as good a changeling father as she could've asked for, and must have done something right because last year she was promoted to assistant special agent in charge. And now, with her boss photographing monkeys and lizards in a Brazilian rainforest, she was running the biggest case to hit Washington, D.C., in years.

She now watched Len Hardy jotting his notes in the corner of the lab and thought, He'll come through this okay.

Margaret Lukas knew that it could happen.

Just ask a changeling . . .

"Hey," a man's voice intruded on her thoughts.

She looked across the room and realized that Parker Kincaid was speaking to her.

"We've done the linguistics," he said. "I want to do the physical analysis of the note now. Unless you've got something else in mind."

"This's your inning, Parker," she said. And sat down beside him.

First, he examined the paper the note was written on.

It measured 6 by 9 inches, the sort intended for bread-and-butter notes. Paper size has varied throughout history but 8½ by 11 has been standard in

America for nearly two hundred years. Six by 9 was the second-most-common size. Too common. The size alone would tell Parker nothing about its source.

As for composition of the paper he noted that it was cheap and had been manufactured by mechanical pulping, not the kraft – chemical pulping – method that produced finer-quality papers.

"The paper won't help us much," he announced finally. "It's generic. Nonrecycled, high-acid, coarse pulp with minimal optical brighteners and low luminescence. Sold in bulk by paper manufacturers and jobbers to retail chains. They package it as a house brand of stationery. There's no watermark and no way to trace it back to a particular manufacturer or wholesaler and then forward to a single point of sale." He sighed. "Let's look at the ink."

He lifted the note carefully and placed it under one of the lab's compound microscopes. He examined it first at ten- then at fifty-power magnification. From the indentation the tip of the pen made in the paper, the occasional skipping and the uneven color, Parker could tell that the pen had been a very cheap ballpoint.

"Probably an AWI – American Writing Instruments. The bargain-basement thirty-nine-cent-er." He looked at his teammates. No one grasped the significance.

"And?" Lukas asked.

"That's a *bad* thing," he explained emphatically. "Impossible to trace. They're sold in just about every discount and convenience store in America. Just like the paper. And AWI doesn't use tags."

"Tags?" Hardy asked.

Parker explained that some manufacturers put a chemical tag in their inks to identify the products and to help trace where and when they'd been manufactured. American Writing Instruments, however, didn't do this.

Parker started to pull the note out from under the microscope. He stopped, noticing something curious. Part of the paper was faded. He didn't think it was a manufacturing flaw. Optical brighteners have been added to paper for nearly fifty years and it's unusual, even in cheap paper like this, for there to be an unevenness in the brilliance.

"Could you hand me the PoliLight?" he asked C. P. Ardell.

"The what?"

"There."

The big agent picked up one of the boxy ALS units – an alternative light source. It luminesced a variety of substances that were invisible to the human eye.

Parker pulled on a pair of goggles and clicked on the yellow-green light.

"It gonna irradiate me or anything?" the big agent said, only partly joking, it seemed.

Parker ran the PoliLight wand over the envelope. Yes, the right third was lighter than the rest. He did the same with the note and found there was a lighter L-shaped pattern on the top and right side of the paper.

This was interesting. He studied it again.

"See how the corner's faded? I think it's because the paper – and part of the envelope too – were bleached by the sun."

"Where, at his house or the store?" Hardy asked.

"Could be either," Parker answered. "But given the cohesion of the pulp I'd guess the paper was sealed until fairly recently. That would suggest the store."

"But," Lukas said, "it'd have to be a place that had a southern exposure."

Yes, Parker thought. Good. He hadn't thought of that.

"Why?" Hardy asked.

"Because it's winter," Parker pointed out. "There's not enough sunlight to bleach paper from any other direction."

Parker paced again. It was a habit of his. When Thomas Jefferson's wife died, his oldest daughter, Martha, wrote that her father paced "almost incessantly day and night, only lying down occasionally, when nature was completely exhausted." When Parker worked on a document or was wrestling with a particularly difficult puzzle the Whos often chided him for "walking in circles again."

The layout of the lab was coming back to him. He walked to a cabinet, opened it and pulled out an examining board and some sheets of collecting paper. Holding the note by its corner, he ran a camel-hair brush over the surface to dislodge trace elements. There was virtually nothing. He wasn't surprised. Paper is one of the most absorbent of materials; it retains a lot of substances from the places it's been but generally they remain firmly bound into the fibers.

Parker took a large hypodermic syringe from his attaché case and punched several small disks of ink and paper out of the note and the envelope. "You know how it works?" he asked Geller, nodding at the gas chromotograph/mass spectrometer in the corner.

"Oh, sure," he said. "I took one apart once. Just for the fun of it."

"Separate runs – for the note and the envelope," Parker said, handing him the samples.

"You got it."

"What's it do?" C. P. asked again. Undercover and tactical agents generally don't have much patience for lab work and know little about forensic science.

Parker explained. The GC/MS separated chemicals found at crime scenes into their component parts and then identified them. The machine rumbled alarmingly – in effect it burned the samples and analyzed the resulting vapors.

Parker brushed more trace off the note and envelope and this time managed to collect some material. He mounted the slides on two different Leitz compound scopes. He peered into one, then the other, turned the focusing knobs, which moved with the slow sensuality of oiled, precision mechanisms.

He stared at what he saw then looked up, said to Geller, "I need to digitize images of the trace in here." Nodding at a microscope. "How do we do that?"

"Ah, piece of proverbial cake." The young agent plugged optical cables into the base of the microscopes. They ran to a large gray box, which sprouted cables of its own. These cables Geller plugged into one of the dozen computers in the lab. He clicked it on and a moment later an image of the particles of trace came on the screen. He called up a menu.

Said to Parker, "Just hit this button. They're stored as JPEG files."

"And I can transfer them on e-mail?"

"Just tell me who they're going to."

"In a minute – I'll have to get the address. First, I want to do different magnifications."

Parker and Geller captured three images from each microscope, stored them on the hard drive.

Just as he finished, the GC/MS beeped and data began to appear on the screen of the computer dedicated to the unit.

Lukas said, "I've got a couple of examiners standing by in Materials and Elemental." These were the Bureau's two trace evidence analysis departments.

"Send 'em home," Parker said. "There's somebody else I want to use."

"Who?" Lukas asked, frowning.

"He's in New York."

"N.Y.P.D.?" Cage asked.

"Was. Civilian now."

"Why not somebody here?" Lukas asked.

"Because," Parker answered, "my friend's the best criminalist in the country. He's the one set up PERT."

"*Our* evidence team?" C. P. asked.

"Right." Parker looked up a number and made a call.

"But," Hardy pointed out, "it's New Year's Eve. He's probably out."

"No," Parker said, "he hardly ever goes out."

"Not even on holidays?"

"Not even on holidays."

"Parker Kincaid," the voice in the speaker phone said. "I wondered if someone from down there might be calling in."

"You heard about our problem, did you?" Parker asked Lincoln Rhyme.

"Ah, I hear everything," he said, and Parker remembered that Rhyme could bring off dramatic delivery like no one else. "Don't I, Thom? Don't I hear everything? Parker, you remember Thom, don't you? Long-suffering Thom?"

"Hi, Parker."

"Hi, Thom. He giving you grief?"

"Of course I am," Lincoln said gruffly. "I thought you were retired, Parker."

"I was. Until about two hours ago."

"Funny about this business, isn't it? The way they never let us rest in peace."

Parker had met Rhyme once. He was a handsome man, about Parker's age, dark hair. He was also paralyzed from the neck down. He consulted out of his townhouse on Central Park West. "I enjoyed your course, Parker," Rhyme said. "Last year."

Parker remembered Rhyme, sitting in a fancy candy-apple-red wheelchair in the front row of the lecture hall at the John Jay College of Criminal Justice in New York. The subject was forensic linguistics.

Rhyme continued, "Do you know we got a conviction because of you?"

"I didn't."

"There was a witness at a killing. He couldn't see the killer; he was hiding. But he heard the perp say something to the vic just before he shot him. He said, 'If I were you, you prick, I'd say my prayers.' Then – this is interesting, Parker, are you listening?"

"You bet." When Lincoln Rhyme spoke, you listened.

"Then during the interrogation at police HQ he said to one of the detectives, 'If I were going to confess it wouldn't be to you.' You know how we got him?"

"How, Lincoln?"

Rhyme laughed like a happy teenager. "Because of the subjunctive voice! 'If I *were* you.' Not 'If I *was* you.' 'If I *were* going to confess.' Statistically only seven percent of the general population uses the subjunctive voice any more. Did you know that?"

"As a matter of fact I do," Parker said. "That was enough for a conviction?"

"No. But it was enough for a confession as part of a plea bargain," Rhyme announced. "Now let me guess. You've got this unsub shooting people in the subway and your only clue to him is the – what? A threat letter? An extortion note?"

"How's he know that?" Lukas asked.

"Another country heard from!" Rhyme called. "To answer the question: I know that there's a note involved because it's the only logical reason for Parker *Kincaid* to be calling *me* . . . Who – excuse me, Parker – *whom* did I just answer?"

"Special Agent Margaret Lukas," she said.

"She's ASAC at the District field office. She's running the case."

"Ah, the Bureau of course. Fred Dellray was just over here to visit," Rhyme said. "You know Fred? Manhattan office?"

"I know Fred," Lukas answered. "He ran some of our undercover people last year. An arms sale sting."

Rhyme continued. "So, an unsub, a note. Now, talk to me, one of you."

Lukas said, "You're right. It's an extortion scheme. We tried to pay but the primary unsub was killed.

Now we're pretty sure his partner – the shooter – may keep going."

"Oh, that's tricky. That's a problem. You've processed the body?"

"Nothing," Lukas told him. "No ID, no significant trace."

"And my belated Christmas present is a piece of the case."

"I GC'd a bit of the envelope and the letter—"

"Good for you, Parker. Burn up the evidence. They'll want to save it for trial but you burn up what you have to."

"I want to send you the data. And some pictures of the trace. Can I e-mail it all to you?"

"Yes, yes, of course. What magnification?"

"Ten, twenty and fifty."

"Good. When's the deadline?"

"Every four hours, starting at four, going to midnight."

"Four P.M.? Today?"

"That's right."

"Lord."

She continued, "We have a lead to the four o'clock hit. We think he's going after a hotel. But we don't know anything more specific than that."

"Four, eight and twelve. Your unsub was a man with a dramatic flair."

"Should that be part of his profile?" Hardy asked, jotting more notes. Parker supposed the man would probably spend all weekend writing up a report for the mayor, the police chief and the City Council – a report that would probably go unread for months. Maybe forever.

"Who's that?" Rhyme barked.

"Len Hardy, sir. District P.D."

"You do psych profiling?"

"Actually I'm with Research. But I've taken profiling courses at the Academy and done postgraduate psych work at American University."

"Listen," Rhyme said to him, "I don't *believe* in psych profiles. I believe in *evidence*. Psychology is slippery as a fish. Look at me. I'm an oven of neuroses. Right, Amelia? . . . My friend here's not talking but she agrees. All right. We've got to *move* on this. Send me your goodies. I'll get back to you as soon as I can."

Parker took down Rhyme's e-mail address and handed it to Geller. A moment later, the agent had uploaded the images and the chemical profiles from the chromatograph/spectrometer.

"*He's* the best criminalist in the country?" Cage asked skeptically.

But Parker didn't respond. He was gazing at the clock. Somewhere in the District of Columbia those people that he and Margaret Lukas were willing to sacrifice had only thirty minutes left to live.

10

This hotel is beautiful, this hotel is nice.

The Digger walks inside, with puppies on his shopping bag, and no one notices him.

He walks into the bar and buys a sparkling water from the bartender. It tickles his nose. Funny . . . He drinks it down and leaves money and a tip, the way the man who tells him things told him to do.

In the lobby the crowds are milling. There're functions here. Office parties. Lots of decorations. More of those fat babies in New Year's banners. My, aren't they . . . aren't they . . . aren't they cute?

And here's Old Man Time, looking like the Grim Reaper.

He and Pamela . . . *click*. . . . and Pamela went to some parties in places like this.

The Digger buys a *USA Today*. He sits in the lobby and reads it, the puppy bag at his side.

He looks at his watch.

Reading the articles.

USA Today is a nice newspaper. It tells him many interesting things. The Digger notices the weather around the nation. He likes the color of the high-pressure fronts. He reads about sports. He thinks he used to do some sports a long time ago. No, that was his friend, William. His friend enjoyed sports. Some other friends too. So did Pamela.

The paper has lots of pictures of nice basketball players. They look very big and strong and when they dunk balls they fly through the air like whirligigs. The Digger decides he must not have played sports. He isn't sure why Pamela or William or anyone would want to. It's more fun to eat soup and watch TV.

A young boy walks past him and pauses.

He looks down at the bag. The Digger pulls the top of the bag closed so the boy won't see the Uzi that's about to kill fifty or sixty people.

The boy is maybe nine. He has dark hair and it's parted very carefully. He's wearing a suit that doesn't fit well. The sleeves are too long. And a happy red Christmas tie bunches up his collar awkwardly. He's looking at the bag.

At the puppies.

The Digger looks away from him.

"If anybody looks at your face, kill them. Remember that."

I remember.

But he can't help looking at the boy. The boy smiles. The Digger doesn't smile. (He recognizes a smile but he doesn't know what it is exactly.)

The boy, with his brown eyes and the little bit of a smile on his face, is fascinated with the bag and the puppies. Their happy ribbons. Like the ribbons the fat New Year's babies wear. Green and gold ribbons on the bag. The Digger looks at the bag too.

"Honey, come on," a woman calls. She's standing beside a pot of poinsettias, as red as the rose Pamela wore on her dress at Christmas last year.

The boy glances once again at the Digger's face. The Digger knows he should look away but he just stares back. Then the boy walks to the crowd of people around tables filled with little dots of food. Lots of crackers and cheese and shrimps and carrots.

No soup, the Digger notices.

The boy walks up to a girl who is probably his sister. She's about thirteen.

The Digger looks at his watch. Twenty minutes to four. He takes the cell phone out of his pocket and carefully punches the buttons to call his voice mail. He listens. "You have no new messages." He shuts the phone off.

He lifts the bag onto his lap and looks out over the crowd. The boy is in a blue blazer and his sister is wearing a pink dress. It has a sash on it.

The Digger clutches the puppy bag.

Eighteen minutes.

The boy is standing at the food table. The girl is talking to an older woman.

More people enter the hotel. They walk right past the Digger, with his bag and his nice newspaper that shows the weather all across the nation.

But no one notices him.

The phone in the document lab began ringing.

As always, when a telephone chirped and he was someplace without the Whos, Parker felt an instant of low-voltage panic though if one of the children had had an accident Mrs. Cavanaugh would of course have called his cell phone and not the Federal Bureau of Investigation.

He glanced at the caller ID box and saw a New York number. He snagged the receiver. "Lincoln. It's Parker. We've got fifteen minutes. Any clues?"

The criminalist's voice was troubled. "Oh, not much, Parker. Speaker me . . . Don't you linguists hate it when people verb nouns?"

Parker hit the button.

"Somebody grab a pen," Rhyme called. "I'll tell you what I've got. Are you ready? Are you *ready?*"

"We're ready, Lincoln," Parker said.

"The most prominent trace embedded in the letter is granite dust."

"Granite," Cage echoed.

"There's evidence of shaving and chiseling on the stone. And some polishing too."

"What do you think it's from?" Parker asked.

"I don't know. How would I know? I don't *know* Washington. I know New York."

"And if it *were* in New York?" Lukas asked.

Rhyme rattled off, "New building construction, old building renovation or demolition, bathroom, kitchen and threshold manufacturers, tombstone makers, sculptors' studios, landscapers . . . The list's endless. You need somebody who knows the lay of the land there. Understand? That's not you, is it, Parker?"

"Nope. I—"

The criminalist interrupted him. "—know documents. You know unsubs too. But not geography."

"That's true."

Parker glanced at Lukas. She was gazing at the clock. She looked back at him with a face devoid of emotion. Cage had mastered the shrug; Lukas's waiting state was the stony mask.

Rhyme continued. "There're also traces of red clay and dust from old brick. Then there's sulfur. And a lot of carbon – ash and soot, consistent with cooking meat or burning trash that has meat in it. Now – the data from the *envelope* showed a little of the same trace substances I found on the letter. But also something more – significant amounts of salt water, kerosine, refined oil, crude oil, butter—"

"Butter?" Lukas asked.

"That's what I said," Rhyme groused. He added sourly, "Don't know the brand. And there's some organic material not inconsistent with mollusks. So, all the evidence points to Baltimore."

"Baltimore?" Hardy asked.

From Lukas: "How do you figure that?"

"The seawater, kerosine, fuel oil and crude oil mean it's a port. Right, right? What else could it be? Well, the port nearest to D.C. that does major crude oil transfer is Baltimore. And Thom tells me – my man knows food – that there are tons of seafood restaurants right on the harbor. Bertha's. He keeps talking about Bertha's Mussels."

"Baltimore," Lukas muttered. "So he wrote the note at home, had dinner on the waterfront the night before. He came to D.C. to drop it off at City Hall. Then—"

"No, no, no," Rhyme said.

"What?" Lukas asked.

Parker, the puzzle master, said, "The evidence is fake. He staged it, didn't he, Lincoln?"

"Just like a Broadway play," Rhyme said, sounding pleased Parker had caught on.

"How do you figure?" Cage asked.

"There's a detective I've been working with – Roland Bell. N.Y.P.D. Good man. He's from North Carolina. He's got this expression. 'Seems a little kind of too quick and too easy.' Well, all that trace . . . There's too *much* of those elements. Way too much. The unsub got his hands on some trace and impregnated the envelope. Just to send us off track."

"And the trace on the letter?" Hardy asked.

"Oh, no, that's legit. The amount of material in the fibers was consistent with ambient substances. No, no, the letter'll tell us where he lived. But the envelope . . . ah, the envelope tells us something else."

Parker said, "That there was more to him than meets the eye."

"Exactly," the criminalist confirmed.

Parker summarized. "So, where he lived there's the granite, clay dust, brick dust, sulfur, soot and ash from cooking or burning meat."

"All that dust – might be a demolition site," Cage said.

"That seems the most likely," Hardy said.

"Likely? How could it be likely?" Rhyme asked. "It's a *possibility*. But then isn't *everything* a possibility until one alternative's proven true? Think about *that* . . ." Rhyme's voice faded slightly as he spoke to someone in the room with him, "No, Amelia, I'm not being pompous. I'm being accurate . . . Thom! Thom! Some more single-malt. Please."

"Mr. Rhyme," Lukas said, "Lincoln. . . . This is all good and we appreciate it. But we've got ten minutes until the shooter's next attack. You have any thoughts about which hotel the unsub might've picked?"

Rhyme answered with a gravity that chilled Parker. "I'm afraid I don't," he said. "You're on your own there."

"All right."

Parker said, "Thank you, Lincoln."

"Good luck to all of you. Good luck." With a click the criminalist disconnected the phone.

Parker looked over the notes. Granite dust . . . sulfur . . . Oh, they were wonderful clues, solid clues. But the team didn't have nearly enough time to follow up on them. Not before 4 P.M. Maybe not even before eight.

He pictured the shooter standing in a crowd of people, his gun ready. About to pull the trigger. How many would die this time?

How many families?

How many children like LaVelle Williams?

Children like Robby and Stephie?

Everyone in the half-darkened lab remained silent, as if paralyzed by their inability to see through the shroud obscuring the truth.

Parker glanced at the note again and had a feeling that it was mocking him.

Then Lukas's phone rang. She listened and her mouth blossomed into the first genuine smile Parker had seen on her face that day.

"Got him!" she announced.

"What?" Parker asked.

"Two of Jerry's boys just found some rounds of the black-painted shells under a chair at the Four Seasons Hotel in Georgetown. Every available agent and cop're on their way there."

11

03.50

"I s it crowded?"

"The hotel?" Cage said in response to Parker's question, looking up from his cell phone. "Hell, yes. Our man says the lobby bar's full – some kind of reception. Then in the banquet rooms downstairs there're four New Year's Eve parties going on. Lot of companies're closing up early. Must be a thousand people there."

Parker thought of what an automatic weapon could do in a closed space like a banquet room.

Tobe Geller had patched the operation radio frequency through speakers. In the lab the team could hear Jerry Baker's voice. "This is New Year's Leader Two to all units. Code Twelve at the Four Seasons on M Street. Code Twelve. Unsub is on premises, no description. Believed armed with a fully auto Uzi and suppressor. You are green lighted. Repeat, you are green lighted."

Meaning they were free to shoot without making a surrender demand.

Dozens of troops would be inside the hotel in minutes. Would they catch him? Even if not, Parker figured, they might spook him into fleeing without harming anyone.

But then they *might* catch him. Arrest him or, if he resisted, kill him. And the horror would be over; Parker could return home to his children.

What were they doing now? he wondered.

Was his son still troubled by the Boatman?

Oh, Robby, how can I tell you not to worry? The Boatman's been dead for years. But look here, now, tonight, we've got another Boatman, who's even worse. That's the thing about evil, son. It crawls out of its grave again and again and there's no way to stop it . . .

Silence from the radio.

Waiting was the hardest. That's what Parker had forgotten in his years of retirement. You never got used to waiting.

"The first cars are just getting there," Cage called out, listening to his cell phone.

Parker bent over the extortion note again.

Mayor Kennedy—
The end is night. The Digger is loose and their is no way to stop him.

Then he glanced at the envelope.

He was looking at the smudges of trace evidence. Looking at the ESDA sheets again, the faint images of the indented writing.

Rhyme's words echoed.

But the envelope tells us something else.
There was more to him than meets the eye . . .

And Parker heard himself earlier – telling Lukas

that Quantico's psycholinguistic profile was wrong, that the unsub was in fact brilliant.

His head shot up. He looked at Lukas.

"What?" she asked, alarmed at his expression.

He said evenly, "We're wrong. We've got it wrong. He's not going to hit the Four Seasons."

The others in the room froze, stared at him.

"Stop the response. The police, agents – wherever they are – stop them."

"What are you talking about?" Lukas asked.

"The note – it's lying to us."

Cage and Lukas looked at each other.

"It's leading us away from the real site."

"'It's'?" C. P. Ardell asked uncertainly. Looked at Lukas. "What does he mean?"

Parker ignored him and cried, "Stop them!"

Cage lifted his phone. Lukas motioned with her hand to stop.

"Do it!" Parker shouted. "The response teams have to stay mobile. We can't tie them up at the hotel."

Hardy said, "Parker, he's *there*. They found the rounds. That can't be a coincidence."

"Of course it's not a coincidence. The Digger *left* them there. Then he went someplace else – to the real target. Someplace that's *not* a hotel." He looked at Cage. "Stop the cars!"

"No," Lukas said. Anger now blossomed in her thin face.

But Parker, staring up at the note, continued. "It's too smart to leave a reference to the hotel accidentally. It tried to fool us with the trace on the envelope. The same's true with the indented writing. The *t-e-l*."

"We hardly even *found* the indented writing," Lukas

countered. "We wouldn't have if you hadn't been helping us."

"It knows—" The talk of the note personified seemed to make them uncomfortable. He said, "The *unsub* knew what he'd be up against. Remember my linguistic profile?" He tapped the picture of the dead unsub. "He was brilliant. He was a strategist. He *had* to make the evidence subtle. Otherwise we wouldn't believe it. No, no, we have to stop the tactical teams. Wherever they are. And wait until we can figure out where the real target is."

"Wait?" Hardy said, exasperated, lifting his hands.

C. P. whispered, "It's five minutes to four!"

Cage shrugged, glanced at Lukas. It was her call.

"You have to," Parker snapped.

He saw Lukas lift her stony eyes to the clock on the wall. The minute hand advanced one more notch.

The hotel was nicer than *this* place.

The Digger looks around him and there's something about this theater he doesn't like.

The puppy bag seemed . . . seemed right when he was in the nice hotel.

It doesn't look right here.

This is the . . . this is the . . . *click* . . . is the Mason Theater, just east of Georgetown. The Digger is in the lobby and he's looking at the wood carvings. He sees flowers that aren't yellow or red but are wood, dark like dark blood. Oh, and what's this? Snakes. Snakes carved in the wood. And women with big breasts like Pamela's.

Hmmm.

But no animals.

No puppies here. No, no.

He'd walked into the theater without anybody stopping him. The performance was nearly over. You can walk into most theaters toward the end of a show, said the man who tells him things, and nobody notices you. They think you're there to pick up somebody.

All the ushers here ignore him. They're talking about sports and restaurants and New Year's Eve parties.

Things like that.

It's nearly four.

The Digger hasn't been to a concert or a play for several years. Pamela and he went . . . *click* . . . went to someplace to hear music. Not a play. Not a ballet. What was it? Someplace where people were dancing. Listening to music . . . People in funny hats like cowboys wear. Playing guitar, singing. The Digger remembers a song. He hums to himself.

> *When I try to love you less,*
> *I just love you all the more.*

But nobody's singing today. This show *is* a ballet. A matinee.

They rhyme, he thinks. Funny. Ballet . . . matinee . . .

The Digger looks at the wall – at a poster. A scary picture he doesn't like. Scarier than the picture of the entrance to hell. It's a picture of a soldier with a huge jaw and he's wearing a tall blue hat. Weird. No . . . *click* . . . no, no, I don't like that at all.

He walks through the lobby, thinking that Pamela would rather see men in cowboy hats than soldiers with big jaws like this one. She'd get dressed up in clothes bright as flowers and go out to see the men in cowboy hats sing. The Digger's friend William wore hats like that sometime. They all went out together. He thinks they had fun but he's not sure.

The Digger eases to the lobby bar – which is now closed – and finds the service door, steps through and makes his way up the stairs that smell like spilled soda. Past cardboard boxes of plastic glasses and napkins and Gummi Bears and Twizzlers.

I love you all the more . . .

Upstairs, at the door that says BALCONY, the Digger steps into the corridor and walks slowly over the thick carpet.

"Go into box number fifty-eight," said the man who tells him things. "I bought all the seats in the box so it'll be empty. It's on the balcony level. Around the right side of the horseshoe."

"Shoe?" the Digger asked. What does he mean, shoe?

"The balcony is curved like a horseshoe. Go to a box."

"I'll go . . ." *Click.* ". . . go to a box. What's a box?"

"It'll be behind the curtains. A little room over-looking the stage."

"Oh."

Now, nearly 4 P.M., the Digger walks slowly toward the box and nobody notices him.

A family is walking past the concession stand; the father is looking at his watch. They're leaving early.

The mother is helping her daughter put her coat on as they walk and they both look upset. There's a flower in the girl's hair but it's not yellow or red; it's white. Their other child, a young boy of about five, glances at the concession stand and stops. He reminds the Digger of the boy in the nice hotel. "No, it's closed," the father says. "Let's go. We'll miss our dinner reservation."

And the boy looks like he's going to cry and he's led away by his father without Gummi Bears or Twizzlers.

The Digger is alone in the corridor. He thinks he feels bad for the boy but he isn't sure. He walks to the side of the horsehoe. There's a young woman in a white blouse walking toward him. She holds a flashlight.

"Hello," she says. "Lost?"

She looks at his face.

The Digger nuzzles the side of the puppy bag against her breast.

"What— ?" she starts to ask.

Phut, phut . . .

He shoots her twice and when she drops to the carpet he grabs her hair and drags her inside the empty box.

He stops just on the other side of the curtain.

My, this *is . . . click . . .* this *is* nice. Hmmm.

He looks out over the theater. The Digger doesn't smile but he now decides that he likes this place after all. Dark wood, flowers, plaster, gold and a chandelier. Hmmm. Look at that. Nicer than the nice hotel. Though he thinks it's not the best place for him to shoot. Concrete or cinderblock walls would be better; that way the bullets would ricochet more and the sharp bits of lead would rattle around inside the skull of the theater and cause oh so much more damage.

He watches people dancing on the stage. Listens to the music from the orchestra. But he doesn't really hear it. He's still humming to himself. Can't get the song out of his cranium.

> *I look into the future.*
> *I wonder what's in store.*
> *I think about our life,*
> *and I love you all the more.*

The Digger pushes the body of the woman against the velvet curtain. He's hot and he undoes his coat even though the man who tells him things told him not to. But he feels better.

He reaches into the puppy bag and wraps his fingers around the grip of the gun. Takes the suppressor in his left hand.

He looks down over the crowds. At the girls in pink satin, boys in blue blazers, women with skin showing in V's at their necks, bald men and men with thick hair. People aim little binoculars at the people on the stage. In the middle of the theater's ceiling is a huge chandelier, a million lights. The ceiling itself is painted with pictures of fat angels flying through yellow clouds. Like the New Year's baby . . .

There aren't that many doors and that's good. Even if he doesn't shoot more than thirty or forty people, others will die crushed in the doorway. That's good.

That's good . . .

Four o'clock. His watch beeps. He steps forward,

grips the suppressor through the crinkly bag, glances at a puppy's face. One puppy has a pink ribbon, one has a blue. But no red and no yellow, the Digger thinks as he starts to pull the trigger.

Then he hears the voice.

It's behind him in the corridor, through the pretty velvet curtain. "Jesus Christ," the man's voice whispers. "We got him! He's here." And the man pulls the curtain aside as he lifts his black pistol.

But the Digger heard him just in time and he throws himself against the wall and when the agent fires, the shot misses. The Digger cuts him nearly in half with a one-second burst from the Uzi. Another agent, behind the first one, is wounded by the stream of bullets. He looks at the Digger's face and the Digger remembers what he has to do. So he kills that agent too.

The Digger doesn't panic. He never panics. Fear isn't even a piece of dust to him. But he knows some things are good and other things are bad and not doing what he's been told to do is bad. He wants to shoot into the crowd but he can't. There are more agents rushing onto the balcony floor. The agents have FBI windbreakers on, bulletproof vests, some have helmets, some have machine guns that probably shoot just as fast as his Uzi.

A dozen agents, two dozen. Several turn the corner and run toward where the bodies of their friends lie. The Digger sticks the bag out through the curtain into the lobby and holds the trigger down for a moment. Glass breaks, mirrors shatter, Twizzlers and Gummi Bears fly through the air.

He should . . . *click* . . . should shoot into the audience. That's what he's supposed to . . .

Supposed to do . . . He . . .

For a moment his mind goes blank.

He should . . . *click.*

More agents, more police. Shouting.

There's so much confusion . . . Dozens of agents will soon be in the corridor outside the box. They'll throw a hand grenade at him and stun him and maybe shoot him to death and the bullets won't rattle around – they'll go straight through his heart and it will stop beating.

Or they'll take him back to Connecticut and shove him through the entrance to hell. He'll stay there forever this time. He'll never see the man who tells him things ever again.

He sees people jumping from the balcony onto the crowds below. It's not far to fall.

Shouting, the agents and the policemen.

They're everywhere.

The Digger unscrews the suppressor and aims the gun at the chandelier. He pulls the trigger. A roar like a buzzsaw. The bullets cut the stem and the huge tangle of glass and metal tumbles to the floor, trapping people underneath. A hundred screams. Everyone is panicked.

The Digger eases over the balcony and drops onto the shoulders of a large man, fifteen feet below. They fall to the floor and the Digger springs to his feet. Then he's being rushed through the fire door with the rest of the crowd. He still clutches the shopping bag.

Outside, into the cool air.

He's blinded by the spotlights and flashing lights from the fifty or sixty police cars and vans. But there aren't many police or agents outside. They're mostly in the theater, he guesses.

He jogs with a middle-aged couple through an alley away from the theater. He's behind them. They don't notice him. He wonders if he should kill them but that would mean mounting the suppressor again and the threads are hard to align. Besides, they don't look at his face so he doesn't *need* to kill them. He turns into another alley and in five minutes is walking along a residential street.

The bag tucked neatly under the arm of his black or blue coat.

His dark cap snug over his ears.

> *I'd love you if you're sick.*
> *I'd love you if you're poor.*

The Digger's humming.

> *Even when you're miles away*
> *I love you all the more . . .*

•   •   •

"Man, Parker," Len Hardy said, shaking his head with youthful admiration, "Good job. You nailed it."

C. P. Ardell meant the same when he said, "Don't fuck around with this man, no how, no way."

Margaret Lukas, listening to her phone, said nothing to Parker. Her face was still emotionless but she glanced at him and nodded. It was her form of thanks.

Yet Parker Kincaid didn't want gratitude. He wanted facts. He wanted to know how bad the shooting had been.

And if the body count included the Digger's.

On a console, speakers clattered with static as Jerry Baker and the emergency workers stepped on each other's transmissions. Parker could understand very little of what they said.

Lukas cocked her head as she listened to her phone. She looked up and said, "Two agents dead, two wounded. An usher killed and one man in the audience was killed by the chandelier, a dozen injured, some serious. Some kids were hurt bad in the panic. Got trampled. But they'll live."

They'll live, Parker thought grimly. But their lives'll never be the same.

Daddy, tell me about the Boatman . . .

Parker asked, "And he got away?"

"He did, yes," Lukas said, sighing.

"Description?"

She shook her head and looked at Cage, who was on his phone too. He muttered, "Nope, nobody got a damn look at him. Well, two people did. But they're the ones he capped."

Parker closed his eyes and let his head fall back against the gray padding of the office chair. It had to have been the one he'd ordered years ago; there was a certain musty, plasticky smell about it that brought back memories – some of the many that were surfacing tonight.

Memories he had no desire to experience.

"Forensics?" he asked.

"PERT's going over the place with a microscope," Cage said. "But – I don't get it – he's firing an automatic weapon and there're no shell casings."

Parker said, "Oh, he's got the gun in a bag or something. Catches the casings."

"How do you know that?" Hardy asked.

"I don't. But it's what *I'd* do if I were him. Anybody at the hotel get a look at him leaving the bullets?"

"Nope," Cage muttered. "And they've canvassed everybody there. One kid said he saw the boogeyman. But he couldn't remember anything about him."

Boogeyman, Parker thought wryly. Just great.

It'd been a photo finish.

Lukas had finally agreed to go along with Parker, saying icily, "All right, all right, we'll stop the response. But God help you if you're wrong, Kincaid." She'd ordered the teams to hold their positions. Then they spent a frantic few minutes trying to guess where the Digger might've gone. Parker had reasoned that he'd leave the bullets at the hotel not long before four – so he'd have ten minutes tops to get to the real target. The killer couldn't rely on getting a cab on a holiday afternoon and buses in the District were very unpredictable; he'd have to walk. That meant about a five-block radius.

Parker and the team had pored over a map of Georgetown.

Suddenly he'd looked at the clock and said, "Are there matinees today in the theaters?"

Lukas had grabbed his arm. "Yes. I saw some in the *Post* this morning."

Tobe Geller was a music fan and he mentioned the Mason Theater, which was only a five-minute walk from the Four Seasons.

Parker ripped open a copy of the *Washington Post* and found that a performance of *The Nutcracker* had started at two and would be letting out around four. A crowded theater would be just the target for the

Digger. He asked Lukas to call Jerry Baker and have him send all the troops there.

"All of them?"

"All of them."

God help you if you're wrong, Kincaid . . .

But he hadn't been wrong. Still, what a risk he'd taken . . . And though many lives had been saved some had been lost. And the killer had escaped.

Parker glanced at the extortion note. The man who'd written it was dead but the note itself felt very much alive. It seemed to be sneering at him. He felt a crazy urge to grab an examination probe and drive it into the note's heart.

Cage's phone rang again and he answered it. Spoke for a few minutes – whatever the news was it seemed encouraging, to judge from his face. Then he hung up. "That was a shrink. Teaches criminal psychology at Georgetown. Says he's got some info about the name."

"The 'Digger'?" Parker asked.

"Yeah. He's on his way over."

"Good," Lukas said.

Cage asked, "What's next?"

Lukas hesitated for a moment then asked Parker, "What do you think? You don't have to limit your thoughts to the document."

He said, "Well, I'd find out if the box in the theater he shot from was empty and if it was, did the unsub buy out the whole box – so the Digger'd have a good shooting position? And then I'd find out if he used a credit card."

Lukas nodded at C. P., who flipped open his phone and called Jerry Baker and posed the questions to him.

He waited for a moment then listened to his response. C. P. disconnected. "Nice try." He rolled his eyes.

"But," Parker speculated, "he bought the tickets two weeks ago and paid cash."

"*Three* weeks ago," the agent muttered, rubbing the shiny top of his head with a rough palm. "And paid cash."

"Hell," Parker snapped in frustration. Nothing to do but move on. He turned to the notes he'd taken of Lincoln Rhyme's observations. "We'll need some maps. Good ones. Not like this." He tapped the street map that they'd used to try to figure out where the Digger had gone from the Four Seasons. Parker continued, "I want to figure out where the trace in the letter came from. Narrow down the part of town he was staying in."

Lukas nodded at Hardy. "If we can do that we'll get Jerry's team and some of your people from District P.D. and do a canvas. Flash his pic and see if anybody's seen him at a house or apartment." She handed Geller a copy of the coroner's photo of the unsub in the morgue. "Tobe, make a hundred prints of this."

"Will do."

Parker looked over the list of trace Rhyme had identified. Granite, clay, brick dust, sulfur, ash . . . Where had the materials come from?

The young clerk who'd brought them the note earlier – Timothy, Parker recalled – appeared in the doorway.

"Agent Lukas?"

"Yes?"

"Couple things you ought to know about. First of all, Moss?"

Gary Moss. Parker remembered the memo about the children who'd nearly been burned to death.

"He's kind of freaked out. He saw a janitor and thought it was a hitman."

Lukas frowned. "Who was it? One of our people?"

"Yeah. One of the cleaning staff. We checked it out. But Moss's totally paranoid. He wants us to get him out of town. He thinks he'll be safer."

"Well, we can't get him out of town. He's not one of our priorities at the moment."

"I just thought I'd tell you," Timothy responded.

She looked around and seemed to debate. She said to Len Hardy. "Detective, you mind holding his hand for a while."

"Me?"

"Would you?"

Hardy didn't look happy. This was yet another subtle slap in the face. Parker recalled that the hardest part of his job when he was running the division was dealing not with elusive documents but with the delicate egos of his employees.

"I guess," Hardy said.

"Thanks." Lukas gave him a smile. Then she said to Timothy, "You said there was something else?"

"Primary Security wanted me to tell you. There's a guy downstairs? A walk-in."

"And?"

"He says he knows something about the Metro shooter."

Whenever there was a major crime like this, Parker recalled, the wackos crawled out of the woodwork – sometimes to confess to the crimes, sometimes to help. There were several "reception" rooms near the main entrance in headquarters for people like this. When anyone with knowledge of a crime dropped into the FBI the good citizen was taken into one of these visitor rooms and pumped for information by an expert interrogator.

"Credentials?" Lukas asked.

"Claims he's a journalist, writing about a series of unsolved murders. License and Social Security check out. No warrants. They didn't take it past a stage-two check."

"What's he say about the Digger?"

"All he said is that this guy's done it before – in other cities."

"In other cities?" C. P. Ardell asked.

"What he says."

Lukas looked at Parker, who said, "I think we better talk to him."

II

THE CHANGELING

The first step in narrowing the field of suspects of a
questioned writing is the identification of the national,
class, and group characteristics. Further elimination of
suspects is made when obvious individual characteristics
are identified, tabulated and evaluated.

—Edna W. Robertson,
Fundamentals of Document Examination

---◆◆◆◆◆---

12

"So he's in D.C. now, is he?" the man asked.

They were downstairs in Reception Area B. Which is what the sign on the door reported in pleasant scripty type. Within the Bureau, however, it was called Interrogation Room Blue, after the shade of the pastel decor inside.

Parker, Lukas and Cage sat across the battered table from him – a large man with wild, gray hair. From the linguistics of his sentence Parker knew the man wasn't from the area. Locals always call the city "the District," never "D.C."

"Who would that be?" Lukas asked.

"You know who," answered the man coyly. "I call him the Butcher. What do *you* call him?"

"Who?"

"The killer with a man's mind and the devil's heart," he said dramatically.

This fellow might have been a nut but Parker decided that his words described the Digger pretty well.

Henry Czisman was in clean but well-worn clothes. A white shirt, straining against his large belly, a striped tie. His jacket wasn't a sports coat but was the top of a gray pinstripe suit. Parker smelled the bitter scent of cigarettes in the clothes. A battered briefcase sat on the table. He cupped a mug of ice water on the table in front of him.

"You're saying the man involved in the subway and theater shootings is called the Butcher?"

"The one who actually did the shootings, yes. I don't know his accomplice's name."

Lukas and Cage were silent for a moment. She was scrutinizing the man closely and would be wondering how Czisman knew the Digger had a partner. The news about the dead unsub had not been released to the press.

"What's your interest in all this?" Parker asked.

Czisman opened the briefcase and took out several old newspapers. The *Hartford News-Times.* They were dated last year. He pointed out articles that he'd written. He was – or had been – a crime reporter.

"I'm on a leave of absence, writing a true-crime book about the Butcher." He added, "I'm following the trail of destruction."

"True crime?" Cage asked. "People like those books, huh?"

"Oh, they love 'em. Best-sellers. Ann Rule. That Ted Bundy book . . . You ever read it?"

"Might have," Cage said.

"People just eat up real-life crime. Says something about society, doesn't it? Maybe somebody ought to do a book about *that.* Why people like it so much."

Lukas prompted, "This Butcher you were mentioning . . ."

Czisman continued. "That was his nickname in Boston. Earlier in the year. Well, I think one paper called him the Devil."

The Devil's teardrop, Parker thought. Lukas was glancing at him and he wondered if she was thinking the same. He asked, "What happened in Boston?"

Czisman looked at him. Glanced at his visitor's pass. It had no name on it. Parker had been introduced by Cage as a consultant, Mr. Jefferson.

"There was a shooting at a fast food restaurant near Faneuil Hall. Lucy's Tacos."

Parker hadn't heard of it – or had forgotten, if the incident had made the news. But Lukas nodded. "Four killed, seven injured. Perp drove up to the restaurant and fired an automatic shotgun through the window. No motive."

Parker supposed that she'd read all the Violent Criminal Apprehension Program bulletins.

She continued, "If I recall, there was no description of that perp either."

"Oh, he's the same. You bet he is. And, no, there was no description. Just guesses. He's probably white. But not necessarily. How old? Thirties or forties. Height? Medium. Build? Medium. He could be anybody. Not like those ponytailed bodybuilding bad guys in made-for-TV movies. Pretty easy to spot them. But the Butcher . . . He's just an average man on the street. Pretty scary, isn't it?"

Lukas was about to ask a question but Czisman interrupted. "You said there was no motive in the restaurant shooting, Agent Lukas?"

"Not according to VICAP."

"Well, did you know that ten minutes after the Butcher finished lobbing rounds through the plate glass window and killing the women and children, a jewelry store was robbed four miles away?"

"No. That wasn't in the report."

Czisman asked, "And did you know that every tactical officer for two miles around was at the restaurant? So even though the owner of the jewelry store hit the silent alarms the police couldn't get to the store in their normal response time of four minutes. It took twelve. In that time the thief killed the owner and a customer. They were the only witnesses."

"The thief, he was the Butcher's accomplice?"

Czisman said, "Who else would it be?"

Lukas sighed. "We need any information you have. But I don't sense you're really here out of civic duty."

Czisman laughed.

She added, "What exactly do you want?"

"Access," he said quickly. "Just access."

"To information."

"That's right. For my book."

"Wait here," she said, rising. She gestured Parker and Cage after her.

Just off Room Blue on the first floor of headquarters Tobe Geller was sitting in a small, darkened room, in front of an elaborate control panel.

He had watched the entire interview with Henry Czisman on six different monitors.

Czisman would have no idea he was being watched because the Bureau didn't use two-way mirrors in its interrogation rooms – the sort you see in urban police stations. Rather, on the walls of the room were three prints of Impressionist paintings. They happened to have been picked not by a GSA facilities planner or a civilian interior designer but by Tobe Geller himself and several other people from the Bureau's Com-Tech group. They were prints of paintings by George Seurat, who pioneered the pointillist technique. Six of the tiny dots in each of the three paintings were in fact miniature video camera lenses, aimed so precisely that every square inch of the interrogation room was covered.

Conversations were also recorded – on three different digital recorders, one of which was linked to a computer programmed to detect the sequence of sounds of someone drawing a weapon. Czisman, like all interviewees, had been searched and scanned for a gun or knife but in this business you could never take too many precautions.

Lukas had instructed Geller, though, that his main job was not so much security as data analysis. Czisman would mention a fact – the robbery in Boston, for instance – and Geller would instantly relay the information to Susan Nance, a young special agent standing by upstairs in Communications. She in turn would contact the field office and seek to verify the information.

Czisman had never drunk from the mug of water Cage had placed in front of him but he did clutch it nervously, which is what everyone did when they sat in FBI interrogation rooms. The mug had a pressure-sensitive surface and a microchip, battery and transmitter in the handle. It digitized Czisman's fingerprints and transmitted them to Geller's computer.

He in turn sent them to the Automated Fingerprint
Identification System database for matching.

One of the video cameras – in a print of Seurat's
famous *Sunday Afternoon on the Island of La Grande
Jatte*, which was a complicated painting that every
interviewee tended to look at frequently – was locked
onto Czisman's eyes and was performing retinal
scans for "veracity probability analysis" – that is, lie
detection. Geller was also doing voice stress analysis
for the same reason.

Lukas now directed Cage and Kincaid into the
observation room.

"Anything yet?" Lukas asked Geller.

"It's prioritized," he said, typing madly.

A moment later his phone rang and Lukas slapped
the speaker phone.

"Tobe?" a woman's voice asked.

"Go ahead," he said. "The taskforce is here."

"Hi, Susan," Lukas said. "It's Margaret. Go ahead.
Give us the deets. What've you got?"

"Okay, prints came back negative on warrants,
arrests, convictions. Name Henry Czisman is legit,
address in Hartford, Connecticut. Bought his house
twelve years ago. Property taxes are up to date and
he paid off the mortgage last year. The image you
beamed up matches his Connecticut driver's license
photo ninety-five percent likely."

"Is that good?" Kincaid interrupted.

"*My* present picture matches ninety-two percent,"
Nance responded. "I've got longer hair now." She
continued. "Employment record through Social Security Administration and IRS shows him working as a
journalist since 1971 but some years he had virtually

no income. Listed his job those years as free-lance writer. So he's taken plenty of time off. Paid no quarterly estimated this year, which he's done in the past. And that suggests he's got no reportable income at all this year. Ten years ago he had very high medical deductions. Looks like it was treatment for alcohol abuse. Became self-employed a year ago, quit a fifty-one-thousand-dollar-a-year job at the Hartford paper and is apparently living off savings."

"Quit, fired or took a leave of absence?" Kincaid asked.

"Not sure." Nance paused. She continued. "We couldn't get as many credit card records as we wanted, because of the holiday, but he's staying at the Renaissance under his name. And he checked in after a noon flight from Hartford. United Express. No advanced purchase. Made the reservation at ten A.M. this morning."

"So he left just after the first shooting," Lukas mused.

"One way ticket?" Kincaid's question anticipated her own.

"Yes."

"What do we think?" Lukas asked.

"Goddamn journalist is all, I'd say," Cage offered.

"And you?" She glanced at Kincaid.

He said, "What do I think? I say we deal with him. When I analyze documents I need every bit of information I can get about the writer."

"If you *know* it's really the writer," Lukas said skeptically. She paused. Then said, "He seems like a crank to me. Are we that desperate?"

"Yes," Kincaid said, glancing at the digital clock

above Tobe Geller's computer monitor, "I think we are."

In the stuffy interrogation room once more, Lukas said to Czisman, "If we talk off the record now . . . and if we can bring this to a successful resolution . . ."

Czisman laughed at the euphemism, motioned for the agent to continue.

"If we can do that then we'll give you access to materials and witnesses for your book. I'm not sure how much yet. But you'll have some exclusivity."

"Ah, my favorite word. Exclusivity. Yes, that's all I'm asking for."

"But everything we tell you now," Lukas continued, "will be completely confidential."

"Agreed," Czisman said.

Lukas nodded at Parker, who asked, "Does the name Digger mean anything to you?"

"Digger?" Czisman shook his head. "No. As in gravedigger?"

"We don't know. It's the name of the shooter – the one you call the Butcher." Lukas said.

"I only call him the Butcher because the Boston papers did. *The New York Post* called him the Devil. In Philadelphia he was the Widow Maker."

"New York? Philly too?" Lukas asked, troubled by this news.

"Jesus," Cage muttered. "A pattern criminal."

Czisman said, "They've been working their way down the coast. Headed where, don't we wonder? To Florida for retirement? More likely the islands somewhere."

"What happened in the other cities?" Parker asked.

"The International Beverage case?" Czisman responded. "Ever hear of it?"

Lukas was certainly current on her criminal history. "The president of the company, right? He was kidnapped."

"Details?" Parker asked her, impressed at her knowledge.

Czisman looked at Lukas, who nodded for him to continue. "The police had to piece it together but it looks like – nobody's exactly sure – but it looks like the Butcher took the president's family hostage. The wife told her husband to get some money together. He agreed—"

"Was there a letter?" Parker asked, thinking there might be another document he could examine. "A note?"

"No. It was all done by phone. Well, the president tells the kidnapper he'd pay. Then he calls the police, and hostage rescue surrounds the house, yada yada yada, the whole nine yards, while the president goes to his bank to get the ransom. But as soon as they opened up the vault a customer pulls out a gun and begins shooting. Killed everyone in the bank: the International Beverage president, two guards, three customers, three tellers, two vice presidents on duty. The video camera shows another man, with him, walking into the vault and walking out with a bag of money."

"So there was nobody in the house?" Lukas asked, understanding the scheme.

"Nobody alive. The Butcher – the Digger – had already killed the family."

Parker said, "He hit them at the weakest point in

the kidnapping process. The police would have the advantage in a negotiation or in an exchange of the money. He preempted them." He didn't say aloud what he was thinking: that it was a perfect solution to a difficult puzzle – *if* you don't mind killing.

"Anything in the bank's security video that'd help us?" Cage asked.

"You mean, what color were their ski masks?"

Cage's shrug meant, I had to ask anyway.

"What about Philly?" Lukas asked.

Czisman said cynically, "Oh, this was very good. The Digger starts taking the bus. He'd get on, sit next to someone and fire one silenced shot. He killed three people, then his accomplice made the ransom demand. The city agreed to pay the ransom but set up surveillance to nail him. But the accomplice knew which bank the city had its accounts in. As soon as the rookies escorting the cash stepped outside the door of the bank the Digger shot them in the back of the head and they escaped."

"I never heard about that one," Lukas said.

"No, they wanted it kept quiet. Six people dead."

Parker said, "Massachusetts, New York, Pennsylvania, Washington. You're right – he was on his way south."

Czisman frowned. *"Was?"*

Parker glanced at Lukas. She told Czisman, "He's dead."

"What?" Czisman seemed truly shocked.

"The partner – not the Digger."

"What happened?" Czisman whispered.

"Hit-and-run after he dropped the extortion note off. And before he could collect his extortion money."

Czisman's face grew still for a long moment. Parker supposed he was thinking: There goes the exclusive interview with the perp. The huge man's eyes darted around the room. He shifted in his chair. "What was his scheme this time?"

Lukas was reluctant to say but Czisman guessed. "The Butcher shoots people until the city pays the ransom . . . But now there's nobody to pay the money to and so the Butcher's going to keep right on shooting. Sounds just like their MO. You have any leads to where his lair might be?"

"The investigation is continuing," Lukas said warily.

Czisman stared at one of the prints. A pastoral landscape. He kneaded the water mug manically.

Parker asked, "How did you follow him here?"

"I read everything I can find about crimes where somebody has no qualms about killing. Most people do, you know. Unless their *raison d'être* is killing – like Bundy or Gacy or Dahmer. No, most professional criminals will hesitate to pull the trigger. But the Butcher? Never. And when I'd hear about a multiple homicide that was part of a robbery or extortion I'd go to the city where it had happened and interview people."

Lukas asked, "Why hasn't anybody made the connection?"

Czisman shrugged. "Isolated crimes, small body counts. Oh, I told the police in White Plains and Philly. But nobody paid much attention to me." He laughed bitterly, waved his arm around the room. "Took – what? – twenty-five dead before anybody'd perk up their ears and listen to me."

Parker asked, "What can you tell us about the Digger? Hasn't *anybody* gotten a look at him?"

"No," Czisman said, "he's a wisp of smoke. He's there and then he's gone. He's a ghost. He—"

Lukas had no patience for this. "We're trying to solve a crime here. If you can help us we'd appreciate it. If not, we better get on with our investigation."

"Sure, sorry, sorry. It's just that I've lived with this man for the past year. It's like climbing a cliff – it could be a mile high but all you see is a tiny spot of rock six inches from your face. See, I have a theory why people don't notice him."

"What's that?" Parker asked.

"Because witnesses remember *emotion.* They remember the frantic robber who's shooting someone in desperation, the cop who's panicked and firing back, the woman screaming because she's been stabbed. But you don't remember calm."

"And the Digger's always very calm?"

"Calm as death," Czisman said.

"Nothing about his habits? Clothes, food, vices?"

"No, nothing." Czisman seemed distracted. "Can I ask what *you've* learned about the accomplice? The dead man?"

"Nothing about him either," Lukas said. "He had no ID on him. Fingerprints were negative."

"Would you . . . Would it be all right if I took a look at the body? Is it in the morgue?"

Cage shook his head.

Lukas said, "Sorry. It's against the regs."

"Please?" There was almost a desperation to the request.

Lukas, though, was unmoved. She said shortly, "No."

"A picture maybe," Czisman persisted.

Lukas hesitated then opened the file and took out the photo of the unsub at the accident site near City Hall and handed it to him. His sweaty fingers left fat prints on the glossy surface.

Czisman stared for a long moment. He nodded. "Can I keep this?"

"After the investigation."

"Sure." He handed it back. "I'd like to do a ride-along."

Where a reporter accompanies police on an investigation.

But Lukas shook her head. "Sorry. I'll have to say no to that."

"I could help," he said. "I might have some insights. I might have some thoughts that'd help."

"No," Cage said firmly.

With another look at the picture Czisman rose. He shook their hands and said, "I'm staying at the Renaissance – the one downtown. I'll be interviewing witnesses. If I find something helpful I'll let you know."

Lukas thanked him and they walked him back to the guard station.

"One thing," Czisman said, "I don't know what kind of deadlines he" – Czisman nodded toward Lukas's file, meaning the unsub – "came up with. But now that he's gone there's no one to control the Butcher . . . the Digger. You understand what that means, don't you?"

"What?" she asked.

"That he might just keep on killing. Even after the last deadline."

"Why do you think that?"

"Because it's the one thing he does well. Killing. And everybody loves to do what they do well. That's a rule of life now, isn't it?"

They huddled once more in the surveillance room, in a cluster around Tobe Geller and his computer.

Lukas said into the speakerphone, "How 'bout the other crimes he mentioned?"

Susan Nance responded, "Couldn't get any of the case agents in Boston, White Plains or Philly. But the on-duty personnel confirmed the cases are all open. Nobody heard of the name Butcher, though."

"Forensics?" Parker asked, just as Lukas started to ask, "Foren— ?"

"Nothing. No prints, no trace. And the witnesses . . . well, the ones who *lived* said they never really saw either the unsub or the Digger – if it was the Digger. I've put in requests for more info on the shootings. They're calling case agents and detectives at home."

"Thanks, Susan," Lukas said.

She hung up.

Geller said, "I'm getting the other analysis . . ." He looked at the screen. "Okay . . . Voice stress and ret scans – normal readings. Stress is awfully low, especially for somebody being cross-examined by three feds. But I'd give him a clean bill of health. Nothing consistent with major deception. But then, with practice you can beat most polygraphs with a Valium and a daydream about your favorite actress."

Lukas's phone rang. She listened. Looked up. "It's security. He's almost out of primary surveillance range. We let him go?"

Parker said, "I'd say yes."

"Agreed," Cage said.

Lukas nodded. She said into her phone. "No detention for subject." She hung up then glanced at her watch. "The shrink? The guy from Georgetown?"

"He's on his way," Cage said.

Now Geller's phone rang. He answered and spoke for a moment. After he hung up he announced, "Com-Tech. They've found a hundred and sixty-seven working Web sites that have information about packing silencers and full-auto machine-pistol conversions. Guess what? Not one of 'em'll hand over e-mail addresses. They don't seem inclined to help out the federal government."

"Dead end," Lukas said.

"Wouldn't do us much good anyway," Geller noted. "Com-Tech added up the hit counter totals from about a hundred of the sites. More than twenty-five thousand people've logged on in the last two months."

"Fucked-up world out there," Cage muttered.

The door opened. Len Hardy walked inside.

"How's Moss?" Lukas asked.

"He's okay. There were two hang-ups on his voice mail at home and he thought they might've been death threats."

Lukas said, "We should have Communications—"

Hardy, eyes on the elaborate control panels, interrupted. "I asked one of your people to check 'em out. One was from Moss's brother. The other was a telemarketer from Iowa. I called 'em both back and verified them."

Lukas said, "That's just what I was going to ask, detective."

"Figured it was."

"Thanks."

"District of Columbia at your service," he said.

Parker thought the irony in his voice was fairly subdued; Lukas didn't seem to notice it at all.

Parker asked, "What're we doing about that map? We've got to analyze the trace."

Geller said, "The best one I can think of is in the Topographic Archives."

"The Archives?" Cage asked, shaking his head. "There's no way we can get in there."

Parker could only imagine the difficulty of finding civil servants willing to open up a government facility on a holiday night.

Lukas flipped open her phone.

Cage said, "No way."

"Ah," she said, "you don't have the corner on miracles, you know."

13

04.50

The brass clock.

It meant so much to him.

Mayor Jerry Kennedy looked at it now, resting prominently on his desk in City Hall.

The gift was from students at Thurgood Marshall Elementary, a school square in the war zone of Ward 8, Southeast D.C.

Kennedy had been very touched by the gesture. No one took Washington the City seriously. Washington the political hub, Washington the federal government, Washington the site of scandal – oh, that was what captured everyone's attention. But no one knew, or cared, how the city itself ran or who was in charge.

The children of Thurgood Marshall had cared, however. He'd spoken to them about honor and working hard and staying off drugs. Platitudes, sure. But a few of them, sitting in the pungent, damp auditorium, had gazed up at him with the look of sweet admiration on their faces. Then they'd given him the clock in appreciation of his talk.

Kennedy touched it now. Looked at the face: 4:50.

So, the FBI had come close to stopping the madman. But they hadn't. Some deaths, some injuries. And more and more panic around the city. Hysteria. There'd already been three accidental shootings – by people carrying illegal pistols for protection. They thought they'd seen the Digger on the street or in their backyards and had just started shooting, like feuding neighbors in West Virginia.

And then there were the press reports berating Kennedy and the District police for not being up to the challenge of a criminal like this. For being soft on crime and for hiding out. One report even suggested that Kennedy had been unavailable – on the phone trying to get tickets to one of his beloved football games – while the theater shooting was going on. The reviews of his TV appearance were not good either. One interviewee, a political commentator, had actually echoed Congressman Lanier's phrase, "kowtowing to terrorists." He'd also worked the word "cowardly" into his commentary. Twice.

The phone rang. Wendell Jefferies, sitting across from the mayor, grabbed the receiver first. "Uh-huh. Okay . . ." He closed his eyes, then shook his head. He listened some more. He hung up.

"Well?"

"They've scoured the entire theater and can't find an iota of evidence. No fingerprints. No witnesses – no reliable ones anyway."

"Jesus, what is this guy, invisible?"

"They've got some leads from this former agent."

"*Former* agent?" Kennedy asked uncertainly.

"Document expert. He's found something but not much."

The mayor complained, "We need soldiers, we need police out on every street corner, we don't need paper pushers."

Jefferies cocked his smooth head cynically. The possibility of police on every street corner of the District of Columbia was appealing of course but was the purest of fantasies.

Kennedy sighed. "He might not have heard me. The TV broadcast."

"Possibility."

"But it's twenty million dollars!" Kennedy argued with his unseen foe, the Digger. "Why the hell doesn't he contact us? He could have twenty *million* dollars."

"They nearly got him. Maybe next time they will."

At his window Kennedy paused. Looked at the thermometer that gave the outside temperature. Thirty-three degrees. It had been thirty-eight just a half hour ago.

Temperature falling . . .

Snow clouds were overhead.

Why are you here? he silently asked the Digger. Why here? Why now?

He raised his eyes and looked at the domed wedding cake of the Capitol Building. When Pierre L'Enfant came up with the "Plan of the City of Washington" in 1792 he had a surveyor draw a meridional line north and south and then another exactly perpendicular to it, dividing the city into the four quadrants that remain today. The Capitol building was at the intersection of these lines.

"The center of the cross hairs," some gun-control advocate had once said at a congressional hearing where Kennedy was testifying.

But the figurative telescopic sight might very well be aimed directly at Kennedy's chest.

The sixty-three-square-mile city was foundering and the mayor was passionately determined not to let it go under. He was a native Washingtonian, a dying species in itself – the city population had declined from a high of more than 800,000 to around a half million. It continued to shrink yearly.

An odd hybrid of body politic, the city had only had self-rule since the 1970s (aside from a few-year period a century earlier, though corruption and incompetence had quickly pushed the city into bankruptcy and back under congressional domination). Twenty-five years ago the federal lawmakers turned the reins over to the city itself. And from then on a mayor and the thirteen-member City Council had struggled to keep crime under control (at times the District had the worst murder rate in America), schools functioning (students testing lower than in any other major city), finances in check (forever in the red), and racial tensions defused (Asian versus black versus white).

There was a real possibility that Congress would step in once more and take over the city; the lawmakers had already removed the mayor's blanket spending power.

And that would be a disaster – because Kennedy believed that only his administration could save the city and its citizens before the place erupted into a volcano of crime and homelessness and shattered families. More than 40 percent of young black men in D.C. were somewhere "in the system" – in jail, on probation or being sought on warrants. In the 1970s one-quarter of families in the District had been headed by a single parent; now the figure was closer to three-quarters.

Jerry Kennedy had had a personal taste of what might happen if the city continued its downward trajectory. In 1975, then a lawyer working for the District school board, he'd gone to the Mall – the stretch of grass and trees presided over by the Washington monument – for Human Kindness Day, a racial unity event. He'd been among the hundreds injured when racial fighting broke out among the crowd. It was on that day that he gave up plans to move to Virginia and run for Congress. He decided to become the mayor of the nation's capital. By God, he was going to fix the place.

To Kennedy the answer was very simple. And that answer was education. You had to get the children to stay in school and if you could do that then self-esteem and the realization that they could make choices about their lives would follow. (Yes, knowledge *can* save you. It had saved him. Lifting him out of the poverty of Northeast D.C., boosting him into William and Mary Law School. It got him a beautiful, brilliant wife, two successful sons, a career he was proud of.)

No one disagreed with the basic premise that education could save people of course. But *how* to solve the puzzle of making sure the children learned was a different matter. The conservatives bitched about what people *ought* to be like and if they didn't love their neighbors and live by family values then that was their problem. We home-school; why can't everybody? The liberals whined and pumped more money into the schools but all the cash did was slow the decay of the infrastructure. It did nothing to make students stay *in* those buildings.

This was the challenge for Gerald David Kennedy. He couldn't wave a wand and bring fathers back to mothers, he couldn't invent an antidote to crack cocaine, he couldn't get guns out of the hands of people who lived only fifteen miles from the National Rifle Association's headquarters.

But he did have a vision of how to make sure kids in the District continued their education. And his plan could pretty much be summarized by one word: bribery.

Though he and Wendell Jefferies called it by another name – Project 2000.

For the past year Kennedy, aided by his wife, Jefferies and a few other close associates, had been negotiating with members of the Congressional District Committee to impose yet another tax on companies doing business in Washington. The money would go into a fund from which students would be paid cash to complete high school – provided they remained drug free and weren't convicted of any crimes.

In one swoop, Kennedy managed to incur the political hatred of the entire political spectrum. The liberals dismissed the idea as a potential source of massive corruption and had problems with the mandatory drug testing as a civil liberties issue. The conservatives simply laughed. The corporations to be taxed had their own opinion, of course. Immediately, the threats started – threats of major companies pulling out of the District altogether, political action committee funds and hard and soft campaign money vanishing from Democratic party coffers, even hints of exposing sexual indiscretions (of which there were none – but try telling that to the media after they've gotten their hands on blurry videotapes of a man and a woman walking into a Motel Six or Holiday Inn).

Still, Kennedy was more than willing to take the risk. And in his months of bargaining on Capitol Hill to get the measure through committee it appeared that the measure might actually pass, thanks largely to popular support.

But then that city employee – Gary Moss – had summoned up his courage and gone to the FBI with evidence of a huge kickback scheme involving school construction and maintenance. Early investigations showed that wiring and masonry were so shoddy in some schools that faculty and students were at serious risk. The scandal kept growing and, it turned out, involved a number of contractors and subs and high-ranking District officials, some of them Kennedy appointees and longterm friends.

Kennedy himself had extolled Moss and thrown himself into the job of rooting out the corruption. But the press, not to mention his opponents, continued to try to link him to the scandal. Every news story about payoffs in the "Kennedy administration" – and there were plenty of them – eroded the support for Project 2000 more and more.

Fighting back, the mayor had done what he did best: He gave dozens of speeches describing the importance of the plan, he horse-traded with Congress and the teachers' union to shore up support, he even accompanied kids home from school to talk to their astonished parents about why Project 2000 was important to everyone in the city. The figures in the polls stabilized and it seemed to Kennedy and Wendy Jefferies that they might just hold the line.

But then the Digger arrived . . . murdering with impunity, escaping from crowded crime scenes, striking again. And who got blamed? Not the faceless FBI. But everyone's favorite target: Jerry Kennedy. If the madman killed any more citizens, he assessed, Project 2000 – the hope for his city's future – would likely become just a sour footnote in Kennedy's memoirs.

And this was the reason that Jefferies was on the phone at the moment. The aide put his hand over the receiver.

"He's here," Jefferies said.

"Where?" Kennedy asked sourly.

"Right outside. In the hallway." Then he examined the mayor. "You're having doubts again?"

How trim the man was, Kennedy thought, how perfect he looks in his imported suit, with his shaved head, his silk tie frothing at his throat.

"Sure, I'm having doubts."

The mayor looked out of another window – one that didn't offer a view of the Capitol. He could see, in the distance, the logotype tower of Georgetown University. His undergrad alma mater. He and Claire lived not far away from the school. He remembered, last fall, the two of them walking up the steep stairway the priest had tumbled down at the end of *The Exorcist*.

The priest who sacrificed himself to save the girl possessed by a demon.

Now, there's an omen for you.

He nodded. "All right. Go talk to him."

Jefferies nodded. "We'll get through this, Jerry. We will." Into the phone he said, "I'll be right out."

In the hallway outside of the mayor's office a handsome man in a double-breasted suit leaned against the wall, right below a portrait of some nineteenth-century politician.

Wendell Jefferies walked up to him.

"Hey, Wendy."

"Slade." This was the man's first name, his *real* given name, believe it or not, and – with the surname Phillips – you'd think his parents had foreseen that their handsome infant would one day be a handsome anchorman for a TV station. Which in fact he was.

"Got the story on the scanner. Dude lit up two agents, did a Phantom of the Opera on a dozen poor bastards in the bleachers."

On the air, with an earplug wire curling down his razor-cleaned neck, Phillips talked differently. In public he talked differently. With white people he talked differently. But Jefferies was black and Slade wanted him to think he talked the talk.

Phillips continued. "Capped one, I think."

Jefferies didn't point out to the newscaster that in gangsta slang the verb "cap" meant "shoot to death" not "chandelier to death."

"Nearly got the perp but he booked."

"That's what I heard," Jefferies said.

"So the man's gonna rub our uglies and make us feel

better?" This was a reference to Kennedy's impending press conference.

Jefferies had no patience today to coddle the likes of Slade Phillips. He didn't smile. "Here it is. This quote dude's gonna keep going. Nobody knows how dangerous he is."

"How dangerous is—"

Jefferies waved him quiet. "This is as bad as it gets."

"I know that."

"Everybody's going to be looking at him."

Him. Uppercase *H*. Jerry Kennedy. Phillips would understand this.

"Sure."

"So, we need some help," Jefferies said, lowering his voice to a pitch that resonated with the sound of money changing hands.

"Help."

"We can go twenty-five on this one."

"Twenty-five."

"You bargaining?" Jefferies asked.

"No, no. Just . . . that's a lot. What do you want me to do?"

"I want him—"

"Kennedy."

Jefferies sighed. "Yes. *Him.* To get through this like he's a hero. I mean, *the* hero. People're dead and more people're probably gonna die. Get the focus on him for visiting vics and standing up to terrorists and, I don't know, coming up with some brilliant shit about catching the killer. And get the focus *off* him for fuckups."

"Off— ?"

"The mayor," Jefferies said. "Kennedy's not the one—"

"No, he's not the one running the case." Phillips cleared his baritone voice. "Is that what you were going to say?"

"Right," Jefferies said. "If there's any glitch make sure he wasn't informed and that he did his best to make it right."

"Well, it's a Feebie operation, right? So we can just—"

"That's true, Slade, but we don't want to go blaming the Bureau for anything."

"We don't? Why exactly?"

"We just don't."

Finally Slade Phillips, used to reading off of a TelePrompTer, had had it. "I don't get it, Wendy. What do you want me to do?"

"I want you to play real reporter for a change."

"Sure." Phillips began writing copy in his head. "So Kennedy's taking a tough line. He's marshaling cops. He's going to the hospitals . . . Wait, without his wife?"

"*With* his wife," Jefferies said patiently.

Phillips nodded toward the press room. "But wait – they were saying . . . I mean, the guy from the *Post* said Kennedy *didn't* visit anybody. They were going to op-ed him on it."

"No, no, he went to the families who wanted to remain anonymous. He's been doing it all day."

"Oh, he has?"

It was amazing what $25,000 could buy you, Jefferies thought.

Phillips added, "That was good of him. Real good."

"Don't overdo it," Jefferies warned.

"But what do I do for footage? I mean, if the story's about him at the hospitals—"

Jefferies snapped, "Just show the same five seconds of tape over and over again like you guys always do. I don't know, show the ambulances at the Metro."

"Oh. Okay. What about the fuckup part? Why do you think there'll be a fuckup?"

"Because in situations like this there's always a fuckup."

"Okay, you need somebody to point a finger at. But not—"

"Not the feds."

"Okay," said Phillips. "But how exactly do I do that?"

"That's *your* job. Remember: who, what, when, where and why. You're the reporter." He took Phillips by the arm and escorted him down the hallway. "Go report."

14

05.00

"Y ou don't look good, Agent Lukas."
    "It's been a long day."
Gary Moss was in his late forties, heavy-set, with short-cropped kinky hair, just going gray. His skin was very dark. He was sitting on the bed in Facility Two, a small apartment on the first floor of headquarters. There were several apartments here, used mostly for visiting heads of law enforcement agencies and for the nights when the director or dep director needed to camp out during major operations. He was here because it was felt that, given what Moss knew and whom he was soon to testify against, he would survive about two hours if placed in District custody.

The place wasn't bad. Government issue but with a comfortable double bed, desk, armchair, tables, kitchen, TV with basic cable.

"Where's that young detective? I like him."

"Hardy? He's in the war room."

"He's mad at you."

"Why? Because I won't let him play cop?"

"Yeah."

"He's not investigative."

"Sure, he told me. He's a desk driver, like me. But he just wants a piece of the action. You're trying to catch that killer, aren't you? I saw about it on TV. That's why y'all've forgotten me."

"Nobody's forgotten about you, Mr. Moss."

The man gave a smile but he looked forlorn and she felt bad for him. But Lukas wasn't here just to hold hands. Witnesses who feel unhappy or unsafe sometimes forget things they've heard and seen. The U.S. attorney running the kickback case wanted to make sure that Gary Moss was a very happy witness.

"How're you doing?"

"Miss my family. Miss my girls. Doesn't seem right, when they've had a scare like that, I can't be there for them. My wife'll do a good job. But a man should be with his family, times like this."

Lukas remembered the girls, twins, about five. Tiny plastic toys braided into their hair. Moss's wife was a thin woman, with the wary eyes you'd expect of someone who's just watched her house burn to the ground.

"You celebrating?" She nodded at a gold, pointed hat with Happy New Year printed on it. There were a couple of noisemakers too.

Moss picked up the hat. "Somebody brought it for me. I said what was I supposed to do with half of Madonna's bra?"

Lukas laughed. Then she grew serious. "I just called on a secure phone. Your family's fine. There're plenty of people looking out for them."

"I never thought anybody'd try to hurt me or my family. I mean, when I was deciding to go to the FBI about what I found at the company. I figured I'd get fired but I never thought people'd want to hurt us."

He hadn't? The kickback scheme involved tens of millions of dollars and would probably result in the indictment of dozens of company employees and city officials. Lukas was surprised that Moss had survived long enough to make it into federal protection.

"What were you going to be doing tonight?" she asked. "With your family."

"Go to the Mall and watch the fireworks. Let the girls stay up late. They'd like that more than the show. How 'bout you, Agent Lukas? What'd you have planned?"

Nothing. She had nothing planned. She hadn't told anybody this. Lukas thought about several of her friends – a woman cop out in Fairfax, a firefighter in Burke, several neighbors, a man she'd met at a wine tasting, someone she'd met in dog class where she'd tried futilely to train Jean Luc. She was more or less close with all of these people and a few others. Some she gossiped with, some she'd shared plenty of wine with. One of the men she slept with occasionally. They'd all asked her to New Year's Eve parties. She'd told them all that she was going to a big party in Maryland. But it was a lie. She wanted to spend the last night of the year alone. And she didn't want anybody to know this – largely because she couldn't have explained why. But for some reason she looked at Gary Moss, a brave man, a man trapped in the firestorm of Washington, D.C., politics and she told him the truth. "I was going to be spending it with my pooch and a movie."

He didn't offer any cloying sympathy. Instead he said brightly, "Oh, you have a dog?"

"Sure do. Black Lab. She's pretty as a fashion model but board-certified stupid."

"How long you had her?"

"Two years. Got her on Thanksgiving."

Moss said, "I got my girls a mutt last year. Pound puppy. We thought we'd lost her in the firebombing but she got out. Had the good sense to leave us behind and just take off, got away from the flames. What movie were you gonna watch?"

"Don't know for sure. Some chick flick, probably. Something good and sappy that'd make me cry."

"Didn't think FBI agents were allowed to cry."

"Only off duty. What we're going to do, Mr. Moss, is keep you here until Monday then you'll be moved to a safe house run by the U.S. Marshals."

"Ha. Tommy Lee Jones. *The Fugitive*. Wasn't that a good movie?"

"I didn't see it."

"Rent it sometime."

"Maybe I will. You'll be fine, Gary. You're in the safest place you could possibly be. Nobody can get to you here."

"Long as those cleaning men stop scaring the shit out of me." He laughed.

He was trying to be upbeat. But Lukas could see the man's fear – it was as if it pulsed though the prominent veins on his bony forehead. Fear for himself, fear for his family.

"We'll get some good dinner brought in for you."

"A beer maybe?" he asked.

"You want a six-pack?"

"Hell, yes."

"Name your brand."

"Well, Sam Adams." Then he asked uncertainly, "That in the budget?"

"Provided I get one of them."

"I'll keep it nice 'n' cold for you. You come back and get it after you catch that crazy guy."

He toyed with the hat. For a moment she thought he might put it on but must have realized that the gesture would look pathetic. He tossed it onto the bed.

"I'll be back later," she told him.

"Where you going?"

"To look at some maps."

"Maps. Hey, good luck to you, Agent Lukas."

She walked through the door. Neither wished the other a happy New Year.

Outside, in the cool air, Parker, Cage and Lukas walked along the dimly lit sidewalk on the way to the Topographical Archives, six blocks from headquarters.

Washington, D.C., is a city of occasional beauty and some architectural brilliance. But at dusk in winter it becomes a murky place. The budget Christmas decorations did nothing to brighten the gray street. Parker Kincaid glanced up at the sky. It was overcast. He remembered that snow was predicted and that the Whos would want to go sledding tomorrow.

They'd trim the bushes in the backyard, as he'd promised Robby, and then drive out west, toward the Massanutten Mountains, with their sleds and a thermos of hot chocolate.

Lukas interrupted these thoughts by asking him, "How'd you get into the document business?"

"Thomas Jefferson," Parker answered.

"How's that?"

"I was going to be a historian. I wanted to specialize in Jeffersonian history. That's why I went to UVA."

"He designed the school, didn't he?"

"The original campus he did. I'd spend days in the archives there and at the Library of Congress. One day I was in Charlottesville, in the library, looking over this letter Jefferson had written to his daughter, Martha. It was about slavery. Jefferson had slaves but he didn't believe in slavery. But this letter, written just before he died, was adamantly proslavery and recanted his earlier opinions. He said that slavery was one of the economic cornerstones of the country and should be retained. It seemed strange to me – and strange that he'd write it to his daughter. He loved her dearly but their correspondence was mostly domestic. The more I read it the more I began to think the handwriting didn't look quite right. I bought a cheap magnifying glass and compared the writing with a known."

"And it was a fake?"

"Right. I took it to a local document examiner and he analyzed it. Caused quite a stir – somebody slipping a forgery into the Jefferson archives, especially one like that. I got written up in the paper."

"Who'd done it?" Lukas asked.

"Nobody knows. It was from the sixties – we could tell that because of the absorption of the ink. The archivists think that the forger was a right-winger who'd planted the letter to take some of the wind out of the civil rights movement. Anyway, from then on I was hooked."

Parker gave Lukas his curriculum vitae. He had an M.S. in forensics from George Washington University. And he was certified by the American Board of Forensic Document Examiners in Houston. He was also in the American Society of Questioned Document Examiners, the National Association of Document Examiners and the World Association of Document Examiners.

"I did free-lance work for a while but then I heard that the Bureau was looking for agent-examiners. Went to Quantico and the rest is history."

Lukas asked, "What appealed to you about Jefferson?"

Parker didn't even consider this. He responded, "He was a hero."

"We don't see many of them nowadays," Cage said.

"Oh, people aren't any different now than they ever were," Parker countered. "There've never been many heroes. But Jefferson was."

"Because he was a renaissance man?" Lukas asked.

"Because of his character, I think. His wife died in childbirth. Just about destroyed him. But he rose above it. He took over raising his daughters. He put the same amount of effort into deciding what kind of dress to buy Mary as he did in planning an irrigation system for the farm or interpreting the Constitution. I've read almost all of his letters. Nothing was too much of a challenge for him."

Lukas paused, looking at a window display of some chic designer clothes, a black dress. He noted she wasn't admiring it; her eyes took in the outfit the way she'd looked at the extortion note, analytically.

Parker was surprised something like this would distract her. But Cage said, "Margaret here's one hell of a, whatta you call it, designer. Makes her own clothes. She's great."

"Cage," she chided absently.

"You know anybody who does that?"

No, Parker didn't. He said nothing.

She turned away from the window and they continued down Pennsylvania Avenue, the stately Capitol ahead of them.

Lukas asked him, "And you really turned down an SAC?"

"Yep."

A faint laugh of disbelief.

Parker remembered the day that Cage and the then deputy director came into the office to ask him if he'd leave the document department and run a field office. As Cage had observed on his front porch earlier that day, Parker was not only good at analyzing documents; he was good at catching bad guys too.

An agent or an assistant U.S. attorney would come to him with a simple question about a document. Maybe a suspected forgery, maybe a possible link between a perp and a crime scene. And sitting in his bonsai-tree-filled office Parker would relentlessly cross-examine the unfortunate law enforcer, who only wanted some technical information on the document. But that wasn't enough for Parker.

Where'd you find the letter? No, no – which drawer? Does the unsub have a wife? Where does she live? Did he have a dog? What were the circumstances of his last arrest?

As one question led to another Parker Kincaid was soon talking less about whether the handwriting matched a signature in a DMV application and more about where the unsub would logically be hiding out. And he was nearly always right.

But he'd had to turn the offer down. A special agent in charge works long hours and, at that time in his life, he needed to be home. For the children's sake.

But none of *this* he wanted to share with Lukas.

He wondered if she'd ask more but she didn't. She pulled out her cell phone and made a call.

Parker was curious about the Topographic Archives. He asked, "What exactly—?"

"Quiet," Lukas whispered abruptly.

"What— ?" he began.

"Be quiet. Keep walking. And don't turn around."

He realized that she wasn't talking on the phone at all but merely pretending to.

Cage asked her, "You got him too? I put him twenty yards back."

"Closer to thirty. No visible weapons. And he's skittish. Erratic movement."

Parker realized that that had been why Lukas had been chatting him up and why she'd stopped and gazed at the dresses in the window – she'd suspected somebody'd been following them and she wanted the person lulled into thinking she didn't know. He too glanced back into a window they passed and saw a man trotting across the street – to the same sidewalk they were on.

Parker now noticed that both Cage and Lukas

were holding their pistols. He hadn't seen them draw the weapons. They were black automatics and on the sights were three tiny green dots that glowed. His service pistol had been a clunky revolver and what he remembered most about it was hating the regulation that required him to be armed at all times; the thought of having a loaded gun anywhere near the Whos disturbed him terribly.

Lukas muttered something to Cage and he nodded. To Parker she said, "Act natural."

Oh, sure . . .

"You think it's the Digger?" he asked.

"Could be," she said.

"Plan?" Cage whispered.

"Take him," she responded calmly.

Lord, Parker thought. The Digger was behind them! With his machine gun. He'd been staking out headquarters and had learned they were primary on the case. We nearly got him at the theater; maybe the unsub had told him to take out the investigators if it looked as if they were getting close.

"You take the street," Lukas said to Cage. "Kincaid, you cover the alley. In case there's backup."

"I—"

"Shhh."

"On three. One . . . two . . .

"But I—" Parker began.

"Three."

They separated fast. Cage stepped into the street, stopping cars.

Lukas turned and sprinted in the direction they'd just come from. "Federal agent!" she shouted. "You, you there! Freeze, hands on top of your head!"

Parker glanced into the alley and wondered what he was supposed to do if he saw an accomplice there. He pulled out his cell phone, punched in 911 and put his thumb over the SEND button. It was all he could think of.

He looked behind him, at Lukas. Beyond her, the man stopped abruptly then turned and took off in a dead run down the middle of the street.

"Hold it!"

Lukas was racing along the sidewalk. The man veered to the right, disappeared into traffic. She tried to follow but a car turned the corner quickly; the driver didn't see her and nearly slammed into her. Lukas flung herself back onto the sidewalk, inches from the fender.

When she started after him again the man was gone. Parker saw her pull her phone out and speak into it. A moment later three unmarked cars, with red lights flashing on the dashboard, skidded into the intersection. She conferred with one of the drivers and the cars sped off.

At a slow jog she returned to Parker. Cage joined them. Lukas lifted her hands in exasperation.

Cage shrugged. "You get a look at him?"

"Nope," Parker answered.

"I didn't either," Lukas muttered. Then she glanced at Parker's hands. "Where's your weapon?"

"My what?"

"You were covering the alley. We had a shake going down and you didn't draw your weapon?"

"Well, I don't have one. That's what I was trying to tell you."

"You're not armed?" she asked incredulously.

"I'm civilian," Parker said. "Why would I have a gun?"

Lukas gave a disdainful look to Cage, who said, "Assumed he had one."

She bent down and tugged up her jeans cuff. Pulled a small automatic out of an ankle holster. She handed it to Parker.

He shook his head. "No thanks."

"Take it," she insisted.

Parker glanced at the gun in her hand. "I'm not comfortable with guns. I was Sci-Crime, not tactical. Anyway, my service weapon was a revolver, not an automatic. Last time I fired one was on the range in Quantico. Six, seven years ago."

"All you do is point and pull," she said, angry now. "The safety's off. First shot is double action, second single. So adjust your aim accordingly." Parker wondered where her sudden anger came from.

He didn't take the weapon.

She gave a sigh, which left her mouth as a long tendril of steam in the cooling temperature. She said nothing but pushed the gun further out toward him.

He decided the battle wasn't worth it. He reached out and took the gun. Glanced at it briefly and slipped it in his pocket. Lukas turned, without saying anything, and they continued up the street. Cage gave him a dubious look, forewent a shrug and made a call on his cell phone.

As they walked along the street Parker felt the weight of the pistol in his pocket – a huge pull, much greater than the dozen ounces the gun actually weighed. Yet it gave him no comfort to have this weapon at his side. He wondered why. A moment passed before he realized. Not because the hot piece of metal reminded him that the Digger might have been behind them a moment ago, intent on killing him and Cage and Lukas. Or even because it reminded him of the Boatman four years ago, reminded him of his son's terror.

No, it was because the gun seemed to have some kind of dark power, like the magic ring in one of J. R. R. Tolkien's books, a power that had possessed him and was carrying him further and further away from his children with every passing minute. A power that could separate him from them forever.

The Digger is in an alley.

He is standing still, looking around him.

There are no agents or police around here. Nobody looking for him. Nobody to shoot him. Or capture him and send him back to Connecticut, where he likes the forests but he hates the barred rooms they make him sit in for hours and hours and do nothing, where people steal his soup and change the channels of the TV away from commercials about cars and puppies so they can watch sports.

Pamela said to him, "You're fat. You're out of shape. Why don't you take up running? Go buy some Nike . . ." *Click*. ". . . some Nike jogging shoes. Go do that. Go to the mall. I've got things to do."

The Digger now thinks he sees Pamela for a minute. He squints. No, no, it's merely a blank wall in the alley.

Do you promise to love, honor, cherish and . . . *click* . . . and obey?

He was jogging with Pamela one day, a fall day,

through red leaves and yellow leaves. He tried to keep up, sweating, his chest hurting the way his brain hurt after the bullet bounced around in his cranium. Pamela ran ahead and he ended up jogging by himself. Ended up walking home alone.

The Digger is worried about what went wrong at the theater. He's worried about all the police and agents and worried that the man who tells him things will be unhappy because he didn't kill as many people as he was supposed to.

The Digger hears sirens in the distance. Many sirens.

He starts through the alley. Lets the shopping bag swing in his arm. The Uzi is inside the bag and it's heavy again because he reloaded it.

Ahead of him, in the alley, he sees some motion. He pauses. There's a young boy. He's black and skinny. He's about ten years old. The boy is listening to someone talk to him. Someone the Digger can't see.

Suddenly the Digger hears Pamela's voice: "Have . . . have . . . have . . . children with you? Have . . . have . . . have . . . your baby?"

> *If we had us a child or three or four,*
> *you know I'd love you all the more.*

Then the memory of the song goes away because there's a tearing sound and the gun and the suppressor fall through the bottom of the shopping bag. He bends down to pick up the gun and as he does he looks up.

Hmmm.

This isn't funny.

The young boy and an older man, dressed in dirty clothes, the man who was talking to the boy, are walking up the alley. The man is bending the boy's arm upward. The boy is crying and his nose is bloody.

They are both looking at the Digger. The boy seems to be relieved. He pulls away from the man and rubs his shoulder. The man grabs the boy's arm again.

The man looks down at the Uzi. He gives the Digger a crooked smile. Says, "Whatever you doing, ain' my business. I'ma just go on my way."

"Leggo my arm," the boy whines.

"Shuddup." The man draws back his fist. The boy cowers.

The Digger shoots the man twice in the chest. He falls backward. The boy jumps back at the loud sound. The suppressor is still on the ground.

The Digger aims the gun at the boy, who is staring at the body.

"If somebody sees your face . . ."

The Digger starts to pull the trigger.

"Have . . . have . . . have . . . children with you?" The words rattle around in his skull.

The boy is still staring down at the body of the man who was beating him. The Digger starts to pull the trigger again. Then he lowers the gun. The boy turns and looks at the Digger. He whispers, "Yo, you cap him! Man, just like nothin', you cap him."

The boy is staring right at the Digger's face. Ten feet away.

Words rattling around. Kill him he's seen your face kill him, killhimkillhimkillhim.

And things like that.

The Digger says, "Hmmm." He stoops and picks up the spent shells and then the suppressor and wraps it and the gun in the torn puppy bag and walks out of the alley, leaving the boy beside a garbage pile, staring at the body.

Go back to the motel and . . . *click* . . . go back to the motel and wait.

He'll have some soup and wait. He'll listen to his messages. See if the man who tells him things has called to tell him he can stop shooting.

When I hear you coming through the door . . .

Some soup would be nice now.

I know I love you all the more.

He made soup for Pamela. He was making soup for Pamela the night she . . . *click*. It was Christmas night. Twelve twenty-five. One two two five. A night like this. Cold. Colored lights everywhere.

Here's a gold cross for you, he said. And this box is for me? . . . A present? Oh, it's a coat! Thank you thank you thank you . . .

The Digger is standing at the stoplight, waiting for the green.

Suddenly he feels something touch his hand.

The Digger isn't alarmed. The Digger never gets alarmed.

He grips the gun in the torn puppy bag. He turns slowly.

The boy stands beside him, holding the Digger's left hand tightly. He's looking straight ahead.

Love you love you love you . . .

The light changes.
The Digger doesn't move.

All the more . . .

"Yo, we can walk," says the boy, now staring at the puppies on the torn bag. The Digger sees the green figure in the WALK/DON'T WALK light.

The green figure seems happy.

Whatever happy is.

Holding hands, the two of them walk across the street.

15

The District of Columbia Topographic and Geologic Archives is housed in a musty old building near Seventh and E Streets.

It also, not coincidentally, is located near a little-known Secret Service facility and the National Security Council's Special Operations Office.

There's no reference to the Archives in any tourist literature and visitors who notice the sign on the front of the building and walk inside are politely told by one of the three armed guards at the front desk that the facility is not open to the public and that there are no exhibitions here but thank you for your interest. Have a nice day. Goodbye.

Cage, Parker and Lukas – on her ever-present phone – waited in the lobby. She shut off the unit. "Nothing. He just disappeared."

"No witnesses?"

"A couple of drivers saw a man in dark clothes running. They think he was white. They think he was medium build. But nobody'd swear to it. Jesus."

Cage looked around. "How'd you get us in here, Lukas? I couldn't get us in here."

Now it was Lukas's turn to shrug cryptically. It seemed that New Year's Eve was the day to call in markers and incur debts.

They were joined by Tobe Geller, who entered the facility at a slow trot. He nodded a greeting to the other members of the team. Then their fingerprints were checked by an Identi-Scanner and their weapons secured in a lock box. They were all directed through to an elevator. They stepped into the car. Parker expected to rise but this elevator, it seemed, went no higher than the first floor. Lukas hit the button marked B7 and the car descended for what seemed like forever.

They stepped out into the Archives proper. Which turned out not to be stacks of dusty old books and maps – which Parker, Certified Document Examiner, had been looking forward to checking out – but a huge room filled with high-tech desks, telephones, microphones and banks of twenty-four-inch NEC computer screens. Even tonight, New Year's Eve, two dozen men and women sat in front of these screens, on which glowed elaborate maps, typing on keyboards and speaking into stalk mikes.

Where the hell am I? Parker wondered, looking around and concluding that the issue of access to the Archives had nothing to do with finding a civil servant with a key to the front door.

"What *is* this?" he asked Geller.

The young agent glanced tactfully at Cage, who

nodded his okay to tell all. Geller replied, "Topographic and cartographic database of a hundred square miles around the District. Ground zero's the White House, though they don't like it when you say that. In case of natural disaster, terrorist attack, nuclear threat – what*ever* – this's where they figure out if it's best for the government to sit tight or get out of town and if so how they ought to do it. What routes are safest, how many congressmen'll survive, how many senators. That sort of thing. Like the war room in *Fail Safe*. Way cool, hmm?"

"What're *we* doing here?"

"You wanted maps," he said, looking excitedly at all the equipment the way only a born hacker would do, "and this's the most comprehensive physical database of any area in the world. Lincoln Rhyme was saying we needed to know the area. Well, *we* may not. But they do." He nodded affectionately toward a long row of six-foot-high computer towers.

Lukas said, "They're letting us use the facility, under protest, provided we don't take any printouts or downloads with us."

"We get searched on the way out," Geller said.

"How come you know so much about it?" Parker asked Geller.

"Oh, I sort of helped set it up."

Lukas added, "Oh, by the way, Parker, you've never heard of this place."

"Not a problem," said Parker, eying the two machine-gun-armed guards by the elevator door.

Lukas said, "Now, what're the materials Rhyme found?"

Parker looked at the notes he'd taken. He read, "Granite, sulfur, soot, ash, clay and brick."

Tobe Geller sat down at a monitor, turned it on, typed madly on a keyboard. An image of the Washington, D.C., area came on the screen. The resolution was astonishing. It looked three-dimensional. Parker thought, absurdly, how Robby and Stephie would love to play Mario Bros. on a monitor like this.

Lukas said to Parker, "Where do we start?"

"One clue at a time," he responded. "The way you solve puzzles."

Three hawks have been killing a farmer's chickens . . .

"First, granite, brick dust and clay," he mused. "They point to demolition sites, construction . . ." He turned to Geller. "Would they be on this database?"

"No," the young agent responded. "But we can track down somebody at Building Permits."

"Do it," Parker ordered.

Geller made the call on a landline – no cell phone would work this far underground and, besides, like all secure facilities in Washington, Parker supposed, the walls were shielded.

"What next?" Parker wondered. "Sulfur and soot . . . That tells us it's industrial. Tobe, can you highlight areas based on air pollutants?"

"Sure. There's an EPA file." He added cheerfully, "It's to calculate penetration levels of nerve gas and bioagent weapons."

More buttons.

The business of the District of Columbia is government, not industry, and the commercial neighborhoods were devoted mostly to product warehousing and distribution. But on the screen portions of the city began to be highlighted – in, appropriately, pollution-tinted yellow. The majority were in the Southeast part of town.

"He's probably *living* near there," Lukas reminded. "What industrial sites are adjacent to areas of houses and apartments?"

Geller continued to type, cross-referencing the indus- trial neighborhoods with residential. This eliminated some but not many of the manufacturing areas; most of them were ringed with residential pockets.

"Still too many," Lukas said.

"Let's add another clue. The ash," Parker said. "Basically burnt animal flesh."

Geller's hands paused above the keyboard. He mused, "What could *that* be?"

Lukas shook her head. Then asked, "Are there any meat-processing plants in any of those areas?"

This was a good suggestion, one Parker himself had been about to make.

Geller responded, "None listed."

"Restaurants?" Cage suggested.

"Probably too many of them," Parker said.

"Hundreds," Geller confirmed.

"Where else would there be burnt meat?" Lukas asked no one in particular.

Puzzles . . .

"Veterinarians," Parker wondered. "Do they dispose of the remains of animals?"

"Probably," Cage said.

Geller typed then read the screen. "There are dozens. All over the place."

Then Lukas looked up at Parker and he saw that the chill from earlier was gone, replaced by something else. It might have been excitement. Her blue eyes were stones still, perhaps, but now they were radiant gems. She said, "How about *human* remains?"

"A crematorium!" Parker said. "Yes! And the polished granite – that could be from tombstones. Let's look for a cemetery."

Cage gazed at the map. He pointed. "Arlington?"

The National Cemetery took up a huge area on the west side of the Potomac. The area around it must be saturated with granite dust.

But Parker pointed out: "It's not near any industrial sites. Nothing with significant pollution."

Then Lukas saw it. "There!" She pointed a finger, tipped with an unpolished but perfectly filed nail. "Gravesend."

Tobe Geller highlighted the area on the map, enlarged it.

Gravesend . . .

The neighborhood was a part of the District of Columbia's Southeast quadrant. Parker had a vague knowledge of the place. It was a decrepit crescent of tenements, factories and vacant lots around Memorial Cemetery, which had been a slave grave-yard dating back to the early 1800s. Parker pointed to another part of Gravesend. "Metro stop right here. The unsub could've taken the train directly to Judiciary Square – City Hall. There's a bus route nearby too."

Lukas considered it. "I know the neighborhood – I've collared perps there. There's a lot of demo-lition and construction going on. It's anonymous too. Nobody asks any questions about anybody else. And a lot of people pay cash for rent, without raising suspicion. It'd be the perfect place for a safe house."

A young technician near them took a phone call and handed the receiver to Tobe Geller. As the agent listened to the caller his young face broke into an enthusiastic smile. "Good," he said into the phone. "Get it to the document lab ASAP." He hung up. "Get this . . . Somebody got a videotape from the Mason Theater shooting."

"A tape of the Digger?" Cage asked enthusiastically.

"They don't know *what* it's of exactly. Sounds like the quality's pretty bad. I want to start the analysis right away. Are you going to Gravesend?"

"Yep," Parker said. Looked at his watch. Two and a half hours until the next attack.

"MCP?" Geller asked Lukas.

"Yeah. Order one."

Parker recalled: a mobile command post. A camper outfitted with high-tech communications and surveillance equipment. He'd worked in one several times, analyzing documents at crime scenes.

"I'll have a video data analyzer installed," Geller said, "and get going on the tape. Where will you be?"

Lukas and Parker said simultaneously, "There." They found they were pointing at the same vacant lot near the cemetery.

"Not many apartments around there," Cage pointed out.

Parker said, "But it's close to the stores and restaurants."

Lukas glanced at him and nodded. "We should narrow down the search by canvassing those places first. They'll have the most contact with locals. Tobe, pick up C. P. and Hardy and bring 'em with you in the MCP."

The agent hesitated, a dubious look on his face. "Hardy? We really need him?"

Parker had been wondering the same thing. Hardy seemed like a nice enough guy, a pretty good cop. But he was way out of his depth in this case and that meant he, or somebody else, might get hurt.

But Lukas said, "If it's not him the District'll just put somebody else on board. At least we can control Hardy. He doesn't seem to mind sitting in the back seat."

"Politics suck," Cage muttered.

As Geller pulled on his jacket Lukas said, "And that shrink? The guy from Georgetown? If he's not at headquarters yet have somebody drive him over to Gravesend."

"Will do." Geller ran for the elevator, where he was, as he'd predicted, thoroughly searched.

Lukas stared at the map of Gravesend. "It's so damn big."

"I've got another thought," Parker said. He was thinking back to what he'd learned about the unsub from the note. He said, "We think he probably spent time on a computer, remember?"

"Right," Lukas said.

"Let's get a list of everybody in Gravesend who subscribes to an online service."

Cage protested, "There could be thousands of 'em."

But Lukas pointed out, "No, I doubt it. It's one of the poorest parts of the city. Computers'd be the last thing people'd spend money on."

Cage said, "True. Okay, I'll have Com-Tech get us a list."

"There'll still be a lot of territory to cover," Lukas muttered.

"I've got a few other ideas," Parker said. And walked to the elevator door, where he too was diligently searched like a suspected shoplifter by the humorless guards.

Kennedy paced in a slow circle around the dark green carpet in his office.

Jefferies was on his cell phone. He clicked it off.

"Slade's got a few ideas but nothing's going to happen fast."

Kennedy gestured toward the radio. "Well, they were damn fast to report that I've been sitting on my butt while the city's getting the hell shot out of it. They were fast to report that I didn't lift the hiring freeze at the police department so we'd have more money for Project 2000. Jesus, the media's making it sound like *I'm* an accomplice."

Kennedy had just been to three hospitals to see the people wounded in the Digger's attacks and their families. But none of them seemed to care about his visit. All anyone asked was why wasn't he doing more to catch the killer?

"Why aren't you at FBI headquarters?" one woman had demanded tearfully.

Because they haven't fucking invited me, Kennedy thought furiously. Though his answer was a gentle "I'm letting the experts do their job."

"But they're *not* doing their job. And you're not either."

When he left her bedside Kennedy didn't offer to shake hands; her right arm had been so badly shot up it had been amputated.

"Slade'll come up with something," Jefferies now said.

"Too little, too late. Now, *that* man is too damn pretty," Kennedy spat out. "Pretty people . . . I never trust them." Then he heard the paranoid words and he laughed. Jefferies did too. The mayor asked, "Am I turning into a crank, Wendy?"

"Yessir. It's my duty to tell you your brains've gone to grits."

The mayor sat down in his chair. He looked at his desk calendar. If it weren't for the Digger he would have been attending four parties tonight. One at the French embassy, one at his alma mater, Georgetown University, one at the city workers' union hall, and – the most important, where he'd actually ring in the New Year – the African-American Teachers' Association in the heart of Southeast. This was the group that was lobbying hard to get his Project 2000 accepted among rank and file teachers throughout the District. He and Claire needed to be there tonight, as a show of support. And yet it would be impossible for him to attend any parties, do any celebrating, with that madman stalking the citizens of his city.

A wave of anger passed through him and he grabbed the phone.

"What," Jefferies asked cautiously, "are you going to do?"

"*Something*," he answered. "I'm going to goddamn do something." He began dialing a number from a card on his Rolodex.

"What?" asked Jefferies, now even more uneasy.

But by then the call to FBI headquarters had been connected and Kennedy didn't respond to his aide.

He was patched through several locations. A man's voice answered. "Yes."

"This's Mayor Jerry Kennedy. Who'm I speaking to?"

A pause. Kennedy, who often made his own phone calls, was used to the silence that greeted his salutation. "Special Agent C. P. Ardell. What can I do for you?"

"That Agent Lukas, she's still in charge of the METSHOOT operation?"

"That's right."

"Can I speak to her?"

"She's not here, sir, no. I can patch you through to her cell phone."

"That's all right. I'm actually trying to reach the District liaison officer, Detective Hardy."

Agent Ardell said, "Hold on. He's right here."

A moment later a voice said tentatively, "Hello?"

"This Hardy?"

"Len Hardy, that's right."

"This's your mayor again."

"Oh. Well. How are you, sir?" Caution was added to the youth in the man's voice.

"Can you update me on the case? I haven't heard a word from Agents Lukas or Cage. You have any idea where the Digger's going to hit next?"

Another pause. "Nosir."

The pause was too long. Hardy was lying about something.

"No idea at all?"

"They aren't exactly keeping me in the loop."

"Well, your job's liaison, right?"

"My orders are just to write a report on the operation. Agent Lukas said she'd contact Chief Williams directly."

"A report? That's ass covering. Listen to me. I have a lot of confidence in the FBI. They do this shoot-'em-up stuff all the time. But how close are they to stopping this killer? Bottom line. No bullshit."

Hardy sounded uneasy. "They have a few leads. They think they know the neighborhood where the unsub's safe house is – the guy who was killed by the truck."

"Where?"

Another pause. He pictured poor Hardy twisting in the wind, feds on one side, his boss on the other. Well, too fucking bad.

"I'm not supposed to give out tactical information to anyone, sir. I'm sorry."

"It's *my* city that's under attack and *my* citizens who're being slaughtered. I want answers."

More silence. Kennedy looked up at Wendell Jefferies, who shook his head.

Kennedy forced his anger down. He tried to sound reasonable as he said, "Let me tell you what I have in mind. The whole point of this scheme was for those men to make money. It's not to kill."

"I think that's true, sir."

"If I can just have a chance to talk to the killer – at this safe house or where he's going to hit at eight – I think I can convince him to give up. I'll negotiate with him. I can do that."

Kennedy did believe this. Because one of his talents

(in this respect *like* his namesake from the sixties) was his ability to persuade. Hell, he'd sweet-talked two dozen of the toughest presidents and CEOs in the District into accepting the tax that would fund Project 2000. He'd even talked poor Gary Moss into naming names in the Board of Education scandal.

Twenty minutes with this killer – even staring down the barrel of that machine gun of his – would be enough. He'd work out some kind of arrangement.

"The way they're describing him," Hardy said, "I don't think he's the sort you can negotiate with."

"You let me be the judge of that, Detective. Now, where's his safe house?"

"I . . ."

"Tell me."

The line hummed. Still, the detective said nothing.

Kennedy's voice lowered. "You don't owe the feds a thing, son. You know how they feel about you being on the task force. You're a step away from fetching coffee."

"That's wrong, sir. Agent Lukas's made me part of the team."

"Has she?"

"Pretty much."

"You don't feel like a third wheel? I'm asking that 'cause *I* feel like one. If Lanier had his way – you know Congressman Lanier?"

"Yessir."

"If he had his way my only job tonight'd be sitting in the reviewing stand on the Mall watching fireworks . . . You and me – the District of Columbia's *our* city. So, come on, son, where's that goddamn safe house?"

Kennedy watched Jefferies cross his fingers. Please . . . It would be perfect. I show up there, I try to talk the man into coming out with his hands up. Either he surrenders or they kill him. And either way, my credibility survives. Either way, I'm no longer the mayor who watched the murder of his city on CNN while he kicked back with a beer.

Kennedy heard voices from the other end of the line. Then Hardy was back. "I'm sorry, Mayor, I have to go. There're people here. I'm sure Agent Lukas will be in touch."

"Detective . . ."

The line went blank.

Gravesend.

The car carrying Parker and Cage bounded over gaping potholes and eased to a stop at a curb where trash and rubble spilled into the street. The burnt-out torso of a Toyota rested, ironically, against a fire hydrant.

They climbed out. Lukas had driven in her own car, a red Ford Explorer, and was already at the vacant lot that was the rendezvous point. She was standing with her hands on her trim hips, looking around.

The smells of urine and shit and burning wood and trash were very strong.

Parker's parents, who became world travelers after his father had retired from teaching history, had once found themselves in a slum in Ankara, Turkey. Parker still could remember the letter he'd received from his mother, who was an ardent correspondent. It was the last letter he'd received from them before they'd died. It was framed and up on the wall

of his study downstairs, next to the Whos' wall
of fame.

They're impoverished, the people here, and that,
more than racial differences, more than culture,
more than politics, more than religion, turns their
hearts to stone.

He thought of her words now, as he looked over
the desolation of the area.

Two black teenagers, who'd been leaning against
a wall graffiti'd with gang colors, looked at the men
and women arriving – obviously law enforcers –
and walked away slowly, uneasiness and defiance
on their faces.

Parker was troubled – though not by the danger;
by the hugeness of the place. It was three or four
square miles of slums and row houses and small
factories and vacant lots. How could they possibly
find the unsub's safe house in this much urban
wilderness?

There were some riddles that Parker had never been
able to figure out.

Three hawks . . .

Smoke wafted past him. It was from fires in the
oil drums where the homeless men and women and
the gangstas burned wood and trash for warmth. He
saw more hulks of stripped cars. Across the street
was a building that seemed deserted; the only clue
to habitation was a bulb burning behind a red towel
covering a broken window.

Just past the Metro stop, over a tall, decaying brick
wall, the chimney of the crematorium rose into the
night sky. There was no smoke rising from it but
the sky above the muzzle rippled in the heat. Perhaps

its fires always burned. Parker shivered. The sight reminded him of old-time pictures of—

"Hell," Lukas muttered. "It looks like hell."

Parker glanced at her.

Cage shrugged in agreement.

A car arrived. It was Jerry Baker, wearing a bulky windbreaker and body armor. Parker saw that, as befit a tactical agent, he was also wearing cowboy boots. Cage handed him the stack of computerized pictures of the unsub – the death mask portrait from the morgue. "We'll use these for the canvas. At the bottom? That's the only description we have of the Digger."

"Not much."

Another shrug.

More unmarked cars and vans began to pull up, their dashboard flashers reflecting in the bands of storefront windows. FBI government-issue wheels. White-and-teal District police cars too, their light bars revolving. There were about twenty-five men and women in total, half of them federal agents, half uniformed cops. Baker motioned to them and they congregated around Lukas's truck. He distributed the printouts.

Lukas said to Parker, "Want to brief them?"

"Sure."

She called, "If you could listen to Agent Jefferson here."

It took a second before Parker recognized the reference to his stage name. He decided he would've been a failure at undercover work. He said, "The man in the picture you've got there was the perp responsible for the Metro and Mason Theater shootings. We think he was working out of a safe house somewhere here in Gravesend. Now, he's dead but his accomplice – the shooter – is still at large. So we need to find the safe house and find it fast."

"You have a name?" one of the District cops called.

"The unsub – the dead one – is a John Doe," Parker said, holding up the picture. "The shooter's got a nickname. The Digger. That's all. *His* description's on the bottom of the handout."

Parker continued. "You can narrow down the canvassing area some. The safe house is probably near a demolition or construction site and won't be far from the cemetery. He also recently bought some paper like this—" Parker held up the clear sleeves holding the extortion note and the envelope. "Now, the paper was sun-bleached so it's possible that he bought it in a store that displays their office supplies in or near a south-facing window. So hit every convenience store, drugstore, grocery store and newsstand that sells paper. Oh, and look for the type of pen he used too. It was an AWI black ballpoint. Probably cost thirty-nine or forty-nine cents."

That was all he could think of. With a nod he handed off to Lukas. She stepped in front of the agents. Looked over them, silent, until she had everyone's attention. "Now, listen up. Like Agent Jefferson said, the unsub's dead but the shooter sure as hell isn't. We don't know if he's in Gravesend and we don't know if he's living in the safe house. But I want everybody here to assume he's ten feet behind you and has a clear path to target. He's got no problem lighting up law enforcement personnel. So as you go through the neighborhood I want everyone to be looking for ambush positions. I want weapon hands free, I want jackets and coats unbuttoned, I want holster thongs unsnapped."

She paused for a moment. She had their complete attention, this thin woman with silver-blond hair.

"At eight o'clock – yep, that's right, just over two hours – our perp is going to find someplace that's filled with people and he's going to empty his weapon at them again. Now I do *not* want to work that crime scene and have to look into the eyes of someone who's just lost a parent or a child. I do *not* want to have to tell them I'm sorry but we couldn't find this beast before he killed again. That is *not* going to happen. *I'm* not going to let it. And *you're* not."

Parker found himself drawn into her words, delivered in a firm, even voice. He thought about the Band of Brothers speech from Shakespeare's *Henry V*, which had been Robby's introduction to theater. The boy had memorized the speech the day after they returned from Kennedy Center.

"All right," Lukas said. "Any questions?"

"Anything more on his armament?"

"He's been armed with a full-auto Uzi loaded with long clips and a suppressor. We have no further information."

"How green-lighted are we?" one agent asked.

"To light up the shooter?" Lukas replied. "*Totally* green-lighted. Anything else?" No one raised a hand. "Okay. We're on emergency frequency. I don't want any chatter. Don't report in that you *haven't* found anything. I don't care about that. You see the suspect, call for backup, clear your background and engage. Now go find me that safe house."

Parker himself felt oddly moved by these words. It had been years since he'd fired a weapon but he suddenly wanted a piece of the Digger himself.

Lukas directed teams of agents and officers to those parts of Gravesend she wanted them to canvas. Parker was impressed; she had a remarkable sense of the geography of this neighborhood. Some people, he reflected, are just natural-born cops.

Half of the agents started off on foot, the rest climbed into their cars and sped away. Leaving Cage, Lukas and Parker standing on the curb. Cage made a call. He spoke for a moment. Hung up.

"Tobe's got an MCP. They're on their way. He's analyzing the tape from the theater. Oh, and that psychologist from Georgetown's on his way over here too."

Most of the streetlights were out – some shattered from bullets, it looked like. Pale green illumination lit the street from the fluorescent lights of the few stores that were open. Two agents were canvassing across the street. Cage looked around and saw two young men rubbing their hands over an oil drum in which a fire burned. Cage said, "I'll talk to them." He walked into the vacant lot. It seemed that they wanted to leave but figured that would look more suspicious. Their eyes locked onto the fire as he approached and they fell silent.

Lukas nodded toward a pizza parlor half a block away. "I'll take that," she said to Parker. "You want to wait here for Tobe and the shrink?"

"Sure."

Lukas started up the street, leaving Parker alone.

The temperature was continuing to fall. There was

now a sharp edge to the air: that frostiness that he enjoyed so much in the autumn – evoking memories of driving the children to school while juggling mugs of hot chocolate, shopping for Thanksgiving dinner, picking pumpkins in Loudon County. But tonight he was aware only of the painful sting in his nostrils and on his ears and fingertips; the sensation was like a razor slash. He stuffed his hands in his pockets.

Maybe because most of the agents had left, the locals were returning to the streets. Two blocks away, a nondescript man in a dark coat stepped out of a bar and walked slowly up the street then stepped into the darkened alcove of a check-cashing outlet – to pee, Parker guessed.

A tall woman, or transvestite, obviously a hooker, walked out of the alley where she'd been waiting for the crowd to disperse.

Three young black men pushed out of an arcade and cracked open a bottle of Colt 45 malt liquor, laughing hard as they disappeared down an alley.

Parker turned away and happened to glance across the street.

He saw a thrift store. It was closed and at first he didn't pay much attention to the place. But then he noticed boxed sets of cheap stationery on shelves near the cash register. Could this be where the unsub had bought the paper and envelope for the note?

He stepped to the window of the store and gazed through the greasy glass, cupping his hands against the glare of the one nearby streetlight that still worked and trying to see the packages of paper. His hands shook in the chill. Beside him a rat nosed through a pile of trash. Parker Kincaid thought, This is crazy. I have no business being here.

But, still, he lifted his sleeve and, using the fleece cuff of his bomber jacket, wiped the grimy glass in front of him as carefully as a diligent window cleaner so that he'd have a better view of the merchandise inside.

16

05.55

"Maybe I seen him. Yeah, maybe."

Margaret Lukas felt her heart pump faster. She pushed the picture of the unsub closer and the counterman at the Gravesend pizza place – a chubby Latino in tomato-sauce-stained whites – continued to study it carefully.

"Take your time," she said. Please, she thought. Let's have a break here . . .

"Maybe. I no so sure. What it is, we get tons 'n' tons of people in here. You know?"

"It's very important," she said.

She'd remembered that the coroner had found steak in the belly of the unsub. There was no steak on the menu here. Still, it was the only twenty-four-hour restaurant on the street near the Metro stop and she figured that the unsub might have stopped in at some point in the past few weeks. Maybe he'd even planned the extortion scheme here – he might've sat under this sickly light at one of the chipped tables to draft the note as he looked around at the sad people eating greasy food and thought, arrogantly, how much smarter he was than they. How much richer he was about to be.

She laughed to herself. Maybe he'd been as smart and arrogant as she was. As much as Kincaid.

Three of them, all alike.

Three hawks on a roof. One's dead; that leaves two on the roof. You and me, Parker.

The clerk's brown eyes lifted, gazed into her blue ones. His dropped bashfully to the paper again. It seemed to be a personal defeat when he finally shook his head. "No, I no think so. Sorry. Hey, you want a slice? The double cheese, it's fresh. I just made it."

She shook her head. "Anybody else working here?"

"No, just me tonight. I got the holiday. You did too, looks like." He struggled for something to say. "You work many holidays?"

"Some," she said. "Thanks."

Lukas walked to the front door. She paused, looked outside.

The agents from the field office were canvassing across the street. Cage was talking to more gangstas in the vacant lot and Kincaid was ogling some thrift store as if the crown jewels were in the window.

The other agents were dispersed where she'd sent them. But had she been right? she wondered. Who knew? You can read all the books on investigative techniques ever written but the bottom line is improvisation. It *was* just like solving one of Kincaid's puzzles. You had to look beyond the formulas and rules.

In front of her, through the greasy windows, she

could see the dilapidated streets of Gravesend fade
into smoke and darkness. It seemed so large and
impenetrable.

She wanted Tobe Geller here, she wanted the
Georgetown psychologist, she wanted the list of on-
line subscribers . . . Everything was taking too long!
And there were far too few leads! Her hand balled
into a fist, a nail pushing into her palm.

"Miss?" came the voice behind her. "Miss Agent?
Here."

She turned. The anger dissipating like steam. The
counterman was offering her a Styrofoam cup of
coffee. In his other hand were two packets of sugar, a
little plastic container of half-and-half and a stirrer.

The man had brushed his hair back with his hands
and looked at her with a forlorn puppy gaze. He said
simply, "It's getting colder out."

Touched by his oblique admiration, she smiled,
took the cup and poured in one sugar.

"Hope you get some celebrating in tonight," he
said.

"You too," she said. And pushed out of the door.

Walking down the cold streets of Gravesend.

She sipped the bad coffee, felt the hot steam waft
around her mouth. It *was* getting colder.

Well, keep going, she thought. Get colder and
colder. Today had been far too like autumn for her.
Please . . . Snow like mad.

Scanning the street. The two agents from the field
office were out of sight, probably on an adjacent block.
Cage too had vanished. And Kincaid was still gazing
into the store near the staging area.

Kincaid . . .

And what exactly was *his* story. Turning *down* a special-agent-in-charge slot? Lukas couldn't understand that – an SAC was the next destination on *her* roadmap to the dep director spot. And beyond. Still, even though she didn't comprehend his not wanting the position, she respected him more for saying no than if he'd taken the job without wanting it.

What *did* explain the walls he'd put up around his life? She couldn't guess but she saw them clearly; Margaret Lukas knew walls. He reminded her of herself – or rather of her *selves*, plural. Jackie and Margaret both. Thinking of the changeling story she'd read years ago, she wondered what kind of books Parker read to his children. Dr. Seuss of course – because of his nickname for them. And probably Pooh. And all the Disney spin-offs. She pictured him in that cozy suburban house – a house very similar to the one Jackie had lived in – sitting in the living room, a fire burning in the fireplace, reading to them as they lay sprawled at his side.

Lukas's eyes happened to fall on a young Latino couple walking down the sidewalk toward the staging area. The wife bundled in a black scarf, the husband in a thin jacket with a Texaco logo on the chest. He pushed a baby carriage, inside of which Lukas caught a sight of a tiny infant, packed in swaddling, only its happy face visible. She thought instinctively about what kind of flannel she'd buy to sew the child a pair of pajamas.

Then the couple moved on.

Okay, Parker, you like puzzles, do you?

Well, here's one for you. The riddle of the wife and the mother.

How can you be a wife without a husband? How can you be a mother without a child?

It's a tricky one. But you're smart, you're arrogant, you're the third hawk. You can figure it out, Parker.

Lukas, alone on the nearly deserted street, leaned against a lamppost, curled her arm around it – her right arm, ignoring her own orders to keep shooting hands free. She gripped the metal hard, she gripped it desperately. Struggled to keep from sobbing.

A wife without a husband, a mother without a child . . .

Give up, Parker?

I'm the answer to the riddle. Because I'm the wife of a man lying in the cold ground in Alexandria Cemetery. Because I'm the mother of a child lying beside him.

The riddle of the wife and mother . . .

Here's another: How can ice burn?

When an airplane drops from the sky into a field on a dark November morning, two days before Thanksgiving, six days before your birthday, and explodes into a million fragile bits of metal and plastic and rubber.

And flesh.

That's how ice can burn.

And that's how I became a changeling.

Oh, puzzles *are* easy when you know the answer, Parker.

So simple, so simple . . .

Hold on, she thought, letting go of the lamppost. Taking a deep breath. Locking away the urge to cry. Enough of that.

One thing Special Agent Lukas didn't tolerate was

distraction. She had two rules she repeated endlessly to new recruits in the field office. The first was "You can never have too many deets." The second was "Focus."

And "focus" was what she now ordered herself to do.

Another breath. She looked around. Saw some motion in a vacant lot nearby – a young kid, wearing gang colors. He stood over an oil drum, waiting for some of his homeys. He had a teenager's attitude – which was a hell of a lot more dangerous than a thirty-year-old's, she knew. He gave her the eyeball.

Then up the street, a block away, she thought she saw a man in the alcove of a check-cashing store. She squinted. Was anybody there? Somebody hiding in the shadows?

No, there was no more motion. It must've been her imagination. Well, this's the place to get spooked.

Gravesend . . .

She tossed out the remains of the coffee and walked toward the teenager in the vacant lot to see if he knew anything about their mysterious unsub. Pulling the computer printout from her pocket, she wove easily around rusting auto parts and piles of trash – the same way *Jackie* Lukas used to maneuver through the perfume counters at Macy's on her way to a drop-dead sale in women's sportswear.

Parker stepped away from the thrift store, disappointed.

The stationery he'd seen inside wasn't the same as the extortion note or the envelope. He looked around the streets. He was shivering hard. He thought:

Stephie's outgrown her down jacket. I'll have to get her a new one. And what about Robby? He had the fiberfill, the red one, but maybe Parker would get the boy a leather bomber jacket. He liked his father's.

He shivered again and rocked on his feet.

Where the hell was that van? They needed the on-line service subscriber list. And the demolition and construction permit information. He wondered too what the tape of the shooting would show.

Parker looked around once more at the devastated streets. No Lukas, no Cage. He watched a young couple – they looked Hispanic – wheeling a baby carriage toward him. They were about thirty feet away. He thought about the times just after Robby was born when he and Joan would take after-dinner strolls like that.

Again his eye caught the man huddling in the check-cashing alcove. Absently wondered why he was still there. He decided to be useful and fished in his pocket for a picture of the unsub. He'd do some canvassing himself.

But something odd was happening. . .

The man looked up and, though Parker couldn't see clearly in the dim light and smoke from the oil drums, reached into his coat and pulled something out, something black, shiny.

Parker froze. It was the man who'd followed them near the Archives!

It was the Digger!

Parker reached into his pocket, for the gun.

But the gun wasn't there.

He remembered the pistol pressing into his hip as he sat in Cage's car and he'd adjusted it in his pocket. It must have fallen out into the front seat.

The man glanced at the couple, who were between him and Parker, and lifted what must have been the silenced Uzi.

"Get down!" Parker cried to the couple, who stopped walking and stared at him uncertainly. "Down!"

The Digger turned toward him and lifted the gun. Parker tried to leap into the shadows of an alley. But he tripped over a pile of trash and fell heavily to the ground. His breath was knocked out of him and he lay on his side, gasping, unable to move, as the man walked steadily closer. Parker called to the couple once more but his voice came out as a breathy gasp.

Where was Cage? Parker couldn't see him. Or Lukas or any of the other agents.

"Cage!" he called but his voice was still merely a whisper.

The Digger approached the couple, only ten feet from him. They still didn't see him.

Parker tried to climb to his feet, waving desperately to the young man and woman to get down. The Digger moved forward, his round face an emotionless mask. One squeeze of the trigger and the couple and their baby would die instantly.

The killer aimed his gun.

"Get . . . down!" Parker rasped.

Then a woman's brash voice was shouting, "Freeze, federal agents! Drop the weapon or we'll shoot!"

The attacker turned, gave a choked cry as the couple spun around. The husband pushed his wife to the ground and shielded the baby carriage with his body.

"Drop it, drop it, drop it!" Lukas continued, screaming now, moving forward steadily, hand extended in front of her, drawing a perfect target on the man's large chest.

The Digger dropped the gun and his hands shot into the air.

Cage was running across the street, his own weapon in his hand.

"On your face!" Lukas shouted. "On your face!"

Her voice was so primitive, so raw, that Parker hardly recognized it.

The man dropped like a log.

Cage was speaking into his phone, summoning backup. Parker could see several other agents sprinting toward them. He climbed unsteadily to his feet.

Lukas was crouched on the ground, her gun pressed into the killer's ear.

"No, no, no," he wailed. "No, please . . ."

She cuffed him, using only her left hand, the gun never wavering from its target.

"What the hell're—" he choked.

"Shut up!" Lukas snapped. She pushed her weapon harder into the man's head. Steam rose from the man's groin; he'd emptied his bladder in fear.

Parker held his side, struggling to fill his lungs.

Lukas, breathing deeply herself, backed away and holstered her weapon. She stepped into the street, eyes contracted and icy, glancing at Parker then at the suspect. She walked to the shaken couple and spoke to them for a few moments. Wrote their names in her notebook and sent them on their way. The father glanced uncertainly at Parker then ushered his wife down a side street, away from the staging area.

As Cage frisked the attacker one of the other agents walked over to the man's weapon and picked it up.

"Not a gun. It's a video camera."

"What?" Cage asked.

Parker frowned. It *was* a camera. It had broken in the fall to the concrete.

Cage stood. "He's clean." He flipped through the man's snakeskin wallet. "Andrew Sloan. Lives in Rockville."

One of the other agents pulled out his radio and called in a warrants request – federal, Maryland and Virginia.

"You can't—" Sloan began to protest.

Lukas took a step forward. "You keep your mouth shut until we tell you to answer!" she raged. "Understand?" Her anger was almost embarrassing. When he didn't answer she crouched and whispered in Sloan's ear, "You got me?"

"I got you," he responded in a numb voice.

Cage pulled one of Sloan's business cards from his wallet. Showed it to Lukas and Parker. It read NORTHEAST SECURITY CONSULTANTS. Cage added, "He's a private eye."

"No warrants," said the agent who'd called in the request.

Lukas nodded at Cage.

"Who's your client?" Cage asked.

"I don't have to answer."

"Yeah, Andy, you do have to answer," Cage said.

"My client's identity is confidential," Sloan recited.

Two more agents arrived. "Under control?" one asked.

"Yeah," Cage muttered. "Get him up."

They pulled him roughly into a sitting position. Left him on the curb. Sloan glanced down at the front of his pants. The wet spot didn't embarrass as much as infuriate him. "Asshole," he muttered to Cage. "I got a law degree. I know my rights. I wanta take a video of you beating off in the bushes, I can do it. I'm on a public street here and—"

Lukas came up behind him, bent down. "Who . . . is . . . your . . . client?"

But Parker leaned forward, motioned Cage out of the streetlight so he could get a better look. "Wait. I know him."

"You do?" Lukas asked.

"Yeah. I saw him at the Starbucks near me. And I think someplace else too in the last couple of days."

Cage kicked the man gently in the leg. "You been following my friend here? Huh? You been doing that?"

Oh, no, Parker thought, finally understanding. Oh, Jesus . . . He said, "His client's Joan Marel."

"Who?"

"My ex-wife."

There was no reaction in Sloan's face.

Parker was in despair. He closed his eyes. Shit, shit, shit . . . Until tonight every foot of tape the private eye might've shot would have shown Parker to be a diligent father. Going to PTO meetings, chauffeuring twenty miles a day to school and sports practices, cooking, shopping, cleaning, wiping tears and working on Suzuki piano with the Whos.

But tonight . . . of all nights. Sloan was an eye-witness to Parker's being right smack in the middle of one of the city's most dangerous police actions.

In harm's way, his children lied to and entrusted to a baby-sitter on a holiday . . .

Mr. Kincaid, as you know, the court system will bend over backwards to place the children with their mother. In this case, however, we are inclined to place them with you, subject to the caveat that you can assure the court there will be no possibility that your career will in any way jeopardize the well being of Robby and Stephanie . . .

"That right?" Cage asked Sloan ominously.

"Yeah, yeah, yeah. She hired me."

Cage saw Parker's expression and asked, "This a problem?"

"Yeah, it's a problem."

It's the end of the world . . .

Cage surveyed the private eye. "The custody fight thing?" he asked Parker.

"Yes."

In disgust Lukas said, "Get him outa here. Give him back his camera."

"It's broke," Sloan snapped. "You're going to pay for it. Oh, you bet you are."

Cage undid the cuffs. Sloan stood unsteadily. "I think I sprained my thumb. It hurts like a bitch."

"I'm sorry about that, Andy," Cage said. "And how're your wrists?"

"They hurt. I gotta tell you, I'm going to have to file a complaint. She put 'em on way too tight. I've cuffed people. You don't have to make 'em that tight."

What the hell was he going to do, Parker was thinking. He stared at the ground, hands shoved into his pockets.

"Andy," Cage asked, "were you the one following us on Ninth Street tonight? An hour ago?"

"Maybe I was. But I wasn't breaking any laws there either. Look it up, Officer. In public I can do whatever I want."

Cage walked up to Lukas. He whispered to her. She grimaced, looked at her watch then nodded reluctantly.

"Look, Mr. Sloan," Parker said. "Is there anyway we could talk about this?"

"Talk? What talk? I give my client the tape, I tell her what I saw. That's all there is to it. I may sue *you* too."

"Andy, here's your wallet." Cage walked up to him and handed it back. Then the tall agent lowered his head and whispered into Sloan's ear. Sloan started to speak but Cage held up a finger. Sloan continued to listen. Two minutes later Cage stopped talking. He looked into Sloan's eyes. Sloan asked one question. Cage shook his head, smiling.

The agent walked back to Lukas and Parker, Sloan right behind.

Cage said, "Now, Andy, tell Mr. Kincaid who your employer is."

Parker, still lost in his hopelessness, listened with half an ear.

"Northeast Security Consultants," the private eye said, hands together in front of him as if he were still cuffed.

"And what's your position with them?"

"I'm a security specialist."

Cage asked, "And who's the client you're working for tonight?"

"Mrs. Joan Marel," he said matter-of-factly.

"What did she hire you for?" Cage asked like a cross-examining attorney.

"To follow her husband. I mean, her ex-husband. And to get evidence against him for a child custody action."

"And have you seen anything that Mrs. Marel could use to her advantage in that action?"

"No, I haven't."

This got Parker's attention.

The man continued, "In fact Mr. Kincaid seems to me to be a . . ." Sloan's voice faltered.

Cage prompted, "Flawless."

"Flawless father . . ." Sloan hesitated. He said, "You know, I'd probably say 'perfect.' I'd feel more comfortable saying that."

"All right," Cage said. "You can say 'perfect.'"

"A perfect father. And I've never witnessed anything . . . uhm." He thought for a moment. "I've never witnessed him *do* anything that would jeopardize his children or their happiness."

"And you didn't get any videotape of him doing anything dangerous?"

"Nosir. I didn't take any tape at all. I didn't see anything that might be helpful to my client by way of evidence."

"What are you going to go back and tell your client? About tonight, I mean?"

Sloan said, "I'm going to tell her the truth."

"Which is?"

"That Mr. Kincaid went to visit a friend in the hospital."

"What hospital?" Cage asked Sloan.

"What hospital?" Sloan asked Parker.

"Fair Oaks."

"Yeah," Sloan said, "that's where I went."

"You'll work on that?" Cage asked. "Your delivery was a little rough."

"Yeah. I'll work on it. I'll get it down real good."

"Okay, now get the hell out of here."

Sloan ejected the tape from what was left of the video camera. He handed it to Cage, who tossed it into a burning oil drum.

The private eye disappeared, looking back uneasily, as if to see which of the agents was going to shoot him in the back.

"How the hell'd you do that?" Parker muttered.

Cage offered a shrug Parker didn't recognize. He understood it to mean "Don't ask."

Cage the miracle worker . . .

"Thanks," Parker said. "You don't know what would've happened if—"

"Kincaid, where the hell was your weapon?" Lukas's abrupt voice interrupted him. He turned to her.

"I thought I had it. It must be in the car."

"Don't you remember procedure? Every time you deploy at a scene you check to make sure your weapon is with you and functioning. You learned that the first week in the Academy."

"I—"

But Lukas's face was again contracted with cold fury. In a gruff whisper: "What do you think we're doing here?"

Parker began, "I keep telling you I'm not tactical . . . I don't think in terms of weapons."

"'Think in terms'?" she spat out cynically. "Look,

Kincaid, you've been living life on Sesame Street for the last few years. You can go back to that world right now and God bless and thanks for the help. But if you're staying on board you'll carry your weapon and you'll pull your share of the load. *You* may be used to baby-sitting but we're not. Now, you going or staying?"

Cage was motionless. Not even the faintest shrug moved his shoulders.

"I'm staying."

"Okay."

Lukas looked neither satisfied with his acquiescence nor apologetic for her outburst. She said, "Now get that weapon and let's get back to work. We don't have much time."

17

06.15

The large Winnebago camper rocked along the streets of Gravesend.

It was the MCP. The mobile command post. And it was plastered with bumper stickers: NORTH CAROLINA AKC DOG SHOW. WARNING: I BRAKE FOR BLUE RIBBONS. BRIARDS ARE OUR BUSINESS.

He wondered whether the stickers were intentional – to fool perps – or if the Bureau had bought the van secondhand from a real breeder.

The camper eased up to the curb and Lukas motioned Cage and Parker inside. One whiff of the air told him that it *had* belonged to dog owners. Still, it was warm inside – with the cold and the scare from the private eye Parker was shivering hard and he was glad to be out of the chill.

Sitting at a computer console was Tobe Geller. He was staring at a video monitor. The image on the screen was broken into a thousand square pixels, an abstract mosaic. He tapped buttons, spun the trackball on his computer, typed in commands.

Detective Len Hardy sat nearby and C. P. Ardell, in his size 44 jeans, was wedged into one of the booths against the wall. The psychologist from Georgetown University hadn't yet arrived.

"The video from the Mason Theater shooting," Geller said, not looking away from the screen.

"Anything helpful?" Lukas asked.

"Nuthin' much," the young agent muttered. "Not yet anyway. Here's what it looks like full screen, real time."

He hit some buttons and the image shrank, became discernible. It was a dim view of the interior of the theater, very jumbled and blurry. People were running and diving for cover.

"When the Digger started shooting," C. P. explained, "some tourist in the audience turned on his camcorder."

Geller typed more and the image grew slightly clearer. Then he froze the tape.

"There?" Cage asked, touching the screen. "That's him?"

"Yep," Geller said. He started the tape again, running it in slow motion.

Parker could see virtually nothing distinct. The scene was dark to begin with and the camera had bobbed around when the videotaper had huddled for cover. As the frames flipped past, in slow motion, faint light from the gun blossomed in the middle of the smudge that Geller had identified as the Digger.

Hardy said, "It's almost scarier, not exactly seeing what's going on."

Parker silently agreed with him. Lukas, leaning forward, stared intently at the screen.

Geller continued. "Now, this one's about the clearest."

The frame froze. The image zoomed in but as the pixel squares grew larger they lost all definition. Soon the scene was just a hodgepodge of light and dark squares. "I've been trying to enhance it to see his face. I'm ninety percent sure he's white. But that's about all we can say."

Parker had seen something. "Back out again," he said. "Slowly."

As Geller pushed buttons the squares grew smaller, began to coalesce.

"Stop," Parker ordered.

The image was of the Digger from the chest up.

"Look at that."

"At what?" Lukas asked.

"I don't see anything," Hardy said, squinting.

Parker tapped the screen. In the center of what was probably the Digger's chest were some bright pixels, surrounded by slightly darker ones in a V-shape, which were in turn surrounded by very dark ones.

"It's just a reflection," Lukas muttered, distracted and impatient. She looked at her watch.

Parker persisted. "But what's the light reflecting *off* of?"

They stared for a moment. Then: "Ha," Geller said, his handsome face breaking into a grin. "Think I've got it."

"What, Tobe?" Parker asked.

"Aren't you a good Catholic, Parker?"

"Not me." He was a lapsed Presbyterian who found the theology of *Star Wars* more palatable than most religions.

"I went to a Jesuit school," Hardy said. "If that helps."

But Geller wasn't interested in anyone's spiritual history. He pushed himself across the tiny space in his wheeled office chair. "Let's try this." He opened a drawer and took out a small digital camera, handed it to Parker. He plugged it into a computer. He then bent a paper clip into the shape of an X, unhooked two buttons of his shirt and held the clip against his chest. "Shoot me," he said. "Just push that button."

Parker did and handed the camera back. Geller turned to the computer, typed and a dark image of the young agent came up on the screen. "Handsome fella," said Geller. He hit more buttons, keeping the bright silver of the paperclip in the center of the screen as he zoomed in. The image disappeared into exactly the same arrangement of bright squares as in the picture of the Digger.

"Only difference," Geller pointed out, "is that his has a yellowish tint. So our boy's wearing a gold crucifix."

"Add that to our description of the shooter, send it out," Lukas ordered. "And tell them we've confirmed he's white." Cage radioed Jerry Baker with the information and told him to pass the word to the canvassers.

The Digger's only identifying characteristic – that he wore a cross.

Was he religious?

Was it a good-luck charm?

Or had he ripped it from the body of one of his victims as a trophy?

Cage's phone rang. He listened. Hung up. Shrugged, discouraged. "My contact at the FAA. They've called all the fixed-base operators in the area about chopper rentals. Man fitting the description of the unsub contracted to charter a helicopter from a company in Clinton, Maryland. Gave his name as Gilbert Jones."

"*Jones?*" C. P. asked sarcastically. "I mean, shit, *that's* original."

Cage continued. "He paid cash. The pilot was supposed to pick up some cargo in Fairfax then there'd be another hour leg of the flight but Jones didn't tell him where. Was supposed to call instructions in to the pilot at ten-thirty this morning. But he never did. The pilot checks out okay."

"Did Jones give him an address or phone number?"

Cage's shrug said, He did but they were both fake.

The door opened and a man in an FBI windbreaker nodded to Lukas.

"Hi, Steve," she said.

"Agent Lukas. I've got Dr. Evans here. From Georgetown."

The psychologist.

The man stepped inside. "Evening," he said. "I'm John Evans." He was shorter than his calm, deep voice suggested. His dark hair was shot with gray and he had a trim beard. Parker liked him immediately. He wore a smile as easy as his old chinos and gray cardigan sweater and he carried a heavy, battered backpack instead of a briefcase. His eyes were very quick and he examined everyone in the camper carefully before he was halfway through the door.

"Appreciate your coming down," Lukas said to him. "This is Agent Cage and Agent Geller. Agent Ardell's over there. Detective Hardy. My name's Lukas." She glanced at Parker, who nodded his okay to give his real name. "And this's Parker Kincaid – he's a document expert used to work for the Bureau." She added,

"He's here confidentially and we'd appreciate your not mentioning his involvement."

"I understand," Evans said. "I do a lot of anonymous work too. I was going to put up a Web site but I figured I'd get too many cranks." He sat down. "I heard about the incident at the Mason Theater. What exactly's going on?"

Cage ran through a summary of the shootings, the death of the unsub, the extortion note and the killer.

Evans looked at the death-mask picture of the unsub. "So you're trying to figure out where his partner's going to hit next."

"Exactly." Lukas said. "All we need is fifteen minutes and we can get a tactical team on the premises to take him out. But we *need* that fifteen minutes. We've got to get a leg up here."

Parker asked, "You've heard the name before? 'The Digger'?"

"I have a pretty big criminal data archive. When I heard about the case I did a search. There was a man in California in the fifties. Called the Gravedigger. He was killed in prison a few months after he went inside. Obispo Men's Colony. Wasn't part of a cult or anything like that . . . Some members of an acting troupe called the Diggers in San Francisco in the sixties were arrested a dozen times for petty larceny – basically just shoplifting. Nothing serious. Then there was a motorcycle gang in Scottsdale called the Gravediggers. They were involved in a number of felonious assaults. But they disbanded in the mid-seventies and I don't have any record of any of the individual bikers."

Lukas said to Geller, "Call Scottsdale P. D. and see if there's anything on them."

The agent made the call.

"Now, the only reference to 'the Digger,' singular, is a man in England in the 1930s. John Barnstall. He was a nobleman – a viscount or something like that. Lived in Devon. He claimed he had a family but he seemed to live alone. Turned out Barnstall'd killed his wife and children and two or three local farmers. He'd dug a series of tunnels under his mansion and kept the bodies down there. He embalmed them."

"Gross," Hardy muttered.

"So the press called him the Digger – because of the tunnels. A London gang in the seventies took the name from him but they were strictly small change."

"Any chance," Lukas asked, "that either the unsub or the Digger himself had heard about Barnstall? Used him as a sort of role model."

"I can't really tell at this point. I need more information. We'd have to identify patterns in their behavior."

Patterns, Parker reflected. Discovering consistent patterns in questioned documents was the only way to detect forgeries: the angle of the slant in constructing letters, penstroke starts and lifts, the shape of the descenders on lower case *y, g* and *q*, the degree of tremble. You could never judge a forgery in isolation. He told Evans, "One thing you should know – this might not be the first time the Digger and his accomplice have done this."

Lukas said, "A free-lance writer contacted us. He's convinced the shootings're part of a pattern of similar crimes."

"Where?"

"Boston, the New York suburbs and Philadelphia.

Always the same – larceny or extortion were the main crimes, with tactical murders to support them."

Evans asked, "He was after money?"

"Right," Parker said. "Well, jewelry once."

"Then it doesn't sound like there's any connection with Barnstall. His diagnosis was probably paranoid schizophrenia, not generalized antisocial behavior – like your perpetrator here. But I'd like to know more about the crimes in the other cities. And find out some more about his MO today."

Hardy said, "What we're doing here is trying to find his safe house. It could have a lot of information in it."

Lukas shook her head, disappointed. "I was hoping the name Digger meant something. I thought it might be the key."

Evans said, "Oh, it still might – if we get more data. The good news is that the name isn't more common. If the *accomplice* – the dead man – came up with the name Digger, that tells us something about *him*. If it was the *Digger's* nickname for himself then that tells us something about *him*. See, naming – designating – is very important in arriving at psych profiling."

He looked at Parker. "For instance, when you and I describe ourselves as 'consultants' there're some psychological implications to that. We're saying that we're willing to abdicate some control over the situation in exchange for a certain insulation from responsibility and risk."

That's one hundred percent right, Parker thought.

"You know," Evans said, "I'd be happy to hang around for a while." He laughed again, nodded at the morgue picture. "I've never analyzed a corpse before. It'll be quite a challenge."

"We could sure use the help," Lukas said. "I'd appreciate it."

Evans opened his backpack and took out a very large metal thermos. He opened the lid and poured black coffee into the lid cup. "I'm addicted," he said. Then he smiled. "Something a psychologist shouldn't admit, I suppose. Anybody want some?"

They all declined and Evans put the thermos away. The doctor pulled out his cell phone and called his wife to let her know he'd be working late.

Which reminded Parker of the Whos and he took out his own phone and called home.

"Hello?" Mrs. Cavanaugh's grandmotherly voice asked when she answered the phone.

"It's me," Parker said. "How's the fort?"

"They're driving me into bankruptcy. And all this *Star Wars* money. I can't figure out what it is. They're keeping me confused on purpose." Her laugh included the children, who would be nearby.

"How's Robby doing?" Parker asked. "Is he still upset?"

Her voice lowered. "He got sort of moody a few times but Stephie and I pulled him out of it. They'd love for you to be home by midnight."

"I'm trying. Has Joan called?"

"No." Mrs. Cavanaugh laughed. "And funny thing, Parker . . . But if she *were* to call and I happened to see her name on the caller ID, I might be too busy to answer. And she might think you were all at a movie or Ruby Tuesday for the salad bar. How would you feel about that?"

"I'd feel really good about that, Mrs. Cavanaugh."

"I thought you might. That caller ID is a great invention, isn't it?"

"Wish I had the patent," he told her. "I'll call later." They hung up.

Cage had overheard. He asked, "Your boy? He okay?"

Parker sighed. "He's fine. Just having some bad memories from . . . you know, a few years ago."

Evans lifted an eyebrow and Parker said to him, "When I was working for the Bureau a suspect broke into our house." He noticed Lukas was listening too.

"Your boy saw him?" Evans asked.

Parker said, "It was Robby's window the perp tried to break into."

"Jesus," C.P. muttered. "I hate bad stuff when it happens to kids. I fucking hate that."

"PTSD?" Lukas asked.

Posttraumatic stress disorder. Parker had been worried that the boy would suffer from the condition and had taken him to a specialist. The doctor, though, had reassured him that because Robby had been very young and hadn't actually been injured by the Boatman he probably wasn't suffering from PTSD.

Parker explained this and added, "But the incident happened just before Christmas. So this time of year he has more memories than otherwise. I mean, he's come through it fine. But . . ."

Evans said, "But you'd've given anything for it not to have happened."

"Exactly," Parker said softly, looking at Lukas's troubled face and wondering why she was familiar with the disorder.

The therapist asked, "He's all right, though. Tonight?"

"He's fine. Just got a little spooked earlier."

"I've got kids of my own," Evans said. He looked at Lukas, "You have children?"

"No," she said. "I'm not married."

Evans said to her, "It's as if you lose a part of your mind when you have children. They steal it and you never get it back. You're always worried that they're upset, they're lost, they're sad. Sometimes I'm amazed that parents can function at all."

"Is that right?" she asked, distracted once more.

Evans returned to the note and there was a long moment of silence. Geller typed on his keyboard. Cage bent over a map. Lukas toyed with a strand of her blond hair. The gesture would have been coy and appealing except for her stony eyes. She was someplace else.

Geller sat up slightly as his screen flashed. "Report back from Scottsdale . . ." He read the screen. "Okay, okay . . . P. D. knew about the gang, the Gravediggers, but they have no contact with anybody who was in it. Most of 'em are retired. Family men now."

Yet another dead end, Parker thought.

Evans noticed another sheet of paper and pulled it toward him. The Major Crimes Bulletin – about Gary Moss and the firebombing of his house.

"He's the witness, right?" Evans asked. "In that school construction scandal."

Lukas nodded.

Evans shook his head as he read. "The killers didn't care if they murdered his children too . . . Terrible." He glanced at Lukas. "Hope they're being well looked after," the doctor said.

"Moss is in protective custody at headquarters and his family's out of state," Cage told him.

"Killing children," the psychologist muttered, shaking his head, and pushed the memo away.

Then the case began to move. Parker remembered this from his law enforcement days. Hours and hours – sometimes days – of waiting; then all at once the leads begin to pay off. A sheet of paper flowed out of the fax machine. Hardy read it. "It's from Building Permits. Demolition and construction sites in Gravesend."

Geller called up a map of the area on his large monitor and highlighted the sites in red as Hardy called them out. There were a dozen of them.

Lukas called Jerry Baker and gave him the locations. He reported back that he was dispersing the teams there.

Ten minutes later a voice crackled through the speaker in the command post. It was Baker's. "New Year's Leader Two to New Year's Leader One."

"Go ahead," Lukas said.

"One of my S&S teams found a convenience store. Mockingbird and Seventeenth."

Tobe Geller immediately highlighted the intersection on the map.

Please, Parker was thinking. Please . . .

"They're selling paper and pens like the kind you were describing. And the display face the window. Some of the packs of paper're sun-bleached."

"Yes!" Parker whispered.

The team leaned forward, gazing at the map on Geller's screen.

"Jerry," Parker said, not bothering with the code names that the tactical agents were so fond of, "one of the demolition sites we told you about – it's two blocks east of the store. On Mockingbird. Get the canvassers going in that direction."

"Roger. New Year's Leader Two. Out."

Then another call came in. Lukas took it. Listened. "Tell *him*." She handed the phone to Tobe Geller.

Geller listened, nodding. "Great. Send it here – on MCP Four's priority fax line. You have the number? Good." He hung up and said, "That was Com-Tech again. They've got the ISP list for Gravesend."

"The what?" Cage asked.

"Subscribers to Internet service providers," Geller answered.

The fax phone rang and another sheet fed out. Parker glanced at it, discouraged. There were more on-line subscribers in Gravesend than he'd anticipated – about fifty of them.

"Call out the addresses," Geller said. "I'll type them in." Hardy did. Geller was lightning fast on the keyboard and as quickly as the detective could recite the addresses a red dot appeared on the screen.

In two minutes they were all highlighted. Parker saw that his concern had been unfounded. There were only four subscribers within a quarter-mile radius of the convenience store and the demolition site.

Lukas called Jerry Baker and gave him the addresses. "Concentrate on those four. We'll meet you at the convenience store. That'll be our new staging area."

"Roger. Out."

"Let's go," Lukas called to the driver of the MCP, a young agent.

"Wait," Geller called. "Go through the vacant lot there." He tapped the screen. "On foot. You'll get there faster than in cars. We'll drive over and meet you."

Hardy pulled his jacket on. But Lukas shook her head. "Sorry, Len . . . What we talked about before? I want you to stay in the MCP."

The young officer lifted his hands, looked at Cage and Parker. "I want to do *something*."

"Len, this could be a tactical situation. We need negotiators and shooters."

"*He's* not a shooter," Hardy said, nodding at Parker. "He's forensic. He'll be on the crime scene team."

"So I'm just sitting here, twiddling my thumbs. Is that it?"

"I'm sorry. That's the way it's got to be."

"Whatever." Pulled his jacket off and sat down.

"Thank you," Lukas said. "C. P., you stay here too. Keep an eye on the fort."

Meaning, Parker guessed, make sure Hardy doesn't do anything stupid. The big agent got the message and nodded.

Lukas pushed open the door of the camper. Cage stepped outside. Parker pulled on his bomber jacket and followed the agent. As he climbed outside Lukas started to ask, "You have— ?"

"It's in my pocket," he answered shortly, slapping the heavy pistol to make sure, and caught up with Cage, who was moving through the smoky vacant lot at a slow trot.

Henry Czisman took a tiny sip of his beer.

He was certainly no stranger to liquor but he wanted at this particular moment to be as sober as possible. But a man in a bar in Gravesend on New Year's Eve had better be drinking or else incur the suspicion of everybody in the place.

The big man had nursed the Budweiser for a half hour.

Joe Higgins' was the name of the bar and Czisman noted with irritation that the punctuation was incorrect. That only plural nouns take solely the *s* apostrophe to form the possessive. The name of the place should be *Joe Higgins's*.

Another sip of beer.

The door opened and Czisman saw several agents walk inside. He'd been expecting someone to come in here for the canvass and he'd been very concerned that it might be Lukas or Cage or that consultant, who would recognize him and wonder why he was dogging them. But these men he'd never seen before.

The wiry old man beside Czisman continued. "So then I go, 'The block's cracked. What'm I gonna do with a cracked block? Tell me what am I gonna do?' And he ain' have no answer for that. Gee willikers. The fuck he think I was gonna do, not see it?"

Czisman glanced at the scrawny guy, who was wearing torn gray pants and a dark T-shirt. December 31 and he didn't have a coat. Did he live nearby? Upstairs. The man was drinking whiskey that smelled like antifreeze.

"No answer, hm?" Czisman asked, eyes on the agents, studying them.

"No. And I tell him I'ma fuck him up he don't gimme a new block. You know?"

He'd bought the black guy a drink because it would look less suspicious to the agents to see a black guy and a white guy with their heads down over a beer and a slimy whiskey in a bar like Joe Higgins', with or without the correct possessive case, rather than just a white guy by himself.

And when you buy somebody a drink you have to let them talk to you.

The agents were showing a piece of paper – probably the picture of the Digger's dead accomplice – to a table of three local crones, painted like Harlem whores.

Czisman looked past them to the Winnebago parked across the street. Czisman had been staking out FBI headquarters on Ninth Street when he'd seen the three agents hurry outside, along with a dozen others. Well, they wouldn't let him go for a ride-along – so he'd arranged for his own. Thank God there'd been a motor-cade of ten or so cars and he'd just followed them – through the red lights, driving fast, flashing his brights, which is what you're supposed to do as a cop when you're in pursuit but don't have a dashboard flasher. They'd parked in a cluster near the bar and, after a briefing, had fanned out to canvass for information. Czisman had parked up the street and had slipped into the bar. His digital camera was in his pocket and he'd taken a few shots of the agents and cops being briefed. Then there was nothing to do but sit back and wait. He wondered how close they were to finding – what had he called it? – the Digger's lair.

"Hey," said the black guy, only now noticing the agents. "Who they? Cops?"

"We're about to find out."

A moment later one of them came up to the bar. "Evening. We're federal agents." The ID was properly flashed. "I wonder if either of you've seen this man around here?"

Czisman looked at the photo of the dead man he'd seen in FBI headquarters. He said, "No."

The black guy said, "He looks dead. He dead?"

The agent asked, "You haven't seen anyone who might resemble him?"

"No sir."

Czisman shook his head.

"There's somebody else we're looking for too. White male, thirties or forties. Wearing a dark coat."

Ah, the Digger, thought Henry Czisman. Odd to hear somebody he'd come to know so well described from such a distant perspective. He said, "That could be a lot of people around here."

"Yessir. The only identifying characteristic we know about him is that he wears a gold crucifix. And that he's probably armed. He might have been talking about guns, bragging about them."

The Digger wouldn't *ever* do that, Czisman thought. But he didn't correct them and said merely, "Sorry." Shook his head.

"Sorry," echoed the whiskey drinker.

"If you see him could you please call this number?" The agent handed them both cards.

"You bet."

"You bet."

When the agents left, Czisman's drinking buddy said, "What's that all about?"

"Wonder."

"Something's always going down 'round here. Drugs. Bet it's drugs. Anyway, so I gotta truck with a busted block. Wait. I tell you 'bout my truck?"

"You started to."

"I'ma tell you 'bout this truck."

Suddenly Czisman looked at the man beside him carefully and felt that same tug of curiosity that'd driven him to journalism years ago. The desire to know people. Not to exploit them, not to use them, not to expose them. But to understand and explain them.

Who was this man? Where did he live? What were his dreams? What sort of courageous things had he done? Did he have a family? What did he like to eat? Was he a closet musician or painter?

Was it better, was it more just, for him to live out his paltry life? Or was it better for him to die now, quickly, before the pain – before the *sorrow* – sucked him down like an undertow?

But then Czisman caught a glimpse of the Winnebago door opening and several people hurrying outside. That woman – Agent Lukas – stepped out a moment later.

They were running.

Czisman tossed money down on the bar and stood.

"Hey, you don' wanna hear 'bout my truck?"

Without a word the big man stepped quickly to the door, pushed outside and started after the agents as they jogged through the decimated lots of Gravesend.

18

B y the time the team met up with Jerry Baker two
of his agents had found the safe house.

It turned out to be a shabby duplex two doors from
an old building that was being torn down – one of the
construction sites they'd found. Clay and brick dust
were everywhere.

Baker said, "Showed a couple across the street the
unsub's picture. They've seen him three or four times
over the past few weeks. Always looked down, walked
fast. Never stopped or said anything to anybody."

Two dozen agents and officers were deployed around
the building.

"Which apartment was his?" Lukas asked.

"Bottom one. Seems to be empty. We've cleared the
top floor."

"You talk to the owner? Got a name?" Parker asked.

"Management company says the tenant is Gilbert
Jones," an agent called.

Hell . . . The fake name again.

The agent continued: "And the Social Security number was issued to somebody who died five years ago. The unsub signed up for the on-line service – name of Gilbert Jones again – with a credit card in that name but it's one of those credit-risk cards. You put money in a bank to cover it and it's only good as long as there's money there. Bank records show that this is his address. Priors were all fake."

Baker asked, "Entry now?"

Cage looked at Lukas. "Be my guest."

Baker conferred with Tobe Geller, who was carefully monitoring the screen on his laptop. Several sensors were trained on the downstairs apartment.

"Cold as a fish," Tobe reported. "Infrareds aren't picking up anything and the only sounds I'm registering are air in the radiator and the refrigerator compressor. Ten to one it's clean but you can screen body heat if you really want to. And some bad guys can be very, very quiet."

Lukas added, "Remember – the Digger packs his own silencers so he knows what he's doing."

Baker nodded, then pulled on his flak jacket and helmet and called five other tactical agents over to him. "Dynamic entry. We'll cut the lights and move in through the front door and the rear bedroom window simultaneously. You're green-lighted to neutralize if there's any threat risk at all. I'm primary through the door. Questions?"

There were none. And the agents moved quickly into position. The only noise they made was the faint jingling of their equipment.

Parker held back, watching Margaret Lukas, in profile, staring intently at the front door. She turned suddenly and caught him watching her. Returned a cool look.

Hell with her, Parker thought. He was angry at the dressing down she'd given him about the gun. It'd been completely unnecessary, he thought.

Then the lights went out in the duplex and there was a loud bang as the agents blew in the front door with 12-gauge Shok-Lok rounds. Parker watched the beams from the flashlights, hooked to the ends of their machine guns, illuminate the inside of the apartment.

He expected to hear shouting at any minute: Freeze, get down, federal agents . . . ! But there was only silence. A few minutes later Jerry Baker walked outside, pulling his helmet off. "Clean."

The lights went back on.

"We're just checking for antipersonnel devices. Give us a few minutes."

Finally an agent called out the front door, "Premises secure."

As Parker ran forward he prayed a secular prayer: Please let us find *something* – some trace evidence, a fingerprint, a note describing the site of the next attack. Or at the very least something that gives us a hint where the unsub lived so we can search public records to find a devil's teardrop above an *i* or a *j* . . . Let us finish this hard, hard work and get back home to our families.

Cage went in first, followed by Parker and Lukas. The two of them walked side by side. In silence.

The apartment was cold. The lights were glaring. It was a depressing place, painted with pale green enamel. The floor was brown but much of the paint had flaked away. The four rooms were mostly empty. In the living room Parker could see a computer on a stand, a desk, a musty armchair shedding its stuffing, several tables. But to his dismay he could see no notes, scraps of paper or other documents.

"We got clothes," an agent called from the bedroom.

"Check the labels," Lukas ordered.

A moment later: "Are none."

"Hell," she spat out.

Parker glanced at the living room window and wondered about the unsub's dietary habits. Cooling in the half-open window were four or five large jugs of Mott's apple juice and a battered cast-iron skillet filled with apples and oranges.

Cage pointed to them. "Maybe the bastard was constipated. Hope it was real painful."

Parker laughed.

Lukas called Tobe Geller and asked him to come check out the computer and any files and e-mail the unsub had saved on the hard drive.

Geller arrived a few minutes later. He sat down at the desk and ran his hand through his curly hair, examining the unit carefully. Then he looked up, around the room. "Place stinks," he said. "Why can't we get some upscale perps for a change? . . . What *is* that?"

Parker smelled it too. Something sweet and chemical. Cheap paint on hot radiators, he guessed.

The young agent gripped the computer's electric cord and wound it around his left hand. He explained, "It might have a format bomb inside – if you don't log on just right it runs a program and wipes the hard drive. All you can do then is unplug and try to override it later in the lab. Okay, let's see . . ."

He clicked on the power switch.

The unit buzzed softly. Geller was ready to yank the

cord from the socket but then he smiled. "Past the first hurdle," he said, dropping the cord. "But now we need the password."

Lukas muttered, "Won't it take forever to figure out?"

"No. It'll take . . ." Geller pulled the housing off the computer, reached inside and took out a small computer chip. Suddenly the screen reported, *Loading Windows 95*. Geller said, "About *that* much time."

"That's all you have to do to beat a password?"

"Uh-huh." Geller opened his attaché case and pulled out a dark-blue Zip drive unit. He plugged this into a port on the computer and installed it. "I'm going to download his hard drive onto these." He tossed a half dozen Zip disks onto the desk.

Lukas's cell phone rang. She answered. Listened. Then she said, "Thanks." She hung up, not pleased. "Pen registers from the phone line here. All he's called is the connection for the on-line service. Nothing else coming in or going out."

Damn. The man had been smart, Parker reflected. A puzzle master in his own right.

Three hawks have been killing a farmer's chickens . . .

"Found something in the bedroom," a voice called. An agent wearing latex gloves walked into the living room. He was holding a yellow pad with writing and markings on it. Parker's heart sped up a few beats when he saw this.

He opened his attaché case and pulled on his own latex gloves. He took the pad and set it on the table next to Geller, bent the desk lamp over it. With his hand glass he studied the first page and noticed immediately that it had been written by the unsub – he'd stared at the extortion note so much that he knew the handwriting as well as his own and the Whos'.

The devil's teardrop over a lower case *i* . . .

Parker scanned the sheet. Much of it was doodlings. As a document examiner, Parker Kincaid believed in the psychological connection between our minds and our hands: personality revealed not by how we form letters (that graphoanalysis nonsense that Lukas seemed so fond of) but through the substance of what we write and draw when we're not really thinking about it. How we take notes, what little pictures we make in the margins when our minds are occupied elsewhere.

Parker had seen thousands of renderings on the documents he'd examined – knives, guns, hanged men, stabbed women, severed genitals, demons, bared teeth, stick figures, airplanes, eyes. But he'd never seen what their unsub had drawn here: mazes.

So he *was* a puzzle master.

Parker tried one or two. Most of them were very complicated. There were other notations on the page but he kept getting distracted by the mazes, his eye drawn to them. He felt the compulsion to solve them. This was Parker's nature; he couldn't control it.

He felt someone nearby. It was Margaret Lukas. She was staring at the pad.

"They're intricate," she said.

Parker looked up at her, felt her leg brush against him. The muscles in her thigh were very strong. She'd be a runner, he guessed. Pictured her on Sunday mornings in her workout spandex, sweaty and flushed, walking through the front door after her three miles . . .

He turned back to the maze.

"Must've taken him a long time to make it," she said, nodding at the maze.

"No," Parker said. "Mazes are hard to solve but they're the easiest puzzles to make. You draw the solution path first and then once that's finished you just keep adding layer and layer of false routes."

Puzzles are always easy when you know the answer . . .

She glanced at him once more then walked away, helped a crime scene tech cut open the mattress, searching for more evidence.

Just like life, right?

Parker's eyes returned to the yellow pad. He lifted the top sheet and on the next page he found a dense page of notes, hundreds of words in the unsub's writing. Toward the bottom of the page he saw a column. The first two entries were:

Dupont Circle Metro, top of the escalator, 9 A.M.
George Mason Theater, box No. 58, 4 P.M.

My God, he thought, this's got the *real* targets on it. It's not a decoy! He looked up and called to Cage, "Over here!"

Just as Lukas stepped into the doorway and shouted, "I smell gas! Gasoline. Where's it coming from?"

Gas? Parker glanced at Tobe, who was frowning. He realized that, yes, *that* was the smell they'd detected earlier.

"Oh, Jesus." Parker looked at the bottles of apple juice.

It was a trap – in case the agents got into the safe house.

"Cage! Tobe! Everybody out!" Parker leapt to his feet. "The bottles!"

But Geller glanced at them and said, "It's okay . . . Look: there's no detonator. You can—"

And then the stream of bullets exploded through the window, tearing the table into shreds of blond wood, shattering the bottles and spraying rosy gasoline over the walls and floor.

```
06.50
```

A thousand invisible bullets, a million.
More bullets than Parker'd ever seen or heard in all his weeks on the range at Quantico.

Glass, wood, splinters of metal shot through the living room.

Parker huddled on the floor, the precious yellow pad still on the desk. He tried to grab it but a cluster of slugs pummeled the floor in front of him and he leapt back against the wall.

Lukas and Cage crawled out the front door and collapsed into the hallway, weapons drawn, looking for a target out the window. Shouting, calls for backup, cries for help. Tobe Geller pushed back from the desk but the chair legs caught on the uneven floor and he tumbled backward. The computer monitor imploded as a dozen slugs struck it. Parker went for the yellow pad again but dropped to his belly as a line of bullets snapped into the walls, heading straight for him. He dodged the volley and lay flat on the floor.

Thinking, as he had before tonight, that he was nearly as afraid of being wounded as he was of dying. He couldn't stand the thought of the Whos seeing him hurt, in the hospital. And he, unable to take care of them.

There was a pause in the fusillade and Parker started for Tobe Geller.

Then the Digger, somewhere outside, on a rooftop maybe, lowered his aim and fired toward the metal pan that the fruit rested in. It too had been placed there for a purpose. The bullets clanged off it and sparks shot into the gasoline. With a huge roar the pungent liquid ignited.

Parker was blown out the door into the hallway by the explosion. He lay on his side beside Cage and Lukas.

"No, Tobe!" Parker cried, trying to get back inside. But a wave of flame filled the doorway and forced him back.

They crouched in the windowless corridor. Lukas on one phone, Cage on another. ". . . maybe the roof ! We don't know . . . Call D.C.F.D . . . One agent down. Make that two . . . He's still out there. Where the hell is he?"

And the Digger kept firing.

"Tobe!" Parker shouted again.

"Somebody!" Geller called. "Help me."

Parker caught a glimpse of the young man on the other side of the raging flames. He lay curled on the floor. The apartment was awash with fire but still the Digger kept shooting. Pumping round after round from the terrible gun into the flaming living room. Soon Geller was lost to sight. It seemed that the table where the yellow pad rested was consumed in flames. No, no! The clues to the last sites were burning to ash!

Voices from somewhere:

". . . where is he?"

". . . going on? Where? Silencer and flash suppressor. Can't find him . . . No visual, no visual!"

"Fuck no, he's still shooting! We've got somebody down outside! Jesus . . ."

"Tobe!" Cage shouted and he too tried to run back into the apartment, which was filled with swirling orange flames, mixed with black, black smoke. But the agent was driven back by the astonishing heat – and by yet another terrifying row of black bullet holes snapping into the wall near them.

More shooting. And still more.

". . . that window . . . No, try the other one."

Cage cried, "Get the fire trucks here! I want 'em here now!"

Lukas called, "They're on their way!"

Soon the sound of the transmissions was lost in the roar of the fire.

Through the noise they could just make out poor Tobe Geller's voice. "Help me! Please! Help me . . ." Growing softer.

Lukas made one last attempt to get inside but got only a few feet before a ceiling beam came down and nearly crushed her. She gave a scream and fell back. Staggering, choking on smoke, Parker helped her toward the front door as a tornado of flames poured into the corridor and moved relentlessly toward them.

"Tobe, Tobe . . ." she cried, coughing fiercely. "He's dying . . ."

"We've gotta get out," Cage shouted. "Now!"

Foot by foot they made their way toward the front door.

In a madness of panic and hypoxia from the burning air Parker kept wishing he were deaf so he couldn't hear the cries from the apartment. Kept wishing he were blind so he couldn't see the loss and sorrow the Digger had brought them, all these good people, people with families, people with children like his.

But Parker Kincaid was neither deaf nor blind and he was very much here, in the heart of this terror – the pistol in his right hand and his left arm around Margaret Lukas as he helped her through the smoke-shrouded corridor.

Look, Kincaid, you've been living life on Sesame Street *for the last few years . . .*

". . . no location . . . no visible flash . . . Jesus, what *is* this . . ." Jerry Baker was shouting, or someone was.

Near the doorway Cage stumbled. Or someone did.

A moment later Parker and the agents were tumbling down the front stairs into the cold air. Despite their racking coughs and vision blurry with tears Cage and Lukas dropped into defensive positions, like the rest of the agents out here. They wiped their eyes and scanned building tops, searching for targets. Parker, kneeling behind a tree, followed their lead.

Crouching beside the command post van, C. P. Ardell held an M-16 close to his thick cheek and Len Hardy brandished his small revolver. The detective's head was moving back and forth, fear and confusion in his face.

Lukas caught Jerry Baker's eye and in a whisper she called, "Where? Where the hell is he?"

The tactical agent motioned toward an alley behind them and then returned to his walkie-talkie.

Cage was retching painfully from the smoke he'd swallowed.

Two minutes passed without a shot.

Baker was speaking into his Motorola, "New Year's Leader Two. . . . Subject was east of us, seemed to be shooting downward at a slight angle. Okay . . . Where? . . . Okay. Just be careful." He said nothing for a long moment, his eyes searching the buildings nearby. Then he cocked his head as somebody came back on the line. Baker listened. He said, "They're dead? Oh, man . . . He's gone?"

He stood up, holstered his weapon. He walked over to Cage, who was wiping his mouth with a Kleenex. "He got into the building behind us. Killed the couple who lived upstairs. He disappeared down the alley. He's gone. Nobody got a look at him."

Parker glanced toward the mobile command post, saw John Evans in the window. The doctor was looking at the grim spectacle with a curious expression on his face: the way a child sometimes looks at a dead animal, emotionless, numb. He may have been an expert in the theory of criminal violence but perhaps had never witnessed its practical application firsthand.

Parker then looked back at the building, which was now engulfed in flames. Nobody could survive the inferno.

Oh, Tobe . . .

Sirens cut through the night. He could see flashing lights reflected along both ends of the street as the fire engines sped closer. All the evidence gone too. Hell, it'd been in his hand! The yellow pad with the locations of the next two targets on it. Why the hell hadn't he glanced at it ten seconds earlier? Why had he wasted precious seconds looking at the mazes? Again Parker sensed that the document itself was the enemy and had intentionally distracted him to give the Digger time to attack them.

Hell. If he—

"Hey," somebody shouted. "Hey, over here! Need some help!"

Parker, Lukas and Cage turned toward an agent in an FBI windbreaker. He was running down a narrow alley beside the burning duplex.

"There's somebody here," the agent called.

A figure lay on the ground, on his side, surrounded by an aura of blue smoke.

Parker assumed the man was dead. But suddenly he lifted his head and cried, "Put it out!" in a gruff whisper. "Damnit, put it out!"

Parker wiped smoke tears from his eyes.

The man lying on the ground was Tobe Geller.

"Put it out!" he called again and his voice dissolved into a hacking cough.

"Tobe!" Lukas ran toward him, Parker beside her.

The young agent must have jumped through the flames and out the window. He'd been in the Digger's line of fire out here in the alley but maybe the killer hadn't seen him. Or hadn't bothered to shoot a man who was obviously badly wounded.

A medic sprinted up to him and asked, "Where you hurt? You hit anywhere?"

But all Geller would offer was his crazed shout. "Put it out, put out the fire!"

"You bet they will, son. The trucks are here. They'll

have it out in no time." The medic crouched down. "But we've got to get—"

"No, goddamnit!" Geller pushed the medic aside with surprising strength and looked directly at Parker, "The pad of paper! Put the fire out!" He was gesturing toward a small fire near his leg. *That's* what the young agent had been shouting about, not the building.

Parker glanced at it. He saw one of the unsub's elaborate mazes go up in flames.

It was the yellow pad. In a split-second decision Tobe Geller had forgone his computer disks and grabbed the unsub's notes.

But it was now on fire, the page with the notes on it was curling into black ash. Parker tore his jacket off and carefully laid it over the pad to extinguish the flames.

"Look out!" somebody called. Parker looked up just as a huge piece of burning siding crashed to the ground three feet from him. A cloud of orange sparks swarmed. Parker ignored them and carefully lifted his jacket off the pad, surveying the damage.

Flames began spurting through the wall behind them. The whole building seemed to sink and shift.

The medic said, "We gotta get out of here." He waved to his partner, who ran up with a gurney. They eased Geller onto the stretcher and hurried off with him, dodging falling debris.

"We gotta pull back!" a man in a black fireman's coat shouted. "We're going to lose the wall! It's gonna come down on top of you!"

"In a minute," Parker answered. He glanced at Lukas. "Get out of here!"

"You can't stay here, Parker."

"The ash is too fragile! I can't move it." Lifting the

pad would crumble the ash into powder and they'd lose any chance to reconstruct the sheets. He thought of the attaché case inside the apartment, now destroyed, and the bottle of parylene in it, which he could've used to harden the damaged paper and protect it. But all he could do now was cover the ash carefully and hope to reassemble it in the lab. A gutter fell from the roof and stabbed the ground, end first, inches away from him.

"Now, mister!" the fireman shouted.

"Parker!" Lukas called again. "Come on!" She retreated a few yards but paused, staring at him.

Parker had an idea. He ran to the duplex next door pulled off the storm window and broke the glass with a kick. He picked up four large pieces. He returned to the pad, which lay like a wounded soldier on the ground, and dropped to his knees. He carefully sandwiched the two sheets of scorched paper – the only ones with writing on them – between pieces of glass. This was how document examiners in the Bureau used to protect the samples sent to them for analysis before the invention of thin plastic sheets.

Chunks of burning wood fell around him. He felt a stream of water as the firemen trained a hose on the flames above him.

"Stop it!" he shouted to them, waving his arm. Worried that the water would further damage the precious find.

Nobody paid him any attention.

"Parker," Lukas shouted. "Now! The wall's about to come down!"

More two-by-fours crashed to the ground. But still he remained motionless, on his knees, carefully tucking bits of ash into the sandwich of glass.

Then, as timbers and bricks and fiery siding fell around him, Parker slowly rose and, holding the glass sheets in front of him, he walked away from the flames, perfectly upright and taking gentle steps, like a servant carrying a tray of wine at an elegant cocktail party.

Another picture.

Snap.

Henry Czisman stood in an alleyway across the street from the burning building. Sparks were flying leisurely into the sky like fireworks seen from miles away.

How important this was. Recording the event.

Tragedy is so quick, so fleeting. But sorrow isn't. Sorrow is forever.

Snap.

He took another picture with his digital camera.

A policeman lying on the ground. Maybe dead, maybe wounded.

Maybe playing dead – when the Digger comes to town people do whatever they must to stay alive. They tuck their courage away and huddle until long after it's safe to get up. Henry Czisman had seen this all before.

Picture: the wall of the duplex falling in a fiery explosion of beautiful embers.

Picture: a trooper with three fingers of blood cascading down the left side of her face.

Picture: the illumination from the flames reflected in the chrome of the fire trucks.

Snap, snap, snap . . . He couldn't take enough shots. He was driven to record every detail of the sorrow.

He glanced up the street and saw several agents talking to passersby.

Why bother? he thought. The Digger's come and the Digger's gone.

He knew he too should go. He definitely couldn't be seen here. So he started to slip his camera into the pocket of his jacket. But then he glanced back at the burning building and saw something.

Yes, yes. I want that. I *need* that.

He lifted the camera, pointed it and pushed the button.

Picture: the man who called himself Jefferson, though that was not his name – the man who was now so intertwined in this case – was resting something on the hood of a car, bending forward to read it. A book? A magazine? No, it glistened like a sheet of glass. All you could really see in the picture was the rigid attention of the man as he wrapped his leather jacket around the glass the way a father might bundle up his infant for a trip outside in the cold night air.

Snap.

So. Protect the mayor.

And don't trash the feds.

Anchorman Slade Phillips was in a coffee shop on Dupont Circle. There were still several dozen emergency vehicles parked nearby, lights flashing through the gray evening. Yellow police tape was everywhere.

Phillips had shown his press pass and gotten through the line. He'd been terribly shaken by what he'd seen at the foot of the escalator. The sludge of blood still drying. Bits of bone and hair. He—

"Excuse me?" A woman's voice asked. "You're Slade Phillips. WPLT."

Anchorpeople are forever doomed to be known by

both names. Nobody ever says Mister. He looked up from his coffee at the flirty young blonde. She wanted an autograph. He gave her one.

"You're so, like, good," she said.

"Thank you."

Go away.

"I want to bc in TV someday too."

"Good for you."

Go away.

She stood for a moment and when he didn't ask her to join him she walked away on high heels, in a gait that reminded Phillips of an antelope's.

Sipping decaf. All the carnage in the Metro – he couldn't get it out of his mind. Jesus . . . Blood everywhere. The chips in the tile and dents in the metal . . . Bits of flesh and bits of bone.

And shoes.

A half-dozen shoes had lain bloody at the base of the escalator. For some reason they were the most horrifying sight of all.

This was the kind of story most journalists dream about in their ambitious hearts.

You're a reporter, go report.

Yet Phillips found he had no desire to cover the crime. The violence repulsed him. The sick mind of the killer scared him. And he thought: Wait. I'm *not* a reporter. He wished he'd said this to that slick prick, Wendy Jefferies. I'm an entertainer. I'm a soap opera star. I'm a personality.

But he was too deep in Jefferies's pocket for that kind of candor.

And so he was doing what he was told.

He wondered if Mayor Jerry Kennedy knew about

his arrangement with Jefferies. Probably not. Kennedy was a stand-up son of a bitch. Better than all the previous mayors of the District rolled into one. Because if Slade Phillips wasn't a Peter Arnett or Tom Brokaw at least he knew people. And he knew that Kennedy *did* want a chance to fix as much of the city as he could before the electorate threw his ass out. Which would undoubtedly be in the next election.

And this Project 2000 of his . . . Man, it took some balls to tax the corporations in the city even more than they were already taxed. Bad blood there. And Kennedy was also coming down like a Grand Inquisitor on that school construction scandal. Rumors were that he'd wanted to pay that whistle-blower, Gary Moss, an additional bonus from District coffers for coming forward and risking his life to testify (an expense Congressman Lanier had refused to approve, of course). There were rumors too that Kennedy was going to crucify anyone involved in the corruption – including long-time friends.

So Phillips could rationalize taking some of the heat off Kennedy's office. It was for a higher good.

More decaf. Convinced that real coffee would affect his gorgeous baritone, he lived on unleaded.

He looked out the window and saw the man he was waiting for. A slight guy, short. He was a clerk at FBI headquarters and Phillips had been currying him for a year. He was one of the "sources who wish to remain anonymous" that you hear about all the time – sources whose relationship to honesty was a bit dicey. But what did it matter? This was TV journalism and a different set of standards applied.

The clerk glanced at Phillips as he stepped into the

coffee shop, looking around cautiously like a bumbling spy. He pulled off his overcoat, revealing a very badly fitting gray suit.

The man was basically a mailboy though he'd told Phillips that he was "privy" (oh, please . . .) to most of the Bureau's "primary decision-making activities."

Ego's such a bitch, Phillips thought. "Hello, Timothy."

"Happy New Year," the man said, sitting down and looking like a butterfly pinned to the wall.

"Yeah, yeah," Phillips said.

"So what's good tonight? They have moussaka? I love moussaka."

"You don't have time to eat. You have time to talk."

"Just a drink?"

Phillips flagged down a waitress and ordered more decaf for him and regular for Timothy.

"Well—" He looked disappointed. "I meant a beer."

The anchorman leaned forward. Whispered, "The crazy guy. The Metro shooter. What's going on with it?"

"They don't know too much. It's weird. Some people're talking about a terrorist cell. Some people're talking right-wing militia. Couple people think it's just a straight extortion scheme. But there isn't any consensus."

"I need some focus," Phillips said.

"Focus? What do you mean 'focus'?" Timothy glanced at a nearby table, where a man was eating moussaka.

"Kennedy's taking a hit on this. That's not fair."

"Why the hell not? He's a goon."

The anchorman wasn't here to debate the mayor's competence. Whatever history decided about the tenure of Gerald D. Kennedy, Slade Phillips was being paid $25,000 to suggest to the world that the mayor *wasn't* a goon. So he continued, "How's the Bureau handling it?"

"It's a tough case," said Timothy, who aspired to be an FBI agent but was forever destined to fall just short of every goal he set for himself in life. "They're doing their best. They got the perp's safe house. You hear?"

"I heard. I also heard he pulled an end run and shot the shit out of you."

"We've never been up against anything like this before."

We?

Phillips nodded sympathetically. "Look, I'm trying to help you guys out. I don't want to go with the story the station's got planned. That's why I wanted to talk to you tonight."

Timothy's puppy-dog eyes flickered and he asked, "Story? They've got planned?"

"Right." Phillips said.

"Well, what *is* it?" Timothy asked. "The story?"

"The screw-up at the Mason Theater."

"What screw-up? They stopped him. Hardly anybody got killed."

"No, no, no," Phillips said. "The point is they could've capped the shooter. But they let him get away."

"The Bureau didn't screw up," Timothy said defensively. "It was a high-density tac op. Those're a bitch to run."

High-density tac op. Tactical operation, Phillips

knew. He also knew that Timothy had probably learned the phrase not at FBI headquarters but from a Tom Clancy novel.

"Sure. But add that to the other rumor . . ."

"What other rumor?"

"That Kennedy wanted to pay the perps but the Bureau set up some kind of trap. Only they fucked up and the shooter found out about it and now he's killing people just to kill them."

"That's bullshit."

"I'm not saying—" Phillips began.

"That's not fair." Timothy came close to whining. "I mean, we got agents all over town ought to be home with their families. It's a holiday. I've been taking faxes to people all night. . . ." His voice faded as he realized the veil covering his true function at FBI headquarters had slipped.

Phillips said quickly, "I'm not saying *I* feel that way. I'm just saying that's the story they've got planned. This asshole's *killing* people. They need to point fingers."

"Well . . ."

"Is there anything *else* to focus on? Something other than the Bureau."

"Oh, that's what you meant by focus."

"Did I say focus?"

"Yeah, earlier you did . . . How about the District metro police? They could be the screw-up factor."

Phillips wondered how much money Wendy Jefferies would pay for a story that the District police, which ultimately reported to Mayor Kennedy, was the quote screw-up factor.

"Keep going. That one doesn't excite me."

Timothy thought for a moment. Then he smiled. "Wait. I have an idea."

"Is it a good idea?" Phillips asked.

"Well, I was at HQ? And I heard something odd." Timothy frowned, his voice fading.

The anchorman said, "Hey, that moussaka *does* look good. How 'bout we get some?"

"Okay," said Timothy. "And, yeah, I think it's a good idea."

III

THREE HAWKS

———◆◆◆◆———

A study of variations in the writing is especially important. These qualities should all be carefully examined. Repeated words should be compared and natural variation or unnatural uniformity looked at.

—Osborn and Osborn,
Question Document Problems

20

The capital of the free world.

The heart of the last superpower on earth.

And Cage nearly shattered an axle once again as his government-issue Crown Victoria crashed into another pothole.

"Goddamn city," he muttered.

"Careful," Parker ordered, nodding toward the glass sheets wrapped carefully and sitting on his lap like a newborn baby. He'd looked briefly at the yellow sheets. But they were badly damaged and he couldn't see any reference to the third and fourth targets. He'd have to analyze them in the lab.

Over crumbling pavement, under streetlights burnt out months ago and never replaced, past the empty poles that once held directional signs, which had long ago been stolen or blown down.

More potholes.

"I don't know why I live here." Cage shrugged.

Accompanied by Parker and Dr. John Evans, the

agent was speeding back to headquarters through the dark streets of the District of Columbia.

"And it snows, we're fucked," he added.

Snow removal wasn't one of the District's strong suits either and a blizzard could hamper Jerry Baker's tactical efforts if they found the Digger's hidey-hole or the site of the next attack.

Evans was on his cell phone, apparently talking to his family. His voice was singsong, as if he were talking to a child but from the snatches of the conversation it seemed that his wife was on the other end of the line. Parker thought it was odd that a psychologist would talk to another adult this way. But who was he to talk about relationships? When Joan was drunk or moody Parker had often found himself dealing with her the way he would a ten-year-old.

Cage juggled his own phone and called the hospital. He asked about Geller's condition.

When he hung up he said to Parker, "Lucky man. Smoke inhalation and a sprained toe from jumping out the window. Nothing worse than that. They're going to keep him in overnight. But it's just a precaution."

"Should get a commendation," Parker suggested.

"Oh, he will. Don't you worry."

Parker was coughing some himself. The pungent taste of the smoke was sickening.

They continued on for another half-dozen blocks before Cage gave Parker a telling "So."

"So," Parker echoed. Then: "What does that mean?"

"Wooee, we having a good time yet?" the agent said and slapped the steering wheel.

Parker ignored him and tucked a tiny scrap of burnt paper back under the glass protecting the unsub's notes.

Cage sped around a slow-moving car. After a few moments he asked, "How's your love life these days? You seeing anybody?"

"Not right now."

It had been nine months, he reflected, since he'd been going with someone regularly. He missed Lynne. She was ten years younger than he, pretty, athletic. They'd had a lot of fun together – jogging, dinners, day trips to Middleburg. He missed her vivacity, her sense of humor (the first time she'd been over to his house she'd glanced at a signature of Franklin Delano Roosevelt and, with perfect deadpan delivery, said, "Oh, I've heard of him. He's the guy started the Franklin Mint. I've got the thimble collection."). But the maternal side of her hadn't blossomed even though she was nearly thirty. When it came to his children, she had fun going to the museums and the cineplex, but Parker could see that any more of a commitment to the Whos – and to him – would soon become a burden to her. Love, like humor, Parker believed, is all in the timing. In the end they drifted apart with the agreement that in a few years, when she was ready for children, they might reconsider something more permanent. (Both knowing, of course, that, as lovers, they were saying goodbye for good.)

Cage now said, "Uh-huh. So you're just sitting at home?"

"Yeah," Parker said. "With my head in the sand like Ozzie the Ostrich."

"Who?"

"It's a kids' book."

"Don't you get the feeling there's stuff going on around you and you're missing it?"

"No, Cage, I don't. I get the feeling that my kids're growing up and I'm *not* missing it."

"That's important. Uh-huh. I can see where that would be kind of important."

"*Very* important."

Evans, still on the phone, was telling his wife he loved her. Parker tuned the words out. They depressed him.

"Whatta you think about Lukas?" Cage finally asked.

"What do I think? She's good. She'll go places. Maybe to the top. If she doesn't implode first."

"Explode?"

"No, implode. Like a lightbulb."

"That's good." Cage laughed. "But that's not what I'm asking. Whatta you think about her as a woman?"

Parker coughed. Shivered at the memory of the bullets and the flames. "You trying to set us up, Lukas and me?"

"Of course not." Then: "It's just I wish she had more friends. I'd forgot that you're a fun guy. You could hang out together some."

"Cage—"

"She's not married. No boyfriends. And, I don't know if you noticed," the wily agent said, "but she's good-looking. Don't you think?"

Sure, I think. For a lady cop . . . Of course Parker was attracted to her – and by more than just her appearance. He remembered a certain look in her eyes as she watched Robby run up the stairs earlier in the day. The way to a man's heart is through his children . . .

But what he told Cage was, "She can't wait till this case is over and she doesn't have to see me again."

"You think?" he asked, but cynically this time.

"You heard her – about my weapon."

"Hell, she just didn't want to send you back to your kids with your ass in a sling."

"No, it's more than that. I've been stepping on her toes and she doesn't like it. But I've got news for her. I'm going to keep on stepping if I think I'm right."

"Hey, there you go."

"What do you mean."

"That's just what *she'd* say. Aren't you two a pair . . ."

"Cage, take a break."

"Look, Margaret's only agenda is collaring perps. There's a ton of ego in her, sure, but it's good ego. She's the *second*-best investigator I know." Parker ignored the glance that accompanied this sentence. Cage thought for a moment. "You know what's good about Lukas? She takes care of herself."

"What does that mean?"

"I'll tell you. Couple months ago her house got broken into."

"Where's she live?"

"Georgetown."

"That happens there, yeah," Parker said. As much as he enjoyed the District he'd never live there, not with the children. Crime was terrible.

Cage continued, "She comes home from the office and sees the door's been jimmied. Okay? Her dog's in the backyard and—"

"She's got a dog? What kind?"

"I don't know. How do I know? Big black dog. Lemme finish. She makes sure her dog's okay then, instead of calling it in, she goes back to her van, puts on body armor, takes her MP-5 and secures the house herself."

Parker laughed. The thought of any other thin, attractive blonde stalking through a townhouse, armed with a laser-sighted machine gun, would have seemed absurd. But for some reason it was perfectly natural with Lukas. "Still don't get your point, Cage."

"No point. I'm only saying Lukas doesn't need anybody to take care of her. People being together, Parker – you know, men and women – don't you think it works out best that way? Nobody taking care of anybody else? That's a rule. Write it down."

Parker supposed the agent was talking about Joan. Cage had seen Parker and Joan together a number of times. And, sure, Parker had been drawn to his ex-wife because she *was* looking for someone to take care of her, and Parker – newly orphaned when they met – was desperate to nurture. Parker thought back several hours, Lukas addressing the troops in Gravesend. Maybe that was what had stirred him so much, listening to her: not so much her expertise as her independence.

They drove in silence for a moment.

"MP-5?" Parker asked, picturing the heavy black Heckler & Koch machine gun.

"Yep. Said her biggest worry was if she had to light up the perp she might ruin some of her wall decorations. She sews too. Makes these quilts you wouldn't believe."

"You told me that before. The perp – she bag him?"

"Naw. He'd booked."

Parker recalled her anger in Gravesend. He asked Cage, "Then what do you think it is? Why she's been on my case?"

After a moment the agent answered, "Maybe she envies you."

"Envies me? What do you mean?"

But he wouldn't answer. "That's not for me to say. Just hold that thought and when she gives you any static cut her some slack."

"You're making no sense, Cage. She envies me?"

"Think of it like one of your puzzles. Either *you* figure it out or she'll tell you the answer. That's up to her. But I'm not giving you any clues."

"Why would I want to know the answer to Margaret Lukas?"

But Cage only skidded around another canyon of a pothole and said nothing.

Evans closed his phone, poured himself another cup of coffee from the thermos. It must have held a half gallon of coffee. This time Parker accepted the offered cup and drank several sips of the strong brew.

"How's the family?" Parker asked him.

"I owe the kids big time." The shrink smiled ruefully.

"How many do you have?"

"Two."

"Me too," Parker said. "How old?"

"In their teens. They're a handful." He didn't give any details and didn't want to say anything more. "Yours?"

"Eight and nine."

"Ah, you've got a few years of peace and quiet."

Cage said, "Grandkids are the best. Take it from me. You play with 'em, get 'em all dirty, let 'em spill ice cream on themselves, spoil 'em crazy and then you send 'em home to their parents. You go have a beer and watch the game. How can you beat that?"

They drove for a few moments in silence and finally Evans asked, "That incident you mentioned. With your son? What happened?"

"You ever hear about the Boatman?" Parker asked.

Cage glanced at Parker warily. Then back to the road.

Evans said, "Remember something from the papers. But I'm not sure."

Parker was surprised; the killer had been featured in the news for months. Maybe the doctor was new to the area. "He was a serial killer in Northern Virginia, Southern Maryland. Four years ago. He'd kidnap a woman, rape and murder her and leave the body in a dinghy or rowboat. The Potomac a couple times. The Shenandoah. Burke Lake in Fairfax. We had leads to this guy who lived in Arlington but we couldn't make a case. Finally I was able to connect him to one of the murders through a handwriting sample. SWAT arrested him. He was convicted but he escaped on the way to federal detention. Well, around that time I was in the middle of the custody battle with my ex. The court had awarded me temporary custody. The kids, the housekeeper and I were living in a house in Falls Church. Then one night, around midnight, Robby starts screaming. I run into his room. There's the Boatman, trying to break in."

Evans nodded, frowning in concentration. His eyes were pale and they studied Parker closely.

Even now, years later, Parker's heart trembled at the memory: Not only at the image of the square, glazed face looking through the bedroom window but at his son's distilled terror. The tears streaming from his huge eyes, his shaking hands. He didn't tell Evans and Cage about the five minutes – they seemed like hours – of absolute horror: shepherding his children into the housekeeper's room, guarding the door while listening to the Boatman stalk through the house. Finally, with the Fairfax County cops still not there, he stepped into the hallway, his service revolver in hand.

He realized that Evans was looking at him even more closely. He felt like a patient. The doctor noted Parker's expression and looked away. He asked, "And you shot him?"

"Yes. I did."

The gun is too loud! Parker had thought manically, as he fired, knowing how the explosions were adding to Robby's and Stephanie's terror.

The gun is too loud!

As Cage pulled up to headquarters Evans slipped the thermos back into his backpack and put a hand on Parker's arm. He gave the document examiner another close look. "Know what we're gonna do?"

Parker lifted an eyebrow.

"We're gonna catch this son of a bitch and both of us get back home to our families. Where we ought to be."

Parker Kincaid thought: Amen.

Inside the document lab at headquarters the team was reassembled.

Margaret Lukas was on the phone.

Parker glanced at her. Her cryptic look toward him in return brought to mind Cage's comments in the car.

Maybe she envies you . . .

She looked back down at the notes she was scribbling. He noticed her handwriting. The Palmer Method. Enviable precision and economy. No nonsense.

Hardy and C. P. Ardell stood nearby, also speaking on cell phones.

Parker set the glass sheets on the examination table.

Lukas shut off her phone. She looked at Cage and the others. "The safe house's completely gone. PERT's going through it but there's nothing left. The computer and the disks were totaled."

Cage asked, "How 'bout the building the Digger shot from?"

"As clean as the Texas Book Depository," she said bitterly. "They got shell casings this time but he wore—"

"Latex gloves," Parker said, sighing.

"Right. When he loaded the clips. And leather when he was in the apartment. Not a bit of trace."

A phone rang and Lukas answered. "Hello? . . . Oh, okay." She looked up. "It's Susan Nance. She's gotten more information back from Boston, White Plains and Philly about the other attacks Czisman was telling us about. I'll put her on the speaker."

She hit a button.

"Go ahead, Susan."

"I've tracked down the case detectives. They tell me that just like here there were no solid forensics. No prints, no witnesses. All of the cases're still open. They got the pictures of the unsub we sent and nobody recognizes him. But they all said something similar. Something odd."

"Which was?" Parker asked. He was carefully cleaning the glass that held the burnt yellow sheets.

"Basically that the violence was way out of proportion to the haul. Boston, the jewelry store? All he took was a single watch."

"Just *one* watch?" C. P. Ardell asked. "Was that all he had a chance to boost?"

"No. Looks like that was all he *wanted.* It was a Rolex but still . . . Worth only about two thousand. In White Plains he got away with thirty thousand. Philly, the bus murder scheme? The ransom was only for a hundred thousand."

And he's asking $20 million from D.C., Parker thought. The unsub was going for bigger and bigger hauls.

Lukas was apparently thinking the same. She asked Evans, "Progressive offender?"

Progressive offenders were serial criminals who committed successively more serious crimes.

But Evans was shaking his head. "No. He *seems* to be but progressives are always lust driven. Sadosexual murderers mostly." He rubbed the back of his bony hand against his beard. The hairs were short – as if he'd only started to grow it recently – and his skin must have itched. "They become increasingly more violent because the crime doesn't satisfy their need. But you rarely see progressive behavior in profit crimes."

Parker sensed the puzzle here was much more complicated than it seemed.

Or much simpler.

Either way, he felt the frustration of not being able to see any possible solutions.

Parker finished cleaning the glass and turned his attention to the evidence. He studied what was left of the two pages. He saw, to his dismay, that much of the ash had disintegrated. The fire damage was worse than he'd thought.

Still it would be possible to read some of the unsub's

writings on the larger pieces of ash. This is done by shining infrared light on the surface of the ash. Burnt ink or pencil marks reflect a different wavelength from that of burnt paper and you usually can make out much of the writing.

Parker carefully set the glass panes holding the yellow sheets side by side in the infrared Foster + Freeman viewer. He crouched and picked up a hand glass he found on the table (thinking angrily: The goddamn Digger just destroyed my five-hundred-dollar antique Leitz).

Hardy glanced at the sheet of paper on the left. "Mazes. He drew mazes."

Parker ignored that sheet, though, and examined the one with the reference to the Mason Theater. He guessed that the unsub had also written down the last two targets – the one at 8 P.M. and the one at midnight. But these pieces were badly jumbled and flaked.

"Well, I've got a few things visible," he muttered. He squinted, trained the handglass on another part of the sheet. "Christ," he spat out. Shook his head.

"What?" C. P. asked.

"Oh, the targets the Digger's already hit are perfectly legible. The Metro and the Mason Theater. But the next two . . . I can't make them out. The midnight hit, the last one . . . that's easier to read than the third. Write this down," he said to Hardy.

The detective grabbed a pen and pad of yellow paper. "Go ahead."

Parker squinted. "It looks like, 'Place where I . . .' Let's see. 'Place where I . . . took you.' Then a dash.

Then the word 'black.' No, '*the* black.' Then there's a hole in the sheet. It's gone completely."

Hardy read back, "'Place where I took you, dash, the black . . .'"

"That's it."

Parker looked up. "Where the hell is he talking about?"

But no one had any idea.

Cage looked at his watch. "What about the eight o'clock hit? That's what we oughta be concentrating on. We have less than an hour."

Parker scanned the third line of writing, right below the Mason Theater reference. He studied it for a full minute, crouching. He dictated, "'. . . two miles south. The R . . .' That's an uppercase *R*. But after that the ash is all jumbled. I can see a lot of marks but they're fragmented."

Parker took the transcription and walked to a chalkboard mounted on the wall of the lab. He copied the words for everyone to read:

. . . two miles south. The R . . .
. . . place where I took you – the black . . .

"What's it mean?" Cage asked. "Where the hell was he talking about?"

Parker didn't have a clue.

He turned away from the board and leaned over the glass sheets, as if he were staring down a bully in a schoolyard.

But the fragment of paper won the contest easily.

"Two miles south of what?" he muttered. "'R.' What's 'R'?"

He sighed.

The door to the document lab swung open and Parker did a double take. "Tobe!"

Tobe Geller walked unsteadily into the room. The young man had changed clothes and seemed to have showered but he smelled smoky and was coughing sporadically.

"Hey, boy, you got no business being here," Cage said.

Lukas said, "Are you crazy? Go home."

"To my pathetic bachelor quarters? Having broken my date with undoubtedly my now-former girlfriend tonight? I don't think so." He started to laugh, then the sound dissolved into a cough. He controlled it and breathed deeply.

"How you doing, buddy?" C. P. Ardell asked, hugging Geller firmly. In the huge agent's face you could see the heartfelt, mano-a-mano concern that tactical agents have no trouble displaying.

"They don't even make a degree for my burns," Geller explained. "It's like I got New England tan. I'm fine." He coughed again. "Well, aside from the lungs. Unlike certain presidents I *did* inhale. Now. Where are we?"

"That yellow pad?" Parker said ruefully. "Hate to say it but we can't make out very much."

"Ouch," the agent said.

"Yeah, ouch."

Lukas walked to the examination table. Standing next to Parker. He couldn't smell the scented soap any longer, only acrid smoke.

"Hm," she said after a moment.

"What?"

She pointed to the fragments of jumbled ash. "Some of these little pieces might fit after the letter *R*, right?"

"They might."

"Well, what's that remind you of?"

Parker looked down. "A jigsaw puzzle," he whispered.

"Right," she said. "So – you're the puzzle master. Can you put them back together?"

Parker surveyed the hundreds of tiny fragments of ash. It could take hours, if not days; unlike a real jigsaw puzzle the edges of the pieces of ash were damaged and didn't necessarily match the adjoining pieces.

But Parker had a thought. "Tobe?"

"Yo?" The young agent coughed, dusted a burnt eyebrow.

"There're computer programs that solve anagram puzzles, aren't there?"

"Anagrams, anagrams? What're those again?"

It was tattooed C. P. Ardell who answered – a man whose most intellectual activity you'd guess would be comparing prices of discount beer. "Assembling different words out of a set of letters. Like n-o-w, o-w-n, w-o-n."

Geller said, "Oh, sure there are. But then *you'd* never use software to help you solve a puzzle, would you, Parker?"

"No, that'd be cheating." He smiled to Lukas. Whose stone face offered nothing more than a momentary glance and returned to the fragments of ash.

Parker continued, "After the sequence '. . . two miles. The R . . .' See all those bits of letters on the ash? Can you put them back together?"

Geller laughed. "It's brilliant," he said. "We'll scan a handwriting sample from the note. That'll give us standards of construction for all of his letters. Then I'll shoot the pieces of ash on the digital camera with an infrared filter, drop out the tonal value of the burnt paper. That'll leave us with fragments of letters. And I'll have the computer assemble them."

"Will it work?" Hardy asked.

"Oh, it'll work," Geller assessed with confidence. "I just don't know how long it'll take."

Geller hooked up the digital camera and took several pictures of the ash and one of the extortion note. He plugged the camera into a serial port on a computer and began to upload the image.

His fingers flew over the keys. Everybody remained silent.

Which made the braying sound of Parker's phone a moment later particularly startling.

He jumped in surprise and opened his cell phone. He noted the caller ID was his home number.

"Hello?" he answered.

His heart froze as Mrs. Cavanaugh said in a taut voice, "Parker."

In the background he heard Robby sobbing.

"What is it?" he asked, trying not to panic.

"Everybody's okay," she said quickly. "Robby's fine. He just got a little scared. He thought he saw that man in the backyard. The Boatman."

Oh, no . . .

"There was nobody there. I turned the outdoor lights on. Mr. Johnson's dog got loose again and was jumping around in the bushes. That was all. But he's scared. Really scared."

"Put him on."

"Daddy? Daddy!" The boy's voice was limp with fear. Nothing upset Parker more than this sound.

"Hey, Robby!" Parker said brightly. "What happened?"

"I looked outside." He cried for a moment more. Parker closed his eyes. His son's fear was like his own. The boy continued. "And I thought I saw him. The Boatman. It was . . . I got scared."

"Remember, it's just the bushes. We're going to cut them down tomorrow."

"No, this was in the garage."

Parker was angry with himself. He'd lazily left the garage door up and there was plenty of junk inside that could resemble an intruder.

Parker said to his son, "Remember what we do?"

No answer.

"Robby? Remember?"

"I've got my shield."

"Good for you. How 'bout the helmet?" Parker glanced up and saw Lukas staring at him raptly. "You have your helmet?"

"Yes," the boy answered.

"And what about the lights?"

"We'll put them on."

"How many lights?" Parker asked.

"Every last one," the boy recited.

Oh, it was so hard, hearing his son's voice . . . And knowing what he had to do now. He looked around the lab, at the faces of these people who had become his own band of brothers tonight. And he thought, You can – with luck and strength – pry yourself loose from wives or lovers or colleagues. But not from your children. Never from your children. They have your heart netted forever.

Into the phone he said, "I'll be right home. Don't worry."

"Really?" the boy asked.

"As fast as I can drive."

He hung up. Everyone was looking at him, motionless.

"I have to go," he said, eyes on Cage. "I'll be back. But I have to go now."

"Is there anything I can do?" Hardy asked.

"No, thanks, Len," Parker answered.

"Jesus, Parker," Cage began, looking up at the clock. "I'm sorry he's scared but—"

Margaret Lukas lifted her hand and silenced the older agent. She said, "There's no way the Digger could know about you. But I'll send a couple of agents to stay outside your house."

He thought that she was saying this as a preface to talking him into staying. But then she added quietly, "Your little boy? Go home. Make him happy. However long it takes."

Parker held her eyes for a moment. Wondering: Had he found a clue to the maze of Special Agent Lukas?

Or was this only a false trail?

He started to thank her but he sensed suddenly that any show of gratitude, any response at all, would throw off this tenuous balance between them. So he simply nodded and hurried out the door.

As he left, the only sound in the lab was Geller's raspy voice speaking to his computer. "Come on, come on, come on." The way a desperate handicapper pleads with a losing horse at the track.

```
07.20
```

Pixel by pixel.

Watching the images fall into place on Tobe Geller's screen. Still a jumble.

Margaret Lukas paced, thinking about anagrams, about ash. Thinking about Parker Kincaid.

When he got home how would he comfort his son? Would he hold him? Read to him? Watch TV with him? Would he be the sort of father who talked to him about problems? Or would he try to distract the boy, take his mind off his fear? Bring him a present to bribe away his sorrow?

She had no idea. All Margaret Lukas knew was that she wanted Kincaid back here now, standing close to her.

Well, part of her did. The other part of her wanted him never to come back, to stay hidden forever in his little suburban fortress. She could—

No, no . . . Come on. Focus.

Lukas turned to compact Dr. Evans, watched him

examining the extortion note carefully, rubbing his hand over his stubbly beard. His pale eyes were unsettling and she decided she wouldn't want him to be *her* therapist. He poured more coffee from his thermos. Then he announced, "I've got some thoughts about the unsub."

"Go ahead," she told him.

"Take 'em with a grain of salt," the doctor cautioned. "To do this right I'd need a ton more data and two weeks to analyze it."

Lukas said, "That's the way we work here. Kick around ideas. We're not holding you to anything."

"I think, from what we've seen, the Digger's just a machine. We'd call him 'profile-proof.' It's pointless to analyze him. It'd be like doing a profile of a gun. But the perp, the man in the morgue, he was a different story. You know organized offenders?"

"Of course," Lukas said. Criminal psychology 101.

"Well, he was a *highly* organized offender."

Lukas's eyes strayed to the extortion note as Evans described the man who'd written it.

The doctor continued. "He planned everything out perfectly. Times, locations. He knew human nature cold – he knew the mayor was going to pay, for instance, even though most authorities wouldn't have agreed to. He had backup plans upon backup plans. The firebomb at the safe house, I'm thinking of. And he found the perfect weapon – the Digger, a functioning human being who does nothing but kill. He took on an impossible task and he probably would've succeeded if he hadn't been killed in that accident."

"We had the bags rigged with tracers, so, no, he probably wouldn't have gotten away," Lukas pointed out.

"Oh," Evans said, "I'll bet he had some plan to counter that."

Lukas realized that this was probably right.

The doctor continued. "Now, he asked for twenty million. And he was willing to kill hundreds of people to get it. He wasn't a progressive offender but he *did* raise the stakes because he knew – well, he *believed* – he could get away. He believed he was good – but he *was* good. In other words his arrogance was backed up by talent."

"Making the prick all the more dangerous," C. P. grumbled.

"Exactly. No false sense of ego to trip him up. He was brilliant—"

"Kincaid said he was highly educated," Lukas said, wishing again that the document examiner were here to kick these ideas around with. "He tried to disguise it in the note but Parker saw right through it."

Evans thought for a moment. "What was he wearing when they brought him into the morgue?"

C. P. found the list and read it to the doctor.

Evans summarized, "So, cheap clothes."

"Right."

"Not exactly the sort of outfit you'd expect from somebody with the intelligence to set this whole thing up and who was asking for twenty million dollars."

"True," Cage said.

"Which means what?" Lukas asked.

"I see a class issue here," Evans explained. "I think he preferred to kill rich people, society people. He saw himself as better than them. Sort of a heroic common man."

Hardy pointed out, "But in the first attack he had the Digger gun down everybody, not just the wealthy."

Evans said, "But consider where. Dupont Circle. It's Yuppieville there. Hardly Southeast. And the Mason Theater? Tickets for the ballet must've been selling for sixty bucks each. And there was the third location too," Evans reminded. "The Four Seasons. Even though he didn't hit it he sent us there. He was familiar with it. And it's very upscale."

Lukas nodded. It seemed obvious to her now and she was upset she hadn't realized it earlier. She thought again about Parker – how he approached puzzles. Thinking broadly. It was so hard sometimes, though.

Focus . . .

"I think he was angry at the rich. At society's elite."

"Why?" Cage asked.

"I don't know yet. Not on the facts we have. But he did hate them. Oh, he was full of hate. And we should remember that when we're trying to figure out what his next target will be."

Lukas pulled the morgue shot of the unsub closer, stared at him.

What *had been* in his mind? What *were* his motives?

Evans glanced at her and gave a short laugh.

"What?" Lukas asked.

He nodded at the extortion note. "I feel like it's the note I've been analyzing. Like *that's* the perpetrator."

She'd been thinking just the same.

Exactly what Parker Kincaid had said too.

Focus . . .

"Hold on, folks," Geller said. "We're getting some-thing." Everyone leaned toward the screen on which they could see the words ". . . two miles south. The R . . ."

Behind that phrase the computer was inserting combinations of the letters from the fragments of ash. It would reject them if the penstroke of one letter didn't match a stroke from the one to its left. But the system had now added a letter *i* behind the *R*. Another one was forming behind that.

"It's that funny *i* with a dot Parker was telling us about," Geller said.

"The devil's teardrop," Lukas whispered.

"Right," Geller said. "Then after that . . . a letter *t*. Is that a *t*? Damn tears, I can't see *anything*."

"Yep," Lukas said. "definitely a *t*. *R-i-t*."

"What's that next letter?" Hardy asked, leaning toward the screen.

"I can't tell." Lukas muttered. "It's too fuzzy. A short letter – without any – what'd Parker call them? – ascenders or descenders."

She leaned over the tech's shoulders. The smell of smoke on him was strong. On the screen the letters were very faint, but, yes, there definitely was an *i* and a *t*. The next one though was just a blur.

"Damn," Geller muttered. "The computer says that that's the letter that fits. The strokes match. But I can't make it out. Anybody see better than me?"

"Looks like a zigzag or something," Lukas said. "An *a* or *x* maybe?"

Cage's head shot up. "Zigzag? Could it be a *z*?"

"Ritz!" Hardy blurted. "Maybe the Ritz-Carlton?"

"That's got to be it!" Lukas said, nodding at Evans. "He's going after more rich people."

"Sure!" Evans said. "And it makes sense – given

his tendency to fool us – he'd figure we'd eliminate hotels because he used one before."

In the office chair Geller rolled to a different computer. In five seconds he had a Yellow Pages telephone directory on the screen. "Two Ritzes in the area. One at Tysons Corner. And one in Pentagon City."

Lukas said, "Parker said he'd stick to the District. Pentagon City's closest."

She called Jerry Baker and told him about the latest target. "I want every tactical agent in the District and Northern Virginia mobilized. And send skeleton crews to the hotel at Tysons." She added, "You're not going to like it but no hoods and helmets."

She meant: without Nomex hoods and Kevlar helmets – shorthand in the Bureau for going plainclothes.

"You sure?" Baker asked uncertainly. When officers dress for undercover surveillance they can't wear as much body armor as in an overt tactical operation. It's far riskier, especially with a perp armed with an automatic weapon.

"Has to be, Jerry. We've almost nailed this guy once and he's gonna be skittish as a deer. He sees anything out of the ordinary he's going to bolt. I'll take responsibility."

"Okay, Margaret. I'll get on it."

She hung up.

She found Len Hardy staring at her. His face suddenly seemed older, tougher. She wondered if he was going to confront her again about his being on a tactical team. But he asked, "You're running the operation plainclothes?"

"Right. Is there a problem with that, Detective?"

"Does that mean you're not going to evacuate the hotel?"

"No, I'm not," she answered.

"But there'll be a thousand people there tonight."

Lukas said, "It's got to be business as usual. The Digger can't suspect a thing."

"But if he gets past us . . . I mean, we aren't even sure what he looks like."

"I know, Len."

He shook his head. "You can't do it."

"We don't have a choice."

The detective said, "You know what I do for a living – compile statistics. You want to know how many bystanders die in covert tactical operations? There's probably an eighty percent chance of significant fatalities among innocents if you try to take him down in a situation like that."

"What do *you* suggest?" she snapped back, letting him see a flash of temper.

"Keep your people plainclothes but get all the guests out. Leave the employees inside if you have to but move everybody else out."

"The best we could do is get fifty or sixty agents inside the hotel," she pointed out. "The Digger walks in the front door, expecting to see five hundred guests, and he finds that few? He'd take off. And he'd go shoot up someplace else."

"For Christ sake, Margaret," Hardy muttered, "at least get the kids out."

Lukas fell silent, eyes on the note.

"Please," the detective persisted.

She looked into his eyes. "No. If we tried to evacuate *anybody*, word would spread and there'd be panic."

"So you're just going to hope for the best?"

She glanced at the extortion note.

The end is night . . .

It seemed to be sneering at her.

"No," Lukas said. "We're going to stop him. *That's* what we're going to do." A glance at Evans: "Doctor, if you could stay here." Then a glance at Hardy. "You handle communications."

Hardy sighed angrily.

"Let's go," Lukas said to Cage. "I've got to stop by my office."

"For what?" Cage asked, nodding to her empty ankle holster. "Oh, another backup?"

"No, for some party clothes. We've got to blend."

"He's got something good for us." Wendell Jefferies, the sleeves of his custom-made shirt rolled high, revealing health-club-toned arms.

By "he" the aide meant Slade Phillips, Mayor Kennedy knew.

The two men were in the City Hall office. The mayor had just given another embarrassing press conference, attended by only a dozen reporters, who, even as he spoke, took cell phone calls and checked pagers in hopes of getting better news from other sources. Who could blame them? Christ, he didn't have anything to say. All he could report on was the morale of some of the victims he'd been to visit at hospitals.

"He's going on the air at nine," Jefferies now told the mayor. "A special report."

"With what?"

"He won't tell me," Jefferies said. "Somehow he thinks *that* would be unethical."

Kennedy stretched and leaned back in the couch – a fake Georgian settee his predecessor had bought. The finish was chipping off the arms. And the hassock on which his size 12 feet rested was cheap; a piece of folded cardboard was stuffed under one leg to keep it from rocking.

A glance at the brass clock.

Dear your honor, thank you very much for coming to speak with us today. It has been an honor to hear you. You are a very good person for us children and students and we would like to commem . . . commem . . . commemorate your visit with this gift, which we hope you will like . . .

The minute hand clicked forward one stroke. In an hour, he thought, how many more people would be dead?

The phone rang. Kennedy glanced at it lethargically and let Jefferies answer.

"Hello?"

A pause.

"Sure. Hold on." He handed the receiver to Kennedy, saying, "This is interesting."

The mayor took the receiver. "Yes?"

"Mayor Kennedy?"

"That's right."

"This is Len Hardy."

"Detective Hardy?"

"That's right. Is . . . Is anybody else listening?"

"No. It's my private line."

The detective hesitated then said, "I've been thinking . . . About what we were talking about."

Kennedy sat up, took his feet off the couch.

"Go ahead, son. Where are you?"

"Ninth Street. FBI headquarters."

There was silence. The mayor encouraged, "Go on."

"I couldn't just sit here anymore. I had to do something. I think she's making a mistake."

"Lukas?"

Hardy continued, "They found out where he's going to hit tonight. The Digger, the shooter."

"They did?" Kennedy's strong hand gripped the phone hard. Gestured to Jefferies to hand him a pen and paper. "Where?"

"The Ritz-Carlton."

"Which one?"

"They aren't sure. Probably Pentagon City. . . . But, Mayor, she's not evacuating them."

"She's *what*?" Kennedy snapped.

"Lukas isn't evacuating the hotel. She's—"

"Wait," Kennedy said. "They know where he's going to hit and she's not telling anyone?"

"No, she's going to use the guests for bait. I mean, that's the only way to say it. Anyway, I thought about what you said. I decided I had to call you."

"You did the right thing, Officer."

"I hope so, I really hope that. I can't talk any longer, Mayor. I just had to tell you."

"Thank you." Jerry Kennedy hung up and rose to his feet.

"What is it?" Jefferies asked.

"We know where he's going to hit. The Ritz. Call Reggie, I want my car now. And a police escort."

As he strode to the door Jefferies asked, "How 'bout a news crew?"

Kennedy glanced at his aide. The meaning of the

look was unmistakable. It meant: Of *course* we want a news crew.

They're both standing awkwardly, side by side, four arms crossed, in the Digger's motel room.

They're both watching TV.

Funny.

The pictures on the TV look familiar to the Digger.

The pictures are from the theater. The place where he was supposed to spin around like he did in the Connecticut forest and send bullets into a million leaves. The theater where he *wanted* to spin, where he was *supposed* to spin, but he couldn't.

The theater where the . . . *click* . . . where the scary man with the big jaws and tall hat came to kill him. No, that's not right . . . Where the *police* came to kill him.

He watches the boy as the boy watches TV. The boy says, "Shit." For no reason, it seems.

Just like Pamela.

The Digger calls his voice mail and hears the woman's electronic voice say, "You have no new messages."

He hangs up.

The Digger does not have much time. He looks at his watch. The boy looks at it too.

He is thin and frail. The area around his right eye is slightly darker than his dark skin and the Digger knows that the man he killed had hit the boy a lot. He thinks he's happy he shot the man. Whatever happy is.

The Digger wonders what the man who tells him things would think about the boy. The man *did* tell him to kill anybody who got a look at his face. And

the boy *has* gotten a look at his face. But it doesn't . . .
click . . . it doesn't seem . . . *click* . . . seem right to
kill him.

> *Why, it seems to me that every day,*
> *I love you all the more.*

He goes into the kitchenette and opens a can of
soup. He spoons some into a bowl. Looks at the
boy's skinny arms and spoons some more in. Noodles.
Mostly noodles. He heats it in the microwave for
exactly sixty seconds, which is what the instructions
tell him to do to get the soup "piping hot." He sets the
bowl in front of the boy. Hands him a spoon.

The boy takes one bite. Then another. Then he stops
eating. He's looking at the TV screen. His small,
bullet-shaped head lolls from one side to the other, his
eyes droop, and the Digger realizes he's tired. This is
what the Digger's head and eyes do when he's tired.

He and the boy are a lot alike, he decides.

The Digger motions to the bed. But the boy looks
at him fearfully and doesn't give a response. The
Digger motions to the couch and the boy gets up
and goes to the couch. He lies down. Still staring at
the TV. The Digger gets a blanket and drapes it over
the boy.

The Digger looks at the TV. More news. He finds a
channel that has commercials. Selling hamburgers and
cars and beer.

Things like that.

He says to the boy, "What's . . ." *Click*. . . . "What's
your name?"

The boy looks at him with half-closed lids. "Tye."

"Tye." The Digger repeats this several times to himself. "I'm going . . . I'm going out."

"Butyoubeback?"

What does he mean? The Digger shakes his head – his head with the tiny indentation above the temple.

"You comin' back?" the boy mutters again.

"I'm coming back."

The boy closes his eyes.

He tries to think of something else to say to Tye. There're some words he feels he wants to say but he doesn't remember what they are. It doesn't matter anyway because the boy is asleep. The Digger pulls the blanket up higher.

He goes to the closet, unlocks it and takes out one of the boxes of ammunition. He pulls on the plastic gloves and reloads two clips for the Uzi and then he spends fifteen minutes repacking the silencer. He locks up the closet again.

The boy remains asleep. The Digger can hear his breathing.

The Digger looks at the torn puppy bag. He is about to crumple it up and throw it out but he remembers that Tye looked at the bag and he seemed to like it. He liked the puppies. The Digger smooths it and puts it beside the boy so that if he wakes up while the Digger is gone he'll see the puppies and he won't be afraid.

The Digger doesn't need the puppy bag anymore.

"Use a plain brown bag for the third time," the man who tells him things told him.

So the Digger has a brown paper bag.

The boy turns over but is still asleep.

The Digger puts the Uzi into the brown bag, pulls his dark coat and gloves on and leaves the room.

Downstairs he gets into his car, a nice Toyota Corolla.

He loves those commercials.

Ohhhhh, everyday people . . .

He likes those better than *Oh, what a feeling* . . .

The Digger knows how to drive. He's a very good driver. He used to drive with Pamela. She'd drive fast when she drove and he'd drive slow. She got tickets and he never did.

He opens the glove compartment. There are several pistols inside. He takes one and puts it in his pocket. "After the theater," warned the man who tells him things, "there'll be more police looking for you. You'll have to be careful. Remember, if anybody sees your face . . ."

I remember.

Upstairs, in Robby's room, Parker sat with his son. The boy was sitting in bed, Parker in the bentwood rocker he'd bought at Antiques 'n' Things and tried unsuccessfully to refinish himself.

Two dozen toys were on the floor, a Nintendo 64 plugged into the old TV. *Star Wars* posters on the walls. Luke Skywalker. And Darth Vader . . .

Our mascot for the evening.

Cage had said that. But Parker was trying not to think about Cage. Or Margaret Lukas. Or the Digger. He was reading to his son. From *The Hobbit.*

Robby was lost in the story, even though he'd heard his father read it to him a number of times. They gravitated to this book when Robby was frightened because of the scene of slaying a fierce dragon. That part of the book always gave the boy courage.

When he'd walked in the front door of his house not long ago the boy's face had lit up. Parker had taken his son's hand and they'd walked to the back porch. He'd patiently showed him once again that there were no intruders in the backyard or the garage. They decided that crazy old Mr. Johnson had let his dog out again without closing the fence.

Stephie had hugged her father too and asked how his friend was, the sick one.

"He's fine," Parker had said, looking for but finding not a bit of truth to hang the statement on. Oh, the guilt of parents . . . What a hot iron it is.

Stephie had watched sympathetically as Robby and Parker had gone upstairs to read a story. At another time she might have joined them but she instinctively knew now to leave them alone. This was something about children that Parker had learned: They bickered like all healthy youngsters, tried to outshine each other, engaged in typical sibling sabotage. Yet when something affected the core of one child – like the Boatman – the other knew instinctively what was needed. The girl had vanished into the kitchen, saying, "I'm making Robby a surprise for dessert."

As he read, he would glance occasionally at his son's face. The boy's eyes were closed and he looked completely content. (From the *Handbook*: "*Sometimes your job isn't to reason with your children or to teach them or even to offer a sterling example of maturity. You simply must be with them. That's all it takes.*")

"You want me to keep reading?" he whispered.

The boy didn't respond.

Parker left the book on his lap and remained in the

scabby rocking chair, easing back and forth. Watching his son.

Thomas Jefferson's wife, Martha, had died not long after their third daughter was born (the girl herself died at age two). Jefferson, who never remarried, had struggled to raise his two other girls by himself. As a politician and statesman he was often forced to be an absent father, a situation he truly hated. It was letters that kept him in touch with his children. He wrote thousand of pages to the girls, offering support, advice, complaints, love. Parker knew Jefferson as well as he knew his own father and could recall some letters from memory. He thought of one of these now, written when Jefferson was vice president and in the midst of fierce political battles between the rival parties of the day.

Your letter, my dear Maria, of Jan. 21 was received two days ago. It was like the bright beams of the moon on the desolate heath. Environed here in scenes of constant torment, malice and obloquy, worn down in a state where no effort to render service can aver any thing, I feel not that existence is a blessing but when something recalls my mind to my family.

Looking at his son, hearing his daughter bang pans downstairs, he worried, as he often did, if he was raising his own children right.

How often he'd lain asleep at night worrying about this.

After all, he'd separated two children from their mother. That the courts and all of his (and most of Joan's) friends agreed that it was the only sane thing to do made little difference to him. He hadn't become a single father by the quirk of death as Jefferson had; no, Parker had made that decision himself.

But was it truly for the children that he'd done this? Or was it to escape from his own unhappiness? This is what tormented him so often. Joan had seemed so sweet, so charming, before they were married. But much of it, he'd realized, was an act. She was in fact cagey and calculating. Her moods whipped back and forth – cheerful for a while, she'd plunge into days of rage and suspicion and paranoia.

When he'd met Joan he was learning how very different life becomes when you're still young and your parents die. The demilitarized zone between you and mortality is gone. You seek as a mate either someone to take care of you or, as Parker had done, someone to take care of.

Don't you think it works out best that way? Nobody taking care of anybody else? That's a rule. Write it down.

So it wasn't surprising that he sought out a woman who, though beautiful and charming, had a moody, helpless side to her.

Naturally, not long after the Whos were born, when their married life demanded responsibility and sometimes just plain hard work and sacrifice, Joan gave rein to her dissatisfactions and moods.

Parker tried everything he could think of. He went with her to therapy, took over more than his share of work with the children, tried joking her out of her funks, planned parties, took her on trips, cooked breakfasts and dinners for the family.

But among the secrets Joan had kept from him was

a family history of alcoholism and he was surprised to find that she'd been drinking much more than he'd believed. She'd do twelve-steps from time to time and try other counseling approaches. But she always lapsed.

She withdrew further and further from him and the children, occupying her time with hobbies and whims. Taking gourmet cooking classes, buying a sports car, shopping compulsively, working out like an Olympian at a fancy health club (where she met husband-to-be Richard). But she always pulled back; she gave him and the children just enough.

And then there was the Incident.

June, four years ago.

Parker returned home from work at the Bureau's document lab and found Joan away from home, a baby-sitter looking after the Whos. This wasn't unusual or troublesome in itself. But when he went upstairs to play with the children he saw immediately that something was wrong. Stephie and Robby, then four and five, were sitting in their shared bedroom, assembling Tinkertoys. But Stephanie was groggy. Her eyes were unfocused and her face slick with sweat. Parker noticed that she'd thrown up on the way to the bathroom. He put the girl into bed and took her temperature, which was normal. Parker wasn't surprised that the baby-sitter hadn't noticed Stephanie's illness; children are embarrassed when they vomit or mess their pants and often try to keep accidents secret. But the girl – and her brother – seemed much more evasive than Parker would have expected.

The boy's eyes kept going to their toy chest. ("*Watch the eyes first*," his *Handbook* commands. "*Listen to the words second.*") Parker walked toward the chest and Robby started to cry, begging him not to open the lid. But of course he did. And stood, frozen, looking down at the bottles of vodka Joan had hidden there.

Stephanie was drunk. She'd tried imitating Mommy, drinking Absolut – from her Winnie the Pooh mug.

"Mommy said not to say anything about her secret," the boy told him, crying. "She said you'd be mad at us if you found out. She said you'd yell at us."

Two days later he started divorce proceedings. He hired a savvy lawyer and got Child Protective Services involved before Joan made the false abuse claim the attorney thought she'd try.

The woman fought and she fought hard – but it was the way someone fights to keep a stamp collection or a sports car, not something you love more than life itself.

And in the end, after several agonizing months and tens of thousands of dollars, the children were his.

He'd thought that he could concentrate on putting his life back together and giving the children a normal life.

And he had – for the past four years. But now she was at it again, trying to modify the custody order.

Oh, Joan, why are you doing this? Don't you *ever* think about them? Don't you understand that our egos – parents' egos – have to dissolve into benevolent vapor when it comes to our children? If he truly thought it would be better for Robby and Stephie to split their time between Parker and Joan he'd agree in a heartbeat; it would destroy part of him. But he'd do it.

Yet he believed this would be disastrous for them. And so he'd duke it out with his ex-wife in court relentlessly and at the same time shield the children from the animosity of the proceedings. At times like this you fought on two fronts: You battled the enemy and you battled your own overwhelming desire to be a child yourself and share your pain with your children. But this you could never do.

"Daddy," Robby said suddenly, "you stopped reading."

"I thought you were asleep." He laughed.

"My eyelids were just resting. They got tired. But *I'm* not."

Parker glanced at the clock. Quarter to eight. Fifteen minutes until—

No, don't think about that now.

He asked his son, "You have your shield?"

"Right here."

"Me too."

He picked up the book and began to read once more.

22

Margaret Lukas looked over the families at the Ritz-Carlton Hotel.

She and Cage stood in the main entrance, where hundreds of people were gathering for parties and dinner. Lukas was wearing a navy-blue suit she'd designed and made herself. It was cut close to her body, made from expensive worsted wool, and it had a long, pleated skirt. She'd cut a special dart in the jacket to make certain that the Glock 10 on her hip did not ruin the stylish lines of the outfit. It would be perfect for the opera or a fancy restaurant but, as it happened, she had worn it only to weddings and funerals. She called it her married-buried suit.

Fifteen minutes until eight.

"Nothing, Margaret," came the gruff voice in her headset. C. P. Ardell's. He was downstairs at one entrance to the Ritz, the parking garage, pretending to be a slightly drunk holiday reveler. The big agent wore a considerably more mundane costume than Lukas's –

stained jeans and a black leather biker's jacket. On his head was a Redskins hat, which he wore not because of the cold but because he had no hair to obscure the earphone wire of his radio. There were an additional sixty-five plainclothes agents in and around the hotel, armed with more weaponry than you'd find at an El Paso gun show.

All looking for a man for whom they had virtually no description.

Probably white, probably average build.

Probably wearing a gold crucifix.

In the lobby Lukas and Cage scanned the guests, the bellhops, the clerks. Nobody came close to matching their fragile description of the Digger. She realized they were standing with their arms crossed, looking just like well-dressed federal agents on stakeout.

"Say something amusing," she whispered.

"What?" Cage asked.

"We're sticking out. Pretend we're talking."

"Okay," Cage said, smiling broadly. "So whatta you think of Kincaid?"

The question threw her. "Kincaid? What do you mean?"

"I'm making conversation." A shrug. "Whatta you think of him?"

"I don't know."

"Sure you do," Cage persisted.

"He's perp smart, not street smart."

This time Cage's shrug was one of concession. "That's good. I like that." He said nothing more for a moment.

"What're you getting at?" she asked.

"Nothing. I'm not getting at anything. We're pretending to talk is all."

Good, she thought.

Focus . . .

They studied a dozen other possible suspects. She dismissed them for reasons she knew instinctively but couldn't explain.

Street smart . . .

A moment later Cage said, "He's a good man. Kincaid."

"I know. He's been very helpful."

Cage laughed in that surprised way of his – the way that meant: I'm on to you. He repeated, "Helpful."

More silence.

Cage said, "He lost his parents just after college. Then there was that custody battle a few years ago. Wife was psycho."

"That's hard," she said, and made a foray into the crowd. She brushed up against a guest with a suspicious bulge under his arm. She recognized a cell phone immediately and returned to Cage. Found herself asking impulsively, "What happened? With his folks?"

"Car accident. One of those crazy things. His mother'd just been diagnosed with cancer and it looked like they caught it in time. But they got nailed by a truck on Ninety-five on the way to Johns Hopkins for chemo. Dad was a professor. Met him a couple times. Nice guy."

"Was he?" she muttered, distracted again.

"History."

"What?"

"That's what Kincaid's dad taught. History."

More silence.

Lukas finally said, "I just need some phony conversation, Cage, not matchmaking."

He responded, "Am I doing that? Would I do that? I'm only saying you don't meet a lot of people like Kincaid."

"Uh-huh. We've got to stay focused here, Cage."

"I'm focused. You're focused. He doesn't know why you're pissed at him."

"Very simple. He wasn't taking care of himself. I told him that. We settled it. End of story."

"He's decent," Cage offered. "A stand-up guy. And he's smart – his mind's a weird thing. You should see him with those puzzles of his."

"Yeah. I'm sure he's great."

Focus.

But she *wasn't* focusing. She was thinking about Kincaid.

So he had his own capital *I* Incidents – deaths and divorce. A hard wife and a struggle to raise the children by himself. That explained some of what she'd seen before. The walls.

Kincaid . . .

And thinking about him, the document examiner, she thought again about the postcard.

Joey's postcard.

On the trip from which they'd never returned, Tom and Joey had been visiting her in-laws in Ohio. It was just before Thanksgiving. Her six-year-old son had mailed her a postcard from the airport just before they boarded the doomed plane. Probably not a half hour before the 737 had crashed into the icy field.

But the boy hadn't known you needed a stamp

to mail postcards. He must have slipped it into the mailbox before his father knew what he was doing.

It arrived a week after the funeral. Postage due. She'd paid for it and for the next three hours carefully peeled off the Postal Service sticker that had covered up part of her son's writing.

Were having fun mommy. Granma and I made
cookys
I miss you. I love you mommy . . .

A card from the ghost of her son.

It was in her purse right now, the gaudy picture of a sunset in the Midwest. Her wedding ring was stored in her jewelry box but this card she kept with her all the time and would until she died.

Six months after the crash Lukas had taken a copy of the card to a graphoanalyst and had her son's handwriting analyzed.

The woman had said, "Whoever wrote this is creative and charming. He'll grow up to be a handsome man. And brilliant, with no patience for deception. He also has a great capacity for love. You're a very lucky woman to have a son like this."

For ten dollars more the graphoanalyst had tape-recorded her comments. Lukas listened to the tape every few weeks. She'd sit by herself in her dark living room, put a candle on, have a drink – or two – and listen to what her son would have been like.

Then Parker Kincaid shows up at FBI headquarters and announces with that know-all voice of his that graphoanalysis is nonsense.

People read tarot cards too and talk to their dear departed. It's bogus.

It's *not*! she now raged to herself. She *believed* what the graphoanalyst had told her.

She had to. Otherwise she'd go insane.

It's as if you lose a part of your mind when you have children. They steal it and you never get it back . . . Sometimes I'm amazed that parents can function at all.

Dr. Evans's observation. She hadn't let on at the time but she knew it was completely true.

And here was Cage trying to set her up. So, she and Kincaid *were* similar. They were smart (and, yes, arrogant). They were both missing parts of their lives. They both had their protective walls – his to keep the danger out, hers to keep herself from retreating inside, where the worst danger lay. Yet the same instincts that made her a good cop told her – for no reason that she could articulate – that there was no future between them. She had returned to a "normal" life as much as she ever could. She had her dog, Jean Luc. She had some friends. She had her CDs. Her runners' club. Her sewing. But Margaret Lukas was emotionally plateaued, to use the Bureau term for an agent no longer destined for advancement.

No, she knew she'd never see Parker Kincaid after tonight. And that was perfectly all right—

The earphone crackled. "Margaret . . . Jesus Christ." It was C. P. Ardell, stationed downstairs.

Instantly she drew her weapon.

"You have the subject?" she whispered fiercely into her lapel mike.

"No," the agent said. "But we've got a problem. It's a mess down here."

Cage too was listening. His hand strayed to his own weapon and he looked at Lukas, frowning.

C. P. continued. "It's the mayor. He's here with a dozen cops and, fuck, a camera crew too."

"No!" Lukas snapped, drawing the attention of a cluster of partyers nearby.

"They got lights and everything. The shooter sees this, he'll take off. It's like a circus."

"I'll be right there."

"Your honor, this is a federal operation, and I'll have to ask you to leave right now."

They were in the parking garage. Lukas noted immediately that there was a controlled entrance and exit – to get in you needed to take a ticket. That meant that license plates were recorded and that in turn meant that the Digger would probably not come in this way – the unsub would have told him not to leave a record of his visit. But Mayor Kennedy, and his damn entourage, was headed for the main entrance to the hotel, where he and his uniformed bodyguards could be spotted in a minute by the killer.

And for God's sake, a *camera crew*?

Kennedy looked down at Lukas. He was a head taller. He said, "You have to get the guests out of here. Evacuate them. When the killer shows up let me talk to him."

Lukas ignored him and said to C. P., "Any of them get into the hotel itself?"

"No, we stopped 'em here."

Kennedy continued. "Evacuate! Get them out!"

"We can't do that," she said. "The Digger'll know something's wrong."

"Well, tell them to go their rooms at least."

"Think about it, Mayor," she snapped. "Most of them aren't guests. They're just locals – here for dinner and parties."

Lukas looked around the entrance to the hotel and the street outside. It wasn't crowded – the stores were all closed for the holiday. She whispered fiercely, "He could be here at any minute. I'm going to have to ask you to leave." Thought about adding "sir." She didn't.

"Then *I'm* going to have to go over your head. Who's your supervisor?"

"I am," Cage said. No shrugs now. Just a cold glare. "You have no jurisdiction here."

The mayor snapped, "So, who's *your* supervisor."

"Somebody you don't want to call, believe me."

"Let me be the judge of that."

"No," Lukas said firmly, glancing at her watch. "The Digger could be in the building right now. I don't have time to argue with you. I want you and your people out of here now!"

Kennedy looked at his aide – what was his name? Jefferies, she believed. A reporter was nearby, filming the entire exchange.

"I'm not going to let the FBI risk those people's lives. I'm going to—"

"Agent Ardell," she said, "put the mayor in custody."

"You can't arrest him," Jefferies snapped.

"Yes, she can," Cage said angrily now, with the most minute of shrugs. "And she can arrest you too."

"Get him out of here," Lukas said.

"Lockup?"

Lukas considered. "No. Just stay with him and keep him out of our hair until the operation's over."

"I'll call my lawyer and—"

A flash of anger burst inside her, as bright as the one that made her explode at Kincaid. She looked up at him, pointed a finger at his chest. "Mayor, this is *my* operation and you're interfering with it. I'll let you go on your way with Agent Ardell or, so help me, I'll have you detained downtown. It's entirely up to you."

There was a pause. Lukas wasn't even looking at the mayor; her eyes were scanning the parking lot, the sidewalks, the shadows. No sign of anyone who might be the Digger.

Kennedy said, "All right." He nodded toward the hotel. "But if there's any bloodshed tonight, it'll be on your hands."

"Goes with the territory," she muttered, recalling she'd said exactly the same about bloodshed to Kincaid. "Go on, C. P."

The agent led the mayor back to his limo. The two men got inside. Jefferies stared defiantly at Lukas for a moment but she turned quickly, and together she and Cage walked back toward the hotel.

"Shit," Cage said.

"No, I think it's okay. I don't think the Digger could've seen anything."

"That's not what I mean. Think about it – if Kennedy found out we were here, that means we've got a leak. Where the hell do you think it is?"

"Oh, I *know* that." She opened her cell phone and made a call.

* * *

"Detective," Lukas said, struggling to control her anger, "you know that information about tac operations is secure. You want to give me a reason why I shouldn't refer what you did to the U.S. attorney?"

She expected Len Hardy to deny or at least offer some slippery excuse about a mistake or getting tricked. But he surprised her by saying briskly, "Refer whatever you want but Kennedy wanted a chance to negotiate with the shooter. I gave it to him."

"Why?"

"Because you're willing to let, what, a dozen people die? Two dozen?"

"If it meant stopping the shooter then, yeah, that's exactly what I'm willing to do."

"Kennedy said he could talk to him. Talk him into taking the money. He—"

"You know he showed up with a goddamn TV crew?"

Hardy's voice was no longer so certain. "He . . . what?"

"A TV crew. He was playing it for media. If the Digger'd seen the lights, the police bodyguard . . . he'd just leave and find another target."

"He said he wanted to talk to him," Hardy said. "I didn't think he was going to use it for PR."

"Well, he did."

"Did the Digger— ?"

"I don't think he could've seen anything."

Silence for a moment. "I'm sorry, Margaret." He sighed. "I just wanted to do something. I didn't want any more people to die. I'm sorry."

Lukas gripped her phone. She knew she should fire

him, kick him off the team. Probably file a report with the District police commission too. And yet she had an image of the young man returning contritely to his house, a house as silent as the one she returned to in the year after Tom and Joey had died – a silence that hurts like a slap from a lover. He'd spend the holiday alone, forced to suffer a false mourning for Emma – a wife not alive and not dead.

He seemed to sense her weakening and said, "It won't happen again. Give me another chance."

Yes? No?

"Okay, Len. We'll talk about it later."

"Thanks, Margaret."

"We've got to get back on stakeout."

She clicked off the phone abruptly and if Hardy said anything else she never heard it. She returned to the lobby of the Ritz-Carlton.

Lukas slipped her weapon off her hip once more, held it at her side and began to circulate through the crowd. Cage tapped his watch. It was a few minutes to eight.

They looked over the railing at the dark water and joked about the *Titanic*, they ate the shrimp and left the chicken livers, they talked about wine and about interest rates and about upcoming elections and about congressional scandals and about sitcoms.

Most of the men were in tuxedos or dinner jackets, most of the women in dark dresses whose hems hovered an inch above the lacquered deck.

"Isn't this something? Look at the view."

"Will we be able to see the fireworks?"

"Where'd Hank get to? He's got my beer."

The hundreds of partyers had stationed themselves all over the lengthy yacht. There were three decks and four bars and everyone at the New Year's Eve bash was feeling great.

Lawyers and doctors, finding a few hours of peace from their clients' and patients' woes. Parents, enjoying a respite from their children. Lovers, thinking about finding an empty stateroom.

"So what's he going to do I heard he was going to run but the polls suck why should he oh what about Sally Claire Tom did they really get that place in Warrenton well I don't know how he can afford it . . ."

Minutes clicked past and the time grew closer to eight o'clock.

Everyone was happy.

Pleasant people enjoying a party, enjoying the company of friends.

Thankful for the view they'd have of the fireworks at midnight, thankful for the chance to celebrate and be away from the pressures of the nation's capital for the evening.

Thankful for the creature comforts conferred upon them by the crew and caterers on board the luxury yacht the *Ritzy Lady*, which floated regally in her dock on the Potomac, exactly two miles south of the Fourteenth Street Bridge.

23

Robby had moved from J. R. R. Tolkien to Nintendo.

He didn't seem upset anymore and Parker could stand it no longer; he had to find out about the Digger, about the most recent attack. Had Lukas and Cage succeeded? Had they found him?

Had they killed him?

He maneuvered through the toys on the floor and walked downstairs, where Stephie was in the kitchen with Mrs. Cavanaugh. The girl was squinting in concentration as she scrubbed one of Parker's stainless-steel pots. She'd made a caramel corn Christmas tree, sprinkled with green sugar. It sat, charmingly lopsided, on a plate on the counter.

"Beautiful, Who," he told her.

"I tried to put silver balls on it but they fell off."

"Robby'll love it."

He started for the den but saw a hollowness in her face.

He put his arm around the girl. "Your brother's okay, you know."

"I know."

"I'm sorry tonight's gone all ka-flooey."

"That's okay."

Which meant of course that it wasn't quite okay.

"We'll have fun tomorrow . . . But, honey, you know my friend? I may have to go back and see him."

"Oh, I know," Stephie said.

"You do?"

"I could tell. Sometimes you're all the way here and sometimes you're partway here. And tonight, when you came back, you were only partway here."

"Tomorrow I'll be all-the-way here. It's supposed to snow. You want to go sledding?"

"Yeah! Can I make the hot chocolate?"

"I was hoping you would." He hugged his daughter then rose and walked into the den to call Lukas. He didn't want her to overhear his conversation.

But through the curtained window he saw motion on the sidewalk, a man, he thought.

He walked quickly to the window and looked out. He couldn't see anyone – only a car he didn't recognize.

He slipped his hand into his pocket. And kneaded the cold metal of Lukas's gun.

Oh, not again . . . Thinking of the Boatman, remembering that terrible night.

The gun is too loud . . .!

The doorbell rang.

"I'll get it," he called abruptly, glancing into the kitchen. He saw Stephie blink. Once again his brusque manner had startled one of his children. Still, there was no time to comfort her.

Hand in his pocket, he looked through the window in the door and saw an FBI agent he recognized from earlier in the evening. He relaxed, leaned his head against the doorjamb. Breathed deeply to calm himself then opened the door with a trembling hand. A second agent walked up the steps. He remembered Lukas's comment about sending some men to watch the house.

"Agent Kincaid?"

He nodded. Looking over his shoulder to make sure Stephie was out of earshot.

"Margaret Lukas sent us to keep an eye on your family."

"Thanks. Just park out of sight if you would. I don't want to upset the children."

"Sure thing, sir."

He glanced at his watch. He was relieved. If the Digger had struck again, Cage or Lukas would have called. Maybe they'd actually caught the son of a bitch.

"The shooter in the Metro killing?" he asked. "The Digger. They got him?"

The look that passed between the two men chilled Parker.

Oh, no . . .

"Well, sir—"

Inside the house the phone started to ring. He saw Mrs. Cavanaugh answer it.

"The shooter, he got on board a party yacht on the Potomac. Killed eleven, wounded more than twenty. I thought you knew."

Oh, God. No . . .

Nausea churned inside him.

Here I was reading children's books while people were dying. *Life on Sesame Street . . .*

He asked, "Agent Lukas . . . she's all right? And Agent Cage?"

"Yessir. They weren't anywhere near the boat. They found some clue that said 'Ritz,' so they thought the Digger was going to hit one of the Ritz hotels. But that wasn't it. The name of the boat was the *Ritzy Lady*. Bad luck, huh?"

The other agent said, "Security guard got off a couple shots and that scared the shooter off. So it wasn't as bad as it might've been. But they didn't hit him, they don't think."

Bad luck, huh?

No, not luck at all. When you don't solve the puzzle it's not because of luck.

Three hawks . . .

He heard Mrs. Cavanaugh's voice, "Mr. Kincaid?"

He glanced into the house.

Eleven dead . . .

"Phone for you."

Parker walked into the kitchen. He picked up the phone, expecting to hear Lukas or Cage.

But it was a smooth-sounding, pleasant baritone he didn't recognize. "Mr. Kincaid?"

"Yes? Who's this?"

"My name's Slade Phillips, WPLT News. Mr. Kincaid, we're doing a special report on the New Year's Eve shootings. We have an unnamed source reporting that you've been instrumental in the investigation and may be responsible for the mix-up in sending the FBI to the Ritz-Carlton Hotel when in fact the killer had targeted another location. We're going on the air with that story at nine. We want to give you the chance to tell your side. Do you have anything to say?"

Parker inhaled sharply. He believed his heart stopped beating momentarily.

This was it . . . Joan would find out. Everyone would find out.

"Mr. Kincaid?"

"I have no comment." He hung up, missing the cradle. He watched the phone spiral downward and hit the floor with a resounding crack.

The Digger returns to his comfy motel room.

Thinking of the boat – where he spun around like . . . *click* . . . like a whirligig among red and yellow leaves and fired his Uzi and fired and fired and fired . . .

And watched the people fall and scream and run. Things like that.

It wasn't like the theater. No, no, he got a lot of them this time. Which will make the man who tells him things happy.

The Digger locks the motel door and the first thing he does is walk to the couch and look at Tye. The boy is still asleep. The blanket has slipped off him and the Digger replaces it.

The Digger turns the TV on and sees pictures of the *Ritzy Lady* boat. Once again he sees that man he recognizes – the . . . *click* . . . the mayor. Mayor Kennedy. He's standing in front of the boat. He's wearing a nice suit and a nice tie and it looks odd to see him wearing such a fancy suit with all the yellow bags of bodies behind him. He's speaking into a microphone but the Digger can't hear what he's saying because he doesn't have the TV volume on because he doesn't want to wake up Tye.

He continues to watch for a while but no commercials come on and he's disappointed so he shuts off the TV, thinking, "Good night, Mayor."

He begins to pack his belongings, taking his time.

Motels are nice, motels are fun.

They come and clean up the room every day and take away your dirty towels and bring you clean ones. Even Pamela didn't do that. She was good with flowers and good with that stuff you did in bed. That . . . *click, click . . . that* stuff.

Mind jumping, bullets rattling around the cra . . . crane . . . cranium.

Thinking, for some reason, about Ruth.

"Oh, God, no," Ruth said. "Don't do it!"

But he'd been told to do it – to put the long piece of glass in her throat – and so he did. She shivered as she died. He remembers that. Ruth, shivering.

Shivering like on Christmas day, twelve twenty-five, one two two five, when he made soup for Pamela and then gave her her present.

He looks at Tye. He'll take the boy out . . . *click* . . . West with him. The man who tells him things told him he'd call after they finished in Washington, D.C., and tell him where they'd go next.

"Where will that be?" the Digger asked.

"I don't know. Maybe out West."

"Where's the West?" he asked.

"California. Maybe Oregon."

"Oh," responded the Digger, who had no idea where those places were.

But sometimes, late at night, full of soup and smiling

at the funny commercials, he thinks about going out West and imagines what he'll do out there.

Now, as he packs, he decides he'll definitely take the boy with him. Out West out . . . *click*.

Out West.

Yes, that would be good. That would be nice. That would be fun.

They could eat soup and chili and they could watch TV. He could tell the boy about TV commercials.

Pamela, the Digger's wife, with a flower in her hand and a gold cross in between her breasts, used to watch commercials with him.

But they never had a child like Tye to watch commercials with.

"Me? Have a baby with *you?* Are you mad crazy nuts fucked . . ." *Click*. ". . . fucked up? Why don't you go *away?* Why are you still here? Take your fucking present and get out. Go away. Do you . . ."

Click . . .

But I love you all the . . .

"Do you need me to spell it out for you? I've been fucking William for a year. Is this *news* to you? Everybody in town knows except you. If I were going to have a baby I'd have *his* baby."

But I love you all the more.

"What are you doing? Oh Je—
Click.
—sus. Put it down!"

The memories are running like lemmings through the Digger's cranium.

"No, don't!" she screamed, staring at the knife in his hand. "Don't!"

But he did.

He put the knife into her chest, just below the gold cross he'd given her that morning, Christmas morning. What a beautiful red rose blossoms on her blouse! He put the knife in her chest once more and the rose got bigger.

And bleeding bleeding bleeding, Pamela ran for . . . where? Where? The closet, yes, the closet upstairs. Bleeding and screaming, "Oh Jesus Jesus Jesus . . ."

Pamela screaming, lifting the gun, pointing it at his head, her hand blossoming into a beautiful yellow flower as he felt a thud on his temple. *I love you all the* . . .

The Digger woke up sometime later.

The first thing he saw was the kind eyes of the man who would tell him things.

Click, click . . .

He now calls his voice mail. No messages.

Where did he go, the man who tells him things? Where is he?

But there's no time to think about it, about being happy or sad, whatever they are. There's only time to get ready for the last attack.

The Digger unlocks the closet. He takes out a second machine pistol, also an Uzi. He puts on the smelly latex gloves and starts to load the clips.

Two guns this time. And no shopping bags. Two guns and lots and lots of bullets. The man who tells him things told him that this time he has to shoot more people than he's ever shot before.

Because this will be the last minute of the last hour of the last night of the year.

24

08.55

A sweating Parker Kincaid ran into the FBI Document Division lab.

Lukas walked up to him. Her face was paler than he'd remembered it. "I got your message," she said. "That reporter – Phillips – he got to one of the mailroom people. Somehow he found out your real name."

"You *promised*," he raged.

"I'm sorry, Parker," she responded. "I'm sorry. It didn't come from here. I don't know what happened."

Dr. Evans and Tobe Geller were quiet. They knew what was going on but, perhaps seeing the look in Parker's eyes, they wanted no part of it. Cage was not in the room.

Parker had called them on his cell phone as he sped – with a red dashboard flasher borrowed from the agents stationed in front of his house – from Fairfax to downtown. His mind had been racing. How could he control the disaster? All he'd wanted to do was help save some lives. That was his only motive, save some children. And look what had happened . . .

Now his own children would be taken away from him. *The end of the world* . . .

He pictured the nightmare if Joan had even partial custody. She'd soon lose interest in mothering. If she couldn't get a baby-sitter she'd drop them off, alone, at the mall. She'd lose her temper at them. They'd have to fix their own meals, wash their own clothes. He was in despair.

Why the hell had he even *considered* Cage's request for help tonight?

A small TV sat on a table nearby. Parker turned it on to the news. It was just nine. A commercial ended and smiling pictures of the WPLT "news team" flipped onto the screen.

"Where's Cage?" he asked angrily.

"I don't know," Lukas answered. "Upstairs some-where."

Could they move out of the state? he wondered manically. But, no, Joan would fight that and the Virginia courts would still have jurisdiction.

On the screen, that son of a bitch Phillips looked up from a stack of papers and gazed at the camera with a grotesquely sincere expression.

"Good evening. I'm Slade Phillips . . . Eleven people were killed and twenty-nine were wounded an hour ago in the third of the mass shootings that have terrorized Washington tonight. In this special report we'll have exclusive interviews with victims and with police on the scene. In addition, WPLT has obtained exclusive videotape of the scene of the most recent killings – on a yacht anchored in the Potomac River."

Parker, hands clenched, watched silently.

"WPLT has also learned that police and FBI agents were sent to a hotel where it was mistakenly believed that the killer would strike next, leaving too few officers and agents to respond to the shooting on the boat. It's not known for certain who is responsible for this mix-up but informed sources have . . . have reported . . ."

Phillips's voice faded. The anchor cocked his head, probably listening to someone through the flesh-colored earphone stuck in his ear. He glanced camera right and a shadow of a frown crossed his face. There was a brief pause and his mouth registered defeat as he recited, "Informed sources have reported that District of Columbia Mayor Gerald D. Kennedy is being detained by federal authorities, possibly in connection with this unsuccessful operation . . . Now, standing by at the site of the most recent shooting, is Cheryl Vandover. Cheryl, could you tell us—"

Cage walked into the lab, wearing an overcoat. He clicked the TV set off. Parker closed his eyes and exhaled. "Jesus."

"Sorry, Parker," Cage said. "Things fall through the cracks sometimes. But I made a deal with you and we're keeping our end of the bargain. Oh, one thing – don't ever ask me how I did *this* one. You *definitely* don't wanna know. Now, we got one more chance. Let's nail this prick. And this time, no foolin'."

The limo eased up to the curb in front of City Hall like a yacht docking.

Mayor Jerry Kennedy didn't like the simile but he couldn't help it. He'd just been at the Potomac riverside, comforting survivors and surveying the devastation that the Digger had caused. His tall, thin wife, Claire, at his side, they'd been astonished at how the bullets had torn the decks and cabins and tables to pieces. He could only imagine what the bullets had done to the bodies of the victims.

He leaned forward and clicked the TV off.

"How could he?" Claire whispered, referring to Slade Phillips's suggestion that Kennedy had in some mysterious way been responsible for the deaths on the boat.

Wendell Jefferies leaned forward, resting his glossy head in his hands. "Phillips . . . I already paid him. I—"

Kennedy waved him silent. Apparently the aide had forgotten about the huge, bald federal agent in the front seat. Bribing media was undoubtedly a federal offense of some kind.

Yeah, Jefferies had paid Slade Phillips his twenty-five thousand. And, no, they'd never get it back.

"Whatever happens," Kennedy said to Jefferies and Claire solemnly, "I don't want to hire Phillips as my press secretary."

His delivery was, as always, deadpan and it took them a minute before they realized it was a joke. Claire laughed. Jefferies still seemed shell shocked.

The irony was that Kennedy would never have a press secretary again. Former politicians don't need one. He wanted to scream, he wanted to cry.

"What do we do now?" Claire asked.

"We'll have a drink and then go to the African-American Teachers' Association party. Who knows? The Digger might still come forward and want the money. I still may have a chance to meet him face-to-face."

Claire shook her head. "After what happened on the boat? You couldn't trust him. He'd kill you."

Couldn't kill me any deader than the press has done tonight, Kennedy thought.

Claire tacked down her wispy hair with a burst from a small container of perfumed spray. Kennedy loved the smell. It comforted him. The vibrant fifty-nine-year-old woman with keen eyes had been his main advisor since his first days of public office, years ago. It was only that she was white that kept her from being his primary assistant as mayor: a characteristic that she too insisted would put him at a disadvantage in the 60-percent-black District of Columbia.

"How bad is all this?" she asked.

"As bad as it gets."

Claire Kennedy nodded and put her hand on her husband's substantial leg.

Neither spoke for a moment.

"Is there any champagne in there?" he asked suddenly, nodding toward the minibar.

"Champagne?"

"Sure. Let's start celebrating my ignominious defeat early."

"You wanted to teach," she pointed out. Then with a wink she added, "Professor Kennedy."

"And you did too, Professor Kennedy. We'll tell William and Mary we want adjoining lecture halls."

She smiled at him and opened the minibar of the limo.

But Jerry Kennedy wasn't smiling. Teaching would be a failure. A successful job at a Dupont Circle law firm would be a failure. Kennedy knew in his heart that his life's purpose was to make this struggling, oddly shaped chunk of swampy land a better place for the youngsters who happened to be born here, and that his Project 2000 was the only thing faintly within his grasp that would allow that to happen. And now those hopes had been destroyed.

He glanced at his wife. She was laughing.

She pointed to the bar. "Gallo and Budweiser."

What else in the District of Columbia?

Kennedy lifted up on the door handle and stepped out into the cooling night.

The guns are finally loaded.

The silencer he's been using has been repacked and the new one is mounted on the second gun.

The Digger, in his comfy room, checks his pocket. Let's see. He has one pistol with him and two more in the glove compartment of his car. And lots and lots of ammunition.

The Digger takes his suitcase out to the car. The man who tells him things told him that the room was paid for. When it was time to go all he had to do was leave.

He packs his cans of soup and dishes and glasses and takes them in a box to the Everyday People Toyota.

The Digger returns to the room and looks at thin Tye for a few minutes, wonders again where . . . *click* . . . where Out West is then wraps the blanket around him. And carries the boy, light as a puppy, down to the car and puts him in the back seat.

The Digger sits behind the wheel but doesn't start the car right away. He turns around and looks at the boy some more. Tucks the blanket around his feet. He's wearing tattered running shoes.

A memory of someone speaking. Who? Pamela? William? The man who tells him things?

"Sleep . . ."

Click, click.

Wait, wait, wait.

"I want you to . . ." *Click, click.*

Suddenly there is no Pamela, no Ruth with the glass in her neck, no man who tells him things. There is only Tye.

"I want you to sleep well," the Digger says to the boy's still form. *These* are the words he wanted to say to him.

He isn't exactly sure what they mean. But he says them anyway.

> *When I go to sleep at night,*
> *I love you all the more . . .*

He starts the car. He signals and checks his blind spot, then pulls out into traffic.

| 10.05 |

T he last location.

> *place I showed you – the black . . .*

Parker Kincaid stood in front of the blackboard in the Document Division lab. Hands on his hips. Staring at the puzzle in front of him. . . . *place I showed you – the black . . .*

"The black what?" Dr. Evans mused.

Cage shrugged. Lukas was on the phone with the PERT crime scene experts on board the *Ritzy Lady*. She hung up and told the team that, as they'd expected, there were few solid leads. They'd found bullet casings with a few prints on them. They were being run through AFIS, and Identification was going to e-mail Lukas the results. There was no other physical evidence. Witnesses had reported a white man of indeterminate age in a dark coat. He carried a brown bag, which presumably held the machine gun. A bit of fiber had been recovered. It was from the bag, techs from PERT had assessed, but was generic and provided no clues as to the source.

Parker looked around, "Where's Hardy?"

Cage told him about the incident at the Ritz.

"She fire him?" Parker asked, nodding toward Lukas.

"No. Thought she should have but she gave him hell – and then a second chance. He's in the research library downstairs. Trying to make amends."

Parker looked back at Geller. The young agent stared at the screen in front of him as the computer's improvised anagram program vainly tried to assemble letters following the word "black." The ash behind this word, however, was much more badly damaged than that near the *Ritzy Lady* notation.

Parker paced for a moment then stopped. He stared up at the blackboard. He felt the queasy sense of nearly but not quite figuring out a clue. He sighed.

He found himself standing next to Lukas. She asked him, "Your boy? Robby? Is he all right?"

"He's fine. Just a little scared."

She nodded. A computer nearby announced, "You've got mail." She walked to it and read the message. Shook her head. "The prints on the shell casings're from one of the passengers on the boat picking up souvenirs. He checks out." She clicked the SAVE button.

Parker gazed at the screen. "That's making me obsolete."

"What?"

"E-mail," he said. He looked at Lukas and added, "As a document examiner, I mean. Oh, people're writing more than ever because of it, but—"

"But there's less handwriting nowadays," she said, continuing his thought.

"Right."

"That'll be tough," she said. "Lose a lot of good evidence that way."

"True. But for me that's not what's sad."

"Sad?" she looked at him. Her eyes were no longer stony but she seemed wary once again of an inartful term echoing in such an esteemed forensic lab.

"For me," he told her, "handwriting's a part of a human being. Like our sense of humor or imagination. Think about it – it's one of the only things about people that survives their death. Writing can last for hundreds of years. Thousands. It's about as close to immortality as we can get."

"Part of the person?" she asked. "But you said graphoanalysis was bogus."

"No, I mean that whatever somebody wrote is still a reflection of who they are. It doesn't matter how the words are made or what they say, even if they're mistaken or nonsensical. Just the fact that someone thought of the words and their hands committed them to paper is what counts. It's almost a miracle to me."

She was staring at the floor, her head down.

Parker continued. "I've always thought of handwriting as a fingerprint of the heart and mind." He laughed self-consciously at this, thinking that she might have another brusque reaction to a sentimental thought. But something odd happened. Margaret Lukas nodded and looked away from him quickly. Parker thought, for a moment, that another message had flashed on a nearby computer and caught her attention. But there wasn't any. With her head turned away from him he could see her reflection in the screen and it seemed that her eyes were glistening with tears. This was something he never would have expected from Lukas but, yes, she was wiping her face.

He was about to ask her if anything was wrong but she stepped abruptly up to the glass panes holding the burnt yellow sheets. Without giving him a chance to say anything about the tears, Lukas asked, "The mazes he drew? You think there's anything there? Maybe a clue?"

He didn't answer. Just continued to look at her. She turned to him briefly and repeated, "The mazes?"

After a moment he looked down, studied the sheet of yellow paper. Only psychopaths tend to leave cryptograms as clues and even then they rarely do. But Parker decided it wasn't a bad idea to check; they had so little else to go on. He put the glass panes holding the sheet on the overhead projector.

Lukas stood beside Parker, both their arms crossed.

"What're we looking for?" Cage asked.

"Do the lines make any letters?" Lukas asked.

"Good," Parker said. She was starting to get the hang of puzzles. They examined the lines carefully. But they found nothing.

"Maybe," she then suggested, "it's a map."

Another good idea.

Everyone gazed at the lines. As head of the District field office Lukas was an expert on the layout of the city. But she couldn't think of any streets or neighborhoods the mazes corresponded to. Neither could anyone else.

Geller looked back at his computer. He shook his head. "The anagram thing isn't working. There just isn't enough of the ash left to make any letters at all."

"We'll have to figure it out the old-fashioned way."

Parker paced, staring at the blackboard. "'. . . the black . . .'"

"Some African-American organization?" Evans suggested.

"Possibly," Parker said. "But remember the unsub was smart. Educated."

Cage frowned. "What do you mean?"

It was Lukas who answered. "The word 'black' is lowercase. If it were the name of a group he'd probably capitalize it."

"Exactly," Parker said. "I'd guess it's descriptive. There's a good chance it *does* refer to race but I doubt it's a reference to a specific organization."

"But don't forget," Cage said. "He also likes to fool us."

"True," Parker admitted.

Black . . .

Parker walked to the examination table, stared down at the extortion note. Put his hands on either side of it. Stared at the devil's teardrop dot above the letter *i*. Stared at the stark ink.

What do you know? he asked the document silently. What aren't you telling us? What secrets are you keeping? What— ?

"I've got something," the voice called from the doorway.

They all turned.

Detective Len Hardy trotted into the lab, a sheaf of papers under his arm. He'd been running and he paused, caught his breath. "Okay, Margaret, you were right. I don't shoot and I don't investigate. But nobody's a better researcher than I am. So I decided why don't I do that? I've found out some things about the name.

The Digger." He dropped the papers on the desk and started through them. He glanced at the team. "I'm sorry about before. With the mayor. I screwed up. I just wanted to do something to keep people from getting hurt."

"It's all right, Len," Lukas said. "What do you have?"

Hardy asked Dr. Evans, "When you were checking out the name, what databases did you use?"

"Well, the standard ones," the doctor answered. He seemed defensive.

"Criminal?" Hardy asked, "VICAP, N.Y.P.D Violent Felons, John Jay?"

"Those, sure," Evans said.

"That was fine," Hardy said. "but I got to thinking why not try *noncriminal* resources? I finally found it. The database at the Religious History Department at Cambridge University." Hardy opened a notebook.

"That group you mentioned in San Francisco in the sixties?" he asked Dr. Evans. "The one called the Diggers?"

"But I checked them out," the doctor said. "They were just an acting troupe."

"No, they weren't," Hardy responded. "It was a radical underground political and social movement, centered in Haight-Ashbury. I checked out their philosophy and history, and it turns out they took their name from a group in England in the seventeenth century. And *they* were a lot more radical. They advocated abolishing private ownership of land. Here's what's significant. They were mostly economic and social but they allied themselves with another group, which was political and more active – sometimes militant. They were called the 'True Levelers.'"

"'Levelers.'" Cage muttered. "That's a damn spooky name too."

Hardy continued. "They objected to control of the people by an upper-class elite and by a central government."

"But what does it mean for us?" Lukas asked.

Hardy said, "It might help us find the last target. What would he want to hit to quote level our capitalistic society?"

Parker said, "Before we can answer that we need to know why he's got it in for society."

"Religious nut?" Geller said. "Remember the crucifix?"

"Could be," Evans said. "But most religious zealots wouldn't want money; they'd want a half hour on CNN."

"Maybe he had a grudge," Parker said.

"Sure. Revenge." Lukas said this.

"Somebody hurt him," Parker said. "And he wants to get even."

Evans nodded. "It's making sense."

"But who? Who hurt him?" Hardy mused, staring again at the ghostly extortion note.

"He got fired?" Cage suggested. "Disgruntled worker."

"No," Evans said, "a psychotic might kill for that but he wasn't psychotic. He was too smart and controlled."

Geller rasped, "Big business, big corporations, fat cats . . ."

"Wait," Hardy said, "if those were his targets wouldn't he be in New York, not Washington?"

"He was," Cage pointed out. "White Plains."

But Hardy shook his head. "No, remember – White

Plains, Boston, Philly? Those were just trial runs for him. This is his grand finale."

"So why Washington?" Hardy mused. "What's here?"

"Government," Parker said. That's why he's here.

Hardy nodded. "And the Diggers objected to central government. So maybe it isn't upper-class society at all." He glanced at Evans. "But the federal government."

Lukas said, "That's it. It's got to be."

Parker: "The government was responsible for something that hurt him." Looking over the team. "Any thoughts on what?"

"Ideology?" Cage wondered aloud. "He's a communist or part of a right-wing militia cell."

Evans shook his head. "No, he would've delivered a manifesto by now. It's more personal."

Lukas and Hardy caught each other's eyes. It seemed to Parker that they came up with an identical thought at the same time. It was the detective who said, "The death of somebody he loved."

Lukas nodded.

"Could be," the psychologist offered.

"Okay," Cage said, "What could the scenario've been? Who died? Why?"

"Execution?" Hardy suggested.

Cage shook his head. "Hardly ever see federal capital crimes. They're mostly state."

"Coast guard rescue goes bad," Geller suggested.

"Far-fetched," Lukas said.

Hardy tried again, "Government car or truck involved in a crash, postal worker shooting spree, Park Service accident . . . diplomats . . ."

"Military," Cage suggested. "Most deaths involving the federal government are probably military related."

"But," Lukas said, "there must be hundreds of fatalities every year in the armed forces. Was it an accident? A training exercise? Combat?"

"Desert Storm?" Cage suggested.

"How old was the unsub?" Parker asked.

Lukas grabbed the medical examiner's preliminary report. She read, looked up. "Mid-forties."

Black . . .

Then Parker understood. He said, "The black wall!"

Lukas nodded. "The Vietnam Memorial."

"Someone he knew," Hardy said, "was killed in 'Nam. Brother, sister. Maybe his wife was a nurse."

Cage said, "But that was thirty years ago. Could something like this resurface now?"

"Oh, sure," Evans said. "If your unsub didn't work through his anger in therapy it's been festering. And New Year's Eve's a time for resolutions and people taking bold action – even destructive action. There'll be more suicides tonight than on any other night of the year."

"Oh, Jesus," Lukas said.

"What?"

"I just realized – the Memorial's on the Mall. There're going to be two hundred thousand people there. For the fireworks. We've got to close off that part of the park."

"It's already packed," Parker said. "They've been camping out for hours."

"But, Jesus," Cage said, "we need more manpower." He called Artie, the building's night entrance guard, who made an announcement over the PA that all available agents in the building were needed in the lobby for an emergency assignment.

Lukas called Jerry Baker and told him to get his tactical agents to the northwest portion of the Mall. She then paged the deputy director on call for the evening. He called back immediately. She spoke to him for a moment then hung up.

She looked at the team. "The dep director's on his way over. I'm going to meet him downstairs to brief him then I'll meet you at the Memorial."

Cage put his coat on. Geller stood and checked his weapon. It looked alien in his hands, which were undoubtedly much more accustomed to holding a computer mouse.

Lukas said, "Hold on, Tobe. You're going home."

"I can—"

"That's an order. You've already done enough."

He protested a bit more. But in the end Lukas won – though only after promising that she'd call him if she needed any other tech assistance. "I'll have my laptop with me," he said, as if he couldn't imagine ever being more than three feet from a computer.

Lukas walked over to Hardy. "Thanks, Detective. That was damn good police work."

He grinned. "Sorry I fucked up with the mayor. He—"

She waved her hand, acknowledging the apology. Offered a slight smile. "Everything's right as rain." Then she asked him, "You still want a piece of the action tonight?"

"Oh, you bet I do."

"Okay, but keep to the rear. Tell me true . . . You really know how to shoot?"

"I sure as hell do. And I'm pretty good too . . . if it's not windy." The young detective, still grinning, pulled on his trench coat.

Parker, feeling the weight of the gun in the pocket, donned his jacket. Lukas glanced at him dubiously. "I'm going," he said firmly in response to her glance.

She said, "You don't have to, Parker. It's okay. You've done enough too."

He smiled at her. "Just point and shoot, right?"

She hesitated then said, "Just point and shoot."

Here it comes, here it comes . . .

My God, look at them all!

A dozen, two dozen agents running out of FBI head-quarters. Some in bulletproof vests, some not.

Henry Czisman took one last sip of Jim Beam and rested the brown bottle on the back seat of his rental car, which reeked of tobacco and whiskey. He crushed out his Marlboro in the overflowing ashtray.

They ran toward their cars. One by one they started up and sped away.

He didn't follow. Not yet. He waited, patient as an adder.

Then Czisman saw the tall gray-haired agent, Cage, push through the front door. Looking behind him. And, yes! There he was: Parker Kincaid.

Though Czisman had not told the FBI agents every-thing, he had in fact been a journalist for most of his life. And a good one. He could read people as perceptively as any street cop. And, while *they* were undoubtedly running their retinal scans and voice stress analysis on him in their interrogation room he was running his own tests. Less high-tech and more intuitive, his were nonetheless just as accurate as the Bureau's. And one of the things he'd decided was that Jefferson was not Jefferson at all. When the man had left the headquarters in a hurry and gotten into his own car several hours ago Czisman had sent the man's license plate to a private eye in Hartford, Connecticut, and had gotten his real identity. Parker Kincaid. A simple database search on the Internet had revealed he was the former head of the Bureau's Document Division.

If the Bureau was using a former agent as a consultant he must be good. Which meant he was the one worth following. Not bureaucratic Cage. Not unfeeling Lukas.

Pausing to zip up his leather jacket, Kincaid looked around to orient himself then climbed into an unmarked car with Cage and another young agent or officer, an earnest man in a trench coat. They turned on a red light on the dash and sped quickly west and south – toward the Mall.

Czisman easily slipped into the motorcade of cars, which were moving so frantically that no one noticed him. Around Eighteenth Street, though, near Constitution Avenue, the crowds and traffic were so thick that the Bureau vehicles were forced to stop and the agents climbed out, ran to the Mall. Czisman was close behind.

Cage and Kincaid stood together, looking over the crowds. Kincaid pointed toward the west side of the Vietnam monument and Cage nodded toward the east. They separated and moved off in their respective directions, the man in the trench coat trotting away from them both, toward Constitution.

Czisman was a heavy man and out of shape. His breath snapped in and out of his congested lungs and his heart pounded like a piston. But he managed to keep up with Parker Kincaid very easily, pausing only momentarily – to take the pistol from the sweaty waistband of his slacks and slip it into his coat pocket.

———◆———

```
11.20
```

The Digger's coat is heavy.

Heavy from the weight of the guns.

From the weight of the clips, containing hundreds of rounds of .22 . . .

Click, click . . .

. . . of . . . of .22 caliber long-rifle ammunition warning bullets can travel up to one mile do not allow children to shoot unsupervised.

But the Digger would never do that – let a child shoot unsupervised.

Not Tye. Never, ever, ever Tye.

Two nicely packed suppressors. Cotton and rubber, cotton and rubber.

You're the you're the you're best . . .

The machine guns are in the inside pockets of his nice blue or black overcoat, his Christmas present from Pamela. One of the pistols from the glove compartment of his Toyota is in the right outside pocket of his coat. Four more clips for the Uzis are in the left-hand pocket.

No bags, no puppies . . .

He's standing in shadows and none of the people nearby notice him. He looks for police or agents and sees none.

Tye is asleep in the back seat of the car, a block away. When the Digger left him his stick-like arms were folded over his chest.

This is what worries him the most – if the police start shooting or if the Digger has to shoot with the unsilenced pistols Tye might wake up from the sound. And then he won't *sleep well.*

He's also worried that the boy will be cold. The temperature keeps falling. But the Digger remembers that he tripled the blanket over Tye. He'll be all right. He's sleeping. Children are always all right when they're sleeping.

He is standing by himself watching some of the people who are about to die. He calls one last time on his cell phone and the lady who sounds like Ruth before the triangle of glass says, "You have no new messages."

So it's okay to kill these people.

They'll fall to the ground like dark leaves.

Chop chop chop chopchopchop . . .

He'll . . . *click* . . . he'll spin around, like a top, like a toy Tye might like, and he'll spread the bullets throughout the crowd. Bullets from two guns.

Then he'll get into the car and check his messages and if the man who tells him things still hasn't called then he and Tye will drive until they find . . . *click* . . . they find California.

Somebody will tell him where it is.

It can't be that hard to find. It's somewhere out West. He remembers that.

*   *   *

Is the Digger behind him?

In front?

Beside?

Parker Kincaid, separated from the other agents, walked in a large, frantic circle near the Vietnam Memorial, lost in a sea of people. Looking for a man in a dark coat. With a shopping bag. Wearing a crucifix.

Far too many people. Thousands of them. Ten thousand.

Cage was on the other side of the Memorial. Len Hardy was on Constitution Avenue. Baker and the other tactical officers were making a sweep from the other side of the Mall.

Parker was about to stop a group from walking down to the Memorial itself, send them to the safety of a cluster of officers, but then he paused.

He realized suddenly that he hadn't been thinking clearly.

Puzzles. Remember the puzzles.

Three hawks have been killing a farmer's chickens . . .

Then he understood his mistake. He'd been looking in the wrong places. He stepped aside, out of the way of the crowd, and examined the grounds near the Vietnam Memorial. He thought of the unsub's mazes and realized that the man would have known that by the third attack the agents would have *some* description of the Digger. He would've told the killer not to approach the Memorial along one of the sidewalks, where he could be spotted more easily; he should come in through the trees.

Parker turned quickly and disappeared into a thicket of maple and cherry trees. It was still crowded with people making their way to the Mall but he didn't stop to tell them to leave the area. His job now wasn't to be a caretaker, a helping hand, a *father*, he was a hunter – just like that night years ago when he stalked through his house, looking for the Boatman. Kneading the heavy gun in his pocket.

Searching for his prey.

Searching for a faceless man in a dark coat.

A man wearing a cross.

Henry Czisman was thirty feet behind Kincaid, walking past the Vietnam Memorial, when Kincaid turned suddenly and moved into a grove of trees.

Czisman followed, looking around him at the sea of people.

What a target the Digger would have here!

He could cut them down like grass.

Czisman's own pistol was in his hand, pointed at the ground. No one saw it; the crowd was distracted, wondering what was going on – with all the police and federal agents telling them to leave the Mall.

Kincaid walked steadily through the trees, Czisman now perhaps twenty feet behind him. Still, there were people everywhere – dozens separated him from Kincaid – and the document examiner had no idea he was being followed.

They were about thirty feet from the solemn black wall when Czisman saw a man in a dark overcoat step from behind a tree. It was a cautious, furtive movement and suggested that the man had been hiding. And when he walked toward the Memorial he moved too deliberately, his head down, focused on the ground for no reason, as if he were trying not to be noticed. He disappeared into the crowd not far from Kincaid.

Czisman trotted after him.

Suddenly Kincaid turned. He glanced at Czisman, away, then back again with a frown, realizing that he'd seen the face before but couldn't place it. Czisman turned away and ducked behind several large men carrying a cooler. He believed he lost Kincaid. He returned to his search, looking again for the man in the dark overcoat.

Where— ?

Yes, yes, there he was! A man in his forties, completely nondescript. He was unbuttoning the coat, looking around with dull eyes at the crowds around him.

And then Czisman saw the flash. A flash of gold on the man's neck.

He wears a gold cross . . .

The agents in the bar had told him that the Digger wore a cross.

So here he is, Czisman thought. The Butcher, the Widow Maker, the Devil . . .

"Hey!" A voice called.

Czisman turned. It was Kincaid.

Now, he thought. Now!

Czisman lifted his revolver, aimed it toward his target.

"No!" Kincaid shouted, seeing the gun. "No."

But Czisman had no clear shot. There were too many people here. He danced to the side and pushed through a break in the crowd, knocking several people aside. He lost Kincaid.

Twenty feet away, the Digger – oblivious to both men – looked over the crowds like a hunter gazing at a huge flock of geese.

Czisman shoved aside a cluster of college students.

"What the fuck you doing, man?"

"Hey . . ."

Czisman ignored them. Where was Kincaid? *Where?* Still no target! Too many people . . .

The Digger's coat fell open. In one of the inside pockets was a large, black machine gun.

But nobody sees him! Czisman thought. It's as if he's invisible.

Nobody knows. Families, children, just feet away from the killer . . .

The crowd seemed to swell with people. The police were directing everyone toward Constitution Avenue but many of them were remaining – so they wouldn't lose a good view of the fireworks, Czisman supposed.

The Digger was squinting, looking for a place to shoot from. He stepped onto a slight rise in the grass.

Kincaid emerged from the crowd.

Czisman pulled back the hammer of his pistol.

27

11.40

The limo had parked beside the Mall, near the box seats reserved for diplomats and members of Congress.

Mayor Kennedy and his wife climbed out, accompanied by C. P. Ardell.

"You have to dog us like this?" Claire asked the agent.

"It's orders," Ardell said. "You understand."

Claire shrugged.

Understand? Kennedy thought. What he understood was that he was virtually under arrest and that he couldn't even avoid the humiliation of appearing in public in his own city without a baby-sitter.

Any hope that his career would survive tonight was being tidily laid to rest by a few glances at the people who stood near the reviewing stand watching him. The ambiguity of Slade Phillips's news report had been missed, or ignored, and it seemed that everyone here thought Kennedy was practically the Digger's partner.

Cameras flashed, capturing the stark images that would be identified in the papers tomorrow as "Mayor and Mrs. Jerry Kennedy." He waved to some of the people on the viewing stand and, with grave tact, fielded cursory comments such as "Where've you been hiding?" "How you doing, Jerry?" No one here really wanted answers; they were hard at work distancing themselves from the soon-to-be-former mayor.

The other question Kennedy heard was: "Heard you weren't coming to the fireworks tonight, Jerry. What brings you out here?"

Well, what brought him out was Claire.

The secretary of the African-American Teachers' Association had called and, only moderately embarrassed, had said it would be better for him not to attend the party he was supposed to be keynote speaker at. "Probably best for everybody."

Well, he'd have been perfectly content to slink back home. But sitting in his City Hall office beside him on the couch, Claire had had a different idea. "Let's get drunk and go watch the goddamn fireworks."

"I don't know," Kennedy had said dubiously.

"Well, I do. You're not the sulking kind, honey. Go out with your head high."

And he'd thought for a few seconds and decided it was the smartest thing he'd heard all night. She'd tracked down a bottle of Moët and they'd drunk it on the way here.

As they wound through the crowd on the reviewing stand Kennedy shook the hand of Congressman Lanier, who obviously recognized Agent Ardell for exactly what he was – a jailer.

Lanier probably could think of nothing to say that

didn't sound like gloating so he merely tipped his head and offered a very unflirtatious "Claire, you're beautiful tonight."

"Paul," she said and, nodding to the quiet Mrs. Lanier, added, "Mindy."

"Jerry," Lanier asked, "what's the latest on the shootings?"

"I'm still waiting to hear."

"We've got room for you right over there, Mayor," said a junior aide, pointing at a deserted bank of orange folding chairs behind the other viewers. "Your friend too." He glanced at the large agent.

"No, no," Kennedy said. "We'll just sit on the stairs."

"No, please . . ."

But, for the moment at least, Kennedy retained some social autonomy, even if he had no fiscal, and he waved off Lanier and the aide. He sat down beside Claire on the top step, dropping his jacket on the wood for her to sit on. C. P. Ardell seemed dense but he was apparently sensitive enough to know what kind of embarrassment the mayor would be feeling at the presence of a federal agent so the big man sat a few feet away from the mayor and his wife, didn't hover over them.

"Used to come here when I was a kid," the agent said to the mayor. "Every Sunday."

This surprised Kennedy. Most FBI agents were transplants to the area. "You grew up here?"

"Sure did. Wouldn't live in Maryland or Virginia for a million dollars."

"Where's your home, Agent Ardell?" Claire asked him.

"Near the zoo. Just off the parkway."

Kennedy laughed faintly. At least if he had to be

under detention he was glad his turnkey was a loyal citizen.

Feeling warm from the champagne, he moved closer to Claire and took her hand. They looked out over the Mall. Gazed at the hundreds of thousands of people milling about. Kennedy was pleased to see that there was no microphone on the reviewing stand. He didn't want to hear any speeches. Didn't want anybody to offer the mike to him for impromptu remarks – Lord, what on earth could he say? All he wanted was to sit with his wife and watch the fireworks blossom over his city. And forget the agony of this day. In his radio plea to the Digger he'd referred to this as the last day of the year. But it was, apparently, the end of many things: his chance to help the city, the lives of many of his residents, so horribly killed.

The end of his tenure in office too; Lanier and the others in Congress who wanted to snatch the District away from its people would probably be able to leverage the Digger incident into something impeachable – maybe interference with a police investigation, something like that. Add in the Board of Education scandal and Kennedy could be out of office within a few months. Wendell Jefferies and all the other aides would be swept out with him. And that would be the end of Project 2000.

The end of all his hopes for the District. His poor city would be set back another ten years. Maybe the next mayor—

But then Kennedy noticed something odd. That the spectators seemed to be moving east purposefully, as if they were being herded. Why? he wondered. The view was perfect from here.

He turned to Claire, started to mention this but suddenly she tensed.

"What's that?" she asked.

"What?"

"Gunshots," she said. "I hear gunshots."

Kennedy looked into the air, wondering if the sound perhaps was the fireworks, starting early. But, no. All he saw was the dark, cloudy sky, pierced by the white shaft of the Washington Monument.

Then they heard the screaming.

Czisman's shots did what he'd intended.

When he'd realized that nobody had seen the Digger – and that he himself had no clean shot at the killer – he'd fired twice into the air, to scatter the people and clear a line of fire.

The explosions sent the crowd into a panic. Howling, screaming, everyone scattered, knocking the Digger to his knees. In seconds the area immediately in front of the Vietnam Memorial was virtually empty.

Czisman saw Kincaid too, flinging himself to the ground and pulling a small automatic out of his pocket. The man hadn't seen the Digger – a thick stand of evergreens separated them.

That was fine with Czisman. *He* wanted the killer.

The Digger was rising slowly. The machine gun had fallen from his coat and he looked around for it. He caught sight of Czisman and froze, gazing at him with the strangest eyes Czisman had ever seen.

In those eyes was less feeling than in an animal's. Whoever the mastermind behind the killings had been – the one lying on the slab in the morgue – that man wasn't pure evil. He would've had emotions and thoughts and desires. He *might* have reformed, *might* have developed the nub of a conscience that was possibly within him.

But the Digger? No. There was no redemption for this machine. There was only death.

The killer with a man's mind and the devil's heart . . .

The Digger glanced at the gun in Czisman's hand. Then his eyes rose again and he stared at the journalist's face.

Kincaid was rising to his feet, shouting at Czisman, "Drop the weapon, drop the weapon!"

Czisman ignored him and lifted the gun toward the Digger. With a shaking voice he began to say, "You—"

But there was a soft explosion at the Digger's side. A tuft of the man's overcoat popped outward. Czisman felt the hard fist in his chest, dropped to his knees. He fired his own gun but the shot went wide.

The Digger removed his hand from his pocket, holding a small pistol. He aimed at Czisman's chest once more, fired twice.

Czisman flew backward under the impact of the rounds.

As he tumbled to the cold earth, seeing distant lights reflected in the wall of the Vietnam Memorial, he muttered, "You . . ."

Czisman tried to get his gun . . . But where was it? It had fallen from his hand.

Where, where? . . .

Kincaid was running for cover, looking around, confused. Czisman saw the Digger walk slowly toward his machine gun, pick it up and fire a burst toward Kincaid, who dove behind a tree. The Digger trotted away, crouching, through the bushes toward the fleeing crowds.

Czisman groped for his gun. "You . . . you . . . you . . ." But his hand fell to the ground like a rock and then there was only blackness.

A few people . . .

Click, cllck . . .

Funny . . .

A few people were nearby, huddled on the ground, looking around. Frightened. The Digger could easily have shot them but then the police would see him.

"The last time kill as many as you can," said the man who tells him things.

But how many is as many as you can?

One, two, three, four, five . . .

The Digger doesn't think he meant only a half dozen. *The last minute of the last hour of the . . .*

So he's hurrying after them, doing the things he ought to do, looking scared, running the way the crowd does, hunching over. Things like that.

You're . . . you're . . . you're the best.

Who was that man back there? he wonders. He wasn't a policeman. Why was he trying to shoot me?

The Digger has hidden the . . . *click, click . . .* the Uzi under his overcoat, the overcoat that he loves because Pamela gave it to him.

There are shouts nearby but they don't seem to be directed at him so he doesn't pay any attention. Nobody notices him. He's moving through the grass, near the bushes and trees, along that wide street – Constitution Avenue. There are buses and cars and thousands and thousands of people. If he can get to them he can kill hundreds.

He sees museums, like the one where they have the

picture of the entrance to hell. Museums are fun, he thinks. Tye would like museums. Maybe when they're in California, out *West*, they can go to a museum together.

More shouting. People are running. There are men and women and children all over the place. Police and agents. They have Uzis or Mac-10s or, *click*, pistols like the Digger's pistols and like the pistol of the fat man who just tried to shoot him. But these men and women aren't shooting because they don't know who to shoot at. The Digger is just one of the crowd.

Click, click.

How far does he have to go to get to more people?

A few hundred feet, he guesses.

He's trotting toward them. But his path is taking him away from Tye – from the car parked on Twenty-second Street. He doesn't like that thought. He wants to get the shooting over with and get back to the boy. When he gets to the crowd he'll spin like a whirligig, watch the people fall like leaves in a Connecticut forest then go back to the boy.

> *When I travel on the road,*
> *I love you all the more.*

Spin, spin, spin . . .

They'll fall like Pamela fell with the rose on her chest and the yellow flashing flower in her hand.

Fall, fall, fall . . .

More people with guns are running over the grass.

Suddenly, nearby, he hears explosions, cracks and bangs and pops.

Are people shooting at him?

No, no . . . Ah, look!

Above him flowers are blossoming in the air. There's smoke and brilliant flowers, red and yellow. Also blue and white.

Fireworks.

His watch beeps.

It's midnight.

Time to shoot.

But the Digger can't shoot just yet. There aren't enough people.

The Digger keeps moving toward the crowd. He can shoot *some*, but not enough to make the man who tells him things happy.

Crack . . .

A bullet streaks past him.

Now someone *is* shooting at him.

Shouting.

Two men in FBI jackets in the middle of the field to the Digger's right have seen him. They're standing in front of a wooden platform, decorated with beautiful red and blue and white banners, like the ones the fat New Year's babies wear.

He turns toward them and fires the Uzi through his coat. He doesn't want to do this – to put more holes in the beautiful dark coat Pamela gave him but he has to. He can't let anyone see the gun.

The men clutch at their faces and necks as if bees are stinging them and fall down.

The Digger turns and continues moving after the crowds.

Nobody has seen him shoot the men.

He only has to walk a couple of hundred feet further and he'll be surrounded by lots of people, looking around like everybody else, looking for the killer, looking for salvation. And then he can shoot and shoot and shoot.

Spinning like a whirligig in a Connecticut forest.

28

12.00

W hen the first bullets crashed into the wood around him Jerry Kennedy shoved Claire off the platform and onto the cold ground.

He jumped after her and lay on his side, shielding her from the bullets. "Honey?" Kennedy shouted.

"I'm all right!" Her voice was edgy with panic. "What's going on?"

"Somebody's shooting. It must be him! The killer – he must be here!"

They lay side by side, huddling, smelling dirt and grass and spilled beer.

One person on the platform had been hit – the young aide, who'd been shot in the arm as Congressman Lanier leapt behind him for cover. But no one else seemed to be injured. Most of the shots had been wild. The killer had been aiming at the two agents in front of the viewing stand, not at anyone on the platform.

Kennedy could see the agents were dead.

The mayor glanced up and saw C. P. Ardell, holding

his black pistol in front of him, looking over the field. He stood tall, wasn't even crouching.

"Agent Ardell!" Kennedy shouted. "There he is! There!"

But the agent didn't shoot. Kennedy climbed halfway up the stairs, tugged at the man's cuff, pointing. "He's getting away. Shoot!"

The huge agent held his automatic out in front of him like a sharpshooter.

"Ardell!"

"Ahnnnn," the agent was saying.

"What're you waiting for?" Kennedy cried.

But C.P. Ardell just kept saying, "Ahnnnnn, ahnnnn," gazing out over the field.

Then Ardell started to turn, slowly revolving, looking north, then east, then south . . . Looking toward the wall of the Vietnam Memorial, then at the trees, then at the Washington Monument, then at the flag that decorated the backdrop of the viewing platform.

"Ahnnnn."

The agent turned once more, a complete circle, and fell onto his back, staring up at the sky with glazed eyes. Kennedy saw the top of his head was missing.

"Oh, Jesus!"

Claire gave a gasp as a stream of the man's blood cascaded down the stairs and pooled inches from her face.

The agent said "Ahnnnnnn" once more, blew a slick bubble from his mouth. Kennedy took the man's hand. It quivered slightly. Then it was still.

Kennedy stood up. He looked past the podium, which Lanier, his aide, and another congressman were hiding behind. The Mall was dim – there were no lights on because of the fireworks – but in the headlights from the emergency vehicles Kennedy had a view of the chaos. He was looking for the silhouette of the Digger.

"What the hell're you doing in my city?" he whispered. Then his voice rose to a shout, "What the hell are you doing here?"

"Jerry, get down!" Claire pleaded.

But he stayed where he was, scanned the field, trying to find the dark form of the killer once more.

Where was he? Where?

Then he saw a man in the shadows, walking fast along a row of cherry trees not far from Constitution Avenue.

He was making for the crowds farther east on the Mall.

Kennedy stood and pried the pistol from the dead agent's hand.

"Oh, Jerry, no," Claire said. "No! Call on your phone."

"There's no time."

"No . . ." She was crying softly.

He paused, turned to her. Touched her cheek with his left hand and kissed her forehead the way he always did before they shut the light out and went to sleep. Then he leapt over the huddling lumps of a young politico couple and sprinted over the grass.

He thought: I'm going to have a fucking heart attack, I'm going to have a heart attack and die . . . But he didn't slow down.

The familiar sights of the city were around him: The white Washington Monument, the stark cherry trees, the tower of the Smithsonian, the gray neo-Gothic buildings of the museums, the tourist buses . . .

Kennedy gasped and ran, gasped and ran.

The Digger was a hundred feet away from him. Then ninety feet . . .

Eighty feet.

Kennedy watched the killer move closer to the crowd. He pulled a black machine gun from under his coat.

There was a shot from the trees to Kennedy's left. Then another and two more.

Yes! Kennedy thought. They've seen him!

But suddenly a tuft of grass beside Kennedy flew into the air and another bullet snapped over his head.

Jesus! They were shooting at *him*. They'd seen a man with a gun running toward the crowds and assumed he was the killer.

"No, no!" He crouched then pointed toward the Digger. "It's him!"

The killer was in the tree line, moving around to the side of the crowd. In just a minute he'd be only fifty feet from them and could kill hundreds with a single burst from the gun.

Hell with it. Let's just hope the cops're bad shots. Kennedy began to sprint forward again.

There was one more shot in his direction but then someone must have identified him. Shouts over the bullhorn ordered the officers to cease fire.

"Get back!" Kennedy was shouting to the crowd.

But there was nowhere for them to go. They were packed together like cattle. Thousands. Some staring at the fireworks, some looking around, uneasy and confused.

Kennedy steered toward the trees, his chest on fire, speeding toward the place where he'd last seen the Digger.

I'm dying, he thought. He pictured himself on the ground, retching in agony as his heart shut down.

And besides, what on earth am I doing? What kind of idiocy is this? The last time he'd fired a gun had been at summer camp with his son – thirty years ago. He'd fired three shots and missed the target completely, to the boy's shame.

Running, running . . .

Closer to the tree line, closer to the Digger.

Agents had seen where he was headed and must have assumed that he was after the killer. A rough line of a dozen men and women in tactical police gear were jogging toward him.

The Digger stepped out of the bushes, pointing the machine gun toward the crowd. He nodded to himself.

Kennedy stopped running, lifted Ardell's pistol and aimed it toward the killer. He wasn't even sure what to aim at, how the sights on the heavy gun worked. Whether he should aim high or low. But Kennedy was a strong man and he held the gun very steadily in his hand. He remembered how he and his eldest son stood side by side at camp, listening to the camp counselor: "Squeeze the trigger. Don't jerk it." The boys giggling at the word.

And so tonight Jerry Kennedy squeezed.

The explosion was huge and he wasn't prepared for the pistol to buck so high in the air.

Kennedy lowered the gun again. Squinted over the dim field. He laughed out loud.

Christ, I did it! I hit him!

The Digger was on the ground, grimacing and clutching at his left arm.

Kennedy fired again. This bullet missed and he fired another round, two more.

The Digger rolled to his feet. He started to aim at Kennedy but the mayor fired again. This was a miss too – the bullet struck a tree – but it was close and the Digger stumbled backward. He fired a short burst toward Kennedy. All the bullets missed.

The killer looked to his left, where the line of agents and cops was moving toward him. He aimed toward them and must have pulled the trigger. Kennedy heard nothing, saw no flash from the end of the gun. But one agent fell and bits of grass and dirt leapt into the air. The other agents dropped into defensive postures on the ground. They aimed toward him but no one fired. Kennedy saw why – because the crowds were directly behind the Digger. They would surely have hit some people in the crowd.

Only Kennedy had a clear shot.

He stood up from his crouch and fired five more times at the black bundle on the ground, driving the Digger back, away from the crowds.

Then the gun clicked. It was empty.

He squinted, looking past the pistol.

The dark form of the Digger was gone.

Panting now.

Something within the Digger snaps and he forgets everything the man who tells him things told him. He forgets about killing as many people as he can and forgets about people seeing his face and forgets about spinning around like a leafy seed in Connecticut. He wants to get out of here and get back to Tye.

The bullets that man was firing came so close . . . He nearly killed me. And if he gets killed what's going to happen to the boy?

He drops into a crouch and sprints toward a tour bus. The engine is idling, a cloud of exhaust rises from the tailpipe.

His arm hurts so badly.

Pain . . .

Look, there's a red rose on his arm!

But, oh, how it . . . *click* . . . how it hurts.

He hopes he never feels pain like this again. He hopes Tye never ever has to feel pain like this.

He looks for the man who shot him. Why did he do that? The Digger doesn't understand. He's just doing what he's been told.

> *Even if you loved me less,*
> *I'd love you all the more.*

Fireworks blossom over the Mall.

A line of police and agents is moving closer. They start shooting. The Digger climbs up the stairs of the bus and turns, spraying bullets at the cluster of pursuing agents.

There's a huge star burst of orange.

"Oh, my," he says, thinking: Tye would like that.

He breaks a window in the bus and carefully aims his gun.

29

12.15

P arker and Cage crouched behind a squad car.
     Neither of them had much tactical training and
knew it was prudent to leave the shoot-'em-up stuff to
the younger, more experienced agents.

Besides, as Cage had just shouted to Parker a minute ago, it was a goddamn war zone. Bullets flying
everywhere. The Digger had good protection inside the
bus and was firing careful bursts through the shattered
windows. Len Hardy was pinned down with several
other District cops on the other side of Constitution
Avenue.

Cage pressed his side and winced. He hadn't been
hit but a stream of bullets had ripped through the sheet
steel of the car they were using for cover and he'd flung
himself to the ground, landing hard on his side.

"You okay?" Parker asked.

"Rib," the man moaned. "Feels broken. Shit."

Agents had cleared the area around the bus and were
peppering it freely whenever they thought there was a

target. They'd flattened the tires so the Digger couldn't drive away although Parker could see there was no chance of that happening in any case – the broad avenue was one huge traffic jam for a half mile in both directions.

Parker heard snippets of radio transmissions.

"No target presenting . . . Get a flash-bang inside. Who's got a grenade? Two down on Constitution. We got . . . anybody copying? We got two down on Constitution . . . Snipers in position."

Then Cage glanced up over the hood of the torn car.

"Jesus," Cage gasped, "what's the fucking kid doing?"

Parker looked too, toward Constitution Avenue, following the agent's gaze. There was Len Hardy, his tiny gun in his hand, crawling from tree to tree toward the bus, lifting his head and firing a shot occasionally.

Parker said, "He's nuts. He doesn't even have body armor."

"Len!" Cage shouted, then winced at the pain.

Parker took over. "Len! . . . Len Hardy! Get back. Let SWAT handle it."

But he didn't hear them. Or pretended he hadn't.

Cage wheezed, "It's like he's got some kind of death wish."

Hardy stood and sprinted toward the bus, emptying his weapon as he ran. Even Parker knew this wasn't proper procedure for a tactical operation.

Parker saw the Digger move toward the back of the bus, where he'd have a good shot at Hardy. The detective didn't notice. He huddled on the ground, completely exposed, reloading.

"Len!" Parker cried. "Get under cover."

"He doesn't even have Speedloaders," Cage muttered. Hardy was slipping the new shells into his revolver one by one.

The Digger moved closer to the back of the bus.

"No!" Parker muttered, knowing he was going to see the young man die.

"Jesus," Cage cried, gasping.

Then Hardy looked up and must have realized what was happening. He lifted the gun and fired three more times – all the shells he'd been able to reload – and then he stumbled backward.

"He's dead," Cage muttered. "He's dead."

Parker saw the killer's silhouette near the emergency exit in the back of the bus – where he had a perfect shot at Hardy, sprawled on the street.

But before the Digger could fire, an agent rolled out from behind a car and crouched, firing a stream of bullets into the bus. Blood sprayed the inside windows. Then there was a sensuous *whoosh*, and fire erupted inside the bus. A flaming stream of fuel flowed to the curb.

Hardy struggled to his feet and ran for cover behind a District squad car. He sat with his head in his hands, shaken but unhurt.

There was a heartrending scream from inside the bus as the interior disappeared in orange fire. Parker saw the Digger, a mass of boiling flames, rise once then fall into the aisle of the bus.

There were soft snaps from inside – like the popcorn that Stephie had made earlier for her brother's surprise dessert – as the Digger's remaining bullets exploded in the fire. A tree on Constitution Avenue caught fire and illuminated the macabre spectacle with an incongruously cheerful glow.

Slowly the agents rose from cover and approached the bus. They stood at a cautious distance as the last of the burning ammunition detonated and the fire trucks arrived and began pumping foam on the charred hulk of the vehicle.

When the flames had died down, two agents in full body armor made their way to the door of the bus and looked inside.

Suddenly a series of loud bangs shook the Mall.

Every agent and cop nearby dropped into defensive positions, lifting their weapons.

But the sounds were only the fireworks – orange spiders, blue star bursts, white concussion shells. The glorious finale of the show.

The two agents stepped out of the doorway of the bus, pulled their helmets off.

A moment later Parker heard one of the agent's staticky transmission in Cage's radio. "Vehicle is secure," he said. "Subject confirmed dead" was the unemotional epitaph for the killer.

As they walked back to the Vietnam Memorial Parker told Cage about Czisman, how the shooting had started.

"He fired warning shots. He hadn't done that, the Digger would've killed a hundred people right here. Maybe me too."

"What the hell was he up to?"

In front of them a cop was covering Henry Czisman's body.

Cage bent down, grimacing in pain. A medic had poked his abdomen and proclaimed that the fall had resulted in the predicted broken rib. The agent was taped then given some Tylenol 3. The most frustrating part of the injury seemed to be that shrugging was momentarily too painful for him.

The agent pulled the yellow rubberized sheet away from the corpse. He went through the journalist's pockets. Took out his wallet. Then he found something else.

"What's this?" He lifted a book out of the man's jacket pocket. Parker saw that it was a little gem of a book: Leather-bound, hand-stitched pages, not "perfect" – glued – binding as in mass-market books. The paper was vellum, which in Thomas Jefferson's day was smoothed animal skin but nowadays was very high-quality cloth paper. The edges of the paper were marbleized in red and gold.

And inside, the calligraphic handwriting – presumably Czisman's – was as beautiful as an artist's. Parker couldn't help but admire it.

Cage flipped through it, paused at several pages, read them, shaking his head. He handed it to Parker. "Check this out."

Parker frowned, looking at the title, written in gold ink on the cover. *A Chronicle of Sorrow.*

He opened it. Read out loud. "To the memory of my wife, Anne, the Butcher's first victim."

The book was divided into sections. "Boston." "White Plains." And photographs of crime scenes had been pasted inside. The first one was headed "Hartford." Parker turned the page and read, "From the *Hartford News-Times*." Czisman had copied the text of the article. It was dated in November of last year.

Parker read, "'Three Killed in Holdup . . . Hartford

Police are still searching for the man who walked into the offices of the *News-Times* on Saturday and opened fire with a shotgun, killing three employees in the classified advertising department.

"'The only description of the killer was that he was a male of medium build, wearing a dark overcoat. A police spokesman said that his motive may have been to divert law enforcement authorities while his accomplice robbed an armored truck making a delivery to a bank on the other side of town. The second gunman shot and killed the driver of the truck and his assistant. He escaped with $4,000 in cash.'"

Cage muttered, "Killed three people for four G's. That's him all right."

Parker looked up. "One of the clerks killed at the paper was Anne Czisman. She was his wife."

"So he wanted the prick as much as we did," Cage said.

"Czisman was using us to get to the unsub and the Digger. That's why he wanted to see the body in the morgue so much. And that's why he was following me. Bait. He used me as bait."

Revenge . . .

"This book . . . it was his way of dealing with his grief." Parker crouched and reverently pulled the sheet back up over the man's face once more.

"Let's call Lukas," he said to Cage. "Give her the news."

At FBI headquarters Margaret Lukas was in the employees' lobby on Pennsylvania Avenue, briefing the deputy director, a handsome man with a politician's trim graying hair. She'd heard the reports that the

Digger was on the Mall and that there had been shooting. Lukas was desperately eager to get to the Mall herself but since she was primary on the case, protocol dictated that she keep the senior administrators in the Bureau informed.

Her phone buzzed. And she answered fast, superstitiously not letting herself hope that they'd captured him.

"Lukas here."

"Margaret," Cage said.

And she knew immediately from his tone that they'd nailed the killer. It was a sound in a cop's voice you learn early in your career.

"Collared or tagged?"

Arrested or dead, she meant.

"Tagged," Cage responded.

Lukas came as close to saying a prayer of Thanksgiving as she'd come in five years.

"And, get this, the mayor winged him."

"What?"

"Yep, Kennedy. Got off a few shots. That saved lives."

She relayed this news to the deputy director.

"You okay?" she asked Cage.

"Fine," Cage responded. "Cracked a rib while I was covering my ass is all."

But her gut tightened. She heard something in his voice, a tone, a hollowness.

Jackie, it's Tom's mother . . . Jackie, I have to tell you something. The airline just called . . . Oh, Jackie . . .

"But?" she asked quickly. "What happened? Is it Kincaid?"

"No, he's okay," the agent said softly.

"Tell me."

"He got C. P., Margaret. I'm sorry. He's dead."

She closed her eyes. Sighed. The fury steamed through her again, fury that she herself hadn't had a chance to park a bullet in the Digger's heart.

Cage continued. "Not even a firefight. The Digger shot toward where the mayor was sitting. C. P. just happened to be in the wrong place."

And it was the place that *I'd* sent him to, she thought bitterly. Christ.

She'd known the agent for three years . . . Oh, no . . .

Cage was adding, "The Digger capped four other friendlies and we've got three injured. Looks like six civies wounded. Still a half-dozen reported missing but no bodies. They probably just scattered and their families haven't found them yet. Oh, and that Czisman?"

"Who, the writer?"

"Yeah. Digger got him."

"What?"

"He wasn't a writer at all. I mean, he was but that's not what he was doing here. The Digger'd killed his wife and he was using us to get him. The Digger took him out first though."

So, it's been amateur night, she thought. Kincaid, the mayor. Czisman.

"What about Hardy?"

Cage told her that the young detective had made a one-man assault on the bus the Digger'd holed up in. "He got pretty close and had good firing position. Might've been his shots that hit the Digger. Nobody could tell what was going on."

"So he didn't shoot himself in the foot?" Lukas asked.

Cage said, "I'll tell you, it looked like he was hell-bent on killing himself but when it came right down to it he backed off and went for cover. Guess he decided to stick around for a few years."

Just like me, Lukas the changeling thought.

"Is Evans there?" Cage asked.

Lukas looked around. Surprised that the doctor wasn't here. Funny she'd thought he was coming down to the lobby to meet her. "I'm not sure where he is," she answered. "Must be upstairs still. In the document lab. Or maybe the crisis center."

"Find him and give him the good news. Tell him thanks. And tell him to submit a big bill."

"Will do. And I'll call Tobe too."

"Parker and I're gonna do crime scene with PERT then head back over there in forty-five minutes or so."

When she hung up the dep director said, "I'm going down to the Mall. Who's in charge?"

She nearly said, Parker Kincaid. But caught herself. "Special Agent Cage. He's near the Vietnam Memorial with PERT."

"There'll have to be a press conference. I'll give the director a heads-up. He may want to make a statement too . . . Say, you miss a party tonight, Lukas?"

"That's the thing about holidays, sir. There'll always be one next year." She laughed. "Maybe we ought to make up T-shirts with that saying on them."

He smiled stiffly. Then asked, "How's our whistle-blower doing? Any more threats?"

"Moss? I haven't checked on him lately," she said. "But I definitely have to."

"You think there's a problem?" The dep director frowned.

"Oh, no. But he owes me a beer."

In the deserted document lab Dr. John Evans folded up his cell phone. He clicked the TV set off.

So they'd killed the Digger.

The news reports were sporadic but as best Evans could tell there'd been minimal fatalities – not like the Metro shooting and not like the yacht. Still, from the TV images, Constitution Avenue looked like a war zone. Smoke, a hundred emergency vehicles, people hiding behind cars, trees, bushes.

Evans pulled on his bulky parka and walked to the corner of the lab. He slipped the heavy thermos into his knapsack, slung it over his shoulder then pushed through the double doors and started down the dim corridor.

The Digger . . . What a fascinating creature. One of the few people in the world who really was, as he'd told the agents, profile-proof.

At the elevator he paused, looked at the building directory, trying to orient himself. There was a map. He studied it. FBI headquarters was much more complicated than he'd imagined.

His finger hovered over the DOWN button but before he could push it a voice called, "Hi." He turned. Saw somebody walking toward him from the second bank of elevators.

"Hi, there, Doctor," the voice called again. "You heard?"

It was that young detective. Len Hardy. His overcoat was no longer perfectly pressed. It was stained and sooty. There was a cut on his cheek.

Evans pushed the DOWN button. Twice. Impatient. "Just saw it on the news," he told Hardy. He shrugged the backpack off his shoulder. The doctor grunted as he caught the bag in the crook of his arm and began to unzip it.

Hardy glanced absently at the stained backpack. He said, "Man, I'll tell you, I spoke a little too fast there, volunteering to go after that guy. I went a little crazy. Some kind of battlefield hysteria."

"Uh-huh," Evans said. He reached inside the backpack and took out the thermos.

Hardy continued, chatting away. "He nearly nailed me. Shook me up some. I was maybe thirty feet from him. Saw his eyes, saw the muzzle of his gun. Man . . . I was suddenly real happy to be alive."

"That happens," Evans said. Where the hell was the elevator?

Hardy glanced at the silver metal cylinder. "Say, you know where Agent Lukas is?" the detective asked, looking up the dark corridor.

"I think she's downstairs," Evans said, unscrewing the lid to the thermos. "She had to brief somebody. The lobby on Ninth. Didn't you just come that way?"

"I came in through the garage."

The doctor pulled the top off the thermos. "You know, Detective, the way you told everybody about the Diggers and Levelers? You made it sound like you didn't trust me." He turned toward Hardy.

Evans looked down. He saw the black, silenced pistol Hardy was pointing at his face.

"Trust didn't have anything to do with it," Hardy said.

Evans dropped the thermos. Coffee splashed onto the floor. He saw the flash of yellow light from the muzzle of the gun. And that was all he saw.

IV

THE PUZZLE MASTER

— ● ◆ ● —

That handwriting was the worstest thing against me.

—Bruno Hauptmann,
referring to the evidence in his trial for
the Lindbergh baby kidnapping

30

The agent was young enough to still be thrilled at the idea of being an FBI employee. So he didn't mind one bit that he'd been assigned the midnight-to-8 shift New Year's Eve in the Bureau's Security Center on the third floor of headquarters.

There was also the fact that Louise, the agent he was working with, wore a tight blue blouse and short black skirt and was flirting with him.

Definitely flirting, he decided.

Well, okay, she was talking about her cat. But the body language told him it was flirting. And her bra was black and visible through the blouse. Which was a message too.

The agent continued to gaze at the ten TV monitors that were his responsibility. Louise, on his left, had another ten. They were linked to more than sixty security cameras located in and around headquarters. The scenes on the monitors changed every five seconds as the cameras sequenced.

Louise of the black bra was nodding absently as he talked about his parents' place on the Chesapeake Bay. The intercom brayed.

It couldn't have been Sam or Ralph – the two agents he and Louise had replaced a half hour ago; they had total-clearance entry cards and would've just walked inside.

The agent hit the intercom button. "Yes?"

"It's Detective Hardy. District P.D."

"Who's Hardy?" the agent asked Louise.

She shrugged and went back to her monitors.

"Yes?"

The voice crackled, "I'm working with Margaret Lukas."

"Oh, on the Metro shooter case?"

"Right."

The legendary Margaret Lukas. The security agent hadn't been with the Bureau very long but even he knew that Lukas would someday be the first woman director of the FBI. The tech pushed the enter button, spun around to face the door.

"Can I help you?

"I'm afraid I'm lost," Hardy said.

"Happens around here." He smiled. "Where you headed?"

"I'm trying to find the document lab. I got lost on the way to get some coffee."

"Documents? That's the seventh floor. Turn left. Can't miss it."

"Thanks."

"What's this?" Louise said suddenly. "Hey, what *is* this?"

The agent glanced at her as she hit a button to stop the

video camera scan and pointed to one of the monitors. It showed a man lying on his back not far from where they were now, on this floor. The monitors were black and white but a large pool of what was obviously blood ran from his head.

"Oh, Christ," she muttered and reached for the phone. "It looks like Ralph."

From behind them came a soft thunk. Louise gave a sudden jerk and grunted as the front of her blouse disappeared in a mist of blood.

"Oh," she gasped. "What— ?"

Another pop. The bullet struck the back of her head and she pitched forward.

The young agent turned toward the doorway, lifting his hands, crying, "No, no."

In a calm voice Hardy said, "Relax."

"Please!"

"Relax," he repeated. "I just have a few questions."

"Don't kill me. Please—"

"Now," Hardy asked matter-of-factly, "your computers're running Secure-Chek software?"

"I—"

"I'll let you live if you tell me everything I ask."

"Yes." He started crying. "Secure-Chek."

"What version?"

"Six oh."

"And if you don't log-in at regular intervals a Code forty-two goes out over the Inter-Gov System?"

"That's right . . . Oh, look, mister." He glanced at the body of the woman beside him, which twitched twice. Blood flowed into the control panel. "Oh, God . . ."

Speaking slowly, Hardy asked, "You started your shift at midnight?"

"Please, I . . ."

"Midnight?" he repeated, a schoolteacher coaching a child.

The agent nodded.

"What was your first log-in time?"

He was crying hard now. "Twelve twenty-one."

"When's the next time you have to log in?"

"One oh seven."

Hardy glanced at the clock on the wall. He nodded.

Panic in his voice, the young agent continued. "On holidays we use a pattern of increasing intervals, so after the second log-in we—"

"That's all right," Hardy reassured the agent then shot him twice in the head and pushed the button to release the door.

The man who was not Detective Len Hardy, a fictional name, but was in reality Edward Fielding made his way to the elevator.

He had until 1:07 before the automated alarm would go off.

Plenty of time.

The building was virtually deserted but still he walked the way he knew he should walk. With an aura not of urgency but of preoccupation. So if he were to run into one of the few remaining agents here they'd merely glance at his pass and, judging Fielding's demeanor, decide to let him continue on to wherever he was headed on his important business.

He inhaled deeply, took in the smells of the laboratory, the offices, the morgue. Feeling a wrenching thrill to be here – in the center of the law enforcement universe. The corridors of FBI headquarters. He remembered, a year ago, the Digger muttering insistently about going to an art museum in Hartford. Fielding had agreed and the crazed man had stood for an hour in front of a Doré illustration from the *Divine Comedy*: Dante and Virgil about to descend into hell. This is just what Fielding felt now – as if he were on a tour of the underworld.

As he walked through the hallways he spoke silently to his teammates. No, Agent Lukas and Parker Kincaid and Dr. John Evans . . . No, my motive isn't revenge for faded politics or terrorism or exposing social injustice. Nor is it greed. Twenty million? Christ, I could've asked for ten times that.

No, my motive is simply perfection.

The idea of the perfect crime was a cliché, true. But Fielding had learned something interesting when he'd been studying linguistics, looking for just the right words and phrases to use in the extortion note. In an article in the *American Journal of Linguistics* a philologist – a language expert – had written that although serious writers are told to avoid them, clichés have value because they describe fundamental truths in universally comprehensible terms.

The perfect crime.

Fielding's holy chalice.

Perfection . . . It was intoxicating to him. Perfection was everything – the way he ironed his shirts and polished his shoes and trimmed his ear hairs, the way he set up his crimes, the way they were executed.

If Fielding had had an aptitude for the law he'd have been a lawyer and devoted his life to creating the perfect defenses for impossibly guilty clients. If he'd had a lust for the outdoors he'd have taught himself everything there was to learn about mountain climbing and made the perfect solo ascent to the summit of Everest.

But those activities didn't excite him.

Crime did.

This was just a fluke, he supposed, to be born utterly amoral. The way some men are bald and some cats have six toes. It was purely nature, he'd decided, not nurture. His parents were loving and dependable; dullness was their only sin. Fielding's father had been an insurance executive in Hartford, his mother a homemaker. He experienced no deprivation, no abuse. From an early age, though, he simply believed that the law didn't apply to him. It made no sense. Why, he spent hours wondering, should man put restraints on himself? Why shouldn't we go wherever our desires and minds take us?

Though it was some years before he learned it, Fielding had been born with a pure criminal personality, a textbook sociopath.

So while he studied algebra and calculus and biology at St. Mary's High School the young man also worked at his true calling.

And, as in all disciplines, that education had ups and downs.

Fielding, in juvenile detention for setting fire to the boyfriend of a girl he had a crush on (should've parked my car three or four blocks away).

Fielding, beaten nearly to death by two police officers whom he was blackmailing with photos of transvestites giving them blow jobs in their squad car (should have had a strong-arm accomplice with him).

Fielding, successfully extorting a major canned-food

manufacturer by feeding their cattle an enzyme that mimicked a positive test for botulism (though he never picked up the money at the drop because he couldn't figure out how to get away with the cash undetected).

Live and learn . . .

College didn't interest him much. The students at Bennington had money but they left their dorm rooms open and there was no challenge in robbing them. He enjoyed occasional felonious assaults on coeds – it *was* challenging to rape someone in such a way that she doesn't realized she's being molested. But Fielding's lust was for the game itself, not sex, and by his junior year he was focusing on what he called "clean crimes," like robbery. Not "messy crimes," like rape. He buckled down to get his psych degree and dreamt about escaping from Ben & Jerry land and into the real world, where he could practice his craft.

Over the next ten years Fielding, back in his native Connecticut, did just that: honed and practiced. Robbery mostly. He avoided business crimes like check kiting and securities fraud because of the paper trails. He avoided drugs and hijacking because you couldn't work alone and Fielding never met anyone he trusted.

He was twenty-seven when he killed for the first time.

An opportunistic – an impulse – crime, very unlike him. He was having a cappuccino at a coffee shop in a strip mall outside of Hartford. He saw a woman come out of a jewelry store with a package. There was something about the way she walked – slightly paranoid – that suggested the package contained something very expensive.

He got into his car and followed her. On a deserted

stretch of road he accelerated and pulled her over. Terrified, she thrust the bag at him and begged him to let her go.

As he stood there, beside her Chevy, Fielding realized that he hadn't worn a mask or switched plates on his car. He believed that he'd subconsciously failed to do these things because he wanted to see how he'd feel about killing. Fielding reached into the glove compartment, took out a gun and before she even had time to scream shot her twice.

He climbed back into his car, drove back to Juice 'n' Java and had another cappuccino. Ironically, he'd mused, many criminals don't kill. They're afraid to because they think they'll be more likely to be caught. In fact, if they *do* kill they'll be more likely to get away.

Still, police can be good and he was arrested several times. He was released in all those cases except one. In Florida he was collared for armed robbery and the evidence against him was strong. But he had a good lawyer, who got him a reduced sentence on condition that Fielding seek treatment at a mental hospital.

He was dreading the time he had to serve but it turned out to be an astonishing two years. In the Dade City Mental Health Facility, Fielding could taste crime. He could smell it. Many, if not most, of the convicts were there because their lawyers were quick with the insanity defense. Dumb crooks are in prison, smart ones are in hospitals.

After two years and an exemplary appearance before the Medical Review Panel, Fielding returned to Connecticut.

And the first thing he did was get a job as an aide at a hospital for the criminally insane in Hartford.

There he'd met a man named David Hughes, a fascinating creature. Fielding decided he'd probably been a pretty decent fellow until he stabbed his wife to death in a jealous rage on Christmas Day. The stabbing was a dime-a-dozen matter but what was so *interesting*, though, was what happened after hubby gave Pamela several deep puncture wounds in the lungs. She ran to the closet and found a pistol and, before she died, shot Hughes in the head.

Fielding didn't know what exactly had happened inside Hughes's cranium, neurologically speaking, but – perhaps because the aide was the first person Hughes saw when he awoke after surgery – some kind of odd bonding occurred between the two. Hughes would do whatever Fielding asked. Getting coffee, cleaning up for him, ironing shirts, cooking. It turned out that Hughes would do more than domestic chores, though – as Fielding found out one evening just after night-duty nurse Ruth Miller removed Fielding's hand from between her legs and said, "I'm reporting you, asshole."

Soon after that a worried Fielding had muttered to Hughes, "That Ruth Miller. Somebody ought to kill that bitch."

And Hughes had said, "Hmmm, okay."

"What?" Fielding had asked.

"Hmmm, okay."

"You'd kill her for me?"

"Uhm. I . . . sure."

Fielding took him for a walk on the grounds of the hospital. They had a long talk.

A day later Hughes showed up in Fielding's cubicle, covered with blood, carrying a piece of jagged glass and asking if he could have some soup.

Fielding cleaned him up, thinking he'd been a little careless about the when and where of the murder and about getting away afterward. He decided that Hughes was too good to waste on little things like this and so he told the man how to escape from the hospital and how to make his way to a nearby cottage that Fielding rented for afternoon trysts with some of the retarded patients.

It was that night that he decided how he could best put the man to use.

Hartford, then Boston, then White Plains, then Philly. Perfect crimes.

And now he was in Washington.

Committing what was turning out to be the *most* perfect crime, he decided (though reflecting that a linguist like Parker Kincaid would be troubled by the unnecessary modifier).

For the last six months he'd spent nearly eighteen hours a day planning the theft. Slowly breaching FBI security – masquerading as young Detective Hardy from the police department's Research and Statistics Department. (He'd selected his particular pseudonym because studies into the psychological impressions of names reported that "Leonard" was unthreatening and "Hardy" conjured an image of a loyal comrade.) He first infiltrated the Bureau's District of Columbia field office because that office had jurisdiction over major crimes in the District. He got to know Ron Cohen, the special agent in charge, and his assistants. He learned when SAC Cohen would be on vacation and which of his underlings would be – as the currently in-vogue term went – "primary" on a case of this magnitude. That would be, of course, Margaret Lukas, whose life he invaded as inexorably as he worked his way into the Bureau itself.

He'd camp out in conference rooms, copying voluminous crime statistics for his fictional reports, then would make trips to the vending machines and restrooms, glancing at internal FBI memos and phone books and ID documentation and procedure manuals. Meanwhile at his home and at his safe house in Gravesend he was spending time cruising the Internet and learning about government facilities, police procedures and security systems (and, yes, Parker, about foreign dialects).

Fielding made hundreds of calls to interior designers who'd worked at FBI headquarters, to the GSA, to former clerks, outside contractors, security specialists, asking innocent questions, talking about phony employee reunions, arguing about imaginary invoices. He usually managed to extract one vital fact – say, about the layout of the headquarters building, the staffing on holidays, the exits and entrances. He learned the brand and general location of security cameras in headquarters. The number and stations of the guards. The communications systems.

He'd spent a month finding the perfect front man – Gilbert Havel, a bum with no criminal record and virtually no recorded past. A man naive enough to think that someone as brilliant as Fielding needed a partner. A man easy to kill.

It was arduous work. But perfection requires patience.

And then, this morning, the Digger shot the hell out of the Metro and Fielding showed up at the Bureau doorstep, eager to help but suitably indignant about being the third wheel on the investigation. Other agents would have double- or triple-checked his credentials, called police headquarters. But not Margaret Lukas, the poor childless widow. Because here was Len Hardy, soon to be a childless widower, wracked with the same sorrow she'd struggled through five years ago.

Of *course* she accepted him into the fold without a thought.

And they'd never guessed a thing about him.

Just as he'd figured.

Because Edward Fielding knew that combating crime today is the province of the scientist. Even the psychologists who profiled the criminal mind use formulae to categorize their prey. Yet the perpetrator himself – the human being – is so often overlooked. Oh, he knew that the agents, believing the unsub to be dead, would be concentrating so hard on the extortion note, the linguistics, the handwriting, the trace evidence, and their computer programs and fancy equipment that they'd never see the real mastermind standing – literally – three feet behind them.

He now came to the elevator. The car arrived and he got inside. Fielding didn't, however, push the seventh-floor button to go to the document lab. He pushed 1B.

The car began to descend.

The FBI's evidence room is the largest forensic storage facility in the country.

It's operated around the clock and usually there's a staff of two to help the agents log in evidence and sometimes to help them carry the heavier items into the locker area or drive confiscated cars and trucks and even trailered boats into the warehouse connected to the facility.

Tonight, though, there were three agents on duty,

a decision made jointly by the deputy director and Margaret Lukas. This was because of the value of a particular item of evidence sitting in the vault at the moment.

But since it was a holiday the two men and the woman were pretty casual. They were lounging around the log-in window, drinking coffee and talking about basketball. The two men had their backs to the window.

"I *like* Rodman," said one of the male clerks.

"Oh, puh-lease," responded the other.

"Hi," said Edward Fielding, walking up to the window.

"Hey, you hear what happened with that guy on the Mall?" the woman asked him.

"No," Fielding said and shot her in the head.

The other two died reaching for their weapons. Only one managed to get his Sig-Sauer out of the holster.

Fielding reached through the window, buzzed himself in.

He counted eight video security cameras trained on the window, shelves and vault. But they sent their images to the third-floor Security room, where there was no one left alive to see the perfect crime unfolding.

Fielding lifted the keys from the dead woman's belt and opened the vault. It was a large room, about twenty by thirty, and was where agents stored drugs and cash taken from heists. In his months of research for the robbery Fielding had learned that prosecutors are obligated to present to the jury the actual cash seized during, say, a drug bust or kidnapping. This was one reason the agents would have brought the ransom money here. The other was something else he'd anticipated – that Mayor Kennedy, whom Fielding had psychologically profiled, would want to keep the cash available in case the Digger contacted him and demanded the ransom after all.

And here it was, the money.

Perfect . . .

Two huge, green canvas satchels. A red tag dangled from each strap. FEDERAL EVIDENCE. DO NOT REMOVE.

He looked at his watch. He estimated that he'd have twenty minutes before Cage and Kincaid and the other agents returned from the Mall after their shoot-out with the Digger.

Plenty of time. As long as he moved quickly.

Fielding unzipped one bag – it wasn't locked – and dumped the cash on the floor. The satchel was wired with several homing devices, as he'd known it would be. The money wrappers too, he'd learned from Tobe Geller – a trick he hadn't anticipated. He wondered if individual bills themselves had been rigged somehow. He doubted it; Geller had never said anything. Still, to make sure, Fielding reached into his pocket and took out a small silver instrument – a Trans-detect, a scanner that could sense the faintest transmission signal of any wavelength, from visual light to infrared to radio waves. He ran this over the pile of cash, just in case the Bureau techs had managed to insert a transmitter into a bill itself. But there were no signals.

Fielding tossed aside the sensor – he had no need for it any longer – and pulled a silk backpack from under his shirt. It was made of parachute material and he'd sewn it himself. He began to pack the money into the bag.

He'd asked for $20,000,000 because that was a credible amount for a scheme like this and also to give some credence to the motive of revenge for a significant event like the Vietnamese War. Fielding, however, would only be able to carry $4,000,000 – which would weigh seventy-two pounds. Generally unathletic, he'd worked out at a health club in Bethesda, Maryland, for six weeks after he'd come to the area so that he'd be strong enough to carry the cash.

The hundred-dollar bills were all traceable, of course (tracing money was easy now thanks to scanners and computers). But Fielding had considered that. In Brazil, where he would be in several days, the $4,000,000 traceable cash would become $3,200,000 in gold. Which would in turn become $3,200,000 in *untraceable* U.S. dollars and eurodollars.

And over the next few years it would easily grow to $4,000,000 once again and then beyond, the mutual fund industry and interest rates willing.

Fielding had no regrets about leaving the rest of the money. Crime can't be about greed; it must be about craft.

He packed the cash into the bag and slung it over his shoulder.

Stepping into the corridor, staggering under the weight, working his way to the elevator.

Thinking: He'd have to kill the guard at the front door, as well as anyone in the team who was still here. Tobe Geller, he thought, had gone home. But Lukas was still in the building. She definitely would have to die. Under other circumstances killing her wouldn't matter – he'd been very careful about hiding his identity and where he really lived. But the agents were much better than he'd anticipated. My God, they'd actually found the safe house in Gravesend . . . That had shaken Fielding badly. He *never* thought they'd manage that. Fortunately Gilbert Havel had been to the safe house a number of times so neighbors would see Havel's picture when the police were doing their canvassing and assume he was the man who'd rented the place – reinforcing the agents' belief that *he* was the mastermind of the crime.

And nearly finding that the *Ritzy Lady* was the site of the second attack . . . He'd sat in the document lab in horror as the computer had assembled the fragments from the note at the safe house. He'd waited for just the right moment and blurted out, "Ritz! Maybe the Ritz-Carlton?" And as soon as they'd heard that, the solution was set in stone. It would be almost impossible to think of any other possibilities.

That's how puzzle solving works, right, Parker?

And what *about* him?

Oh, he was far too smart, far too much of a risk to remain alive.

As he walked slowly down the deserted corridors he reflected that, while Fielding was the perfect criminal, Kincaid was the perfect detective.

What happens when perfect opposites meet?

But this was a rhetorical question, not a puzzle, and he didn't waste time trying to answer it. He came to the elevator and pushed the UP button.

31

12.45

Margaret Lukas swung open the door to the document lab.

She looked inside. "Hello? Dr. Evans?"

He didn't answer.

Where was he? she wondered.

She paused at the examination table, looked down at the extortion note.

The end is night.

Thinking: Maybe Parker Kincaid wasn't quite correct when he'd said that no one would make this kind of mistake.

In a way the end *is* night. Darkness and sleep and peace.

Night, take me. Darkness, take me . . .

That's what she'd thought when she'd gotten the call from her mother-in-law about the crash that killed Tom and Joey. Lying in bed that windy November night, or two nights later or three – it was all a jumble now – lying by herself, unable to breathe, unable to cry.

Thinking: Night, take me. Night, take me, please. Night, take me . . .

Lukas now stood hunched over the document examining table, gazing down, her short blond strands falling forward past her eyes, like a horse's blinders. Staring at the words of the extortion note, the swirls of the sloppy letters. Lukas remembered watching Kincaid as he'd studied the note, his lips moving faintly, as if he were interviewing a living suspect.

The end is night.

Shaking her head at her own morbidly philosophical mood, she turned and left the lab.

She walked to the elevator. Maybe Evans was waiting at the guard station. She looked absently at the indicator lights as the elevator ascended.

The hallways were deserted and she was aware of the small noises of empty buildings at night. The field office, where she worked, was located near City Hall, some blocks away, and she didn't get here very often. She didn't like headquarters very much. It was too big. And tonight, she reflected, the place was dark and spooky. And it took a lot to make Margaret Lukas spooked. She remembered Kincaid projecting the extortion note onto a screen in the lab and she'd thought: It looks like a ghost. Never would have admitted it. But that was what she thought.

Lukas sensed more ghosts now. Here in these corridors. Ghosts of agents killed in the line of duty. Ghosts of victims of the crimes that were investigated here.

And her own personal ghosts? she thought. Oh, but they were with her all the time. Her husband and son.

They never left. Nor did she want them to. The change-ling needed something to remind her of *Jackie* Lukas.

She glanced down at the floor in front of the elevator. There was a dark stain on the floor. What was it? She smelled sour coffee.

The elevator light flashed and a chime sounded. The door opened. Someone stepped out.

"Oh, hi," Lukas said. "Got some news for you."

"Hey, Margaret," said Susan Nance, juggling a dozen files. "What's up?"

"They just tagged him. Got him on the Mall."

"The *Metshoot* killer?"

"Yep."

The woman gave a thumbs up. "Excellent. Oh, Happy New Year."

"Same to you."

Lukas got on the elevator and descended to the main floor.

At the employee entrance guard station Artie looked up at her and nodded a pleasant greeting.

"Did that Dr. Evans sign out?" she asked him.

"Nope. Haven't seen him."

She'd wait for him here. Lukas sat in one of the comfortable lobby chairs. Sank down into it. She felt exhausted. She wanted to get home. She knew people said behind her back how sad it must be – a woman living alone. But it wasn't sad at all. Returning to the womb of the house was a hell of a lot better than sitting at a bar with girlfriends or going out on a date with the endless fodder of eligible – and dull – men in Washington.

Home . . .

Thinking about the report she'd have to write about METSHOOT.

Thinking about Parker Kincaid.

Focus, she told herself.

Then she remembered that she didn't have to focus anymore.

What *about* him? Well, he wanted to ask her out. She knew he did.

But she'd already decided to say no. He was a handsome, energetic man, filled with the love of children and domestic life. How appealing that seemed. But, no, she couldn't inflict herself on him, couldn't inflict the sorrow that she believed she radiated like toxic fumes.

Maybe Jackie Lukas might have had a chance with a man like Kincaid. But a changeling like Margaret never would.

Artie looked up from his paper. "Oh, forgot to say – Happy New Year, Agent Lukas."

"Happy New Year, Artie."

As the Digger smouldered with a foul reek and the fire department spurted foam onto the scorched cherry tree, as the crowds circled the burnt-out bus, Parker and Cage stood together.

The Digger's gone. So long.

Verses from Dr. Seuss trooped through his mind like some of the author's bizarre creatures.

Parker blamed his mania on a cocktail of exhaustion and adrenaline.

He called the Whos and promised them he'd be home in a half hour. Robby told his father about the air horn someone had blasted at midnight, waking up the Bradleys down the street and causing a neighborhood stir. Stephie described the sparklers in the yard with breathless, sloppy adjectives.

"Love you, Who," he said. "Be home soon."

"Love you too, Daddy," the girl said. "How's your friend?"

"He's going to be fine."

Cage was talking to an evidence tech from PERT and Parker was jockeying to get downwind of the smoke from the bus. There was an unpleasant scent – worse than the burnt rubber of the tires. Parker knew what it was and the thought of inhaling any of the Digger's ashy corpse nauseated him.

A dead psycho smouldering before him, and Parker, at the tail end of an evening like none other he'd ever had . . . Yet it's the mundane things in life that poke up like crocuses. He now thought: Hell, I don't have enough cash to pay Mrs. Cavanaugh. He patted his pockets and dug out a small wad of bills. Twenty-two bucks. Not enough. He'd have to stop at an ATM on the way home.

He glanced at a piece of paper mixed in with the money. It was the transcription of the unsub's writing they'd found earlier in the evening on the burnt yellow pad. The references to the last two sites of the attacks that he'd found on the pad of paper Tobe Geller had saved from the burning safehouse.

> . . . *two miles south. The R* . . .
> . . . *place I showed you. The black* . . .

"What's that?" Cage asked, kneading his wounded rib.

"A souvenir," Parker said, looking down at the words. "Just a souvenir."

*   *   *

Edward Fielding paused at the end of the corridor, gasping under the weight of the money on his back.

He looked toward the reception area thirty feet away and saw the short blond hair of Margaret Lukas. Beyond her was the guard, reading the newspaper. The lights were out in the corridor and even if they'd turned toward him it would have been difficult to see him clearly.

Adjusting the money more comfortably, he clutched the pistol in his right hand and started down the hallway. His leather soles tapping faintly on the tile. He noted that Lukas was facing away from him. He'd put one bullet in her head. Then as the guard looked up, he'd kill him.

Then home free.

Tap tap tap.

He closed the distance to his targets.

Perfect.

32

12.55

Margaret Lukas, gazing at the Christmas tree in the lobby, stretched like a cat.

She listened absently to footsteps coming up the hall behind her.

Two weeks ago the entryway here had been filled with presents that the agents and staffers had donated for homeless families. She'd volunteered to give away some of the toys but at the last minute she canceled and, instead, worked twelve hours on Christmas Day, investigating the killing of a black man by two whites.

Tap, tap, tap . . .

Now she wished she *hadn't* canceled on Christmas. At the time she'd reasoned that giving out toys was frivolous when she could be doing "serious" work. But now she admitted that the thought of seeing small children on the holiday was more harrowing to her than kicking in the door of a redneck gun nut in Manassas Park.

Coward, she told herself.

Tap, tap, tap . . .

She looked out the glass windows. Crowds, people returning from the Mall. She thought about the Digger. Wondered about the shoot-out, about who'd fired the shots that killed him. She'd been in two firefights in her career and remembered mostly confusion. It was so different from in the movies. Never any sense of slow motion – a gunfight in real life was five blurry seconds of utterly terrifying chaos and then it was over with.

The vivid images came *afterward*: caring for the wounded and removing the dead.

Tap . . . tap . . .

A buzzing phone startled her.

In front of her Artie answered and she absently watched his grizzled face.

"Front desk . . . Oh, hello, Agent Cage."

Suddenly the guard was frowning. He glanced at Lukas then focused past her. His eyes went wide. "Well," the guard said uneasily. "Detective Hardy? . . . He's *who?* What do you mean? . . . But he's right here, he's – Oh, Jesus."

Artie was dropping the phone, fumbling for his weapon.

Tap tap taptaptaptap . . .

Instinctively Lukas knew that the footsteps, now running toward them, were an attacker's. She fell forward just as the rounds from the silenced pistol snapped into the back of the couch where she'd been sitting, ripping Naugahyde and bits of stuffing from the upholstery.

She looked behind her, twisting around, scrabbling for cover behind a potted plant.

It was . . . Wait, it couldn't be! It was Hardy.

Firing wildly, Artie shouted, "It's him! He's the

killer. He . . . Oh, my. Oh, no . . ." The guard looked down at his chest. He'd been hit. He slumped to his knees, fell behind the desk.

Another bullet snapped through the back of the couch, near Lukas's head. She curled for cover behind the anemic palm tree so many agents had ridiculed. She cringed as a bullet was loudly deflected by the chrome pot.

Lukas was on automatic. She didn't even try to figure out what had happened or who this man really was. She looked up quickly, searching for a target. But she had to duck fast as another bullet chopped though the thick green blades of leaf inches from her face. She rolled to her left, against the wall, rose and drew a target. In a portion of a second she checked the backdrop behind Hardy and fired three fast shots.

The heavy 10-millimeter slugs just missed him and dug huge chunks out of the wall. Hardy fired twice more at her then vanished back down the corridor.

She ran to the wall beside the hallway, pressed her back against it.

The tapping footsteps receded.

Another voice from the far end of the corridor called, "What's going on? What's going on!"

Somewhere along the hallway a door slammed.

Lukas looked around the corner quickly then went back to cover. She'd seen a man down at the end of the hall, in silhouette. She dropped to her belly, drew a target, shouted, "I'm a federal agent! Identify yourself or I'll fire!"

"Ted Yan," the man called. "In Software Analysis."

Lukas knew him. He was a friend of Geller's, an

agent. But she thought: Great, I've got a computer nerd for backup.

"You alone?" she shouted.

"I'm—"

Silence.

"Ted?"

"No. There're two of us . . . Susan Nance is here with me."

Nance's voice cracked as she called, "Oh, Margaret, he got Louise in Security! She's dead. And Tony Phelps too."

Jesus. What was going on?

Ted said, "We're by the—"

"Okay, quiet," Lukas barked. "Don't give away your position. Did anybody go past you?"

"No," Ted called. "He couldn't've gotten by me. I heard a door slam in the hallway here. He's somewhere between us."

"Cover me," Lukas called.

Watching her back, Lukas ran to the guard station. Artie was unconscious but wasn't bleeding badly. She picked up the phone but Cage was no longer on the line. She hit 911, identified herself as a Justice Department agent and called in a Code 42 at FBI headquarters.

To her knowledge nobody'd ever done this, not in the entire history of the Bureau. It meant an assault on headquarters. It had become a joke over the years – when somebody 42'd, it meant they'd totally screwed up.

"You armed?" Lukas called.

"Service," Ted called. "Both of us."

Meaning their Glocks or SIG-Sauer service pistols. Lukas thought about her MP-5 machine gun, sitting in her truck at the moment. She would have given anything for the weapon but didn't have time to get it now.

She studied the corridor, which was still empty.

Eight doors in the hallway. Five on the right, three on the left.

He's behind one of them.

Here's a puzzle for you, Parker. Which door leads to our Judas?

Three hawks have been killing a farmer's chickens . . .

Holding the gun out in front of her, she eased forward, saw the silhouettes of the other agents at the far end of the corridor. Using hand signals, she motioned them aside, back around the corner. If Hardy burst from a doorway she'd have trouble acquiring a target with Ted and Nance in the background. They'd have the same trouble too and might hesitate to light up Hardy for fear of hitting her. Alone, she'd lose the cross-fire advantage but could shoot freely if he tried to make a run for it.

Lukas moved down the corridor.

Which door? she wondered.

Think . . . Come on! Think!

If Hardy had any sense of orientation he'd know that the five offices on her right were exterior ones; he wouldn't've picked any on the left because he'd risk getting trapped inside the building.

Okay, we'll narrow it down to those on the right.

Of these five, two were labeled RECEPTION – the euphemism for the interrogation rooms like the one in which they'd met with Czisman. Hardy might logically doubt that the FBI would have reception rooms and he might figure that they had something to do with security and would have no access to outside – which in fact they didn't; they were windowless.

The door in the middle was labeled MAINTENANCE. Lukas didn't know exactly where that one led but she supposed it was a janitor's closet with no other exit and concluded that Hardy would have made the same deduction.

That left two doors. Both unmarked and both, she happened to know, leading to small offices for temporary word-processor operators. Both rooms had windows facing the street. One was the office closest to the reception area. The other was closest to Ted and Nance.

But what's the hurry? she asked herself. Just wait for backup.

But Hardy could be breaking through one of the windows right now, close to escaping. Lukas wouldn't risk that this man might get away.

Which door, which one?

She made her choice: The door nearest the lobby. It made sense. Hardy wouldn't have run thirty or forty feet down the corridor with an armed agent behind him before taking cover.

Once she made her decision she forgot all other options.

Puzzles are always easy when you know the answer. Just like life, right?

She tried the knob. But the door was locked.

Were they always locked? she wondered. Or had he locked it from the inside?

No, *he'd* locked it. He *had* to be in there. Where else could he have gone? She ran to the guard station, got the keys from Artie's belt, returned. She slipped the key in the hole as quietly as she could.

Turned the latch.

It clicked with an alarming sound.

Hell. May as well just shout out, Here I come!

One, two . . .

Breathe deep.

She thought about her husband, about her son.

I love you mommy!

And pushed through the door fast.

Crouching, weapon up, pressure on the sharp trigger of the Glock . . .

Nothing . . .

He wasn't here.

Wait . . . the desk . . . It was the only piece of furniture he could be hiding behind.

She stepped around it, swinging her weapon in front of her.

Nothing.

Hell, she'd gotten it wrong. He'd gone through the other door, the far one.

Then, from the corner of her eye, faint motion.

The door directly across the hallway from this one – another door marked MAINTENANCE – had opened slightly. The muzzle of a silenced gun was lowering toward her.

"Margaret!" Susan Nance's voice came from the end of the corridor. Then the woman shouted, "Freeze, you!"

Lukas flung herself to the floor as Hardy's gun fired twice.

But he wasn't aiming at her. The bullets were meant for the plate-glass window. The glass shattered into a thousand pieces.

Nance fired a group of three as Hardy, who ran awkwardly because of a large knapsack on his back,

stumbled through the corridor and into the office where
Lukas crouched. The agent's shots missed. He fired
blindly in Lukas's direction, forcing her under cover.
She rolled to the floor. The slugs clanged into the desk
and Hardy leapt through the empty window frame onto
the deck overlooking Ninth Street. He jumped over
the fence to street level. Lukas returned fire but she
missed too.

She climbed to her feet and ran to the window.

Lukas understood what had happened: Hardy had
tried the door on the window side of the building and
found it locked. He'd waited in a janitor's closet across
the hall, outguessing her – figuring she'd probably pick
the door she did and get the key to open it. He'd
used her.

She'd been dead wrong.

*He aims at the hawk on the left and shoots and
kills it . . .*

Standing on the crisp broken glass on the deck, she
looked up and down the street but could see no sign
of Hardy.

The bullet doesn't ricochet . . .

All she saw was a huge crowd of people returning
from the fireworks, staring in surprise at the shattered
window that framed the attractive blonde with a gun in
her hand.

How many hawks left on the roof? . . .

33

Parker and Cage were in the document lab once more. Joined this time by the dep director.

"Six dead," the dep director muttered. "Lord almighty. Inside headquarters."

Dr. John Evans, shot twice in the face, had been found in a seventh-floor closet. Artie the guard was badly wounded but would live.

"Who the hell *is* he?" the dep director demanded.

The man pretending to be Hardy had left some good fingerprints and they were being run through the Automated Fingerprint Identification System files right now. If his prints were on file anywhere in the country they'd know his identity soon.

Lukas pushed through the door. Parker was alarmed to see a peppering of blood on her cheek.

"You all right?" he asked.

"Artie's," she said in a low murmur, noticing his eyes on the blood. "Not mine." She looked at Parker then Cage for a moment. The stones in her eyes were gone but he couldn't tell what had replaced them. "How did you know?"

Cage glanced toward Parker. "It was him figured it out."

"Tremble," Parker answered. He held out the sheet of paper that he'd found in his pocket when he'd been looking for baby-sitter money. "I noticed there was tremble in his handwriting. That's what happens when somebody tries to disguise their writing. I remembered it was Hardy who'd written down what I dictated but why would he try to fake his writing? There was only one reason – because *he'd* written the extortion note. I checked the lowercase *i* in 'two miles' and the dot was a devil's teardrop. That confirmed it."

"What happened?" the deputy director asked. "The director wants to know. Immediately."

"It was all a setup," Parker said, pacing. Somewhere in his mind the entire plot was quickly falling into place in minute detail. He asked Lukas, "How did Hardy get involved in the case?"

"I *knew* him," she said. "He's been coming by the field office for the past few months. Just flashed a badge and said he needed some stats on felonies in the District for a congressional report. District P.D.'s Research and Statistics does it a couple times a year. It's all public information – not ongoing investigations – so nobody bothered to check. Today he showed up and said he's been assigned as liaison for the case."

"And it's one of those obscure departments," Parker pointed out. "So that if the mayor or the police chief really *did* send somebody from Major Crimes or Investigation over here for liaison he probably wouldn't have known there was no Len Hardy."

Lukas said, "So he's been planning this for two months." Sighing in disgust.

"Probably six," Parker muttered. "Planned every detail. He *was* a goddamn perfectionist. His shoes, his nails, his clothes . . . Flawless."

Cage asked, "But the guy in the morgue, the one we thought was the unsub. Who's he?"

Parker said, "A runner. Somebody Hardy – or whatever his name is – hired to deliver the letter."

"But," Cage said, "he was killed in an accident."

"No, it wasn't an accident," Lukas said, stealing the words from Parker's throat.

Nodding, he said, "Hardy murdered him, ran him down in a stolen truck to make it look accidental."

Lukas continued, "So we'd think the perp was dead and bring the money back to the evidence room. He knew we'd have tracking devices in the bags. Or that we'd try to collar him at the drop."

Cage, wincing again from the cracked rib, said, "He left the transmit bags downstairs. Repacked the money. And ripped off the tracking labels too."

"But he came up with the info about the Digger, didn't he?" the deputy director asked. "Because of him we stopped the shooter before he could do any real damage on the Mall."

"Well, of *course*," Parker responded, surprised they didn't get it.

"What do you mean?" the dep director asked.

"That's why he *picked* the Vietnam Memorial. It's not far from here. He knew we'd be shorthanded and that we'd virtually empty the building to get everybody out, looking for the Digger."

"So he could just waltz into Evidence and pick up

the money," Lukas said bitterly. "It's just what Evans said. That he had everything planned out. I told him that we'd rigged the bags with tracers but Evans said he had some plan to counter that."

Cage asked Parker, "The prints on the note?"

"Hardy never touched it without gloves but he made sure the runner did – so we could verify the body was the unsub's."

"And he picked somebody with no record and no military service," Lukas added, "so we couldn't trace the runner . . . *Jesus*, he thought of everything."

A computer beeped. Cage leaned froward and read. "It's an AFIS report and VICAP and Connecticut State Police files. Here we go . . ." He scrolled through the information. A picture came up on the screen. It was Hardy. "His real name is Edward Fielding, last known address, Blakesly, Connecticut, outside of Hartford. Oh, our friend is not a very nice man. Four arrests, one conviction. Juvie time too but those records're sealed. Treated repeatedly for antisocial behavior. Was an aide and orderly at Hartford State Hospital for the Criminally Insane. He left after a nurse he was accused of sexually harassing was found stabbed to death.

"The hospital administration," Cage continued, reading from the screen, "thinks Fielding talked a patient, David Hughes, into killing her. Hughes was admitted two years ago. Christmas Day. He had severe brain damage following a gunshot wound and was highly suggestible. Fielding probably helped Hughes escape. The Hospital Board and the police were going to investigate Fielding but he disappeared after that. That was in October of last year."

"Hughes is the Digger," Parker announced softly.

"You think?"

"Positive." He continued, "And the Hartford newspaper shooting – what got Czisman started on Fielding's trail – that was in November." Recalling the clipping in Czisman's book. "That was their first crime."

A Chronicle of Sorrow . . .

"But why so much death?" the dep director asked. "It can't just be for the money. He must've had some terrorist leanings."

"Nope," Parker said definitively. "Not terrorism at all. But you're absolutely right. It has nothing to do with the money. Oh, I recognize him."

"You *know* Fielding?"

"No, I mean I recognize the type. He's like a document forger."

"Forger?" asked Lukas.

"Serious forgers see themselves as artists, not thieves. They don't really care about the money. The point is to create a forgery that fools everyone. That's their only goal: a perfect forgery."

Lukas nodded. "So the other crimes – in Hartford and Boston and Philly – they were just exercises. Stealing one watch, a few thousand dollars. It was just to perfect his technique."

"Exactly. And this was the culmination. This time he got a big chunk of money and's going to retire."

"Why do you think that?" Cage asked.

But Lukas knew the answer to that one too. "Because he sacrificed his errand boy so he could escape. He told us where the Digger was."

Recalling how Hardy had fired at the bus, Parker

added, "He may actually have been the one who shot the Digger on the Mall. If they took him alive he might have talked."

"Hardy was laughing at us," Cage said, slamming his fist down on the table. "The whole fucking time he was sitting right next to us and laughing."

"But where is he?" the dep director asked.

Parker said, "Oh, he'll have his escape all planned out. He's outthought us every step of the way. He won't stumble now."

"We can get his picture off the video camera down in the lobby," Cage said. "Get it to all the TV stations."

"At two in the morning?" Parker said. "Who's going to be watching? And we've already missed the newspaper deadlines. Anyway, he'll be out of the country by sunup and on a plastic surgeon's operating table in two days."

"The airports're closed," the dep director pointed out. "He can't get any flights till morning."

"He'll be driving to Louisville or Atlanta or New York," Lukas said. "But we'll put out a bulletin to the field offices. Get agents to all the airports, Amtrak stations and bus terminals. Rental-car companies too. Check DMV and deeds offices for an address. And call Connecticut State Police." She paused, looking at Parker. He could see that she was thinking exactly what he was.

"He's thought of all that," Parker said. "I'm not saying we don't have to do it. But he's anticipated it."

"I know," she said and seemed all the more angry because of her helplessness.

The dep director said, "I'll authorize ten-most-wanted status."

But Parker wasn't listening. He was staring at the extortion note.

"Perfect forgery," he whispered to himself.

"What?" Lukas asked.

He looked at his watch. "I'm going to go see somebody."

"I'm going with you," Lukas said.

Parker hesitated. "Better if you didn't."

"No, I'm going."

"I don't need any help."

"I'm going with you," she said firmly.

And Parker looked into her blue eyes – stone or no stone?

He couldn't tell.

He said, "Okay."

They drove through the streets of the District, mostly deserted now. Parker was at the wheel.

A car paused at an intersection, to their right. In the glare Parker caught Lukas's profile, her thin mouth, her rounded nose, her sweep of throat.

He turned back to the street and drove deeper into Alexandria, Virginia.

Maybe she envies you.

How much he wanted to take her hand, sit with her in a lounge or on his couch at home. Or lie in bed with her.

And talk. Talk about anything.

Perhaps about the secret of Margaret Lukas, whatever that might be.

Or just do what he and the Whos did sometimes –

talk about nothing. Talk silly, they called it. About cartoons or neighbors or the Home Depot sale or recipes or vacations past and vacations planned.

Or maybe he and Lukas would share the war stories that cops – federal or state or crossing guards – loved to boast about.

The secret could wait.

She'd have years to tell him, he thought.

Years . . .

Suddenly he realized that he was considering a connection with her that might last more than a single night or a week or month. What did he have to base this fantasy on? Nothing really. It was a ridiculous thought.

Whatever connection there might be between them – she the soldier, he the hausfrau – was pure illusion.

Or was it? He remembered the Whos in the Dr. Seuss book, the race of creatures living on a dust mote, so small no one could see them. But they were there nonetheless, with all their crazy grins and contraptions and bizarre architecture. Why couldn't love be found in something that seemed invisible too?

He looked at her once again and she at him. He found his hand reaching out tentatively and touching her knee. Her hand closed on his, nothing tentative about it.

Then they were at the address he sought. He removed his hand. He parked the car. Not a word said. Not a look between them.

Lukas climbed out. Parker too. He walked around to her side of the car and they stood facing each other. How badly he wanted to hold her. Put his arms around her, slip his hands into the small of her back, pull her close. She glanced at him and slowly unbuttoned her blazer. He caught a glimpse of the white silk blouse. He stepped forward to kiss her.

She glanced down, unholstered her weapon and buttoned her blazer once more. Squinted as she looked past him, checking out the neighborhood.

"Oh." Parker stepped back.

"Where to?" she asked matter-of-factly.

Parker hesitated, looked at her cool eyes. Then nodded at a winding path that led into an alley. "This way."

The man was about five feet tall.

He had a wiry beard and bushy hair. He wore a ratty bathrobe and Parker had obviously wakened him when he banged fiercely on the rickety door.

He stared at Parker and Lukas for a moment then, without a word, retreated quickly back into the apartment, as if he'd been tugged back by a bungee cord.

Lukas preceded Parker inside. She looked around then holstered her weapon. The rooms were cluttered, filled to overflowing with books and furniture and papers. On the walls hung a hundred signed letters and scraps of historical documents. A dozen bookshelves were chockablock with more books and portfolios. An artist's drawing table was covered with bottles of ink and dozens of pens. It dominated the tiny living room.

"How you doing, Jeremy?"

The man rubbed his eyes. Glanced at an old-fashioned windup alarm clock. He said, "My, Parker. It's late. Say, look at what I've got here. Do you like it?"

Parker took the acetate folder Jeremy was holding up.

The man's fingertips were yellow from the cigarettes he loved. Parker recalled that he smoked only outside, however. He didn't want to risk contaminating his work. As with all true geniuses Jeremy's vices bent to his gift.

Parker took the folder and held it up to a light. Picked up a hand glass and examined the document inside. After a moment he said, "The width of the strokes . . . it's very good."

"Better than good, Parker."

"Okay, I'll grant you that. The starts and lifts are excellent. Also looks like the margins are right and the folio size matches. The paper's from the era?"

"Of course."

"But you'd have to fake the aging of the ink with hydrogen peroxide. That's detectible."

"Maybe. Maybe not." Jeremy smiled. "Maybe I've got something new up my sleeve. Are you here to arrest me, Parker?"

"I'm not a cop anymore, Jeremy."

"No, but she is, isn't she?"

"Yes, she is."

Jeremy took the sheet back. "I haven't sold it. I haven't even offered it for sale." To Lukas he said, "It's just a hobby. A man can have a hobby, can't he?"

"What is it?" Lukas asked.

Parker said, "It's a letter from Robert E. Lee to one of his generals." He added, "I should say, *purporting* to be from Robert E. Lee."

"He forged it?" Lukas asked, glancing at Jeremy.

"That's right."

"I never admitted anything. I'm taking the Fifth."

Parker continued. "It's worth maybe fifteen thousand."

"Seventeen . . . *If* somebody were going to sell it. Which I never would. Parker arrested me once," Jeremy said to Lukas, tweaking his beard with his middle finger and thumb. "He was the only one in the world who caught me. You know how he did it?"

"How?" she asked. Parker's attention was not on the excellent forgery but on Margaret Lukas, who seemed both amused and fascinated by the man. Her anger had gone away for the moment and Parker was very pleased to see that.

"The watermark on the letterhead," Jeremy said, scoffing. "I got done in by a watermark."

"A few years ago," Parker said, "Jeremy . . . let's say, came into possession of a packet of letters from John Kennedy."

"To Marilyn Monroe?" Lukas asked.

Jeremy's face twisted up. "*Those*? Oh, those were ridiculous. Amateurish. And who cares about them? No, these were between Kennedy and Khrushchev. According to the letters, Kennedy was willing to compromise on Cuba. What an interesting historical twist that would have been. He and Khrushchev were going to divvy up the island. The Russians would have half, the U.S. the other."

"Was that true?" Lukas asked.

Jeremy was silent and stared at the Robert E. Lee letter with a faint smile on his face.

Parker said, "Jeremy makes up things." Which happened to be the delicate way he described lying when he was speaking with the Whos. "He forged the letters. Was going to sell them for five thousand dollars."

"Four thousand eight hundred," Jeremy corrected.

"That's all?" Lukas was surprised.

"Jeremy isn't in this business for the money," Parker said.

"And you caught him?"

"My technique was flawless, Parker, you have to admit that."

"Oh, it was," Parker confirmed. "The craftsmanship was perfect. Ink, handwriting attack, starts and lifts, phraseology, margins . . . Unfortunately, the Government Printing Office changed the presidential letterhead in August of 1963. Jeremy got his hands on several of those new sheets and used them for his forgeries. Too bad the letters were dated *May* of '63."

"I had bad intelligence," Jeremy muttered. "So, Parker, is it cuffs and chains? What've I done now?"

"Oh, I think you know what you've done, Jeremy. I think you know."

Parker pulled up a chair for Lukas and one for himself. They both sat.

"Oh, dear," Jeremy said.

"Oh, dear," echoed Parker.

34

Finally, it was snowing.

Large squares of flakes parachuting to the ground. Two inches already, muting the night.

Edward Fielding, lugging the burdensome silk bag of money on his back and carrying a silenced pistol in his right hand, waded through a belt of trees and brush in Bethesda, Maryland. From FBI headquarters he'd driven here via two "switch wheels" – getaway cars that professional thieves hide along escape routes to trick pursuers. He'd stayed on major highways the whole way, keeping exactly to the speed limit. He parked on the other side of this grove of trees and walked the rest of the way. The money slowed him down but he certainly wasn't going to leave the cash in the car, despite the relative safety in this placid, upscale Washington suburb.

He eased through the side yard and paused by a fence separating his rented house from the one next door.

On the street, every car was familiar.

Inside his house, no movement or shadows he didn't recognize.

Across the street, the lights in all the houses facing his were dark except for the Harkins' place. This was normal. Fielding had observed that the Harkins rarely went to bed before 2 or 3 A.M.

He set the knapsack holding the money beside a tree on the property next door to his house. And stood upright, letting his muscles enjoy the freedom from the heavy load. He moved along the fence, checking out the ground in the front, back and side yards around his house. No footprints in the snow there or on the sidewalk in front of the houses.

Fielding picked up the money once again and continued along the walk to his house. There were several security devices he'd rigged to let him know if there'd been any unwanted visitors – homemade tricks, rudimentary but effective: thread across the gate, the front door latch lined up with a tiny fleck of dried paint on the storm door, the corner of the rattan mat curled and resting against the door.

He'd learned these from a right-wing web site on the Internet about protecting yourself from blacks, Jews and the federal government. Despite the snow, which would have revealed any intruders, he checked them carefully. Because that was what you did when you committed the perfect crime.

He unlocked the door, thinking of his next steps. He'd only be here for five or ten minutes – long enough to pack the money into boxes that had contained children's toys, collect his other suitcases then drive, via three safe cars already planted along the route, to Ocean City, Maryland. There he'd get on the chartered boat and be in Miami in two days. Then a chartered plane would take him to Costa Rica and that night he'd fly on to Brazil.

Then he'd—

He wasn't sure where she'd been hiding. Maybe behind the door. Maybe in the closet. Before Fielding even had time to feel the shock of adrenaline flooding through his body the pistol had been ripped from his hand and Margaret Lukas was screaming, "Freeze, freeze, federal agents!"

Fielding found himself not freezing at all but tumbling forward and lying flat on his belly, under her strong grip. Gun in his ear. The cash was pulled off him and his hands were cuffed by two large male agents. Fingers probed through his pockets.

They pulled him to his feet and pushed him into an armchair.

Cage and several other men and women walked through the front door, while yet another agent inventoried the money.

He had a completely mystified expression on his face. She said, "Oh, those trip wires and things? You *do* realize we bookmark the same Web site as everybody else – that Aryan militia crap."

"But the snow?" he asked. Shivering now from the shock. "There were no footprints. How'd you get in?"

"Oh, we borrowed a hook and ladder from the Bethesda Fire Department. The SWAT team and I climbed in through your upstairs window."

Just then Parker Kincaid walked through the front door. Lukas nodded toward him and explained to Fielding, "The fire truck was his idea."

Fielding didn't doubt that it was.

Parker sat down in a chair opposite Fielding and crossed his arms. The detective – Parker couldn't help but think of him that way still – looked older now and diminished. Parker remembered wishing earlier that the unsub were still alive so that he could see how the man's mind worked. One puzzle master to another. It seemed he'd gotten his wish. But now he felt no professional curiosity at all, only revulsion.

Puzzles are always easy when you know the answer.

They become boring too.

Lukas asked him, "How's it feel to know you're going to be in an eight-by-eight cell for the next ten years – until they give you that needle?"

Cage explained, "You wouldn't last very long in general population. Hope you like your own company."

"I prefer it to most people's," Fielding said.

Cage continued, as if Fielding hadn't spoken. "They're also going to want you in Boston and White Plains and Philadelphia too. I guess Hartford as well."

Fielding lifted a surprised eyebrow.

Parker asked, "The Digger was the patient in your hospital, right? The hospital for the criminally insane? David Hughes?"

Fielding didn't want to seem impressed but he was. "That's right. Funny guy, wasn't he?" He smiled at Parker. "Sort of the boogey man incarnate."

Then Parker suddenly understood something else and his heart froze.

Boogeyman . . .

"In the command post . . . I was talking about my

son. And not long after that . . . Jesus, not long after that Robby saw somebody in the garage. That was the Digger! . . . You called him, you sent him to my house! To scare my son!"

Fielding shrugged. "You were too good, Kincaid. I had to get you off the case for a while. When you went off to raid my safe house – finding that was *very* good, by the way – I stepped outside to make a call and left a message that my friend should go visit your little fella. I thought about killing them – well, and you too, of course – but I needed you to be at headquarters around midnight. To make my deductions about the site of the last shooting more credible."

Parker lunged forward and drew back his fist. Lukas caught his arm just before it crashed into Fielding's cringing face.

She whispered, "I understand. But it won't do anybody any good."

Trembling with rage, Parker lowered his hand, stepped to the window, watching the snow. Forced himself to calm. He believed if he'd been alone with Fielding now he could kill the man. Not because of the host of deaths tonight but because he could still hear the hollow fear in Robby's voice. *Daddy . . . daddy . . .*

Lukas touched his arm. He looked at her. She was holding a notebook. She said to Parker, "For what it's worth, he did the same thing to me." She flipped through the pages, tapped several entries. "My house was broken into a few months ago. *He's* the one who did it. He took notes about my life."

Fielding said nothing.

Lukas continued, speaking directly to the killer.

"You found out all about me. You found out about Tom . . ."

Tom? Parker wondered.

"You cut your hair the same way as his. You said you were from outside Chicago, just like him. You read his letters to me . . ." She closed her eyes and shook her head. "'Right as rain.' You stole his expression! And then you told me about having a wife in a coma. Why? So I'd keep you on the team – when everybody else – me included – didn't want you interfering with the case."

"I needed to get inside your defenses, Margaret. I knew what kind of adversary you'd be."

"You stole my past, Fielding."

"What's the past for but to use?" he asked evenly.

"But how could you kill so many people?" Lukas asked in a whisper.

"Appalled?" Fielding asked. He seemed exasperated. "But why not? I mean, Jesus Christ, why not? Why is one death less horrifying than a million? Either you kill or you don't. If you do, then death is just a matter of degree and if it makes sense, if it's *efficient*, then you kill whom you have to kill. Anyone who doesn't accept that is a naive fool."

"Who's the guy in the morgue?" Cage asked.

"His name is Gil Havel."

"Ah, the mysterious Gilbert Jones," Parker said. "He rented the helicopter, right?"

"I *had* to make you believe that I was really going to try to get away with the money from the drop on Gallows Road."

"Where did you find him?"

"In a bar in Baltimore."

"Who was he? Havel."

"He's just some loser. A bum, more or less. I promised him a hundred thousand dollars to deliver a note to City Hall and help me with the helicopter and rent the safe house. I made him think he was my partner."

Parker said, "And you had him walk back to the Metro or bus stop along a particular route. Where you were waiting with the van to run him down."

"You had to believe that the mastermind was dead. So you'd bring the money back to the evidence room . . ."

"What about Kennedy? You sent him to the Ritz."

"The mayor?" Fielding asked. "That was a surprise – when he called me. And a risk. But it worked out well." He nodded analytically. "For one thing, I had to keep you focused on the Ritz-Carlton, not the *Ritzy Lady*. And then my penance for the betrayal was bringing you the bone about the Digger's name . . . You know, you really are something, Kincaid. How'd you figure it out?"

Parker continued, "How did I find out you were the unsub? Because of your handwriting. I had a sample – when I dictated to you from the yellow sheets Tobe saved."

"I was worried about that," Fielding said. "But I couldn't very well balk when you asked me to take notes, could I? But I tried to improvise – I tried to disguise my writing."

"The dot on your lowercase *i* gave you away."

Fielding nodded. "Oh, that's right. The devil's teardrop. I didn't think about that . . . What did you say? That it's always the little things."

"Not always. But usually."

Lukas asked, "The information about the Digger – you had that all along, didn't you? You didn't go to the library."

"Nope. Hell, that's why I *named* Hughes the Digger. So you'd think he had some ridiculous revenge scheme against the government. But . . ." He looked around the room. "How'd you get *here?*"

"To this house?" Parker couldn't resist. "Perfection," he said and watched the arrogant smile slide off the killer's face. He continued. "To escape after the perfect crime, you'd want the perfect passports. You'd find the best forger in the business. He happens to be a friend of mine. Well, let's just say we're close; I put him in prison once."

For a moment Fielding was flustered. "But he didn't know my real name or address."

"No, but you called him," Parker countered.

"Not from here," Fielding said, argumentative, whiny.

Lukas too wanted part of deconstructing the man. "From the phone booth up the street." She nodded toward the corner. "We ran the pen register numbers through Bell Atlantic security." Then she held up a computer picture of Fielding. "We lifted it from the tape in the FBI headquarters security camera. Just showed it to a half-dozen people in the neighborhood tonight and got a beeline to your front door."

"Shit." He closed his eyes.

The little things . . .

Parker said, "There's this saying among forgers that the expression 'You can't think of everything' doesn't count. You *have* to think of everything."

Fielding said, "I knew you were the strong link,

Parker. The biggest risk. I should've had the Digger take care of you right up front."

Cage asked, "You didn't have any problem sacrificing your friend?"

"The Digger? Wouldn't exactly call him a friend." Fielding added, "He was a dangerous person to keep alive. Anyway, you may've guessed, this was going to be my last job. I don't need him anymore."

An agent walked into the doorway. "Okay, Fielding. Your ride's here."

They started to lead him off. He paused at the doorway. Turned back.

"Admit it, Parker, I'm good," he said churlishly. "After all, I nearly did it."

Parker shook his head. "Either an answer to a puzzle's right or it's wrong. There's no 'nearly' about it."

But when he was led out of the door Fielding was smiling.

35

02.20

The workmen were lashing the burnt bus to a flatbed.

The medical examiner had carted off the Digger's body, in whose hands was fused, horribly, a scorched black machine gun.

Edward Fielding sat in federal detention, legs shackled and wrists cuffed.

As Parker said goodnight to Cage, looking around for Margaret Lukas, he noticed Mayor Gerald Kennedy start toward them. He'd been here, with a skeleton crew of journalists, surveying the damage and talking to police and rescue workers.

He walked up to them.

"Your honor," Cage said.

"I have you to thank for that little news story, Agent Cage? Implicating me in the screwup at the boat?"

A shrug. "Investigation had priority, sir. Shouldn't've showed up at the Ritz. Probably would've been better to keep politics out of it."

Kennedy shook his head. "So I understand you've caught the man behind this."

"We did, sir."

Kennedy turned his jowly face to Parker, "And you're Agent—"

"Jefferson, Your Honor. First name's Tom."

"Oh, you're the one I've been hearing about. The document examiner?"

"That's right," Parker said. "I saw you do some pretty nifty shooting there."

"Not nifty enough," the mayor nodded ruefully toward the smoking bus. The mayor asked, "Say, you related to Thomas Jefferson?"

"Me?" Parker laughed. "No, no. It's a common name."

"My aide's name is Jefferies," he said as if making cocktail party conversation.

Then Lukas arrived. She nodded to the mayor and Parker could see the tension in her face, as if she were expecting a confrontation.

But all Kennedy said was, "I'm sorry about your friend, Agent Ardell."

Lukas said nothing. She stared at the scorched bus.

A reporter called, "Mayor, there's a rumor that you chose not to call out the National Guard tonight because you thought it would interfere with tourist traffic. Could you comment on that?"

"No, I couldn't." He too gazed at the bus.

Lukas said, "Tonight didn't turn out very well for anybody, did it?"

"No, Agent Lukas," Kennedy said slowly. "I suspect things like this never do."

He took his wife's hand and walked to their limousine.

Margaret Lukas handed Cage some documents – maybe evidence reports or arrest records. Then, eyes still on the bus, she walked to her truck. Parker wondered, Was she leaving without saying goodbye?

She opened the door, started the engine and put the heater on – the temperature had dropped and the sky was overcast with thick clouds, which were still shedding fat grains of snow. She left the truck's door open, leaned back into the seat.

Cage shook Parker's hand then muttered, "What can I say?" To Parker's surprise the agent threw his arms around him, hugged him once hard, wincing at the pain, then started off down the street. "Night, Lukas," Cage shouted. "Night, Parker. Man, my side hurts. Happy New Year, everybody. Happy goddamn New Year."

Parker zipped up his jacket and walked toward Lukas's truck, noticing that she was looking at something in her hand. Parker wasn't sure what it was. It seemed to be an old postcard that had been folded up. She stared at it. She glanced at Parker then seemed to hesitate. Just before he got to the truck she put the card away in her purse.

She pulled a bottle of beer out of her pocket, a Sam Adams, cracked it open with a church key that rested on the dash.

"They sell those in vending machines at headquarters now?"

"Present from my witness, Gary Moss." She offered it to him. He took a long sip, handed it back. Lukas remained in the Ford but turned sideways, facing Parker. "What a night, hm?"

"What a night," he repeated. He reached forward and offered his hand.

She gripped his solidly. They'd both removed their gloves and though their hands were red from the cold, their flesh was the identical temperature; Parker felt no cold or heat coming from her skin.

Neither of them let go. He enclosed her hand with his left.

"How're the kids?" she asked. "What do you call them again?"

"The Whos."

"Whos. Right. Have you talked to them?"

"They're fine." Reluctantly he released his grip. Was she reluctant too? He couldn't tell. Then he asked, "You'll need a report, I assume?" He remembered all the paperwork U.S. attorneys required to get ready for federal criminal trials. Mountains of it. But Parker didn't mind; after all, documents were his business.

"We will," Lukas responded. "But there's no hurry."

"I'll do one on Monday. I'm finishing a project this weekend."

"Document? Or home improvement?"

"You mean home improvement as in tools?" He laughed. "Oh, I don't do that. Kitchens I know. Workbenches, uh-uh. No, it's a possible forgery. A letter supposedly written by Thomas Jefferson. A dealer in New York wants it analyzed."

"Is it real?"

"My gut feeling is yes. I have some more tests to run. Oh, here." He handed her the pistol.

Lukas, in the skirt now, was no longer dressed for hiding backup weapons on her ankle. She slipped the gun into her glove compartment. Parker's eyes strayed to her profile again.

Why on earth would you envy me? he wondered silently.

Sometimes puzzles answer themselves, in their own time.

And sometimes you just never do find the answer. And that's because, Parker Kincaid had come to believe, you weren't meant to.

"Hey, you doing anything tomorrow night?" he asked suddenly. "Want to have a ridiculously suburban dinner?"

She hesitated. Not moving a muscle. Not even breathing, it seemed. He didn't move either, just kept a faint smile on his lips, the way he waited for the Whos to confess about missing cookies or a broken lamp.

Finally she too smiled but he saw that it was fake – a smile of stone, one that matched her eyes. And he knew what her answer would be.

"I'm sorry," she said formally. "I have plans. Maybe some other time."

Meaning: never. Parker Kincaid's *Handbook for the Single Parent* had a whole chapter on euphemisms.

"Sure," he said, trying to step on the disappointment. "Some other time."

"Where's your car?" Lukas asked. "I'll give you a ride."

"No, that's okay. It's right over there."

He gripped her hand again and resisted the urge to pull her close.

"'Night," she said.

He nodded.

As he walked to his car he looked at her and saw she was waving. It was an odd gesture since her face was emotionless and she wasn't smiling.

But then Parker noticed that she wasn't waving at all. She was wiping off the condensation on the windows, not even looking at him. When she'd cleaned the glass Margaret Lukas put the truck in gear and sped into the middle of the street.

On the way home, driving through the quiet, snow-filled streets, Parker stopped at a 7-Eleven for black coffee, a ham-and-egg on a croissant and cash from the ATM. When he walked in the front door of his house he found Mrs. Cavanaugh asleep on the couch.

He woke her and paid her twice what she asked for. Then escorted her to the door and stood on the front steps, watching her walk over the snow carefully until she disappeared into her own house across the street.

The children had fallen asleep in his bed – his room sported a TV and VCR. The screen was bright blue, circumstantial evidence that they'd watched a movie. He was afraid to see which video had lulled them to sleep – he had a collection of R-rated thriller and sci-fi films – but what popped out when he hit eject was only *The Lion King*. Troubling enough – Robby would forever detest hyenas – but at least it had a noble ending and the violence was largely unseen.

Parker was exhausted – beyond exhaustion. But sleep, he felt, was still an hour or so away.

Despite his urging her not to, Mrs. Cavanaugh had done dishes and cleaned the kitchen – so he couldn't work off energy that way. Instead, he bundled up the trash from around the house and carted it out into the backyard, lugging the green bags over his shoulder like Santa. Thinking: What a crazy life – to have been pointing a gun at someone an hour ago, to have been shot at himself, and now to be back in the middle of suburbia, lost in these domestic chores.

As he eased up the lid of the trash bin Parker glanced into the backyard. He stopped, frowned. There were footprints in the snow.

Recent footprints.

Only a few minutes old, he judged – the edges were still sharp, unsoftened by the falling snow and the wind. The intruder had walked up to the guest room window, then disappeared toward the front of the house.

Parker's heart began thudding.

He carefully set the garbage bag down and walked quietly back into the house.

He closed and locked the kitchen door behind him. Checked on the front door. It was locked. Because of his document business – the value of the specimens and the risk of pollution and dust in the air – the windows in the house were sealed and couldn't be opened; he didn't need to check them.

But whose footprints?

Just kids, maybe.

Or Mr. Johnson looking for his dog.

That's all it was. Sure . . .

But ten seconds later he was on the phone to the federal detention facility in Washington, D.C.

He identified himself as FBI Special Agent Parker Kincaid, a statement only a few years untrue. "I was working on that case tonight with Margaret Lukas."

"Sure. METSHOOT."

"Right. I'm being a little paranoid here," Parker said, "But the suspect – Edward Fielding. He's not out on bail, is he?"

"Bail? No way. He won't be arraigned until Monday."

"He's locked down?"

"Yep. I can see him. On the monitor."

"He asleep?"

"No, just sitting on his bed. Been behaving himself. Talked to his lawyer – that was about an hour ago – then went into his cell and's been there ever since. Why?"

"Just spooked, I guess. Thought I saw the boogeyman."

"Boogeyman. Ha. Hey, Happy New Year."

Parker hung up, relieved.

For about five seconds.

Talking to his lawyer?

Parker didn't know any lawyer in the country who'd be up at this hour on a holiday, talking to a client who wouldn't be arraigned for two days.

Then he thought: Perfection.

"Oh, Jesus," he muttered.

Fielding – the man who had a plan for everything. He must have had a plan for escaping if he was caught.

He lifted the receiver and hit the first digit of 911.

The line went dead.

Motion outside the kitchen door.

He looked up.

Standing on the back porch, gazing at him through the window in the door was a man. He was pale. Wearing a dark coat. Black or blue. There was blood on his left arm but not a lot of blood. Burns on his face but they weren't serious.

The man lifted his silenced machine gun and tapped the trigger, as Parker leapt aside, crashing into the wall and falling to the floor. The doorknob and lock of the back door blew apart under the stream of bullets. Glass splinters exploded into the room.

Leisurely, the Digger pushed the door open and stepped inside, like a friendly neighbor invited over for coffee.

36

03.00

The Digger's cold, the Digger wants to get this over with and leave.

He'd rather be outside. He likes the . . . *click* . . . the . . . the . . . the snow.

He likes the snow.

Oh, look, a nice Christmas wreath and a nice Christmas tree in Parker Kincaid's comfy house. Tye would like this.

Funny . . .

No puppies, no ribbons here. But a nice wreath and a nice tree.

He fires again as Kincaid runs through the doorway.

Did he hit him? The Digger can't tell.

But, no, guess not. He sees Kincaid crawling into another room, shutting out lights, rolling on the floor.

Doing things like that.

The Digger believes he's happy. The man who tells him things called again, an hour ago. Not a message from the voice-mail lady who sounds like Ruth but a real call on his cell phone. He told the Digger that the night wasn't over yet even though the Digger had gone to the black wall and done what he was supposed to do.

Not . . . *click* . . . not over yet.

"Listen to me," said the man who tells him things and so the Digger listened. He was supposed to kill three more people. Someone named Cage and someone named Lukas. And Parker Kincaid. "Kill him first. Okay?"

"Hmmm, okay."

The Digger knows Kincaid. He came to his house earlier tonight. Kincaid has a little boy like Tye except the Digger doesn't like Kincaid's little boy because Kincaid wants to make the Digger go back to the hospital in Connecticut. Kincaid wants to take him away from Tye.

"Then at four-thirty A.M.," said the man who tells him things, "I want you to come to the Federal Detention Center on Third Street. I'll be in the clinic. It's on the first floor in the back. I'll be pretending I'm sick. Kill everyone you see and let me out."

"Okay."

Walking into the dining room, the Digger sees Kincaid roll out from beneath the table and run into the hallway. He fires another stream of bullets. Kincaid's face looks like Ruth's face when he was about to put the glass in her neck and like Pamela's when he put the knife in her chest below the gold cross here's your Christmas present I love you love you all the more . . .

Kincaid disappears into another part of the house.

But he won't leave, the Digger knows. The children are here. A father won't run out on his children.

The Digger knows this because he wouldn't leave Tye. Kincaid won't leave the little blond boy and the dark-haired girl.

If Parker Kincaid lives, the Digger will never get to Cal-i-fornia. Out West.

He steps into the living room, holding the gun in front of him.

Parker rolled away from the Digger, rolled along the floor, elbows scraped, head throbbing from where he hit the edge of the kitchen table, diving away from the bullets.

The Whos! he thought in despair, scrabbling toward the stairs. He wouldn't let the Digger upstairs. He'd die with a death grip on the man's neck if he had to but he would save the children.

But another burst of shots. He turned from the stairs and dove into the living room.

A weapon . . . What could he use? But there were none. He couldn't get into the kitchen and grab a knife. He couldn't get into the garage for the ax.

Why the hell had he given back Lukas's gun?

Then he saw something – one of Robby's Christmas presents, the baseball bat. He snagged it, gripped the taped handle and crawled back toward the stairs.

Where is he? Where?

Then steps, faint. The crunch of the Digger walking over broken glass and pottery.

But Parker couldn't tell where he was.

The hallway?

The dining room? The first-floor den?

What should he do?

If he shouted for the children to leap out the window they'd just come to see what he wanted. He had to get upstairs himself, grab them and jump. He'd try to cushion the fall as best he could. The snow would help and he could aim for the juniper bushes.

Footsteps very close. Crunch. A pause. Another crunch.

Parker looked up.

No! The Digger was at the foot of the stairs, about to climb them, looking up. No expression on his face.

He's profile-proof . . .

Parker couldn't run at him; he'd be in full view and would die before he got three steps toward the man. So he flung the bat into the dining room. It crashed into the china cabinet.

The Digger stopped, hearing the noise. He turned stiffly and walked toward it. Like the alien monster in the old horror film *The Thing*.

When he was nearly to the arched doorway Parker climbed out from behind the couch and charged him.

He was six feet away from his prey when he stepped on one of Robby's toys. It shattered with a loud crunch. The Digger spun around just as Parker rammed into him, knocking him to his knees. He landed a fist on the killer's jaw. The blow was hard but the Digger dodged away and Parker, under the momentum of the swing, fell onto his side. He collapsed on the floor, tried for the Digger's gun. But the man was too fast for him and grabbed the weapon, then struggled to his feet. Parker could do nothing but retreat into the narrow space behind the couch.

His face dripping sweat, hands trembling, he huddled here.

Nowhere else to go.

The Digger backed up, orienting himself. Parker saw something sharp on the floor in front of him. Glistening. A long shard of glass. He grabbed it.

The killer squinted, looking around. He located Parker, who gazed up into the man's dim eyes. Parker thought – no, Margaret Lukas's eyes aren't dead at all; there's a million times more life in them than in this creature's. The killer moved closer. Coming around the back of the couch. Parker tensed. Then he looked past the man – at the Christmas tree. He remembered the three of them, he and the Whos, opening presents on Christmas morning.

It's a good thought to die with, he decided.

But if he was going to die he'd make sure the children didn't. He gripped the long splinter of glass, wrapped his shirt cuff around the lower half. He'd slash the man's jugular vein and pray that he'd bleed to death before he got up the stairs, where the children were sleeping. Not daring to think about the sight the Whos would see in the morning. He tucked his legs under him, gripped his impromptu knife.

It would be all right. They'd survive. That was all that mattered.

He got ready to leap.

The Digger walked around the couch and started to lift the gun.

Parker tensed.

Then: the stunning crack of the single, unsilenced gunshot.

The Digger shuddered. The machine gun fell from

his hands. His eyes focused past Parker. Then his head dropped and he sank to the floor. He fell forward, a bullet hole in the back of his skull.

Parker grabbed the Uzi and pulled it toward him, looking around.

What? he wondered frantically. What had happened?

Then he saw someone in the doorway.

A boy . . . How could that be? He was a young boy. Black. He was holding a pistol. He walked forward slowly, staring at the corpse. Like a cop in a movie he kept the large gun pointed at the Digger's back. He needed both hands to hold it and struggled with the gun's weight.

"He kill mah daddy," the boy said to Parker, not looking at him. "I seen him do it."

"Give me the gun," Parker whispered.

The boy continued to stare at the Digger. Tears were running down his cheeks. "He kill mah daddy. He brought me here, brought me in a car."

"Let me have the gun. What's your name?"

"I seen him do it. He do it right in fronta me. I been waiting t'cap his ass. Found this piece in his car. Trey-five-seven."

"It's okay." Parker said. "What's your name?"

"He dead. Shit."

Parker eased forward but the boy pointed the gun toward him threateningly. Parker froze and backed off. "Just put that down. Would you do that? Please?"

The boy ignored him. His wary eyes scanned the room. They stopped momentarily on the Christmas tree. Then returned to the Digger. "He kill mah daddy. Why he do that?"

Parker slowly rose once more, hands up, palms out. "Don't worry. I'm not going to hurt you."

He glanced upstairs. But the shot had apparently not wakened the Whos.

"I'm just going over there for a minute." He nodded to the tree.

He skirted the boy – and the bloodstain surrounding the Digger's head – and walked to the Christmas tree. He bent down and picked up something and returned, knelt. Parker held his empty right hand out to the boy, palm up. Then with his left he offered him Robby's *Star Wars* Millennium Falcon spaceship.

"I'll trade you."

The boy studied the plastic toy. The gun drooped. He was much shorter than Robby and must have weighed only sixty or seventy pounds. But his eyes were twenty years older than Parker's son's.

"Let me have the gun, please."

He studied the toy. "Man," he said reverently. Then he handed Parker the pistol and took the toy.

Parker said, "Wait here. I'll be right back. Do you want something to eat? Are you hungry?"

The boy didn't answer.

Parker picked up the machine gun and carried it and the pistol upstairs. He put the guns on the top shelf of the closet and locked the door.

Motion beside him. Robby was coming down the corridor.

"Daddy?"

"Hey, young man." Parker struggled to keep his voice from trembling.

"I had a dream. I heard a gun. I'm scared."

Parker intercepted him before he got to the stairs,

put his arm around him and directed him back to the bedroom. "It was probably just fireworks."

"Can we get firecrackers next year?" the boy asked sleepily.

"We'll see."

He heard footsteps outside, slapping on the street in front of the house. Glanced outside. He saw the boy running across the front lawn, clutching the spaceship. He vanished up the street.

Headed for where? Parker wondered. The District? West Virginia? He couldn't spare a moment's thought for the boy. His own son took all his attention.

Parker put Robby in bed, beside his sister. He needed to find his cell phone and call 911. But the boy wouldn't let go of his father's hand.

"Was it a bad dream?" Parker asked.

"I don't know. I just heard this noise."

Parker lay down next to him. He glanced at the clock. It was 3:30. Joan would be here at 10:00 with her social worker . . . Jesus, what a nightmare this was. There were a dozen bullet holes in the walls. Furniture was damaged, the breakfront shattered. The back door was destroyed.

And in the middle of the carpet was a bloody corpse.

"Daddy," Stephie said, mumbling in her sleepy voice.

"It's okay, honey."

"I heard a firecracker. Petey Whelan had firecrackers. His mother told him he couldn't have any but he did. I saw them."

"That's not our business."

Parker lay back, closed his eyes. Felt her slight weight on his chest.

Thinking about the bullet holes, the bullet casings, the shattered furniture. The body.

He imagined Joan's testimony in court.

What could he do? What excuse could he come up with?

What . . . ?

A moment later Parker Kincaid was breathing deeply. Content in the sleep of a parent whose children were close in his arms, and there is no sleep better than that.

When he opened his eyes it was five minutes to ten in the morning.

Parker had been awaked by the sound of a car door slamming and Joan's voice saying, "We're a few minutes early but I'm sure he won't mind. Watch your step – he knew we were coming and he didn't bother to shovel the walk. Typical. Typical."

37

H e rolled from the bed.
Nauseous, head throbbing, he looked out the window.

Joan was walking toward the house. Richard was with her, bringing up the rear, sullen. He didn't want to be here. And another woman too – the social worker. Short, clattering along on stocky heels, looking at the house appraisingly.

They walked to the front door. The bell rang.

Hopeless . . .

He stood in the upstairs hallway, toes curling on the carpet. Well, just don't let her in, he told himself. He'd stonewall. Make her get a court order. That would buy a couple of hours.

Parker paused, looked at his sleeping children. He wanted to grab them and escape out the back door, drive away to West Virginia.

But that would never work, he knew.

The bell rang again.

What can I do? How can I stall?

But Joan would still know something was wrong. Stalling would make the paranoid woman even more suspicious. And what would two hours or three hours buy him?

He took a deep breath and started down the stairs.

What could he possibly say about the bullet holes in the walls? The blood? Maybe he could—

Parker stopped at the landing.

Stunned.

A thin, blond woman in a long, black skirt and white blouse, her back to Parker, was opening the door.

Which was surprising enough. But what truly shocked him was the condition of the house.

Immaculate.

Not a piece of broken porcelain or glass anywhere. Not a bullet hole in any of the walls. They'd been plastered and primed; buckets of paint sat in the corner of the living room on white tarps. The chair that had been peppered with bullets last night had been replaced by a similar one. There was a new breakfront.

And the Digger's corpse – gone. On the spot where he'd died was a new oriental carpet.

With Joan, Richard and the social worker standing in the doorway, the woman in the dark skirt turned. "Oh, Parker," said Margaret Lukas.

"Yes," he answered after a moment.

She smiled in a curious way.

He tried again. "Morning."

"How was your nap?" she asked. Then prompted, "Good?"

"Yes," he said. "It was good."

Lukas turned back and nodded to the visitors. She said to Joan, "You must be Parker's wife."

"Ex-wife," Joan said stepping inside. The social worker – a pudgy brunette – entered next, followed by handsome and impeccably slow-witted Richard.

Parker continued down the stairs and couldn't resist touching a wall where he *knew* he'd seen a cluster of bullets strike last night. The plasterboard was smooth as Stephie's cheek.

He had a terrible pain in his shoulder and head from where he'd dived to the floor last night as the Digger came through the kitchen door. But if not for that he'd have thought the entire attack was a dream.

He realized that Joan was staring at him with a put-out smile on her face. "I said, 'Hello, Parker.'"

"Morning, Joan," he said. "Hello, Richard." Parker walked into the middle of the living room and kissed Joan's cheek, shook her husband's hand. Richard carried a shopping bag of stuffed animals.

Joan didn't introduce Parker to the social worker but the woman stepped forward. She shook his hand. She may or may not have given her name. Parker was too dumbfounded to notice.

Joan looked at Lukas, "I don't think we've met. You're . . ."

"Jackie Lukas. I'm a friend of Parker's."

Jackie? Parker lifted an eyebrow. The agent noticed but said nothing about the name.

Joan glanced at Lukas's trim figure with a neutral look. Then his ex-wife's eyes – the color so reminiscent of Robby's, the cynical expression so different – took in the living room.

"Did you? . . . What did you do? Redecorate or something? I didn't notice it last night."

"I had some free time. Thought I'd fix things up a little."

His ex studied him. "You look awful, Parker. Didn't you sleep well?"

Lukas laughed. Joan glanced at her.

"Parker invites me over for breakfast," Lukas explained, offering the two women a look of female conspiracy. "Then he goes upstairs to wake up the children and what's he do but fall back asleep."

Joan's grunt repeated what she'd said earlier: Typical.

Where was the blood? There'd been a lot of blood.

Lukas asked the guests, "You want some coffee? A sweet roll? Parker made them himself."

"I'll have some coffee," the social worker said. "And maybe I'll have half a roll."

"They're small," Lukas said. "Have a whole one."

"Maybe I just will."

Lukas disappeared into the kitchen and came back a moment later with a tray. She said, "Parker's quite the cook."

"I *know*," Joan answered, unimpressed with her ex-husband's talents.

Lukas handed coffee cups out and asked Parker, "What time did you get back from the hospital last night?"

"Uhm."

"The hospital? Were the children sick?" She asked this with melodramatic concern, glancing at the social worker.

"He was visiting a friend," Lukas responded.

"I don't know what time," Parker said. "It was late?" The answer was largely a question; Lukas was the writer of this scene and he felt he should defer to her script.

"What friend?" Joan demanded.

"Harold Cage," Lukas said. "He'll be all right. Just a broken rib. Isn't that what they said?"

"Broken rib."

"Slipped and fell, right?" Lukas continued her award-winning performance.

"Right," Parker recited. "Slipped and fell."

He sipped the coffee that Lukas had put in his hand.

The social worker ate a second sweet roll. "Say, could I get the recipe for these?"

"Sure," Parker said.

Joan kept a benign smile on her face. She walked around the living room, examining. "The place looks all different." As she passed her ex-husband she whispered, "So, Parker, sleeping with skinny little Jackie, are we?"

"No, Joan. We're just friends."

"Ah."

"I'll get some more coffee," Lukas said.

"I'll help you," Parker said.

In the kitchen he swung the door closed and turned to Lukas. He whispered, "How? How on earth . . . ?"

She laughed – undoubtedly at the expression on his face. "You called Detention last night. Said you were spooked. Night watch called me. I tried to call you. Bell Atlantic said your line'd been cut. Fairfax County SWAT got here around three-thirty on a silent roll-in and found a dead body downstairs and you in bed taking a nap. Who was the shooter who got the Digger? Wasn't you, right?"

"Some kid. He said the Digger killed his father. The Digger brought him here with him. Don't ask me why. The boy just took off . . . Now answer one for me – who was the body on the bus?"

"The bus driver. We figure the Digger kept him alive and then made him run for the exit in the back. Then Digger shot him then the gas tank and when the fire started he climbed out one of the windows. Used the smoke for cover. Got away through the traffic jam. Smarter than he seemed."

But Parker shook his head. "No, it was Fielding. He told the Digger to do that. He wasn't going to sacrifice his boy at all. This wasn't going to be their last job. They probably had years of this ahead of them . . . But the house." Parker waved his arms. "How— ?"

"That was Cage. He made a few calls."

The miracle worker.

"I don't know what to say."

"We got you into this mess. It's the least we could do."

Parker wouldn't argue with that.

"Wait . . . What did you call yourself? Jackie?"

She hesitated. "Nickname," she said. "It's what my family calls me. I don't use it much."

There were footsteps on the stairs, soft thuds as the children came down to the living room. Parker and Lukas could hear the voices through the kitchen door: "Mommy! Hey!"

"Hello, both of you," Joan said. "Here, here . . . This is for you."

Rustling of paper.

"Do you like them?" Joan asked. "Do you?"

Stephie's dubious voice said, "Oh, it's Barney."

Robby laughed out loud. Then he groaned. "And Big Bird."

Parker shook his head at his ex-wife's incompetence and gave Lukas a smile. But she didn't notice. Her head was turned toward the living room, drawn hypnotically toward the sound of the children's voices. After a moment she looked out the window and stared at the falling snow. Finally she said, "So that's your wife. You two don't seem much alike."

Parker laughed. What Lukas really meant was: How the hell did you end up with her?

A legitimate question and one he'd be happy to answer. But doing so would require a lot more time than they had right at the moment. And would also have to be part of a complicated ritual involving her sharing at least *some* of the answers to the puzzle of Margaret – or Jackie – Lukas.

And what a puzzle she was: Parker looked her over – the makeup, the jewelry. The softness of the white silk blouse, the delicate lace of the lingerie beneath it. And she was wearing perfume today, not just fragrant soap. What did it remind him of? He couldn't tell.

She glanced at his perusing eyes.

Caught once again. He didn't care.

Parker said, "You don't look like an FBI agent."

"Undercover," Lukas said, finally laughing. "I used to be really good at it. I played a Mafia hit man's wife once."

"Italian? With that hair?"

"I had Miss Clairol for backup." Neither said anything for a moment. "I'll stay until she leaves. Thought a hint of a domestic life might help you out with the social worker."

"It's above and beyond the call," he said.

She gave a shrug worthy of Cage.

"Look," he said, "I know you said you had plans. But the Whos and I were going to do some yard work."

"In the snow?"

"Right. Cut down some bushes in the backyard. Then we were going sledding? What it is, we don't get much snow here?"

He stopped speaking. Ending declarative sentences with interrogatory inflection . . . And he actually began a sentence with "What it is." The forensic linguist within him was not pleased. *Nervous, are we?* He continued. "I don't know if you'd be interested, but . . ." He stopped once again.

"Is that an invitation?" Lukas asked.

"Uhm. Yes, it is."

"Those plans I had?" she said. "I was going to clean up my house and finish sewing a blouse for a friend's daughter."

"Is that an acceptance?"

A tentative smile. "I guess it is." Silence for a moment. "Say, how's the coffee? I don't make it very often. Usually I just go to Starbucks."

"Good," he answered.

She was facing the window. But her eyes moved once more toward the door; she was listening to the sound of the children. She turned back to Parker. "Oh, I've figured it out."

"What?"

"The puzzle."

"Puzzle?"

"How many hawks were left on the roof. This morning, sitting here, I figured it out."

"Okay. Go ahead."

"It's a trick question. There's more than one answer."

"That's good," Parker said, "but that doesn't mean it's a trick question. It just means you're thinking the right way – you've realized that a legitimate answer is that there are several possible solutions. It's the first thing that puzzle masters learn."

"See," she continued, "you tend to think that all the facts you need are given in the puzzle but there are some that aren't stated."

Absolutely right. He nodded.

"And those facts have to do with the nature of hawks."

"Ah," Parker said, "and what does a hawk's nature have to do with the puzzle?"

"Because," she said, pointing a finger at him and revealing a sliver of girlishness he hadn't seen before, "hawks might be scared off by a gunshot. But they might not. Because – remember? – they were far apart on the roof. That was a clue, right?"

"Right. Keep going."

"Okay, the farmer shoots one bird off the roof but we don't know what the other two do. They both might stay. So then the answer'd be there're two left. Or one might fly off and that'd leave one. Or both might fly off, which'd leave none. So. Those're the three answers."

"Well," Parker responded, "you were right to consider implied facts."

She frowned. "What does that mean? Am I right or not?"

"You're wrong."

"But," Lukas protested, "I have to be right."

"No, you don't." He laughed.

"Well, I'm at least partly right, aren't I?"

"There's no such thing as partly right when it comes to puzzles. You want to know the answer?"

A hesitation. "No. That'd be cheating. I'm going to keep working on it."

It was a good moment to kiss her and he did, briefly, then, as Lukas poured more coffee, Parker returned to the living room to hug his children and tell them good morning on the first day of the year.

Author's Note

In trying to solve Parker's puzzle, Jackie Lukas's mistake was in making an assumption: that the hawk the farmer shot would fall off the roof. It might not have. The question didn't ask how many "living hawks" were left on the roof, just how many "hawks." So the answer is this: Three hawks would remain if the dead hawk didn't fall off and the other two don't fly away. Two hawks, if the dead hawk didn't fall off and one flies away or if the dead hawk does fall off and the other two stay. One hawk, if the dead hawk falls and one of the others flies away or if the dead hawk doesn't fall and the others fly away. No hawks, if the dead hawk falls off the roof and the others fly away.